Bad Girls Don't

· · · · · · · · ·

Cathie Linz

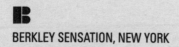

BERKLEY SENSATION, NEW YORK

THE BERKLEY PUBLISHING GROUP
Published by the Penguin Group
Penguin Group (USA) Inc.
375 Hudson Street, New York, New York 10014, USA
Penguin Group (Canada), 90 Eglinton Avenue East, Suite 700, Toronto, Ontario M4P 2Y3, Canada
(a division of Pearson Penguin Canada Inc.)
Penguin Books Ltd., 80 Strand, London WC2R 0RL, England
Penguin Group Ireland, 25 St. Stephen's Green, Dublin 2, Ireland (a division of Penguin Books Ltd.)
Penguin Group (Australia), 250 Camberwell Road, Camberwell, Victoria 3124, Australia (a division
of Pearson Australia Group Pty. Ltd.)
Penguin Books India Pvt. Ltd., 11 Community Centre, Panchsheel Park, New Delhi—110 017, India
Penguin Group (NZ), Cnr. Airborne and Rosedale Roads, Albany, Auckland 1310, New Zealand
(a division of Pearson New Zealand Ltd.)
Penguin Books (South Africa) (Pty.) Ltd., 24 Sturdee Avenue, Rosebank, Johannesburg 2196, South
Africa

Penguin Books Ltd., Registered Offices: 80 Strand, London WC2R 0RL, England

This is a work of fiction. Names, characters, places, and incidents either are the product of the author's imagination or are used fictitiously, and any resemblance to actual persons, living or dead, business establishments, events, or locales is entirely coincidental. The publisher does not have any control over and does not assume any responsibility for author or third-party websites or their content.

BAD GIRLS DON'T

A Berkley Sensation Book / published by arrangement with the author

PRINTING HISTORY
Berkley Sensation mass-market edition / November 2006

Copyright © 2006 by Cathie L. Baumgardner.
Cover art by Masaki Ryo.
Cover design by George Long.
Interior text design by Stacy Irwin.

ISBN: 0-425-21284-X

BERKLEY SENSATION®
Berkley Sensation Books are published by The Berkley Publishing Group,
a division of Penguin Group (USA) Inc.,
375 Hudson Street, New York, New York 10014.
BERKLEY SENSATION is a registered trademark of Penguin Group (USA) Inc.
The "B" design is a trademark belonging to Penguin Group (USA) Inc.

PRINTED IN THE UNITED STATES OF AMERICA

10 9 8 7 6 5 4 3 2 1

Chapter One

· · · · · · · · · · ·

There were plenty of things that aggravated Skye Wright, but seeing a police cruiser in her rearview mirror was right up there.

No worries. She could handle Rock Creek's finest. She'd done it before, when Deputy Timmy Johnson had stopped her for speeding on her way to give belly-dancing lessons. The beanpole law enforcement officer was a sucker for a big smile and a little cleavage. Or a *lot* of cleavage, depending how far over the limit she was traveling.

The halter top she wore gave her ample opportunity to flash a little flesh if necessary.

"Hey, Timmy. You know I was only going a little fast to get your attention . . ."

"It worked."

Uh-oh. This wasn't Timmy. The Studly Do-Right glaring down at her and her cleavage was no sucker. She'd heard about Sheriff Nathan Thornton, but had managed to avoid him. Until now.

"I need to see your license, proof of insurance, and registration," he barked.

Paperwork. She was *so* against paperwork. "Is that really necessary?" She shot him a huge smile. Hey, it was worth a try.

Lawman Nathan did not smile back. "License, proof of insurance, and registration."

Skye shrugged. "Okay, but it's gonna take me a while to find all that, because I've got a lot of stuff in my bag. Hold on . . . my wallet is in here someplace . . ."

She'd barely started digging in her huge Peruvian woven tote when he gave her another order.

"Take your hands out of the bag and please step out of the car."

His *please* wasn't a polite one, so he got no points for saying it as far as she was concerned. Frankly, her attention was focused on trying to remember if she'd even put her wallet in the tote.

"Put your hands where I can see them and step out of the car, ma'am," he commanded, his voice gritty with impatience.

"What?" Had he just called her *ma'am*? No one called her ma'am. She was only twenty-five, not ninety.

"Step out of the car. Now!"

"Okay, okay." She shoved open the car door. "But I don't see how that's going to help me find the paperwork you want."

She jingled but didn't jiggle as she slid out of her used Toyota. He didn't blink at her belly-dancing costume—the black crocheted, fringed halter, the purple silk harem pants. She didn't have her chiffon hip scarf on, but she was wearing the harmonious hip belt, with its loops of coins that made such a delightful sound as she moved.

Studly Do-Right wasn't projecting harmonious vibes at

all. She saw her own reflection in his mirrored sunglasses, which he didn't bother removing. Skye hated not being able to see his eyes. She judged people by their eyes.

Well, maybe *judge* was the wrong word to use. She'd made more than her share of mistakes in her first twenty-five years. Who was she to judge others? She *read* people by their eyes. Yeah, that was a better way to explain it.

Skye had always had strong responses to certain stimuli. And arrogant authority figures like the lawman with the stony expression totally pushed her buttons. But not in a sexual way.

Not that the guy was any slacker in the hottie department. He had all the right physical attributes—dark hair, broad shoulders, narrow waist. His face was sharply angular, but his bottom lip was surprisingly sensual, and his jaw reflected tons of stubbornness. His voice might have been nice, but it was definitely much too bossy for her taste.

"Dump out your purse on the trunk."

There he went again. Being bossy. Skye felt like arguing, but she had places to go and things to do besides stand here arguing with an aggravating cop. She dumped her stuff onto the Toyota's rusty trunk, thrilled to find her wallet was in there after all. So were lots of other things— papers, receipts, unopened junk mail, a few meditation cards, her checkbook (with a negative balance), her daughter's missing minikaleidoscope—and an unopened box of Trojan condoms.

"Here's my license." She handed it to him. "Hello?" She waved it at him. The man seemed obsessed with the contents of her bag. Hadn't Mr. Lawman ever seen condoms before?

"You appear to have a pile of tickets there." He nodded toward the official-looking documents.

So that's what those papers were. Skye knew she'd stuck them someplace. A sudden breeze blew them off her car, which had already had over a hundred thousand miles on it when she'd bought it cheap from the friend-of-a-friend months ago.

"I'll get that." He reached down for the tickets, studying them as he handed them to her.

She grabbed them from him. His fingertips were warm against hers. She didn't care. "Is this going to take long? I'm going to be late for an appointment. The football team is waiting for me."

"You doing a little routine for them?" He made it sound like she was planning on giving all the guys a lap dance.

"I'm giving them lessons."

"I'll just bet you are."

"Yoga lessons and belly dancing. To improve their balance and karma."

"Yeah, karma is real important in football," he drawled. "Right up there with a tough defense and a running game."

"If you don't believe me, call the coach. He's the one who hired me."

"For a little light entertainment."

"No, for enlightenment and physical improvement."

"Yeah, right."

"Not that you'd know anything about enlightenment. Your mind is so closed, I'm surprised it even functions. Are you done with my license?"

"No. Where's your registration and proof of insurance?"

She rolled her eyes. "How should I know?"

"You're supposed to have them with you when you drive. And you're not supposed to drive over the posted speed limit."

"Who decided on thirty-five miles an hour, anyway? That's totally insane. This isn't a residential area and there's hardly any traffic—probably because of the speed trap you've got set up here."

"If you don't have your registration and proof of insurance, I'm going to have to take you back to the station."

"I don't have time for this!" The coin belt around her hips jangled as she stomped her foot. "I can't believe you're being so anal! What's your next step? Handcuffing me? Go ahead!"

• • •

Nathan couldn't believe how rapidly she launched herself into an impassioned rant about police states squashing personal freedoms.

Fearing she'd hurt herself as she vehemently waved her hands around and narrowly missed smacking him in the face, he had no choice but to restrain her after she ignored his repeated requests to calm down.

Naturally, that's when another car pulled up. A big Lincoln Town Car. Owen Dunback, the elderly funeral director, was behind the wheel.

"What's going on here?" Owen asked.

"Police brutality! The man has a handcuff fetish!" Skye declared.

"She's hardly a threat," Owen said.

Nathan disagreed. Skye had threatened his peace of mind before he'd even met her. Rock Creek was a small town. He'd heard all about her and her mishaps.

"There's no need to handcuff her," Owen added.

"She was speeding."

"Then give her a ticket."

"She has a habit of not paying tickets. Has a pile of them in her bag."

"I'll pay them for her." Owen's wrinkled face reflected his concern. "Nate, she has a small child at home."

Nathan made no comment. He felt the pulse jerking in his neck as emotion coursed through him. Here was a woman accustomed to breaking the rules and not caring about the consequences. And she had a child.

No, he couldn't go there. He couldn't relive the searing pain of loss.

Slamming the door on those dark emotions, Nathan kept his focus on the present.

"How fast was she going?" Owen asked.

Nathan had to unclench his jaw to reply. "Ten miles above the speed limit."

"I think he's just got something against belly dancers." Skye swayed in front of him. Her arms might be restrained behind her back, but those hips of hers were making moves that should be illegal. "That right, Mr. Lawman? Do you feel threatened by a woman's cosmic power?"

"Not unless she's carrying a gun."

"I'm not into guns."

"Glad to hear that."

Owen interrupted them. "What do you say, Nate? Issue her a ticket. Or give her a warning. But don't take her to jail."

"Authority figures are always threatened by free spirits," Skye stated.

"Only if they're speeding and driving without the required documentation," Nathan retorted.

She stunned him by handing him the handcuffs. Somehow she'd freed herself. She shrugged. "A little trick I learned from a friend."

Okay, now he was *really* getting pissed. "You've just added resisting arrest to your charges," he growled.

"I wasn't resisting," she denied. "I just politely returned your handcuffs to you."

"That's true," Owen agreed.

"Trust me, when and if I start resisting, you'll know," Skye added with a satisfied smirk.

"That's it. Get in the car." Nathan slapped the handcuffs back on her and stuffed her in the backseat of the squad car.

"Call my mom," Skye called out to Owen. "She's at my place babysitting. Tell her what happened and ask her to gather the gang."

"Sheriff, you're making a mistake," Owen said.

That wasn't the way Nathan viewed it. He knew trouble when he saw it, and Skye was trouble with a capital *T*. She'd been stirring things up since she'd first sauntered into town a few months ago. Nothing illegal that he knew about. Until today.

She drove him nuts singing the Beatles' "Revolution" all the way to the police station. "I picked an old protest song because I figured you wouldn't know any of the newer ones," she said.

Nathan ignored her potshot at his age and pulled in front of the station. He knew from her California driver's license she was twenty-five, five-foot-five, 135 pounds. She had spiky black hair in the photo. That had changed. Her hair was red now. He suspected she was the type always making some weird statement with her appearance—purple hair, mohawks, nose rings, tongue piercings. He'd seen it all, even in a small town like Rock Creek. He'd noticed Skye had a navel ring when she'd twitched her hips at him earlier, but there were no other visible piercings or tattoos.

"Come on." He opened the car door. "The show's over."

"On the contrary." Skye smiled. "It's just beginning."

A crowd was gathered around the entryway to the police station, waving hastily made signs scribbled with markers and crayons.

LET THE BELLY DANCER GO!

FREE SKYE!

LET MY MOMMY GO! This small sign was carried by a little girl. Skye's four-year-old daughter.

Nathan blocked the punch to his heart at the sight of the half-pint kid wearing a tutu with a pajama top, yellow boots, and a tiara.

Get it together, he fiercely ordered himself. *You have a situation here. You need to stay focused on that and not your own demons.*

These weren't wacky outsiders protesting. They were locals. He knew them all. Sue Ellen Riley, known as "Our

Lady of the Outlandish" when she'd lived in Serenity Falls earlier in the year. Owen Dunback. Nancy Crumpler, owner of the auto parts store a block away. Lulu Malick, goth teenager. Algee Washington, the big black guy who'd just opened a second Cosmic Comics store a few doors down from the station.

Then there was Angel Wright, in her New Age grove. Skye's mother. She was reprimanding him with some nonsense about releasing negative energy into the atmosphere, when Sister Mary joined the crowd.

"I got a report of police brutality," the nun said, "and someone needing my guidance."

"That would be him," Skye replied, pointing in Nathan's direction.

Which made Nathan realize she'd taken off the handcuffs and put them on again, with her arms in front of her this time.

Dammit! First chance he got, he was ordering new handcuffs. These were as old as the hills, and clearly defective.

"What's going on here, Nate?" Sister Mary demanded.

"She was speeding."

"So you arrested her?"

"She was driving without proof of insurance or registration. And she's got outstanding tickets in three states out west," Nathan said.

"Which I offered to pay," Owen added.

Sister Mary turned her eagle eye on Nathan. "In that case, what's the problem?"

Despite being a lapsed Catholic, Nathan almost squirmed before stopping himself. "She resisted arrest."

"She knows how to slip out of handcuffs," Owen explained. "She wasn't really resisting."

"Of course she knows how to get out of handcuffs. I taught her myself," Sister Mary declared with a touch of pride. "A little something I picked up from my civil disobedience training during the civil rights movement."

Nathan was speechless, but not for long. "Move aside, everyone!"

Instead, they all sat down, blocking the door. Then they linked arms.

"You really should clean the sidewalks better," Sue Ellen noted with disapproval. "The sidewalks in Serenity Falls are spotless. These are cracked, and there are dandelions in between."

"You've got five seconds to move or I'll have you all arrested." Nathan's voice was steely.

"The cell won't hold us all. It's barely large enough for one. Besides, think of the paperwork. Do you really want to put yourself through that?" Sister Mary asked him. "Wouldn't it be simpler to just get those old tickets paid?"

"She's got a new ticket."

Owen raised his hand. "I'll pay that, too."

"Come on, Nate." Sister Mary was using her coaxing voice now. "Owen's arthritis is causing him pain here."

"I'm okay," Owen stoically maintained.

"Then *my* arthritis is causing *me* pain," Sister Mary stated.

"I can help you with that," Angel said, her curly brown hair bouncing. "I've got some special yoga moves. We'll talk later."

"This is not a joke, people," Nathan growled.

"Of course it's not," Angel replied. "Arthritis is a serious matter."

Nathan glared at her. "I'm talking about your daughter."

Angel beamed proudly. "She's gorgeous, isn't she? A little on the rebellious side, but she has a good heart."

"It's that rebellious side that's gotten her into trouble," Nathan stated.

Skye raised an eyebrow. "I thought you said it was my speeding that got me in trouble. Being rebellious is not illegal."

Maybe not, but Nathan knew that the sexual awareness

thrumming through him as he held Skye by his side was definitely a very serious offense. He suspected this aggravating, belly-dancing female would shake, rattle, and roll his entire law-abiding world if he weren't careful.

Good thing Nathan planned on being *extremely* careful. He'd spent a lifetime following the rules. Skye had clearly spent a lifetime breaking them.

Definitely a bad combination . . .

Nathan needed to regain control of this situation. "Sister Mary and Owen—you two come with me."

"What about me?" Skye rattled her handcuffs.

"We're all going inside to hash this out," Nathan stated.

The sit-in group stood.

"Not all of you," Nathan said hurriedly.

"But you just said . . ." Angel looked confused.

"For a lawman, he's not very bright, is he?" Skye noted with a shake of her head. "Or very concise."

Nathan refused to rise to the bait. "Sister Mary and Owen, come along with Ms. Wright."

Skye blinked with fake innocence. "Do you mean me?"

"Or me?" Angel asked. "Which Ms. Wright were you referring to?"

"The handcuffed one." Nathan put his hand on Skye's elbow to guide her forward.

"You may call her Skye," Angel told him.

No way Nathan wanted to be on a first-name basis with this sexy bundle of trouble. Thanks, but no thanks. "The rest of you wait out here. Or better yet, go home."

"We're practicing our constitutional right to gather."

"Only we're going to gather over at the Dairy Queen across the street," Sue Ellen said. "But don't think that means we're not paying attention to what's going on over here."

"I'm not going to the Dairy Queen," Angel protested. "Sugar is poison. How about some freshly baked yellow-squash cookies instead?" She tugged a bag out of her tote and jiggled it enticingly.

"Let's get this circus going," Skye said, suddenly in a hurry to move inside.

Five minutes later, Nathan surveyed the threesome before him in his office. Sister Mary and Owen were a natural pairing. Both comforted and served people in their time of need. Skye was definitely the odd one out in this trio.

"I don't think you realize the seriousness of this situation," Nathan sternly told her.

"Serious? Global warming is serious," Skye replied. "This is a piece of cake compared to that. In fact, you should be thanking me for saving you from Angel's yellow-squash cookies."

"They *are* an acquired taste," Sister Mary agreed.

Nathan sharply rapped his knuckles on his wooden desk. "People, if we could please focus on the matter at hand here."

"Sure. Speaking of hands, do you want these back now?" Skye handed him the handcuffs, dropping them in the middle of his U.S. Marine Corps "Semper Fi" mouse pad.

"You have a real attitude problem, you know that?" he growled.

Skye shrugged. "So I've been told."

"Just tell me what paperwork I have to sign and I'll do it," Owen said.

Nathan hated seeing the respected business owner dragged into Skye's mess. "Owen, are you sure you want to do that? I mean, this isn't really your problem."

"She's a friend," Owen replied.

"Uh-huh." Nathan sounded dubious.

"Get that look off your face," Skye ordered Nathan. "Owen is one of the good guys."

"Who you're taking advantage of by having him pay for your mistakes instead of taking responsibility for them yourself."

"That was my idea," Owen stoically maintained.

"Don't you have anything to contribute to this conversation, Sister Mary?" Nathan asked.

The nun shook her head and fixed him with a stare. "Not really. You seem to be doing just fine judging everyone's morals all on your own."

"She broke the law."

"*She's* sitting right here," Skye reminded him, waving her hand to get his attention. Her movement made her breasts bounce.

"I haven't forgotten." Impossible to do that with her sitting in front of him wearing that belly-dancing outfit. "You're not exactly the kind of person who fades into the background."

Skye grinned and wiggled her shoulders, making her entire body sing . . . and his entire body harden. "Why, thank you, Sheriff. That's the first compliment you've given me. No doubt it will be the last."

"It appears you two got off on the wrong foot," Sister Mary said. "There certainly are a lot of sparks flying here."

Nathan's eyes shot from the vixen-woman's bustline to the nun's knowing face. "Sparks?"

Skye wiggled her shoulders again. Not that he looked at her again. No, he could tell what she was doing by the sound of all those tiny bells chiming as she moved.

Ask not for whom the bell tolls. It tolls for thee. Nathan didn't remember the author of that quote, but he could sure relate at the moment.

"Sparks," Sister Mary repeated.

"You're mistaken, Sister." His voice was curt.

The sound of a little girl's screeching voice directly outside his office caught everyone's attention. "I gotta pee! Right now! I want my mommy with me!" the kid screamed.

Skye was on her feet and at her daughter's side in two seconds flat.

"Skye isn't dangerous," Sister Mary told Nathan when

he moved to go after her. "Not to the public. Maybe to your peace of mind. But don't hold that against her, Nate."

"You're trying to make this personal. It's not."

"You haven't let anything get personal for a long time now, have you?" Her voice was compassionate.

"Uh, I think I'll go see about a cup of coffee if that's okay?" Owen said.

"Drink it at your own risk," Nathan told him with a smile. "But you're welcome to help yourself. Do you know where it is?"

Owen nodded. "I saw it when we came in."

Once they were alone, Sister Mary looked at Nathan with an expression that reminded him of a bomb-sniffing dog, determined and focused. "It's just us now, Nate."

"Yes, it is." He perched on the corner of his desk and folded his arms across his chest as he faced her.

"So what's this really all about?" Sister Mary demanded.

"Speeding and driving without proper documentation."

"She gets to you, doesn't she? She gets to most people. Skye isn't one to sit on the sidelines of life. She's right there in the middle of the action."

"Yeah, I got that."

"So what bothers you the most about her?"

"The fact that she was speeding."

"Right. She's fast. And that bothers you."

The nun made it sound like he was attracted to the belly-dancing vixen. "There you go again, trying to make it personal."

"And there you go again." Sister Mary wasn't backing down. "Putting up barriers. As I said before, you haven't let anything get personal for some time now."

Nathan shrugged. "Law enforcement works better that way."

"How about life? Does it work better that way too?"

Before he could answer, Nathan's windowless office was suddenly plunged into darkness.

Chapter Two

· · · · · · · · · · ·

Nathan's military and law enforcement training instantly kicked in. A slice of light coming through the partially open office door revealed a solitary figure standing there.

An unidentifiable figure. Not good.

"Doesn't the town pay its electric bills?" Sister Mary was asking even as Nathan shot forward, only to run into someone in the dark. Someone with curves and dancing bells.

Nathan grabbed Skye to prevent her from falling. He was aiming for her shoulders, but somehow his right hand encountered the fullness of her breast en route.

"Don't waste electricity," a child's voice reprimanded him.

"Don't cop a feel in the dark," Skye told Nathan before shoving him away.

"What's 'cop a feel' mean, Mommy?"

"I'll tell you later." Skye flicked the lights back on. She hated the fact that the touch of Studly Do-Right's hand on her breast had shaken her. "My daughter likes to turn the lights off."

"Don't waste electricity, right, Mommy?"

"Right." And sexy zings from Nathan's touch were a definite waste of electricity as far as Skye was concerned.

She gave him the evil eye, aka the Sicilian death stare, just in case he got any ideas about placing his hands anywhere near her breasts again. But she could tell by the stunned look on his face that he hadn't planned on groping her in the first place.

Not that his touch even qualified as a grope. It was more like a quick brush, really. Which made her intense reaction all the more disturbing. What was that all about? She was no prude to go all weak at the knees this way.

Sister Mary broke the sudden, awkward silence by making introductions. "You already know Angel, Skye's mother. And this is Toni, Skye's daughter. She's four."

"You look mean." Toni gave Nathan a miniversion of the Sicilian death stare. "I don't like you."

"She's into expressing her emotions." Angel ruffled her granddaughter's hair.

"Like her mother," Nathan drawled.

"Absolutely," Skye stated proudly.

"I'm sorry if Toni's yelling upset you earlier," Angel said, "but she wanted her mommy."

Nathan nodded. "Yeah, I got that."

"I'll bet you thought I was going to make a run for it, didn't you?" Skye directed her challenging comment to Nathan.

Before he could reply, Owen returned to the room with coffee in hand and an apologetic expression on his face. "I don't mean to be rude, but I've got a funeral I've got to prepare for this afternoon, so if we could get the paperwork going here, I'd really appreciate it."

Nathan was instantly all business. "How much do you owe on all those tickets?" he asked Skye.

"Three hundred and ninety-three dollars." She dug them out of her huge tote bag. "Here, do the math yourself if you don't trust me."

He used the calculator on his tidy desk. "Actually, it comes to three hundred and ninety-two dollars. I'll tell you what." He steepled his fingers. "Pay these old tickets and I'll let you go this time."

Angel's face was serene. "I'm so glad you're trusting your inner vision on this matter, Nathan."

Sister Mary beamed. "Thanks, Nate."

Owen's smile was equally big. "Yes, thank you, Nate."

"Aren't *you* going to thank me?" Nathan asked Skye.

Skye gave him the evil eye once again. "Don't push your luck."

"In that case, I hope you'll consider this experience a warning."

Skye smiled sweetly. "I will if you will."

• • •

"What do you think they're doing over there at the police station?" Sue Ellen asked between slurps of her Blizzard at the Dairy Queen.

Algee shrugged. "Sister Mary will make sure they don't torture Skye."

"Do you know how many people are tortured around the world each year?" Lulu asked. "The statistics are on the Amnesty International website."

Sue Ellen clucked her tongue. "You're just a regular Suzie Sunshine, aren't you?"

Lulu pointed to her Dark Angel tattoo, one of many tattoos covering much of the skin on her arms. "I'm into dark, not light."

"Speaking of dark, I really wish you'd let me do something with your hair," Sue Ellen replied. "That flat black just doesn't do a thing for your pale complexion."

"Keep your evil Mary Kay hands to yourself," Lulu growled.

Sue Ellen didn't take offense. "Isn't it interesting how different we all are, yet we're all friends of Skye?"

"Yeah, it's just fascinating," Lulu drawled.

Algee stood. "Well, if you ladies don't need me any longer, I'd better get back to the store."

Sue Ellen grabbed his massive arm. "You can't leave yet. What if Skye needs our help?"

"With what?" Algee asked. "A prison break?"

Sue Ellen looked horrified. "You don't think they're going to put her in prison, do you?"

"Do you know how many innocent people are thrown into prison every year?" Lulu asked.

"No, and I don't want to know," Sue Ellen retorted, her voice agitated. "All I care about is Skye. And maybe world peace. Oh, and being the top-selling Mary Kay representative in Pennsylvania someday."

"I don't think you're supposed to be staging sit-ins if you're a Mary Kay representative," Lulu said.

"Well, I'm not actually selling the cosmetics yet," Sue Ellen admitted. "It's just one of the many things on my list of life possibilities."

"Did Angel come up with that?" Lulu asked.

"With selling cosmetics?" Sue Ellen laughed and shook her head. "Heavens, no. You know how she is about that sort of thing. No animal testing, only natural ingredients." Then, abruptly, "What are we going to do if they arrest Skye?"

"I'll tell you one thing. I'm not babysitting Toni the Biter," Lulu said.

"I had no idea when I hired you to help out part-time that you were such a wimp," Algee retorted.

Lulu shrugged. "That kid is dangerous."

"She doesn't bite as much as she used to," Algee commented. "You should have seen her six months ago."

"You don't think she'll bite a cop, do you?" Sue Ellen's eyes widened as this new thought raced through her mind. "Can they arrest a three-year-old?"

"She's four," Algee said.

"She's a menace," Lulu said.

"Yeah . . . she is. Just like her mother," Sue Ellen said fondly.

* * *

"One more thing before you go," Nathan told Skye. Angel had already taken Toni outside, leaving Skye alone with the sheriff.

"What? You want your pound of flesh?"

He gave her a visual once-over. "You're certainly showing enough flesh."

"What's that supposed to mean?"

"That your outfit isn't exactly age appropriate."

She stood toe-to-toe with him, which meant she had to tilt back her head to give him the Sicilian death stare, but it was worth the extra effort. "Are you saying I'm too old?" Danger vibrated in every word, cautioning him.

"I'm saying that outfit is much too provocative to wear in front of a group of hormone-crazed teenage boys."

Skye actually had a less revealing outfit she normally wore for the sessions at the high school. It was in her car and she'd planned on changing, but had been running late.

Not that she'd explain any of that to Cop-Man. Instead, she snarled, "Who made you the fashion gestapo?"

"It doesn't take an expert to know what's right and what's wrong."

"You're right."

"I am?" He was clearly surprised by her agreement.

"It doesn't take an expert to see that I'm *right* and you're *wrong*."

"How do you figure that?"

"Explaining that to you would take several hours and, frankly, I don't have the time. Thanks to you, I've totally missed the football session and will have to reschedule."

"Thanks to me and Owen, you're not in jail right now."

"And that's what's really got your tighty-whities all bunched up in a knot, right? The fact that I'm not behind bars. I'll bet in a previous life you ran the dungeon in a dark castle somewhere."

"Speaking of dark, you really should watch your daughter and stop her from turning off the lights like that."

"What's the matter, Mr. Lawman?" she taunted. "You afraid of the dark?"

"I'm used to the dark."

Something in his tone made her pause. The man had just insulted her kid. Sort of. She should be taking his head off right now, not wondering what had caused the pain she'd discerned in his voice a moment ago.

For the first time, she gave him a closer look, digging beneath the authoritative surface. Skye wasn't as good at viewing auras as Angel was, but she wasn't too bad. The reading would be stronger if she and Studly Do-Right were both outside and she were barefoot, in direct contact with the Earth.

She could just imagine his response to her asking him to step outside so she could read his aura, check his chakras, and mediate his meridians.

Yeah, right. Not gonna happen.

She'd have to make do. She was good at that.

Skye knew that her own auric field often strongly interacted with others, sometimes resulting in sparks. Or bonfires, in the case of this lawman.

She opened her internal channels . . . and saw that Sheriff Nathan Thornton had lots of red and black in his aura.

Strong mind and will. Strong passion. Anger. Secrets. Barriers.

"Have you been listening to a word I've said?" he demanded.

Skye blinked, breaking the cosmic connection. Whew! That was like sticking her finger in an electric socket. She knew, because she'd done that finger-in-the-socket thing a few days ago, trying to do a home repair job herself. The feeling was more zap than zing, while the intensity was fierce.

Skye was surprised by what she'd viewed in Nathan's aura. And equally surprised by her reaction to it. She just stood there, trying to gather her scattered thoughts.

"Maybe you should take this." He handed her a flyer.

It took her a second or two to realize it was for a drug rehab center. She crumpled the flyer and shoved it right back at him. "I do *not* take drugs."

"You'd hardly admit it to me if you were."

Okay, her earlier empathy for him was now totally gone. Vaporized. Evaporated faster than a grape Popsicle left in the searing sun of the California desert.

She stashed her New Age auric gaze and replaced it with the death stare.

He had the nerve to raise an eyebrow and appear bored. "Are we done here?"

Skye would like to think so, but her intuition warned her that her run-ins with Nathan were just beginning.

Even so, she said, "We're done."

"Good. As long as we understand one another."

What planet was this guy on? He didn't *understand* one thing about her. He'd jumped to his own conclusions the instant he'd seen her in her belly-dancing costume.

Not age appropriate, huh? She'd make him pay for that comment. Big-time. She just needed to figure out how . . .

• • •

Skye's next stop was the Dunback Funeral Home, where she gave Owen a huge hug in the privacy of his somber office. "I know you're getting prepared for a funeral, so I won't keep you long. I just had to tell you that you're the best, do you know that?"

He blushed. "I was helping you for purely selfish reasons. If they lock you up, who would I dance with to my Benny Goodman records?"

"Any one of half a dozen widows in town, including Lenore Trimble, who've been eyeing you for ages."

"Bah!" He waved her words away. "They're just after my money."

She perched on the corner of his massive desk. "Why don't you think *I'm* after your money? Especially since you just loaned me several hundred dollars."

"Money isn't your thing."

She had to smile. "You're sounding more like me every day, Owen."

"I'll take that as a compliment."

"I'll pay you back. I'll write you out an IOU right now."

"You don't have to do that . . ."

"Yes, I do." Skye searched her tote bag for a piece of paper. The first thing she found was an unopened electric bill. The envelope was already covered with her scribbled notes.

"Really, I trust you," Owen was saying. "I don't need you to write anything on paper."

"I want to do it. I just can't seem to find anything . . ." she muttered in frustration.

"Here." He handed her a notepad with the elegantly scripted heading DUNBACK FUNERAL HOME in black ink on cream vellum.

"Did you get a receipt from Nasty Nathan?" she asked Owen as she searched for a pen in her bag.

"He's really not that bad, normally."

"No? So I bring out the worst in him?"

"Yes. No." Owen was clearly at a loss as he handed her a slim, silver-toned pen.

"He had the nerve to hand me a flyer about drug rehab." Skye was still simmering over that one.

"Maybe he was trying to be helpful."

"You think? In that case, he failed miserably."

They were abruptly interrupted by the arrival of Sue Ellen in a nearly hysterical state. "Oh, Skye, I'm so glad you're alive!"

"Wha . . . at?" Skye could only gasp because Sue Ellen held her in a stranglehold hug that would have done a mighty python proud.

"When I heard you were in the funeral home, I thought you'd died!" Sue Ellen was using her drama-queen voice.

"Why?"

"Because she's morbid," Lulu said as she joined them.

"Me?" Sue Ellen was highly insulted. "*You're* the one who knows the suicide rates of every country in the world. You're the morbid one! I'm the eternal optimist."

"Then why did you think that Skye was dead?" Lulu demanded.

Skye was getting light-headed from lack of oxygen. "Let . . . go!"

"What?" Sue Ellen released her. "Oh, sorry about that. Are you okay?"

"No, she's not okay." Lulu thumped Skye on the back. "You almost strangled her."

"I did not. Did I?" Sue Ellen looked anxiously at Skye.

Skye was too busy breathing to reply or to ask who'd told Sue Ellen she was at the funeral home. She knew from past experience that Sue Ellen had a way of twisting reality around. Really, there was no point even asking why or how Sue Ellen reached some of the conclusions she did. You just had to go with the flow.

"So what happened?" Sue Ellen asked. "We want to hear every detail."

"We do?" Lulu said.

"Where's Toni?" Sue Ellen glanced around nervously. "Did the police keep her?"

"No," Skye replied. "She's with Angel back at my apartment."

"Oh, that's a relief. Lulu was afraid she might have to babysit her if you were incarcerated."

"You make it sound like that's the only thing I was worried about," Lulu protested.

"She was also worried about suicide rates," Sue Ellen said.

"Not that I thought *you'd* do that," Lulu added.

Sue Ellen frowned. "Why would I worry about suicide rates?"

"I meant that Skye wouldn't."

Sue Ellen only looked more confused. "Of course Skye wouldn't worry about suicide rates. She's got enough on her plate."

Lulu just rolled her eyes.

"There." Sue Ellen pointed at her. "Don't you think Lulu would look better without all that black eyeliner?"

"Uh, I've got a funeral to tend to," Owen muttered before leaving them alone in his office.

Skye quickly finished writing her IOU and left it on his desk before gathering her motley crew and heading out the side entrance to his office. The last thing Owen needed was a scene at an impending funeral. And somehow, wherever Skye went, scenes followed.

"Can one of you give me a lift to my car?" she asked.

"I will, I will." Sue Ellen was almost prancing up and down with excitement. "Then you can tell me all about your adventure."

"I'm coming, too," Lulu called out.

Sue Ellen frowned at her. "Don't you have to go to work?"

Lulu shook her head, her pigtails almost smacking her

in the eyes. "I don't start at Cosmic Comics until next week."

"Oh. Well, then, get in." Sue Ellen held open the back door to her pink Cadillac. "Did you ever wonder why the main street in town here is called Barwell Street instead of Main Street like in Serenity Springs?"

"My dad claims it's because there were more bars than churches on the street," Lulu replied. "And that went over *well* with the locals, so it's called Barwell."

"Rock Creek is a lunch-pail kind of town," Sue Ellen proudly declared.

"By that, you mean that it's got a blue-collar mentality?" Skye asked. "I agree with you."

"No, I mean there used to be a lunch-pail factory here, but it closed. We do still have a tank in the World War II memorial area." Sue Ellen gave the armament a wave as they passed by. "But let's get back to your traumatic experience, Skye. Were there sparks?"

"Huh?"

"Sparks," Sue Ellen repeated. "Between you and that sexy sheriff. Someone said he copped a feel. You could report him for that, you know."

"It was an accident. And how did you even hear about it?" Skye demanded.

"Her cousin was getting arrested for a DUI and he overheard some woman telling the sheriff not to cop a feel. We figured it had to be you."

"He's a *second* cousin," Sue Ellen said. "So what happened?"

"Toni turned off the lights. You know how she likes to do that."

Sue Ellen nodded before looking in her rearview mirror. "Put your seatbelt on, missy," she ordered Lulu. "I'm not getting a ticket because of you."

"Skye doesn't have hers on."

Sue Ellen shifted her attention to Skye. "Get yours on too. You should know better."

"She's distracted after getting groped by the sheriff," Lulu said.

"I am not!" Skye said.

"Are, too," Lulu taunted.

Sue Ellen clucked her tongue. "Children, behave. Skye, talk."

"About what?"

"The sparks."

"I gave him the Sicilian death stare. Nancy taught me that."

"Nancy Crumpler from the auto parts store?"

"That's right."

"Show us," Lulu demanded.

Skye had to swivel her heard to face Lulu in the backseat. Lulu shrieked.

Sue Ellen swerved the Caddy. "Don't do that!"

Skye shrugged. "You wanted a demonstration. I showed you."

"Was the sheriff impressed?" Sue Ellen asked.

"Hard to say."

"Yeah, he's a hard one to read," Sue Ellen said.

"And you like hard ones," Lulu said.

"Stop that!" Sue Ellen's order would have carried more weight if she hadn't cracked up with laughter a second later.

"Come on, admit it. Remember that naked firefighter?" Lulu asked Sue Ellen.

"He wasn't naked all the time. He posed in the nude for a fund-raising calendar."

"That wasn't the only thing being raised. He appeared very . . . excited in that photo."

"Oh, yeah." Sue Ellen smacked her lips. "November never looked so good."

"Then why did you two break up?" Lulu asked.

Sue Ellen waved her hand, her lilac acrylic nails gleaming in the sunlight. "He was a player. A bed hopper."

"A lesson well learned, grasshopper," Skye solemnly intoned in her best guru voice.

"I'll bet that sheriff of yours would look mighty fine in the buff. Make a great July pinup. What do you think, Skye?"

"I think the chances of that happening are about as good as me joining the military-industrial complex," Skye replied.

Sue Ellen blinked. "Huh?"

Skye lifted her chin. "I refuse to imagine the man naked. Not after he shoved a drug rehab flyer at me."

Sue Ellen appeared confused. "But, Skye, you imagine *all* men naked."

"I do not!"

"You don't imagine Owen naked, do you?" Lulu sounded horrified at the prospect.

"Of course not." Skye smacked Sue Ellen's right driving arm, making the car swerve again. "Why'd you say that?"

"Because it's true. You're one of the most uninhibited people I know."

"That doesn't mean I . . . never mind," Skye muttered. "Forget it."

Sue Ellen sounded remorseful. "I didn't mean it as an insult."

Skye patted her arm. "I know."

"Calling her a slut isn't exactly a compliment," Lulu noted. "First you think she's dead, then you think she's a slut."

"I didn't call her a slut!" Sue Ellen turned her gaze from the road ahead to Skye beside her. "You know that, right?"

"Hey, watch out!"

Sue Ellen swerved to avoid hitting a squirrel that had sprinted into the street. "Oh no! I didn't hit it, did I?"

"No, it's fine," Skye said. "Look at it, sitting on the curb with tons of Paris Hilton attitude, mocking you."

"Oh no," Sue Ellen groaned.

"I told you, the squirrel is fine," Skye said.

"Not the squirrel."

"Then what?"

Sue Ellen pointed to the police cruiser flashing its lights behind them.

"Ladies." Nathan's voice was solemn. "We meet again."

Chapter Three

· · · · · · · · · · ·

"**We** have to stop meeting like this, Sheriff," Skye drawled. "People will start talking."

"What did I do?" Sue Ellen's voice trembled.

"You were driving erratically." Nathan's voice reflected his disapproval.

"That's because Sue Ellen thought Skye was dead," Lulu said.

"Really?" Nathan leaned down to get a better look through the car window. "She doesn't look dead to me."

Skye batted her lashes at him. "Another compliment, Sheriff?"

"Just the facts, ma'am."

"In that case, why aren't you dragging Sue Ellen out of the car like you did me?" Skye demanded.

"I didn't drag you out," Nathan said calmly. "I asked you very politely to get out of the car. I even said please."

"Right before you handcuffed me. Don't you want to

put the cuffs on Lulu back there?" Skye jabbed her thumb toward the backseat. "With that goth thing going on, Lulu must look very dangerous to you."

"I've been trying to tell Lulu that black lipstick and nail polish aren't very feminine," Sue Ellen said. "Maybe you could help out, Sheriff. From a man's perspective, you know?"

"Not my jurisdiction, ma'am."

"You're not a man?" Skye taunted.

Nathan's voice was stiff. "I meant fashion isn't within my jurisdiction."

Skye wasn't letting him off the hook. "That didn't stop you from telling me what you thought of my clothes today. You weren't pulling any punches then."

"Sparks," Sue Ellen mouthed in the rearview mirror for Lulu's benefit, pointing first at Nathan and then at Skye. "Lots of sparks."

"And what about asking Sue Ellen for her license and all that other paperwork, huh?" Skye said, leaning forward to get a better look at Nathan. He'd actually taken off his sunglasses and stuck them in the top pocket of his shirt. A courtesy he hadn't bothered to show her.

"I don't need you doing my job for me."

"Somebody has to do it, since you seem to be botching things."

"Well, then." Sue Ellen's smile was bright. "I've got my license and registration and proof of insurance right here." She hastily handed the papers to Nathan.

"She also keeps her paper money all facing the same direction in her wallet," Skye told him. "In decreasing amounts. Twenties first, then tens, then fives, then ones."

Nathan didn't seem impressed. "Everyone does that."

"No, they do not. I sure don't," Skye said.

"You keep old speeding tickets in your bag," Nathan countered. "Along with a lot of other stuff."

"Like the box of condoms. Why don't you just say it?"

Skye's voice rose along with her agitation. "You jumped to conclusions about me based on the fact that I was carrying a box of condoms in my bag."

"Skye, you slut, you," Lulu teased from the backseat.

"A safe and smart slut," Skye retorted. "And don't you forget it."

Sue Ellen laughed nervously. "Don't listen to them, Sheriff. They don't really mean anything."

Skye undid her seatbelt, preparing herself for battle if need be. Even sparring with words needed freedom from restraints as far as she was concerned. "You don't have to defend me to him. He already knows what he thinks."

"You seem to be harboring a lot of hostility," Nathan noted.

"You think? Gee, and why might that be?" Skye tapped her finger on her chin. "Oh, wait, I remember now. Because you stopped me, handcuffed me, tossed me in the back of your police cruiser, made me miss an important appointment, which could well have jeopardized my work and therefore my income . . . But wait, there's more. Then you warn Owen about a gold-digging hussy like me and shove a drug rehab flyer in my face on my way out the door."

"Well, when you put it like that . . ." Sue Ellen turned to Nathan. "I guess she does have reason to be harboring some hostility toward you, Nathan. I mean, Sheriff."

"I was just doing my job. And I never said she was a hussy."

"The look on your face said it loud and clear. Are you denying that's what you were thinking?" Skye challenged him.

He was silent.

"I didn't think so." Skye shifted in her seat, the bells on her costume creating a music of their own.

"You're in hot water now." Sue Ellen patted Nathan's hand.

He returned her papers to her. "I'm going to let you off with a warning this time, Sue Ellen."

"Sure, you are." Skye's sarcasm was apparent. "No handcuffs for her."

"He saved them for you," Sue Ellen told her. "Surely that makes you special to him."

"A word of warning to you, ladies," Nathan said.

"That's Lady Hussy to you," Skye shot back.

Was that a smile she saw on his lips? Skye wondered. *No way. There couldn't possibly be a humorous bone anywhere in Studly Do-Right's entire, admittedly well-muscled, body.*

"Try to stay out of trouble for the rest of the day." Having delivered that ultimatum, Nathan walked away.

Lulu swiveled her head to watch him. "I'll tell you one thing, that man has one primo ass."

"He does have a fine butt," Sue Ellen agreed, her eyes glued to the rearview mirror.

"He's a pain in the butt," Skye muttered.

"Sparks," Sue Ellen said. "Definite sparks."

"Sparks and the Sicilian death stare. I saw her give it to him," Lulu said.

"Really? I missed it. When did she do that?"

"When he accused her of 'harboring hostility.'"

"Hello?" Skye waved her arms. "I'm not enjoying you two talking about me as if I weren't here."

Sue Ellen changed the subject. "Seatbelts everyone."

"The pink Batmobile is ready for takeoff," Lulu mocked from the backseat.

"Hey," Sue Ellen said. "I'm not the one who saw *Batman Begins* a dozen times. In an IMAX theater."

"No, you're the one who saw it five times and owns two copies of the DVD," Lulu retorted.

The two continued to argue about the Caped Crusader, and Skye was relieved when they finally got to her trusty and rusty Toyota a few minutes later. "Thanks for the lift, you guys."

"No problem."

She waved as they drove away.

Now where were her keys? She had them somewhere in her tote bag . . .

She was still searching for them when a patrol car slowly pulled up beside her and Nathan got out.

Skye rolled her eyes. "What law did I break this time, huh? Was I breathing too heavily?"

"I don't know. Were you?"

"There some law against that?"

"Depends what made you breathe heavily in the first place."

"It wasn't you."

"No?"

"No. And it wasn't drugs."

"I was just trying to help."

"If that's your idea of help, I'd hate to see your idea of . . ." What was the opposite of help? She couldn't think straight. Not that she'd ever been a fan of linear thinking. She was more into abstracts. Like the image of his jaw. You could do sharp U-turns on that square jaw.

"Of what?" he prompted.

Skye blinked at him. "Huh?"

"You'd hate to see my idea of what?"

"Just about anything."

"That's pretty broad."

"Don't you have some thief to chase down or something?"

"Your shoplifting charge came up when I checked your record earlier."

"So you stopped to pat me down? Make sure I didn't steal anything from the station?" She held out her arms. "What's the matter? Are you missing any staplers or tape dispensers?"

Nathan just gave her a look. And it wasn't a "You're a sexy goddess" look. It was a "You're a loon" look. "We seem to have gotten off on the wrong foot," he said.

"Would that be the foot you planted on my neck?"

"That never happened."

"I was speaking figuratively."

"You've really got a thing against authority figures. Why is that?"

"And you've really got a thing against free spirits. Why is that?" she countered.

"Look, I just stopped to give you something."

"The keys to the city?"

"Your car keys." He handed over the ring. "You left them at the station."

"Why didn't you give them to me when you stopped Sue Ellen?"

"At first, I didn't know you were in the car."

"And once you did?"

"I guess I got distracted."

"No," she scoffed. "You? Distracted? By little ol' me? No way."

"You do have a powerful personality."

"So do you."

"Something we have in common, I guess. The only thing, probably."

Suddenly, she had the overwhelming urge to prove him wrong. "Naw, I'm sure there are other things we have in common. You breathe air. So do I. I read from left to right. So do you. I live in Rock Creek. So do you. See, that's a bunch of things."

There it was again. That hint of a smile. This time, she called him on it. "Hey, I saw that."

"What?" His face was impassive once more.

"That smile. Don't bother denying it. I saw those lips of yours move upward just at the corners there."

"You did, did you?"

"Absolutely. You should smile more often. It's good for you. Relieves stress. Laughing is even better."

"How do you know I don't laugh a lot?"

"You don't seem the jolly type."

"Now who's being judgmental?"

"You're right."

"I am?" He seemed surprised.

"Yeah. Maybe you're a balloon clown on your days off, I don't know."

"A what?"

"A balloon clown. You know, those people who dress up in clown outfits and twist balloons into little dog shapes for kids. Or maybe you're a stand-up comic on the side and you just aren't telling anyone."

"Not likely."

"No?"

"No."

"Why did you take your sunglasses off when you were speaking to Sue Ellen, but you don't remove them when you talk to me?" The question was on her mind, so she asked it. That was the way she was.

"I didn't wear them when I spoke to you in my office."

"You want to know what I think?"

"Not really. But I have a feeling you're going to tell me anyway."

"I think I throw you off balance, so you wear those sunglasses to put a wall between us. To keep me at a distance. What's the matter? Do I scare you?" She shimmied her hips and moved closer.

"Right." He was using that scoffing tone again, but his voice sounded a little huskier this time.

"Intimidate you, maybe?" She made another tempting move.

"Not at all."

"Provoke you? Excite you?"

"None of the above."

"Right."

"Like I said earlier, try to stay out of trouble. Although I have a feeling that might be difficult for you to do."

"Who knows? Maybe I'll surprise you."

Skye thought she heard him mutter "You already have" before he marched back to his patrol car and left her, standing there at the side of the road.

• • •

"She got to you, didn't she?" The comment came from Nathan's administrative assistant, Celeste Fox, the minute he walked into the building. In her early sixties, Celeste acted more like a mother hen than an employee, the way she fussed over Nathan. "That rowdy girl, Skye. I bet you're gonna dream of her in that *I Dream of Jeannie* outfit of hers tonight. Don't give me that look like you don't know what I'm talking about."

"I *don't* know what you're talking about. And it doesn't matter, because we do have work to do."

"It's done."

"It can't be. Law enforcement work is never done."

"Enough of it is for you to take a break. You work too hard, Sheriff." Celeste placed her hands on her ample hips. "What did you have for breakfast?"

"Coffee."

Celeste shook her head and tsked him, something she did a lot. "Breakfast is the most important meal of the day. You shouldn't be skipping that. It's not healthy. I'll bet you skipped lunch, too. Here." She reached over to her desk, picked up a thick sandwich covered in plastic wrap, and shoved it at him. "That's homemade tuna salad on fresh-baked bread. Eat that for lunch. If you keep skipping meals, you're going to end up skinny as a beanpole, like Timmy Johnson."

The name of Nathan's deputy only served to remind him of how Skye had conned the less-experienced officer into doing her bidding. Well, that wasn't going to happen to him. She could shimmy her hips all she wanted. He was immune.

So why was she even in his thoughts? Aggravated with himself, Nathan headed for his office.

Celeste was right on his heels.

"Look, I promise I'll eat the sandwich," he told her. "Later."

"There's no time like the present." She plopped into a chair across from his desk. "You can eat while I tell you about your phone messages."

"I thought they were supposed to repair the voicemail system by this morning."

Celeste nodded. "That was the original plan, yes. But there was a glitch."

Nathan had learned that there was always a glitch where the town of Rock Creek was concerned. "So when will it be fixed?"

Celeste shrugged. "They're saying tomorrow. Possibly. It could happen. Meanwhile, I've been taking your phone messages." She paused to consult her notes. "Your mother called from Nebraska and wanted to know what's on your birthday list. And the mayor wanted to remind you about the city council meeting tomorrow night."

"Right. Anything else?"

"Yes. I just wanted to assure you that I squelched any beginnings of a rumor about you and that rowdy Skye."

"What kind of rumor?"

Celeste lowered her voice and leaned closer. "Apparently, someone overheard her telling you not to . . . 'cop a feel' was the way I believe they put it. Not that you'd ever do such a thing." Her eyes behind her huge glasses reflected her outrage. "Which I informed them in no uncertain terms."

"That was nice of you."

Celeste waved his words away. "Niceness had nothing to do with it. I wasn't going to just stand by and let someone bad-mouth you. I'll bet that hussy-woman Skye threw herself at you. Is that what happened?"

"Uh . . ."

"Am I interrupting something?" The question came from Nathan's best friend and college roommate Cole Flannigan, the local vet.

"No, come on in. I was just about to take a lunch break. Thanks, Celeste." He nodded at her, hoping she'd take the hint that it was time to leave now.

She did, reluctantly, closing the door after her.

"The woman dotes on you, you know," Cole told him with a grin. He turned the straight-backed oak chair around and sat facing Nathan, his arms propped on the back.

"Why do you have to rearrange the furniture every time you walk into a room?" Nathan asked before biting into his sandwich.

"Don't give me any grief. I had to pick up a hundred-pound Newfoundland this morning, and sitting this way makes my back feel better."

"You're gettin' old, man."

"I'm younger than you are," Cole retorted. "I see Celeste gave you lunch again. Hey, remember that pizza-eating contest we had back in college?"

"Yeah, I beat the crap out of you."

"That's not how I recall it."

"Of course not. You were drunk at the time."

"Ah, those were the days, huh?"

"Yeah." Those were the days when Annie was still alive. She'd been Nathan's college sweetheart. After finishing his stint in the Marine Corps, he'd gone back home and enrolled at the University of Nebraska in Omaha, where he majored in criminal justice. That's where he'd met Cole.

Cole had been Nathan's best man when he exchanged wedding vows with Annie in front of a church packed with friends and family. Cole had also stood beside him during the funeral, when they'd lowered Annie's coffin into the ground on a frigid January day.

Cole was the reason Nathan had ended up here in Rock

Creek. He'd had to leave Nebraska to escape the darkness threatening to overtake him after Annie's death. When Cole told him about the opening for sheriff, Nathan had decided to apply for the job.

He'd been surprised to get it. Now he knew why there hadn't been many applicants. The pay wasn't all that great and Rock Creek was a town definitely down on its luck. Not much going on in these parts. Until Skye blew into town.

There she was again. Belly dancing her way into his thoughts. She was definitely . . . challenging.

There was a time in Nathan's life when he'd gone after challenges. That was no longer the case.

At the ripe old age of thirty-one, Nathan had learned the hard way that the saying was true: *Life's a bitch and then you die.*

Only, Annie had died much too young. When that dump truck ran a red light and hit her car broadside, killing her instantly, something within him had died along with her. And it was never coming back.

•   •   •

"I never thought I had to worry about Skye." Angel patted the llama's head as she confided her innermost concerns to her. This morning, Tyler had driven Angel out to the Amish farm where her two llamas were boarded. "And I thought I'd given up worrying, because it attracts problems. Although I did start worrying again with that situation with my daughter Julia. She's the older one. You remember her, right? You stayed in her backyard for a while."

Lucy the Llama blinked her luxurious lashes at Angel and nuzzled her for more treats.

"There was that whole mess with my not telling Julia who her biological father was," Angel continued. "He was too rich. Still is. But Julia seems to be doing okay now. I think Luke will make her happy. I'm not sure what will make Skye happy."

Angel paused to feed Lucy a piece of banana.

"Not that Skye is unhappy, exactly," Angel continued. "She's not a worrier. She's a lot like me. Or how I used to be. I've been getting hot flashes, did I tell you? Despite all the soy I've been taking. I've told Tyler that he's the one making me hot. You've met him. He thinks I'm a little crazy for talking to llamas, but he doesn't really seem to mind. Anyway, I love him. You love Ricky too, huh?"

Ricky joined them, moseying over at a llama-paced stroll.

"You two are the stars of my Luna Llamas business." Their sheared dual-fiber fleece was oil free, which made it a spinner's dream. "Most fiber artists just buy yarn, which I do as well. But I also bought you. And then I sort of went broke. That's why I had to move in with Julia last year. But I'm slowly coming back. People seem to like the hats and scarves I crochet. In fact, I have a waiting list now, so you two keep growing that great dual-fiber fleece. And have a baby. Have a little *cría.*"

Angel paused to rub their ears. "You are such a great couple. Like Julia and Luke. And Tyler and me. And Skye and . . ." Angel frowned. "I don't know who would be right for her. That sheriff sure responded intensely to her presence yesterday. Not that I can see a match there. I mean, I love my daughter dearly, but even I know that she reacts adversely to any kind of authority figure. She has to do things her way."

"Are you talking to the llamas again?" Tyler asked as he joined her near the fence. As always, he was wearing jeans, and his long gray hair was in a single braid. Since it was August, he'd traded his customary flannel shirt for an extremely faded T-shirt.

Tyler was the man in her life. The man she'd discovered in Serenity Falls, of all places. A Rollerblading misfit who worked as a handyman but didn't really fit within the tidy confines of a town like Serenity Falls, recently named one of the Top Ten Best Small Towns in America. Angel considered herself lucky to have found him.

"Did you get tired of waiting in the car for me?"

"Yeah." He hugged her. "I missed you."

"Thanks for coming with me today."

He just smiled down at her, keeping his arms loosely looped around her waist.

She looked at the surrounding rustic landscape. Twin silos rose from beside the barn like a pair of proud parents. In the distance, fields of grain swayed in the gentle summer breeze. The gently rolling hills gave Angel a sense of being safely nestled in Mother Earth's embrace. "It's beautiful out here in the country, isn't it?"

"Serenity Falls isn't exactly the big city."

"No, but it's not the same as living on a farm like this, where the air is fresh and clean."

Tyler inhaled deeply. "Ah, the smell of fresh manure. There's nothing quite like it. Guaranteed to clear your sinuses."

Angel absently rubbed a spot behind Lucy's ear. "I think the Amish have it right."

"So you think you might like living on a farm around here?"

Angel nodded. "How about you?" Her attention shifted to Tyler. "Do you miss Chicago?"

The sun went behind a cloud, shadowing Tyler's face as he shook his head. Since she'd first met him, Tyler had always been a man of few words.

He still didn't talk about his past. He'd told her as little as he could. And she could understand that. At first. But they were closer now. Or at least she was closer to him. She'd fallen in love with him. Head over heels.

He'd told her loved her. Once. Which was a big deal for a quiet guy like him.

But she still had a hard time reading him. And she shouldn't. They were soul mates. She should be able to know what he was thinking without him having to tell her.

Maybe her hot flashes were blocking her usual empathy. She was also having some memory issues. Not that she'd ever had a photographic memory. She'd always thought in clusters. Or in loops, like crocheting. One thought led to another and another, until in the end she had no idea what she'd started out thinking.

"Did you ever call Adam back?"

Tyler's question about Julia's biological father caught Angel totally off guard. "Not yet."

"Don't you want to know why he called you?"

"Not particularly."

"Why not? You had a child with him."

"That he didn't know about until a few months ago."

"Yeah, but he knows now."

"So?"

"So . . . nothing." Tyler's expression closed up before he abruptly added, "He's left his wife."

"What?"

"Adam. I read in the paper that he's left his wife. Filed for divorce. Maybe that's why he's calling you. Because he wants you back."

"I don't care what he wants."

"No?"

"No." Angel turned to face him fully. "Where is all this coming from? Don't you believe that I love you?"

Instead of answering, Tyler leaned down and kissed her. It was only later that Angel realized he'd never answered her question.

· · ·

"Okay, ladies, are you ready to shake your stuff?"

The cinder-block walls of the Rock Creek community center ricocheted the sound of belly-dancing music for Skye's Wednesday class.

"Wait," Fanny Abernathy demanded. At eighty-two, she

was the oldest one in the class. "Turn off the music a minute."

Skye did so.

"Is it true you were arrested for indecent exposure yesterday?" Fanny asked.

"Of course not," Nancy Crumpler answered on her behalf. "Hey, did I ever tell you all about the time I was a dancer in Vegas? Now there's a story."

Her comment surprised Skye. "But your sister is a nun."

"Yeah, she's the good sister. I'm the bad one," Nancy said proudly.

"I can relate to that," Skye said. "My sister Julia is the perfect one in the family."

"The librarian from Serenity Falls? I heard she took off on the back of a Harley with some bad boy six months ago."

"Her one attempt to out-bad me," Skye scoffed. "Not that that was possible. It takes a certain something to be a bad girl, and Julia just doesn't have it."

"What kind of something?" Fanny asked.

"Bad girls make things happen," Skye replied.

"That's right," Nancy agreed.

Skye swiveled her hips. "Bad girls have coast-to-coast confidence."

"They're cheeky. And some have great cheeks." Nancy turned her back to everyone and cupped her firm bottom with her hands before giving them all a wiggle to demonstrate. "There's a reason the sign on Crumpler's Auto Parts says 'We Have the Best Parts Around.' This here"—she pointed to her derriere—"is definitely my best part."

The entire class cracked up. Octogenarian Fanny giggled so hard, they almost had to do a Heimlich on her.

"They're sassy and saucy," Skye continued.

"Are you talking about bad girls or Nancy's bottom?" Fanny demanded.

Skye grinned. "Both. Bad girls don't have a plan for

life. They only know what they want right now, and they go after it."

"So what do you want right now?" Fanny asked.

"To get this class moving."

"Have you heard when your sister is coming back?"

"No."

"Do you think she knows about your being arrested?"

"I wasn't actually arrested."

"A lot of people saw you entering the police station in handcuffs."

"Handcuffs were involved, yes."

"You mean you and the sheriff were just having fun?" Fanny frowned. "That doesn't sound like him. He's not the type to have fun. You know his story, right?"

"I know he's an uptight pain in the butt," Skye said.

"It's not polite to talk about an officer of the law that way."

"She's already told you she's a bad girl," Nancy said.

Fanny shook her head. "Even so . . . Do you know why Nathan is the way he is?"

"No," Skye said. She didn't want to know anything that might make Nathan more appealing. "And I don't care."

"It's a tragic story, really. I can't believe you've been in Rock Creek for several months and you haven't heard about it."

"Successful avoidance on my part," Skye muttered.

Fanny pursed her lips. "But why would you want to do that?"

"Maybe tragedy makes her cry," Nancy suggested. "It makes her mother cry."

"Bad girls probably don't cry, huh?" Fanny looked to Skye for the answer.

"Not unless they're after something," Skye said. "Okay, ladies, let's get down to business here. Prepare to let your inner diva out." .

As Skye went through the familiar movements of her

dance, she felt the stress gradually leave her body. She ordered thoughts of Studly Do-Right to depart as well, but being the stubborn sort . . . he refused.

So she imagined him posing nude for some calendar, figuring that should chase him out of her thoughts. No such luck. He made a mighty fine Mr. May.

• • •

"I'm home!" Skye called out later that afternoon as she walked into her apartment above the deserted Tivoli Theater.

The entire building had been for sale for over a year. No one wanted to buy it. So the once brilliant movie theater remained dark, as it had for quite a while apparently.

The realtor who was selling it was in one of Skye's belly-dancing classes and had given her a very quick tour of the Tivoli when she first moved in. Red velvet seats baggy from thousands of patrons sitting in them. A deep blue ceiling painted with hundreds of faded gold stars. A screen bigger than those in the megaplexes so popular these days.

The reality was that too many businesses in Rock Creek were boarded up with FOR SALE or FOR LEASE signs stuck in their vacant windows. The downtown area along Barwell Street was three blocks long . . . well, only two and a half if you didn't count the south end of town, where the library, village hall, and sheriff's department were all located.

Nearby was the Dairy Queen, and a block down was Angelo's Pizza. These were the only two eating establishments in Rock Creek. No Indian curry places or Thai take-out here. No organic fusion bistros to satisfy Skye's food cravings.

Crumpler's Auto Parts was on the northern end of town. Next up were three empty retail spaces, where Chuck's Meat Market was the most recent to close its doors. Leah's Nail Salon had been around for a while and seemed to be doing okay. Nick's Tavern was still open next to the VFW hall on the corner, and doing a good business.

Another place with plenty of customers was the Sisters

of the Poor Charity Thrift Shop. Which was why Algee said he'd chosen the empty space beside it to open his second Cosmic Comics store.

Gas4Less, a combo gas station/convenience store, was the only other really active business on that block.

Skye could see the thrift shop from her living room window. She'd gotten most of her furnishings from there, and from local garage sales. The lucky bamboo plant by the door was a gift from Angel, who dabbled in feng shui more than Skye did.

The spinning wheel in the corner of the living room was one of the few things Skye had brought with her from the West Coast. Angel was a better spinner than Skye, but Skye still enjoyed doing it when she had the time. Which wasn't often these days. Not when she was scrambling to keep the bill collectors at bay.

Skye didn't have the kind of spirit to fit into the mold of a regular nine-to-five job—not that there were many of those available these days in Rock Creek. Instead, she gave yoga and belly-dancing lessons. She also helped out Algee at the comic-book store on occasion, and her sister's friend Pam at her bridal floral business if she needed an extra hand for an event. But those weren't regular things.

Of course, Skye wasn't into regular things. She was rather proud of that fact.

"Mommy!"

Skye was also proud of her daughter Toni. The kid was just like her. All attitude and cocky confidence.

Skye scooped her up into her arms, where Toni hung on to her like a little monkey—arms around her neck, legs around her waist.

"Who is this princess?" Skye demanded.

Toni straightened her crooked tiara. "I'm Cinderella. I'm making 'viron-mental good shoes with no leather."

"Been telling her your version of the Cinderella story again, huh?" Skye said to Angel, who had joined them.

"Absolutely."

"Cinderella is in the shoe business," Toni recited. "But she's not a capitalist pig even though she's a princess."

Skye smothered her with kisses before setting Toni free.

"What kept you?" Angel said. "Usually you're back from class before now."

Skye shrugged. "I stopped at Gas4Less to get a few instant lottery tickets for Owen as a thank-you present. I hope I don't lose them before I give them to him."

"I don't mind waiting if you want to run over there now," Angel said.

"Really? It'll only take me a minute. And you know how I am about paperwork."

"Go on, give them to him before you lose them."

"I won't be long. I'll be right back," Skye told her daughter before racing down the stairs and across the street to the stately building of the funeral home, where DRIVE SAFE. WE'LL WAIT was displayed on the sign out front.

Skye wasn't good at either thing—playing it safe, or waiting. However, once inside, she did knock on Owen's door and wait for his invitation to enter.

"Hi, Owen. I got you a surprise. Do you have a minute?"

He smiled at her. "For you, always."

"I know how much you're into the lottery, so I got you some of these cards." She spread a handful of them on his desk.

"The Pennsylvania Lottery is the only one that uses the funds to benefit senior citizens, you know," Owen told her.

"So you only participate to help seniors, huh?"

"That's my story and I'm sticking to it. Here." He handed her a few of the cards. "Those are instant winners. Do me a favor and rub them with a coin for me." He handed her a quarter. "My fingers are a little arthritic today."

Skye felt badly for him. "I shouldn't have gotten this kind, then. Sorry."

"That's okay. So what did you get?"

"I have no idea." She held up the ticket to him.

"Not a winner. Try another one."

"You do realize that the chances of your winning is probably something like one in a billion."

"Actually, for this game, the odds are a little better."

"You call this a game?" she scoffed. "Baseball is a game. This is a waste of time."

"Let me see."

Skye showed him.

"Not a winner. There's one left," he said.

"You know what you are?" After rubbing with the coin, Skye didn't even bother looking at the card before showing it to him. "You're an eternal optimist."

"Son of a buck! You know what you are? You're a *winner*!"

Chapter Four

. . . .

"**Right.** It's kind of you to say so, but I've got to go—"

"I'm not kidding!" Owen's face was turning red with excitement. Or maybe he was having a stroke . . .

Great. She'd given him a gift that gave him heart trouble.

"Calm down," she urged him. "Take a deep breath."

"Are you listening to me? You're a winner!"

"Here, sit down." Skye hurried to his side and lowered Owen into the office chair.

He popped right back up. "I don't need to sit down."

"Okay, okay." She was aiming for a soothing voice, but that wasn't one she used very often. She sure didn't want to sound bossy like her good-girl sister.

"You're not hearing me."

Skye tried to be sympathetic. "That's a problem for a lot of people these days, the feeling that they're not being heard. That their views and emotions aren't valued."

"I'm not talking about my views or emotions! I'm talking about the lottery!"

"Which you take seriously." She patted his arm. "I get that. Really I do."

"And do you get that this is a winning ticket?" He waved the card right in front of her nose, his arthritic knuckles almost hitting her. "An instant million-dollar winner!"

"Yeah, right. Very funny, Owen."

"I'm not joking."

"Let me see." The way he was flapping that card around, she couldn't read a word.

A second later, Owen was the one leading a shaken Skye to a chair. She jumped up a second later and hugged him. "I'm so glad for you!"

He blinked. "For me?"

"You're a millionaire!"

"I was already a millionaire. A number of times over."

"Well, now you've got even more."

"It's yours." He held it out to her.

"No, it's not." She gently pushed against his hand. "I gave you the lottery ticket as a gift."

"And I'm giving you the million dollars as a gift."

"That hardly seems a fair exchange."

"Skye, you need the money much more than I do. I've got no family left, aside from my pain-in-the-behind nephew, Milton. And heaven knows I don't want him to have this. Think of what you could do with a million dollars."

She shook her head. Money had never been important to her. She'd never bothered worrying about it. Somehow, some way, something always came through.

"Don't you have a dream that you'd like to see come true?"

"Plenty of them," she replied. "But a million dollars won't bring world peace or end poverty or cure cancer."

"What about a personal dream? One that only *you* would

have. Not a charitable idea or hope, but something that seemed impossible for you to attain before."

She stared at the ticket as if mesmerized before putting out a hand to ward off temptation. "You should donate the money to charity if you don't want it for yourself. A million dollars might not cure cancer, but it would help fund more research."

What kind of bad girl, are you? her inner voice mocked. *Whoever heard of an altruistic bad girl?*

"What are you afraid of?" Owen said.

Now those were fighting words, as far as Skye was concerned. Fear was *not* an emotion she allowed in her vocabulary. "Nothing!"

"And you expect me to believe that you couldn't do a thing with an extra million dollars?"

"*Extra* suggests I had another million stockpiled someplace," she noted dryly. "Which is definitely not the case."

"You could start a college fund for your daughter. Or start a 401K retirement fund for yourself."

"I'm only twenty-five and Toni is only four."

"It's never too soon to start planning for the future."

"I'm more a dreamer than a planner."

"Exactly." Owen pounced on her words. "So dream big." He spread his hands wide. "You could buy whatever you wanted just about. A huge house. New cars. Stocks and bonds."

"Or the Tivoli Theater."

"Or the Tivoli . . ." Owen paused as her words sank in. "The theater? You want to buy the theater? It's been closed for years now."

"I know. I live right above it, remember? And I got to take a look around when I first rented the apartment. The real estate agent let me in for a peek. It's incredible inside. Tattered and bruised after being neglected. But, Owen, those walls talked to me."

"It was one of the first theaters built for 'talkies.' "

Noting the fondness in his voice, she said, "Why don't you buy it, Owen?"

"I've got enough on my hands running the funeral home. I don't need another business. But you could buy it."

"I'm not a businessperson."

"You've got passion and drive and a big dream. You can learn the rest."

"No way."

"You don't think so?"

"I'm not practical."

"Who says you have to be?"

Skye frowned. "I thought business owners had to be practical."

"Depends."

"You're practical."

"Yet here I am, handing over a million-dollar lottery ticket to you to buy the Tivoli Theater."

He had her there. "Sounds pretty crazy," she admitted.

"Anything wrong with that?"

"You are definitely asking the wrong person. I'm not exactly the traditional type."

"Which is why you can dream big. You're always talking about karma. You bought the ticket. It's karma that you be the winner."

"It seems more likely that you've earned the good karma by doing such good deeds, like paying off my speeding tickets."

"You'd do the same for me."

"Yeah, I would," Skye agreed. "The difference is that you'd never have a bunch of unpaid tickets."

"Are you gonna hold that against me?"

"Of course not."

"Then take the ticket. It's yours. Please." His voice softened. "It's really what I want."

"Maybe you should sleep on it . . ."

"Skye, I haven't reached the ripe old age of seventy-three

without knowing that I want. And I want you to have this. Karma and I want you to have this. So take it and make an old man happy." He pressed the card into her hand.

"If you should change your mind . . ."

"I won't."

"But if you should . . ."

"I *won't*."

She'd never heard him speak so emphatically.

"The Tivoli Theater needs you," he added with a twinkle in his light blue eyes. When she'd first met him, his eyes reminded her of Santa's, in a poster she'd seen as a kid. They were the sort of eyes that drew you in, that radiated kindness and positive energy.

She hugged him fiercely. "When I reopen it, you've got a lifetime free pass."

"That works for me."

Skye blinked away a sudden wave of tears. She'd never been the weepy type. She was definitely emotional, but more passionate in nature than vulnerable.

Stepping away from her, Owen reached for a Kleenex from the box on his desk. "Now don't get me started or we'll both end up bawling," he teased her.

"There's no crying in baseball . . . " she began.

"Or funeral directing," he said, completing his favorite saying. "Now go on home and celebrate!"

• • •

Angel was cooking angel-hair pasta when Skye burst into the apartment.

"That took a while." Angel's attention remained on the marinara sauce she was creating on the stove.

"Yeah, well, I went over there broke and came back . . . a millionaire!" Skye danced Angel around the tiny kitchen.

"What are you talking about? You didn't borrow more money from Owen, did you?"

"Of course not. In fact, I'm now in a position to pay him back."

"What do you mean?"

"One of those lottery tickets I got him—turns out it was an instant winner." Skye waved the ticket at Angel, much the way Owen had waved it at her.

Angel looked at the card as if it represented all the evil in the universe. "Money brings trouble."

"Not having money also brings trouble. Like the electric company threatening to discontinue service."

"We don't need much."

"Maybe not, but electricity is nice."

"It starts with electricity and ends with gas-guzzling SUVs and designer watches."

"I'm not buying an SUV or a watch. I'm buying the Tivoli Theater."

"What?"

"The movie theater downstairs. I'm going to buy it. And restore and reopen it."

Angel appeared speechless. Skye knew the condition wouldn't last long.

"A movie theater?" Angel said.

"That's right."

"I hadn't thought of that." Angel sniffed a moment before rushing back to the stove. "My sauce!"

"Are you and Angel playing tag in the kitchen?" Toni demanded as she joined them. She'd traded her customary tiara for a fairy wand filled with sparkling stars. Her feet were bare and she was wearing a two-piece swimsuit with little fish on it.

"No, we're celebrating by dancing." Skye scooped her up in her arms and cradled her so she could press a raspberry kiss onto Toni's bare tummy.

Toni shrieked with laughter. "That tickles!"

"*No.*" Skye stared down at her with mock disbelief. "You mean this tickles?"

She gave her daughter another loud, smacking raspberry kiss, right on her belly button.

"Yes!"

"I had no idea it might tickle. In that case . . . I'll do it again!"

Toni wriggled herself free, giggling gleefully as Skye chased her into the living room and around the round red couch, a castoff found at the thrift shop.

Always a fan of multitasking, Skye spoke to Angel while playing with Toni. "You've run a bunch of businesses, Angel. I'm just following in your footsteps. What do you think?"

"That it appears we're about to embark on another adventure." Angel's expression remained worried as she reached out to hug Skye. "Maybe I should consult the tarot cards and runes."

"You don't have to. My mind is already made up."

Two hours later, Skye's mind was still racing. She read Toni her favorite Olivia the Pig story and put her to bed. Since Skye never wore a watch, she had no idea what time it was. She only knew that she was too wound up to relax.

"I'm just gonna go get some fresh air," Skye told Angel. "Can you stay a bit longer?"

"Sure." Angel looked up from the scarf she was crocheting. "Everything okay? You haven't lost the lottery ticket already, have you?"

"Not unless it's grown legs and walked out of the freezer." Skye often stashed important papers there. "I won't be long."

"The last time you said that, you came back with a million dollars."

Skye just grinned. "Who knows what I'll come back with this time?"

The August night was hot, the muggy air hitting the skin left bare by her blue crop-top and black cotton shorts. Like most of her wardrobe, she'd gotten the items from the thrift shop run by Sister Mary.

Rock Creek didn't have a fancy town square like Serenity Falls did, so Skye couldn't go jogging or strolling through some artistically arranged flower garden in the dark.

Instead, she skipped over the cracked sidewalk and did a sassy salsa dance with the paint-peeling lamppost on the corner. She had to celebrate. Do a happy Snoopy dance. A boogie. Some hip-hop. A waltz that would make Fred Astaire and Ginger Rogers proud. Their movies had probably been shown at the Tivoli in the thirties. All glamour and glitz.

Skye twirled and swirled her way down the deserted street until . . . *smack*! She was stopped midstep by a brick wall.

Wait, not brick. Human. Male. Smells good.

Strong hands. Broad chest.

Her nose was flattened against his shirt, her lips pressed against the warm cotton.

Her inner diva came to life. The one that missed having a man in her bed.

"You okay?"

His voice rumbled, reverberating through her body.

Wait a second. This wasn't a man. This was the cop!

She quickly stepped back. Nathan wasn't wearing his uniform. Jeans and a plain blue T-shirt made him look entirely too . . . good.

Better than good. Great enough to haul into bed.

Not that she'd ever do that. Not with an uptight lawman like him. She might be bad, but she wasn't stupid.

"What are you doing?" Her voice sounded sharp.

"I was about to ask you the same thing." He sounded entirely too laid-back.

"I was dancing. Some law against that?"

"I'm off duty."

"I'm buying the Tivoli Theater." She had no idea where the words came from or why she was blurting them out to him, of all people.

"Really." His tone deleted any sign of a question mark at the end of the glaringly doubtful word.

"Yes, really."

"I thought you didn't have enough money to pay your outstanding tickets yourself."

"I didn't. But things change."

"In a few hours?"

"Absolutely. They can change in the blink of an eye."

Nathan knew that only too well. One minute he'd been happily married, the next he was listening to the call telling him that his wife had died at the scene of a car accident.

"Yeah, I know."

Skye stared at him. Not the way she'd looked before, when he'd arrested her. Then those green eyes of hers had been full of fire and disdain. Now they were speculative. Thoughtful.

"Yeah, you do," she said softly.

He stiffened. "Have people been talking?"

"Huh?"

"About me?"

"They tried," she cheerfully acknowledged, "but I refused to listen to them."

Nathan didn't know what to say to that. This woman had a way of doing that to him. Knocking him off balance. Like the way she'd done when she'd smacked into him while waltzing down the street like some escapee from *Singin' in the Rain*.

He had to admit she did look awesome in those shorts and cropped top. Her bare skin had been smooth and soft beneath his fingertips when he'd caught her.

He had to say something. He couldn't just stand here with his jaw hanging open. And it had to be something coherent.

While he was trying to come up with a sentence that fit his criteria, she continued right on speaking. "Some things I prefer to discover for myself."

"Huh?" *Smooth, Thornton. Real smooth.*

"You can't take other people's opinions about things. You have to form your own impressions. Like when I smacked into you. You want to know what my first impression was?" She didn't bother pausing to wait for his answer. "That you smelled good. Well, first I thought you were a brick wall. But one that smelled good."

"I took a shower." *Brilliant. You and James Bond . . . so good with the ladies. Gag me now. Before I say something else stupid.*

"You used soap."

"Yeah." What kind of comment was that? Of course he was gonna use soap when he took a shower.

"No aftershave. You don't need it. You smell good enough without it. Did you know that the sense of smell is one of the most powerful senses we have?"

Nathan made a noncommittal grunt that could have meant anything. It was his preferred means of communication under normal circumstances. Not that anything about his run-ins with Skye fell under the heading of "normal."

"Most people think we only have five senses. Sight." She paused to bat eyelashes at him. "Smell." She sniffed with that cute nose of hers. "Sound." Her voice went all soft and sexy. "Taste." She licked her lips. "Touch." She ran her index finger down from her throat to her collarbone. "But we actually have six."

"Six?" His voice sounded rusty.

She nodded. "Don't get me wrong. I'm not knocking the other five senses. I'm a real big fan of them. I mean, listening to a Kurt Cobain song while looking at a summer sunset and eating organic strawberries? Heaven. And touch. There's nothing quite like touch." This time she ran her finger down his bare arm. "See what I mean?"

Was she deliberately trying to seduce him? Two could play that game.

"You mean like this?" He ran his index finger down her arm and back up again.

He'd meant to prove a point, but instead he'd just activated his body's launch sequence with amazing speed. Erection begun . . .

Nathan tried to focus on her reaction instead of his own. She could have been outraged. Angry. Disinterested.

But not her. Her eyes widened. So did her smile. "Yeah, just like that. Or maybe a little more slowly . . ."

She swirled her fingers down his arm, her finger dancing arousing him more than any lap dance had in his single days.

"Right. Slowly." He repeated her movement, adding a few seductive moves of his own. Caressing the inside of her elbow made her eyes go all dark and her lips part. "Slowly is good."

"Slowly is great," she murmured before grabbing a handful of his T-shirt and tugging him closer.

Her lips met his head-on.

There was nothing slow about the kiss. It has hot and fast. Open mouths and tangled tongues.

Then it was over.

She scooted backward. "Why'd you do that?"

"*Me?* You were the one—"

"Yes, I was. Bad idea."

"Felt damn good."

"Yes, it did." Skye dazedly touched her lips before frowning. "But still a bad idea."

"Agreed."

"Agreed," she repeated.

Nathan nodded and then walked away, leaving Skye behind, reminding herself once more that while she might be bad, she sure wasn't stupid.

True, her sister . . . her *half* sister Julia wouldn't agree.

But then, Julia had never agreed with the various paths Skye had chosen to take in life.

Julia had never actually called them stupid. She didn't have to. She had a way of looking at you that made her thoughts real clear. As if Skye had a giant *L* plastered in the middle of her forehead. Loser, loser, loser.

Not that Skye cared. Not really. Okay, maybe just a little bit. Big deal.

The bottom line was that Skye and Julia were total opposites. They didn't even share the same father. Julia's biological father was some capitalist billionaire. That bit of recently revealed info explained a lot, as far as Skye was concerned.

It explained why they were so different. Why Julia was so prim and proper. So conservative. So locked into worrying what other people thought. And Skye . . . wasn't.

Skye also wasn't going to exchange saliva with an uptight by-the-book cop like Nathan. Even if he was a damn fine kisser. Not that their kiss had lasted long enough . . .

No, don't go there. No experimenting with this man.

No wasn't a concept that Skye dealt with very well. She hoped that making Nathan forbidden territory didn't just entice her into wanting him even more.

• • •

"I'm worried about Skye," Angel told Tyler later that night as they sat beneath the stars on a park bench in Serenity Falls' quaint town square.

Clasping his hand in hers always made her feel better, but tonight that wasn't working. And, okay, yes, Tyler was still a man of mystery, but Angel didn't care. She knew enough about him to know she loved him with every fiber of her being.

Since she was now a fiber artist—designing, spinning, crocheting, and knitting hats, scarves, and sweaters with a funky twist—she'd started visualizing various threads running through her life.

Angel had followed many convoluted threads in her fifty years. She liked to think they'd all led her here, to this wooden bench in Serenity Falls nestled beside Tyler.

Not that she was a fan of the conservative little town. The place was entirely too anal for her tastes. But she'd found Tyler here, so she couldn't complain too much.

Besides, she was stuck here house-sitting until her oldest daughter Julia returned from her adventures on the back of bad boy Luke Maguire's Harley.

Tyler still hadn't verbally responded to her comment about being worried about Skye. But he'd started rubbing his thumb along the back of her hand in that soothing way he had, as if to reassure her that things would work out.

So much had changed since Angel had blown into town with Skye and Toni almost a year ago. Pivotal moments became snapshots in her inner scrapbook. Her first meeting with Tyler beside the pond behind the library, her first sighting of him Rollerblading to cope with his insomnia late at night, her guilt at not telling Julia about her biological father.

"It's money," Angel murmured, reaching up to touch the amethyst crystal she wore around her neck. Amethyst was said to have a calming effect on the emotions and to increase perception and creative insight. All attributes she could use about now.

"What's money?"

"The reason I'm worried about my daughter."

"So this is about Adam?"

"No, it's about Skye."

"I don't understand. Is she jealous about Julia having a rich father?"

"No way," Angel said. Then she frowned. "At least, I don't think so. We've never really discussed it. Maybe we should. Anyway, that's not what I was talking about."

Tyler just waited.

"Skye was almost arrested yesterday."

"And that's why you're worried?"

Angel shook her head. "Oh no, I was actually very proud of her. We even staged a sit-in to protest the way she was being treated."

"How was she being treated?"

Now Angel patted Tyler's hand. "You sounded so lawyerly there for a moment."

"Shoot me now," Tyler muttered.

"It still hurts you, doesn't it? Thinking about your former life as a prosecutor."

"I'm not the same man anymore."

"You're a much better man."

"Most people wouldn't think that scraping by as a handyman doing odd jobs around town is better."

Angel rubbed her cheek against his shoulder. "Ah, but you already know I'm not most people."

"Yeah, that's one of the things I love about you."

Tyler said he loved things *about* her, but he'd only said he loved her once. She told herself it didn't matter. No way was she rocking the cosmic boat too much at this point.

"But getting back to Skye," Tyler prompted her.

"Yeah, well, it turns out she has a bunch of unpaid tickets from the West Coast."

"Not good."

"Apparently not. But no reason to put her in handcuffs."

"They handcuffed her?"

"The sheriff did. Of course, she slipped right out of them, just like Sister Mary taught her. But that's another story. Anyway, we eventually got the ticket thing sorted out, with Owen loaning her the money to pay them off."

"Owen the funeral director guy?"

Angel nodded. "To show him her appreciation, Skye bought him some of those instant lottery tickets. Apparently, one of them was a winner and he insisted on giving it back to her."

"Generous of him. So how much did she win?"

"A lot." Angel nervously plucked at the floaty, tie-dyed Indian-cotton skirt she wore.

"A hundred?"

Angel could forgive him for starting low, since to her a hundred dollars was a lot of money. "A million."

Tyler almost choked.

Angel patted him on the back and nodded. "I know. It's a lot of money. Not to someone like Adam, maybe . . ."

"Did you return his call yet?"

Angel shook her head.

"Why are you avoiding him? Are you afraid that if you talk to him, your old feelings for him will come back?"

"Of course not!"

"Then what are you afraid of?"

"A lot of things. Global warming, mercury in fish, the disappearance of the rain forest, schoolchildren getting obese from soft drinks in schools."

"Do you hold Adam responsible for all those things?"

"Well, he *is* a capitalist pig."

"With whom you had a child."

"A long time ago."

"It's still a bond the two of you have."

Angel shifted in her seat. "I wish you wouldn't put it that way."

"Why not?"

"Because it makes it seem as if . . ."

"As if the two of you had sex?" he demanded.

Totally stunned by Tyler's comment, Angel leapt to her feet and shouted, "I haven't had sex in thirty years!"

Chapter Five

. . . .

"**You** haven't had sex in thirty years?" Tyler rose to his feet, but took his time doing it. "What do you call what we did last night?"

"I meant that I haven't had sex with Adam in thirty years." Angel's voice was much calmer and a lot quieter now.

Julia might be out of town, but she'd have a hissy fit if she heard via the grapevine that her mother was yelling about sex in the middle of Serenity Falls.

Skye wouldn't care.

Angel's two daughters were polar opposites, which often left Angel feeling like she was being torn apart in the middle.

And now she had Tyler acting weird. "Where is this coming from?"

He just shrugged.

That shrug was the last straw. "I hate it when you do

that. I read your gesture as you telling me that I'm not worthy of a reply."

He looked at her blankly. "What gesture?"

"Your shrug."

This time he rolled his eyes instead.

"That's not a real good substitute," Angel informed him. "Just talk to me. Tell me why you're so manic about Adam all of a sudden."

"It's not all of a sudden," Tyler said softly.

"Well, you haven't acted like this before."

"How am I supposed to compete with one of the richest guys on the planet?"

"There is no competition."

"Yeah, right."

"Is this some male thing I'm missing here?" Angel was totally mystified.

"You're obviously avoiding speaking to him."

"And *that* makes you think I want to have sex with him? I avoid talking to the mayor of Serenity Falls. That doesn't mean I want to have sex with *him*."

"Aren't you curious?"

"About having sex with the mayor? No. Yuck." Angel made a face, the same one she made at the thought of eating a caribou burger. "Am I curious about Adam and what he wants? No, not really. Will it make you feel better if I promise to return his call tomorrow?"

Tyler sighed and kicked a stone in the path.

Angel sighed right along with him. "You're dying to just give me a shrug as an answer, aren't you?"

"Yeah."

"So what, exactly, is it that you want me to do?"

Tyler got a look in his eyes that let her know his thoughts had returned to sex . . . and her . . . with him.

"I can read your mind sometimes," Angel said.

He smiled, slow and sexy. "Yeah, I know."

"But not *all* the time. So when you're feeling insecure or upset about something, you need to *tell* me. Deal?"

Tyler took her in his arms and kissed her, but he never did agree to her deal.

· · ·

"You boys better not let yourself get out-pretzeled by some girl." This was Coach Russ Spears's warning to the members of his football team gathered in the Rock Creek High School gym.

Even though it was still only August, and the new school year hadn't officially begun yet, the gym's walls were already covered with ENTERING TROJAN COUNTRY signs. Or maybe they'd been left up from last year. They did look a little the worse for wear. But then, so did much of Rock Creek, including the high school and the football team.

Although Skye didn't know a lot about sports, she'd been expecting teenage boys as big as buildings and strong enough to bulldoze them down if any structure got in their way.

And, okay, yeah . . . there were a couple of those. And a few beanpoles. A *lot* of beanpoles.

Coach Spears, by comparison, looked like a Buddha, with his protruding belly stretching his Trojans polo shirt to capacity. The coach was deceptive, though. He might be built like a fireplug, but he could move fast when he wanted or needed to. He also had the kind of voice that made others move fast when he ordered them to do so. "So you boys swallow your pride and get into the lettuce position. Pronto."

"Lotus," Skye corrected him. "Not lettuce. Thanks, Coach. I've got it from here."

A kid with red hair, freckles, and wire-rim glasses tentatively raised his hand.

Skye gave him an encouraging smile. "Yes?"

"Coach told us that Adam Vinatieri, the kicker for the Patriots, does yoga."

"Hmmmm." Skye wasn't really into the details of football. She just knew this was a job she enjoyed—teaching yoga.

"Do you think this yogi stuff will help my kicking game?"

"A brain transplant would help your kicking game," one of the hulks said.

"It's yoga, not yogi," Skye said, "and, yes, I do think it will help your kicking game, if you let it. Do you all remember the moving into stillness I talked about last time?"

"Stillness?" The coach frowned. "I want them to have more flexibility. To run faster. Tackle better."

"Right." Whatever.

The coach folded his arms across his barrel chest and fixed her with an intense stare, the look of a man who'd weathered years of dealing with teenagers and wasn't about to put up with any crap. "You know some folks think this is too foo-foo. Then I read about the University of Memphis using yoga for their football team. They get into a meditative state that puts them beyond discomfort. That's where I want these guys—beyond discomfort. Pronto."

"Yoga isn't about pronto. It's about concentration and meditation."

"And sacks," the coach reminded her. "And winning."

"Yoga is process oriented, not goal oriented." Skye paused to turn on the boom box. "It doesn't matter how many times you perform a routine. The importance is that you are focused while performing it."

"How can they focus with that damn music blaring?" the coach complained.

"It's the Dave Matthews Band, and they like it."

The coach's look told her that was the wrong answer.

So she came up with another one. "I mean, it . . . uh . . . helps their concentration so they can win . . . uh . . . more sacks."

"You don't *win* sacks. Never mind. Just get on with it."
He stalked off.

Skye faced the team. This was only her second lesson,
and there were still a few holdouts to the entire concept of
their learning yoga. Rebels. Skye could relate. Being a
rebel herself, she knew exactly which buttons to push to
get them on the *ohm* track.

"If any of you think yoga is for sissies, I'm about to prove
you wrong. You'll be doing a series of exercises designed to
work the entire body, strengthening it, making it more flexi-
ble, and giving you more balance. So let's get started."

Skye began with breathing exercises, worked into stretching exercises, and then led them in a series of poses that had
all of them breaking a sweat by the end of the hourlong session.

The redheaded kicker came to Skye's side while the
other guys were still trying to recover from their power
workout. "Lulu has a shirt like that." He pointed to the
"Got Brains?" T-shirt Skye wore with her cotton yoga
pants.

"Yeah, she does."

"I hear she's got a job at Cosmic Comics." His voice
was kind of quiet and muffled with embarrassment.

"That's right."

He shuffled off without saying anything further.

Skye wanted to wrap things up, so she faced the team,
getting their attention with a wave of her arms. "Remember, you cannot fail. There is no failure in yoga."

"Yeah, well, there is failure in football," Coach Spears
growled as he rejoined them. "And we've had enough of it.
Right, Trojans?"

"Right."

"I didn't hear you," the coach barked. "Right, Trojans?"

"Right, Coach!"

• • •

"Escaped from any handcuffs lately?" Sister Mary greeted Skye as she entered the Sisters of the Poor Charity Thrift Shop later that day.

"Not lately, no. How about you?"

The nun laughed. "My handcuff-escaping days are behind me now."

"Oh, come on. You never know. I mean, you were part of a sit-in just the other day."

"True. I haven't spoken to you since then. How are you doing?"

"Fine. Why?" Skye eyed her suspiciously. "What have you heard?"

"Nothing." Sister Mary countered with a suspicious look of her own. "Why? What should I have heard?"

The nun's words made Skye realize that since she'd spilled the beans about the winning lottery ticket to Nathan last night, he could have blabbed it all over town. But he hadn't. At least not to Sister Mary. Or to anyone else Skye had run into so far today.

Before Skye could reveal her good news, Sister Mary was called away. Her place was taken by Wally Purdy, the assistant manager of the thrift store.

Wally was something of an eccentric, one of the special souls that the nun had taken under her wing over the years. He'd once confessed to Skye that he'd been an alcoholic most of his life, until Sister Mary had convinced him to get help. Skye didn't know how long ago that was, or how old he was. Maybe in his forties? Age didn't really matter to her. Nor did mistakes in a person's past.

Wally had nondescript looks, dull brown hair and eyes, but he made up for that with his outfits. He took pleasure in wearing the most outlandish golf pants paired with an equally jarring shirt. Today, he'd teamed a Hawaiian shirt in shades of green and yellow with pink-and-white pants.

Skye admired Wally's sense of individualism. Plus, she

just plain liked the guy. He had a good heart and he colored outside the lines. Definitely her kind of person.

"Have you come about gravity?" Wally asked.

"Gravity?"

Wally nodded. "The kitten. She fell through a hole in the roof in the back and landed on a chair that had just been donated. That's why I named her Gravity. I know that little girl of yours has been wanting a kitten for some time now. Want to see her?" Without waiting for an answer, Wally reached beneath the counter and pulled out a basket lined with a thick towel.

Curled up inside was the ugliest kitten Skye had ever seen. She was mostly black, with orange splotches all over her face and body. She looked as if she'd fallen into a jar of peanut butter.

Wally beamed. "Isn't she adorable?"

Skye was instantly a goner.

"You're not allowed to have pets in your apartment," Sister Mary reminded her as she rejoined them.

Skye waved her words away. "That policy may be changing soon. Wally, can you take care of Gravity for me awhile?"

"Sure. She can stay with me here at the store and keep me company."

"Just make sure she doesn't get outside. It's a dangerous world for a little thing like her." Skye rubbed the scrawny kitten's ears. The result was a mighty purr that would do a lion proud.

Wally grinned. "Dr. Flannigan the vet has already looked at her and given her some kitten shots. He says she's in good health, just needs some TLC. And he wasn't talking about The Learning Channel, either. He meant tender loving care."

"That's good to know."

Wally nodded. "I thought so too."

"Skye, what makes you think that your landlord is going

to change his 'no pets' policy?" Sister Mary asked. "Or were you thinking of breaking that rule? And don't give me that 'Who, me?' look. You know you like breaking rules. In fact, you thrive on it. Right, Wally?"

"Abs-o-tively, pos-a-lutely." The phrase was Wally's favorite.

"I only break rules that are meant to be broken," Skye said.

Sister Mary appeared doubtful. "Right."

"Like speed limits that make no sense."

The nun immediately pounced. "Ah, I thought we'd get around to him."

"Him?"

"Nate. The man who slapped those handcuffs on you."

"And who looked so pissed off when I escaped from them."

"You shouldn't say *pissed* in front of a nun," Wally whispered to Skye. "It's not proper."

"I'm rarely proper," Skye replied. "Nothing I could say would freak out Sister Mary."

"I wouldn't go quite that far," the nun said. "So, getting back to Nate . . ."

Skye rolled her eyes. "You're not going to talk about sparks, are you? Between Studly Do-Right and me? Because I've already heard it from Sue Ellen."

Wally frowned in confusion. "Who's Studly Do-Right?"

"Never mind." Sister Mary patted his hand. "Why don't you go get some of that kitty chow for your kitten?"

"She's going to be Skye's kitten soon."

"I'm not even going to get into that discussion," Sister Mary said after Wally had departed.

"Why not? I'd rather discuss Gravity than *him*."

"He has a name. Nathan. Or Nate."

"Nathan." Skye shook her head. "That's an old-fashioned name. Old-fashioned, just like him."

"So now you're judging the man based on his name?"

"No, based on the fact that he tried to give me a flyer for drug counseling. He thought I was an addict or something."

"Did you correct him?"

"Abs-o-tively." Skye began to casually browse through a rack of clothes.

"He's a good man."

"And I'm a bad girl. Not meant for an uptight guy like him."

"Why not?"

"Why . . . not?" Skye actually sputtered. She couldn't remember doing that before.

"Yes. Why not?" Sister Mary calmly repeated. "Don't you think you're good enough for him?"

"That's not the issue."

"Isn't it?" Sister Mary gave her one of those intense looks that could zoom straight into your very soul.

"I kissed him," Skye said casually. "We both agreed it was a mistake."

When Sister Mary blinked, Skye was the one who pounced this time. "Aha! I surprised you, didn't I?"

"Were you trying to surprise me?"

"By kissing him?" Skye grinned. "No, actually you didn't enter my thoughts at the time at all."

Sister Mary laughed. "I'm relieved to hear that."

"Look, don't spread it around town that I kissed him."

"I won't."

"And don't go getting any ideas about him and me. Because that's not going to happen."

"Whatever you say."

"You could sound a little more convincing."

"So could you," Sister Mary said with a knowing smile.

On that note, Skye left the thrift store without buying anything and headed over to Cosmic Comics to say hi.

Algee greeted her with his milewide smile.

"So, how's your new employee working out?" Skye blatantly pointed at Lulu before getting distracted by her friend's clever T-shirt slogan. *Alcohol and calculus don't mix. Never drink and derive.* "Hey, that reminds me . . . Lulu, there's a dude on the football team who's got a crush on you."

"Dude?" Lulu raised a pierced eyebrow.

"Dude?" Algee shook his head. "You've been hanging out at Rock Creek High School too long."

"Don't you want to know who it is?" Skye asked Lulu.

"You already told me. Dude. That must be his name. Dud, more likely," she muttered darkly.

"He likes the sayings on your T-shirts."

"I'll bet Dude-boy likes the saying on the cheerleaders' T-shirts better. Printed right over their boobs is the offending comment 'Who Needs Brains When You Have These?' A bunch of us protested, staging a 'girlcott' of the stores that sold the T-shirts."

Algee was amazed. "You're making that up, right? The shirts don't really say that, do they?"

Lulu nodded. "It's called irony. But only if you actually *do* have a brain. Which they don't."

"Lulu doesn't like cheerleaders," Skye said to Algee.

"Yeah," he noted dryly. "I detected that much myself."

"And I haven't even mentioned the Nipplegate incident of last year," Lulu continued. "When cheerleader Brandi's breast popped out of her minuscule halter top in a major wardrobe malfunction."

Recognizing that Lulu was on her way to a rant, Skye decided to sidetrack her throwing out a little bait. "What about the dude who has a crush on you?"

"What about the dude who has a crush on *you*?" Lulu said, no wimp in the baiting department herself.

"I'd rather talk about the one who has a crush on you," Skye replied.

"And I'd rather not."

"Do either of these dudes have a name?" Algee asked.

Skye shrugged. "The football dude is Brock. Or Brad.

Something like that. I'm not that good with names. I've only given the team two lessons."

"Brad is the redheaded kicker and Brock is the jock quarterback," Lulu stated.

"I thought you didn't care who the dude was?"

"I don't. Just like you don't care about the sheriff and all those sparks between you two."

"It's not the same thing at all," Skye said, hands on her hips.

"Time out." Algee covered his ears. "Too much girl talk."

"I agree," Nathan said, strolling out from a side aisle.

Once again, he was out of uniform and looking entirely too sexy in jeans and another plain, slogan-free T-shirt. Skye's gaze was instantly drawn to his mouth and the lips that she'd kissed, tasted, nibbled, wanted to kiss again . . .

Her brief lapse into feebleminded fantasyland aggravated Skye. So naturally she took it out on Nathan. "What are you doing here? Is no place safe anymore?"

"What could be safer than having an officer of the law on the premises?"

"Did you know he was here?" Skye asked Lulu.

She shook her head. "He must have come in before I got here. I only arrived a few minutes ago."

Skye turned with an accusatory glare toward Algee. "Well, *you* must have known he was in here."

"Don't answer that on the grounds that you might incriminate yourself," Nathan advised Algee.

The two men grinned at each other. The room's testosterone level immediately skyrocketed, which drove Skye crazy.

"Oh, get over yourselves," she snapped. "Next thing you know, you'll be slapping butts like the guys on the football team."

"Yeah, what is *that* about?" Lulu asked with a roll of her eyes.

"Men." Skye did an eye roll of her own. "You can't live with them, and you can't . . . shoot them."

"Ain't that the truth." Skye would have felt better had the drawled words not come from Nathan. She just hated his having the last word. Unfortunately, he left before she could come up with something suitably sarcastic.

No problem. She'd get him next time.

• • •

"Adam Kemp here."

Upon hearing Adam's voice, Angel froze, then immediately ended the call she'd just placed to him. She stared down at the cell phone that Julia had gotten for her before leaving town, as if it held the answer to why she'd chickened out and hung up.

Startled when it rang a moment later, she automatically answered. "Hello?"

"Why did you call me and then hang up?" Adam demanded.

"How did you know it was me?"

"I have caller ID. Your cell phone number came up. So I just hit star-six-nine."

Angel had no idea what he was talking about—not that unusual an occurrence, actually. He threw her off balance, which made her defensive. This despite the fact that her horoscope had claimed today was a good day to take action. "Why did you call me?"

"To see why you called me and hung up."

"I was just returning your original call."

"You took your sweet time."

His sarcastic comment irked her. "What do you want?"

"I haven't heard from our daughter Julia in eleven days now. When was the last time she called you?"

"Uhm . . . I don't know." Angel frowned in concentration. "A couple of days ago?"

"Meaning what? Two days? Five days? Three weeks? What?"

"You know I don't pay attention to time the way you do."

"How about our daughter? Do you pay attention to her?"

"Of course I do! And how dare you insinuate otherwise."

"How dare you not even know how long it's been since you've talked to Julia," he shot back.

"She's a grown woman."

"So?"

"So she can take care of herself. She's the practical one in the family. And she has Luke. The last time I spoke to her, she sounded fine."

"I left a message on her cell phone's voicemail telling her to call me."

"Ordering her, most likely. Julia doesn't respond well to orders."

"She must have gotten that from you," Adam retorted.

"Yeah, right. Like you're the obedient type. You don't respond well to orders either."

"True enough. I suppose you've heard that I'm separated from my latest wife."

"Really?" Angel wasn't about to admit she'd heard anything. "I'm sorry to hear that."

"Why?"

"Because it's always sad when things don't work out."

"Were you sad when things didn't work out with us?"

His question stunned her. "That was decades ago."

"Answer the question."

"No."

"No, you weren't sad?"

"No, I'm not answering the question."

"Why not?"

"Because it's none of your business."

"The same way that you figured it was none of my business that I had a daughter?"

"I already explained about that . . ."

"Your brief and incoherent explanation can't make up for all those years I've missed."

"If you're trying to guilt-trip me, you're not going to succeed."

"Because you have no conscience?"

"You're a fine one to talk about conscience! You're in the business of putting other people out of business, of taking away their jobs!"

"I'm in the business of making money."

"No matter what the cost?"

His voice changed. Deepened. "I'm not the monster you've made me out to be. Let me prove it to you."

"What do you mean?" What was he up to?

"Have dinner with me."

"Dinner?"

"You eat, right?"

"I'm a vegetarian."

"Do you eat fish? We could go to a seafood place I know here in Philadelphia and talk about Julia. She told me you've got a photo album of her as a baby."

"It's more like a scrapbook and it covers her entire childhood, not just when she was a baby."

"I'd love to see that."

Angel was about to say she'd mail it to him, but realized she didn't trust Adam to return it.

"Help me understand why you didn't tell me about Julia earlier." His voice became husky, entreating her.

Help me. Man, was Angel a sucker for those words. That was the only reason she reluctantly agreed to meet Adam. That and the fact that a new yarn store had recently opened in Philadelphia. She'd been wanting to visit it. This just gave her an excuse to do so.

The deed done, she hung up.

She was really getting too old to be playing these kind of games. She was having hot flashes and memory lapses.

Soy and black cohosh were her friends, working together to maintain her hormonal balance. So why weren't the damn supplements doing their job? Sometimes she just got so aggravated.

Angel's face burned as she picked up a Seventh Generation catalogue and fanned herself to cool off.

The thing was, most of the time Angel didn't feel all that old. She still felt like the girl who'd met Adam in that ethics class at UCLA. She even looked a little like her still. Sort of.

So what was going on that she was worrying about her age all of a sudden?

She thought about Adam and their making a date for dinner. No, not a date. A meeting. Like a business meeting. Not that she was into business meetings, but he sure was.

That's how she'd view it. As for how to tell Tyler about it . . . she'd figure that part out later.

• • •

Nathan paused after entering Nick's Tavern, wondering if the place had always looked so . . . tacky. The minimal lighting was no doubt meant to keep patrons in the dark, literally, so they wouldn't notice certain things. Like the linoleum floor curling at the edges. Or the dinginess of the decades-old wood paneling with the hole still in it from a fight he'd been called upon to break up over six months ago.

The scary thing was that Nick's Tavern was the best bar in town.

Not that Nathan was into fancy stuff. All he really needed was to meet up with his buddy Cole . . . and order a beer.

"Hey, I heard you had an exciting day the other day," Cole said as he lifted a bottle of Budweiser in his buddy's direction.

"Not really." Nathan paused to order a Heineken.

"No? So, protestors staging a sit-in outside the police station is normal?"

"I didn't say it was a *normal* day. Just not an exciting one."

"I find that hard to believe."

"Why?"

"Because Skye Wright creates excitement wherever she goes."

"Which isn't a good thing."

"Depends. I heard she got to you."

"I need to get a new assistant," Nathan muttered. "Celeste talks too much."

"No one else would take the job."

"She still talks too much."

"Hey, she was just bringing her beagle to me for his shots. We chatted a few minutes."

"About me."

"Your name came up a time or two. Is it true you handcuffed her?"

"Celeste? No. I might be tempted to gag her, though."

"I meant Skye. Did you handcuff Skye?"

"Only as a precautionary measure. I didn't want her hurting herself."

"Did she have a weapon? Other than her belly-dancing costume, I mean?"

Nathan's eyes narrowed. "What do you know about her belly-dancing costume?"

"That she looks damn good in it."

"And you know this how?"

"And you care why?"

Nathan refused to answer. "You know what this town needs? Less gossip and more good take-out."

"You're saying that Nick's microwaved nachos aren't up to your usual culinary standards?"

"I'm saying that it's a good thing I've got a cast-iron stomach."

"Why didn't you tell me about the Skye episode when I stopped by your office the other day?"

"There was nothing to tell."

"Yeah, right."

Nathan hadn't heard anything in town today about any supposed change of Skye's good fortune that would allow her to purchase the Tivoli Theater. Since she'd been dancing down the street in happiness when she'd run into him last night, you'd think she'd have spread the word all over the entire state by now.

Why hadn't she? What was she up to now? Had she just been yanking his chain? Pulling some scam?

Great. She'd sauntered her way right back into his brain. Here he thought he'd been doing so well keeping her locked out . . .

But that kiss was hard to ignore. Not impossible to wipe out, just stubborn and totally memorable. Like her.

Nathan finished the rest of his Heineken and ordered another, noting as he did so that the green bottle matched the color of Skye's eyes.

Dammit, there she was again. Couldn't a guy get a beer without having to deal with an aggravating, hip-twitching woman who'd probably inspired the saying, "When Mr. Happy gets hard, a man's brain goes soft"?

His brain had to be soft to allow her entry again and again.

Kissing her had definitely made Mr. Happy get hard.

Even now, just thinking about her made his body react.

Shifting in his seat, Nathan deliberately focused on another subject. This time he asked Cole the questions. He preferred things that way. "Were you aware that your aunt, Sister Mary, knows how to slip out of handcuffs?"

"Yeah. She taught me when I was a kid."

"And your other aunt, Mrs. Crumpler, was a participant in the sit-in."

"That doesn't surprise me."

"Some family you've got there."

"Yeah," Cole said fondly. "Hey, yours is some family too."

"They don't do sit-ins."

"Your older sister is a doctor with Doctors without Borders, working in Africa. And your other sister is a teacher in Alaska someplace."

"Homer. Homer, Alaska."

Cole looked up from the pile of empty peanut shells he'd neatly stacked. "And your mom makes the best Florentine cookies on the planet."

"Yeah, she does."

"In her spare time, when she's not working as a nurse at the local hospital. And your dad is no slouch. What is this, his thirtieth year with the Nebraska State Police?"

"Yeah. He'll be retiring soon."

"A rock-solid family."

"Right."

Cole frowned. "So where did they go wrong with you?"

Nathan smiled for the first time that night. "They must have gotten the wrong baby at the hospital."

"Nah, that excuse isn't gonna wash. Your mom's a nurse. She'd noticed something like that. Besides, you've got your dad's Roman nose and your mom's stubborn streak."

"And you've got your aunt's nagging streak."

"Which aunt might that be?"

"Sister Mary."

"Ah . . ." Cole nodded knowingly. "So she got on your case, did she?"

"They called her down to the station with the news that I might be torturing someone."

"Well, you do drive Celeste crazy sometimes when you skip meals."

"I meant a prisoner."

"You had a prisoner?"

"Well, not a prisoner per se . . ."

"So who did Sister Mary think you were torturing?" Cole held up one hand. "No, let me guess. The belly-dancing Skye?"

"Affirmative."

"Oh, man, I wish I'd been there to see that."

"See what?"

"Sister Mary torturing you. Trying to pull the truth out of you. She's a nun. You're a lapsed Catholic. She's got that guilt thing going for her big-time."

"I was immune."

"Right. Sure you were." Cole nodded but looked like he didn't believe a word. "How about the belly dancer? Were you immune to her, too?"

"Totally."

"Did you know that your upper lip twitches when you lie?"

If Nathan's upper lip was twitching, it was because of the memory of Skye seductively nibbling on it.

"Did you know that I can't hear a word you say?" Nathan said.

"I heard that you start going deaf after you turn thirty."

"You're only a few years younger than I am."

"Chronologically."

"Right. Mentally you're, what . . . twelve?"

Cole threw a handful of peanut shells at him.

"You throw like a girl, you know that?" Nathan ducked as another handful of shells flew his way.

"Okay, that's it." Cole stood and smacked his hands palm down on the rickety table. "You. Me. In front of the dartboard. Now."

"Sheriff, thank God I found you!"

Nathan was instantly on his feet, facing the newcomer—Owen Dunback's slick nephew, Milton.

"You've got to arrest her immediately," Milton demanded breathlessly.

"Slow down. Arrest who?"

"That sleazy slut who tricked my uncle out of a million dollars!"

Chapter Six

· · · · · · · · · · ·

"A name, Milton." Nathan's voice was firm. "I need a name."

"Who do you think I'm talking about? How many sleazy sluts are there in town seducing my poor uncle?"

Nathan was not impressed with his outburst. "A name."

"Skye Wright. She's embezzled money from him."

"That's a serious charge."

"I realize that."

"What makes you think she embezzled money?"

"Because she has a winning lottery ticket worth a million dollars."

Nathan certainly remembered his earlier conversation with Skye about buying the Tivoli Theater. He thought maybe she'd concocted the story. Apparently not, if what Milton was telling him was true.

"And you know this how?" Nathan asked.

"My uncle told me. He gave her the ticket."

"That's not embezzlement. That's generosity."

"That's not generosity, that's senility!" Milton shoved his hand through his thinning brown hair. He wore it combed over, as if that would hide his shiny scalp.

"If he *gave* her the ticket—"

"He didn't know what he was doing!"

"Is Owen saying he wants the ticket back?"

"*I'm* saying that."

"It's not *your* ticket," Nathan pointed out.

"It's not hers, either."

"It is if Owen gave it to her."

"Think about it, Sheriff. What sane man would give a female like her a million dollars? Unless it was for services provided." Milton's eyes lit up. "Can't you arrest her for that? For prostitution."

"Calm down." Nathan belatedly realized the entire bar crowd was ignoring the baseball game on the TV and was instead listening to them.

"I will not calm down!" Milton's voice rose as if to prove that point.

"Then let's go to the station to discuss this matter."

Milton nodded. "Good idea."

Behind his back, Cole rolled his eyes.

"Later, buddy." Nathan told him.

"I would have beaten you at darts anyway."

"Dreamer."

Cole grinned and shrugged. "Hey, it's a tough job, but somebody's gotta do it."

And Nathan sure wasn't a dreamer. Not anymore. Never again.

• • •

A little after nine that night, Skye opened her apartment door to find Nathan standing there. "We have to talk," he said.

He was wearing the same jeans and T-shirt he'd had on

at Cosmic Comics earlier. No outrageous sayings on this man's chest. Plain navy blue cotton covered his muscular upper torso. She remembered grabbing his T-shirt last night and kissing him as if they were in a mosh pit together. "I thought we weren't going to discuss that kiss."

"We're not."

"Then why are you here?"

"To talk to you."

"About?"

"About that winning lottery ticket."

"Oh. I told you about it earlier."

"No, you just told me you were buying the Tivoli Theater. You didn't tell me how you planned on doing that."

"Oh? So how did you find out? Did Owen tell you?"

"Yes. So did his nephew Milton."

"Milton," Skye repeated slowly. The little weasel. "Right. So you're here to interrogate me. Or handcuff me again." She shoved her wrists at him.

"I'm not going to handcuff you."

"Don't make promises you can't keep," she murmured.

"Can't we just talk?"

"On the record, I'm assuming."

"Right. Just talking like two adults."

"One of whom is an authority freak."

"That must be you."

Skye did a double take. The cop had a sense of humor? When had that happened?

"I was talking about *you*," she said.

"I'm not an authority freak."

"Neither am I."

"Good. Another thing we have in common. That list is getting longer every day."

"Did you talk to Owen about the winning ticket?" Skye asked.

"Yes."

"Then you already know the facts."

"I'd like to hear them from you, as well." He pulled a small notebook from his back pocket.

"To see if our stories match, is that it?"

"Just tell me what happened."

"Why should I?"

"Because I asked you to."

"That kind of logic never worked for me."

"No surprise there," Nathan muttered.

"Meaning what?"

"Meaning you're not logical."

"I am totally logical. Just not by your definition of logic."

"There's only one definition of logic. It's in the dictionary."

"No, there are many definitions, and they are determined by each person's life view."

"Right."

"Could you sound a little more sarcastic?"

"Hey, I'm not into that New Age kind of stuff."

"Like logic, you mean?"

"Logic has nothing to do with New Age beliefs."

"You being an expert and all on New Age beliefs."

"We've gotten off the subject here. Back to that lottery ticket—"

"No, I want to hear more about your barbaric views on this subject."

"On lottery tickets?"

"On"—she used hand quotes—"New Age stuff."

"Look, I'm just a guy from Nebraska trying to do my job—"

"That "Aw shucks, ma'am" routine is not going to work with me, so don't even try it."

"It's not a routine."

"Puh-lease. I've seen you in kick-butt mode. I've kissed you. You're not just a guy from Nebraska."

"I'm not?"

"No. And you already know that damn well, so you sure don't need my telling you."

Nathan wasn't sure what he knew "damn well" anymore. Not when he was around Skye. And he hated that. Hated being at a disadvantage. Hated being anything but rock solid.

He could feel small fissures forming in the shell he'd carefully constructed these past years. Not acceptable.

"Do you need me to be kick-ass before you'll answer my question?" Nathan demanded.

"Which question was that?" Skye countered. "What, exactly, is Milton accusing me of?"

"Why don't you just tell me your side of the story?"

"Why should I?"

"Because it's the right thing to do."

She gave him a look.

Nathan sighed. "Why are you so determined to make things difficult?"

"Me? It's you who is making life difficult. I'll bet you never meditate, right?"

"Right."

"I can tell."

"I'm glad."

"You shouldn't be. You'll live longer if you meditate. It's a great stress reliever."

"Maybe I don't want to live longer."

"Ah."

Now her expression turned speculative, as if he were a puzzle she was intent on figuring out. Well, good luck with that. Because there was no way in hell he was going to let her get to know him well enough to do that. He couldn't figure himself out, so there was no way a flaky belly dancer who could kiss like an angel—a Victoria's Secret angel—could decipher him.

She was smart enough not to ask him why he didn't want to live longer. Not that he would have told her.

She was wearing black shorts that showed off her great legs and a cropped tie-dyed T-shirt that showed off her midriff and naval ring.

"You need a drink," she suddenly announced, then yanked him inside.

He felt as if he'd stepped inside a circus trailer. Color was splashed everywhere—the walls, the rugs, the mounds of pillows scattered all over. Reds, oranges, yellows.

Not that the place was cluttered. On the contrary. Not much furniture, but what was there was memorable.

He recognized the round red couch and worn orange recliner as rejects from the Sisters of the Poor Charity Thrift Shop. And he was pretty sure that his buddy Cole had sold that ugly brass floor lamp at his last garage sale for a buck.

"Here." She handed him a mug filled with liquid.

He sniffed it suspiciously. "What is it?"

"Arsenic tea."

"Very funny."

"It's organic green tea."

"I don't drink tea."

"You only drink that thick, dark sludge at the police station that you call coffee, huh?"

"Black, no sugar, no milk."

"Right. Because you're a guy from Nebraska. A hunky side of beef from the cornfields."

He raised an eyebrow. "Hunky?"

"Who wears tighty-whities. Am I right?"

Nathan mentally counted to ten. He could practically feel the steam pouring out of his ears. Normally, he was a very controlled guy, but she had an uncanny way of getting to him.

"Come on. You can tell me," she coaxed.

"No." His jaw was clenched so tightly he could barely speak. "I can't."

"You're not blushing, are you?"

He narrowed his eyes and put his war face on. "Enough

of this. Is it your claim that Owen gave you the winning lottery ticket?"

"It's not a claim, it's the truth."

"Fine." He slapped the notebook shut. "If you don't want to cooperate with this investigation, I'll note that in my report."

"You do that." She took a sip of the tea she'd poured for him. "What report is that? The one on me? It must be getting pretty thick by now."

"And that pleases you, doesn't it?"

She shrugged and took another sip.

The tea left her lips damp and made him want to kiss her again. Her gaze caught his. The air between them radiated sex.

"Back off, mean man!" a voice barked.

It took Nathan a second to realize that the person with the pipes of a Paris Island Marine Corps drill instructor was none other than Skye's half-pint daughter. She bared her teeth at him. The kid, not Skye.

"It's okay." Skye smoothed her daughter's hair back, inadvertently tilting the little girl's tiara even more. "I thought you were sleeping."

What kind of mom had their kid sleeping in a tiara and a tutu with tights?

"I heard voices."

"Want some tea?" Skye offered her mug to the little girl, who drank while eyeing him suspiciously. She handed the tea back to her mother before ordering, "Make him go away."

"I was just leaving," Nathan muttered. He never muttered. Until he'd met Skye.

"My name is Toni and I don't want you bullying my mommy," Toni told him, hands on her tiny hips. "You do that again and she'll turn you into a toad. She's got a spinning wheel just like Sleeping Beauty. Sleeping Beauty wasn't just a princess. She had a business empire. Tell him, Mommy."

"I don't think he wants to hear a fairy-tale."

"Is he a troll?"

"No." Skye shook her head. "He's an authority figure."

"We don't like those, right?"

Skye nodded. "We question their authority, yes."

Nathan couldn't let that one pass. "That's a nice lesson to teach a kid."

"Toni and I learn from each other."

"So, how does that work? You learn tantrums from her and she learns bad behavior from you?"

"Don't insult my kid." Skye's face reflected her anger.

Toni jumped up and down in excitement, the tiara flying right off her head. "Get him, Mommy. Get him! Turn him into a toad!"

"He's already a toad," Skye said.

Toni paused to stare at him. "No, he's not. Toads look like mean frogs. He still looks like a mean man. I bite," Toni warned Nathan.

"So do I," he growled right back at her.

Great. Now he was in a pissing contest with a little kid. Real mature. Real professional.

He had to get out of there. Before making an even bigger idiot of himself than he'd already done.

As Nathan slammed the door on his way out, he heard the sexy mother and her undisciplined kid giggling. At him. The supposed authority figure. Too bad the only thing he seemed to be an authority on lately was losing control. That had to stop.

• • •

"Did you arrest her?" Milton was waiting at the sheriff's station early the next morning, pouncing on him the instant Nathan entered the front door.

"No." Nathan hadn't gotten much sleep last night and he wasn't in the best of moods by a long shot. He should have used the employees' back entrance, but he hadn't been thinking straight.

"You didn't arrest her?" Milton was furious. "Why not?"

"Because she didn't commit a crime."

"She stole that lottery ticket!"

"Not according to Owen. It was his ticket. He could do what he wanted with it. And he wanted to give it to her. In fact, he alleges that she bought the ticket in the first place as a gift for him."

Milton trailed Nathan into his office, ignoring protests by Celeste. "And you believed that?"

"Why would your uncle lie?"

"To protect her."

Nathan sank into his office chair and waved the fluttering Celeste away, his look intended to reassure her that he could handle this himself. "Please close the door on your way out, Celeste."

She slammed it.

Great. Now he'd have to soothe her ruffled feathers. Later. One drama at a time. "What's your interest in all this, Milton?"

"I'm just trying to protect my uncle, that's all."

The door opened and Owen joined them, waved in by a militant-looking Celeste. She didn't approve of guests entering his office without her first announcing them, so she said, "Owen Dunback to see you, Sheriff."

"Thanks, Celeste, I can handle this. If you'd just close the door again, please?"

She didn't slam it quite so hard this time.

Owen faced his nephew. "What are you doing, Milton?"

"As I just told the sheriff, I'm just trying to protect you."

"By telling people I'm getting senile? Or by besmirching Skye's reputation?"

"Her reputation was bad before I said anything," Milton said stiffly. "Before she even came here."

Owen glared at his nephew. "Just give it up, Milton. I'm warning you, I don't want you spreading these vicious rumors about Skye. Or about me, for that matter. I'm no more senile than you are. In fact, I'd wager I've got my act together more than you do. I'm not the one who still sleeps with a night-light."

Milton's expression instantly turned defensive. "My parents scarred me for life when they took me to see *Poltergeist*."

"Get over it," Owen retorted. "And get over the idea that any of my money is coming your way. Or your wife Robin's way. It's not going to happen."

"Since my parents' deaths, we're your only next of kin."

"That doesn't mean anything. Now stop wasting the sheriff's valuable time with this nonsense."

Milton's face turned beet red before he pivoted, yanked open the door, and marched out, reminding Nathan of a pissed-off rooster.

"I'd like a word with you," Owen said to Nathan.

Nathan nodded toward the still-open office door.

Owen closed it and then sat down. "Did you speak to Skye about this situation?"

"Yes."

"What did she say?"

"She wasn't real cooperative."

"Why should she be? You were as good as accusing her of lying and stealing. Despite the fact that I'd already given you all the relevant information, you insisted on going to see her. I told you it wasn't a good idea. Young people." Owen shook his head. "They just don't listen."

"Did Skye come complaining to you after my visit?"

Owen stared at him in astonishment. "Are you kidding? You don't think Skye is capable of fighting her own battles?"

"Her kid bites."

"I know. Did she get you?"

"No." Nathan shifted some papers on his desk. "Where's the little girl's dad?"

"I don't know. Skye never talks about him. Why did you want to know?"

"Because she seems to be raising her kid without much discipline."

"I wouldn't go there if I were you," Owen warned him. "Skye is very touchy about the subject of her daughter."

"Yeah, I got that."

"I really don't know why you two got off on such bad footing. Might have had something to do with your handcuffing her and hauling her off to jail."

"I didn't haul her and she wasn't in jail. She was here in my office."

"Skye has a thing against authority figures."

"Yeah, I got that, too."

"I'm sorry that my irritating nephew created a problem. I can assure you that there is nothing the least bit shady about my giving Skye that ticket."

"Not many people would hand over a million dollars to someone."

Owen shrugged. "I have more money than I need. She doesn't. But she has a dream."

"To buy the Tivoli Theater."

"She told you?" Owen was clearly surprised.

"Yeah, she mentioned it."

"Skye isn't one to share her dreams."

"She's not exactly the shy sort."

"True, but still . . . When did she tell you about the theater?"

"I bumped into her on the street the other night," Nathan admitted. "It must have been shortly after you gave her the ticket. She seemed pretty excited. She was dancing down the sidewalk."

Owen smiled. "Sister Mary says Skye creates a joyful noise wherever she goes."

"Must be caused by those bells on her belly-dancing costume," Nathan noted.

"Was she wearing that when you bumped into her?"

"No."

"Then her costume didn't cause the joyful noise. It's her. Skye is something special. I wish you could see that."

Nathan could see that. But that didn't mean he liked it.

• • •

"I've gathered you all here today to share some good news." Skye looked out at the expectant faces of her friends—Sue Ellen, Lulu, Sister Mary, Nancy, and Algee. They were all gathered in her living room. "You may have heard some rumors—"

"I didn't believe them," Sue Ellen stated vehemently.

"They're true," Skye said.

"You seduced Owen?" Sue Ellen's lipstick-laden lips curled in an *eeeyuw* expression.

"No, that part isn't true," Skye said quickly. "The part about the million-dollar winning lottery ticket is true."

"And you had us come here because you're going to share your winnings with us?" Lulu looked hopeful.

"No. I'm going to buy the Tivoli Theater and reopen it," Skye announced.

The room was totally silent.

"Back up a minute," Nancy said. "How did you get a million-dollar lottery ticket? I didn't know you gambled."

"I don't," Skye admitted. "But you know how Owen loves the lottery. So I got him a couple of instant-winner cards. As a thank-you for him paying off my traffic tickets."

Nancy frowned. Clearly, this was news to her. "He paid off your tickets?"

"Yes. But I'm going to pay him back from my winnings," Skye quickly assured her.

"So, when you found it was an instant winner, you took the lottery ticket back?"

"He gave it back to me," Skye explained.

"Yeah." Nancy nodded. "That's what Owen said earlier today."

"You mean, you already knew I'd won?"

Everyone nodded.

"Then why didn't any of you say anything before this?"

Sister Mary shrugged. "You said you had something important to tell us. We all figured we'd let you say whatever that was."

Sue Ellen stood and placed her hands on her hips. "I can't believe you didn't say anything before this."

"It only happened two nights ago."

"What if I'd been hit by a bus, huh? What then?" Sue Ellen paused a moment to milk the most drama. "I'd have died not knowing you'd won a million dollars."

Algee spoke for the first time. "Did you say you were buying the Tivoli Theater?"

Skye nodded. "That's right. I sealed the deal this morning with the realtor. Well, once I get the lottery money, the deal will be sealed."

"Sealed the deal?" Sue Ellen placed the back of her hand on Skye's forehead. "Are you running a fever? This doesn't sound like you at all."

Skye laughed. "I'm fine."

"What are you going to do about the rumors that Milton is spreading around town?" Lulu asked. "Want me to TP the front of his tax accounting office with a few rolls of Charmin?"

"I could have a word with him," Algee offered, flexing his impressive biceps. "Put the fear of God into him."

"That's something I'm good at as well," Sister Mary said. "Maybe it would be better if I spoke to him."

"He's a born-again evangelical Baptist," Nancy said. "He's not going to listen to a nun. I know some guys. They used to run a chop shop. Not that I get auto parts from them, but . . . I could ask them to have a word with Milton."

Sister Mary gave her younger sibling a disapproving look. "Mobsters are not the answer."

Nancy looked defensive. "Yeah, that's what you told me when I hooked up with Anthony in Vegas."

"And I was right."

"I don't care what Milton says," Skye stated.

"Is that another bad-girl trait?" Nancy asked.

"Yeah."

"Are you still going to give your belly-dancing lessons?" Nancy said.

Skye was surprised by the question. "Of course. I'm going to honor all my obligations."

"That doesn't sound very bad-girl to me," Lulu said.

"Frankly, I need the money," Skye replied. "I won't get the lottery payout for a few weeks yet."

"Oh." Lulu nodded. "I guess that makes sense. Besides, the football team is counting on you, especially Brad the kicker. Their season begins soon."

"The other day you said you didn't care about any of that."

Lulu shrugged. "I was just stating a fact. Don't make a big deal out of it."

"Winning a million dollars is a big deal," Sue Ellen said.

"So is buying a theater," Sister Mary said.

"Thanks for not telling me I'm out of my mind."

"Would it make any difference to tell you that?" Sister Mary asked.

"No," Skye admitted.

Sister Mary smiled, one of those saintly nun smiles she was so good at. "Then what's the point?"

Skye felt a twinge of guilt. Okay, more than a twinge. "If I were a better person, I'd have donated the money to the Sisters of the Poor."

Sister Mary patted her arm reassuringly. "Owen has been more than generous toward our charitable endeavors."

"I told him he should have donated the money to you

instead of giving it to me." The words were out before Skye could stop them.

Lulu shook her head at Skye. "That really doesn't sound very bad-girl at all. Keep talking like that, and your reputation will be totally ruined."

"Milton is doing his best to ruin my reputation already. He sent the sheriff over here last night to interrogate me."

"The sheriff? Did he bring handcuffs?" Sue Ellen had an eager light in her blue eyes. "Or a whip?"

Skye cracked up. "No, he did not."

"Not that I'd know anything about either of those two things," Sue Ellen hastily assured Sister Mary. "Or where to order them on the Internet."

They were interrupted by a knock on the door. Sister Mary leaned over and opened it. "Ah, Nate. Come on in. We were just talking about you."

Chapter Seven

· · · · · · · · · · ·

"**Why** do I have the impression that you weren't singing my praises?" Nathan said as he cautiously entered the room.

"Maybe because you're paranoid?" Skye suggested.

"Just because he's paranoid, that doesn't mean that people aren't still talking about him," Lulu said. "I have the T-shirt. Oh, wait, I traded it for this one." She pointed to her chest. *Don't talk to me when I'm talking to myself*.

"So, to what do we owe the honor of your visit, Nate?" Sister Mary asked.

At that point, Toni ran into the room with her favorite toy in hand—Ta, the orange tiger Angel had recently crocheted for her. She stopped in her tracks when she saw Nathan. "It's the mean man! I thought you said he'd turn into a toad, Mommy. He bites," the little girl told the room at large. "He told me so."

As Skye watched Nathan's face turn red, she almost felt sorry for him. Almost.

"Maybe I should come back later," he muttered.

"Why? There's nothing you can't say in front of my friends. Have you come here to continue your interrogation?" Skye demanded.

"You didn't by any chance bring handcuffs with you, did you?" Sue Ellen asked hopefully.

"Or a whip?" Lulu said.

Nathan's eyes shot to Sister Mary, who waved away his visible concern. "Don't worry about me."

"He *is* carrying a big gun," Nancy noted with a grin.

"Come on, give the guy a break, would you?" Algee came to Nathan's defense. "Maybe we should all clear out and let him speak to Skye privately. Who knows, maybe he came to apologize to her for mistakenly believing a word that tacky accountant said about her." Algee's inflection clearly indicated that an apology was definitely in order and would be a very good idea. Hint, hint.

Skye was actually impressed with how quickly Algee cleared the room. He offered to take Toni down to the comic-book store with him, but the little girl steadfastly refused to leave her mother's side. Skye's miniprotector eyed Nathan suspiciously.

"So, did you come to apologize, Nathan?" Skye asked.

"In a manner of speaking."

"And what manner might that be?"

"I may have been a little rough on you last night."

"You think?"

"You didn't help matters any."

"Not a direction you want to take if you want this apology to fly," she warned.

Toni's eyes widened. "Does he fly? Like those mean monkeys in *The Wizard of Oz*?"

"No, he can't fly," Skye reassured her.

"I brought something," he stated gruffly.

"Not handcuffs or a whip?"

"No. It's something for the kid. I didn't mean to scare her." His voice got even gruffer.

"You can speak directly to her. She's right here."

Skye saw him swallow, and a wave of emotion suddenly hit her. The raw emotion was coming from the uptight lawman. Toni wasn't the one scared. Nathan was.

But why? What did this mean? Did it have something to do with his wife? Did they have a kid of their own? Maybe she should have paid more attention when people had tried to tell her about him.

Nathan surprised her by squatting so that he was eye-level with Toni. "I didn't mean to scare you. I'm sorry."

Toni's eyes darted up to her mother for direction before taking matters into her own little hands. "Do you promise not to be mean again?" she said sternly.

Nathan nodded. "I'll do my best."

"Okay." Toni patted his cheek. "You're okay now. Just don't be mean again or my mommy will really have to turn you into a toad."

Skye saw his Adam's apple bobble as he rose to his feet. "Here." He shoved a wrapped package into her arms before quickly exiting.

So much pain, so tightly bound inside one man.

"What's in the package, Mommy?"

"I don't know. I guess we'll have to unwrap it to see." As Skye tore off the paper, it occurred to her that she might have to unwrap Nathan's defenses in order to see the man inside.

"Show me, show me!" Toni jumped up and down with excitement.

It was a book. *Kitten's First Full Moon*, about a kitten who thought the moon was a bowl of milk, with wonderful black-and-white illustrations.

Maybe there was more to the guy than met the eye. Not that what met the eye wasn't mighty fine. That big gun and all.

• • •

Later that afternoon, Angel stared down at the tarot cards spread out on the 1950s-style Formica kitchen table in Skye's apartment. "These seem to indicate that you may be in for a rough patch coming up. With some danger."

"I'm in danger of smacking that guy," Skye said.

"What guy?"

"Nathan."

"Why?"

"Because he's starting to seem complicated, and you know how I am about that."

"You're a sucker for that."

"Yeah, I know." Skye bit into an organic Winesap apple she'd gotten from the local farmer's market. "Why couldn't he just stay a pain in the butt? Why did he have to get Toni an adorable kitten book?"

"He got her a book? When?"

"Earlier this afternoon. When he stopped by."

"And that's why you want to smack him?" Angel said. "Because you're attracted to him?"

Skye nodded.

"Violence is never the answer to a problem. Although Adam made me want to smack him when we talked the other day," Angel admitted.

"You talked to Adam? Why?"

"It was about Julia."

"What about her?"

"He wants to meet up for dinner."

"The capitalist pig is after you."

"No, he's not."

"I thought I heard he's separated from his wife."

"I don't care if he is."

"Did you say you'd meet him?" Skye demanded.

Angel nodded sheepishly.

"What were you thinking? Never mind. I think Toni and

I should go with you. That should keep his mind off sex with you."

"Now you're sounding like Tyler."

"What does he think about this dinner idea?"

"I haven't exactly told him yet."

"Remember how much trouble you got into for lying before? About Julia's biological father?"

"I know. I believe in leading an honest life. Really, I do. But sometimes . . ."

"Sometimes what?"

"It's hard. And stressful."

"That's a sign that you should stay far away from Adam. I mean, you didn't see the guy for thirty years."

"I know."

"Julia's not even here, and still she's able to make you miserable."

"This isn't Julia's fault. I know you two girls have some issues . . ."

"More issues than *Time* magazine, as the saying goes. Although I prefer the irreverent satire of the *Onion*."

"You're both just so different."

"Yeah. She's uptight and impossible and I'm always right."

Angel smiled. "She came through for us when we were in a bind a few months ago. She let us stay with her all that time. I'm still living in her house."

"House-sitting while she's off pretending to be a wild thing. As if she could ever really pull that act off."

"She looked pretty natural sitting on the back of that Harley, I must say. I was really surprised. But you didn't see her, did you?"

Skye shook her head.

"Why not?" Angel studied Skye's face. "Why didn't you come see her off?"

"I was busy."

Angel gave her a look.

Skye tossed her apple in the garbage. "I didn't want to, okay?"

"You're not jealous, are you?"

"Of her and Luke? No way. We had zip chemistry."

"No, I meant of her father."

"You mean the fact that she has a billionaire father who's alive, while my father is dead? No. I'd rather have had my dad any day."

"That's what I thought, but I wasn't sure." Angel frowned. "There's still tension in your voice whenever you speak about her."

"Because she drives me crazy."

"Julia says the same about you."

"I know she does. But she's wrong. She always thinks she knows best."

"The curse of being an older sister, perhaps?"

"I don't know what caused it, but it is a curse, all right. And she's so bossy and judgmental. Half the trouble I got into was just to piss her off."

"Well, she's not around now, so you don't have to do anything to get into trouble. Unless that's why you're creating sparks with the sheriff? To aggravate your sister?"

"No. He's able to aggravate me all on his own."

"I suspect you have the same effect on him."

"I also want to grab him and kiss him."

"He looks at you as if he'd like that too. With him doing some of the grabbing, as well. So what's stopping you two from getting together?"

Skye stared at Angel as if she'd just beamed down from another galaxy. "You're kidding, right? Can you see me with a tight-assed authority figure like him?"

"You said yourself that he's complicated."

"So he's a *complicated* tight-assed authority figure."

"That you'd really like to have sex with."

"Possibly."

"So, what do you plan on doing about it?"

"Please." Skye gave her mother a look. "Since when have I ever had a plan?"

"True." Angel enveloped her in a quick hug. "So you're just going to see what happens? See where fate takes you?"

"Or where I take fate. You know I like to lead rather than follow."

"I suspect Nathan feels the same way. About being a leader and not a follower."

"Yeah, I suspect the same thing." Skye grinned. "Which should make things interesting, huh?"

• • •

Angel spent the next day in Philadelphia, exploring some new co-ops and yarn shops before heading for the trendy seafood place Adam had selected. She and Adam arrived at the same time. At first glance, he didn't seem any different than the last time she'd seen him, several months ago. His aura still had lots of red and brown going on. He still radiated power and confidence. His hazel eyes were different, though. She just wasn't sure how.

He ordered a hot appetizer called Dynamite, which combined baked shrimp, scallops, calamari, and shitake mushrooms with spicy mayo. She'd forgotten he liked spicy food as much as she did.

"I read in the paper that your other daughter won a million dollars in the lottery. If she needs any financial advice, I can recommend someone," Adam offered.

"She's bought a theater."

"She what?"

"She bought a movie theater. The Tivoli. In Rock Creek."

"What made her do an idiotic thing like that?"

"It's not idiotic," Angel protested.

Adam narrowed his eyes at her. "Was this *your* idea?"

"No, it was not."

"You don't have to get all het up about it. My question was a valid one, given your business history."

"Hey, it's not easy being a New Age entrepreneur. You're never going to let me forget that, are you? Or forget the fact that I didn't tell you about Julia right away."

"Right away? You waited thirty years!"

"Is that why you invited me to dinner? Because you wanted to accuse me face-to-face?"

"No." Adam rubbed his hand across his face and, for a second, looked amazingly vulnerable. Unless she was imagining things? "I want to understand."

"Do you really, Adam?"

"Yeah, I do." He sounded distressed. "I missed all that baby stuff. Julia's first walk, her first words. And I'll never get it back."

"You could have more children."

"I already told you that I can't."

When she'd let him know about Julia, he'd confessed to a medical condition that had subsequently made him sterile, but he hadn't gone into any details and Angel hadn't wanted to ask. "You could still adopt."

"Where did we go wrong?" His eyes turned melancholy.

"*We?*"

"You and me."

"As I recall, you cheated on me."

"You said you didn't want an exclusive relationship. You were the one who made that statement, not me."

"I didn't really mean it."

"How the hell was I supposed to know that?"

"It was a long time ago, Adam. We've changed."

"You haven't." At her look, he added, "I mean it. You haven't lost your zest for life."

"I appreciate the compliment." She took a gulp of wine. Was he flirting with her? Was she responding? Or was it just another hot flash?

"Did you really think I was such a monster that you had to hide my child from me?"

"Oh, Adam, it's not that simple. I was afraid you'd take her from me. And that you'd raise her to worship the dollar the way your family does. You come from an incredibly powerful family. I had no one."

"No family of your own?"

Angel paused to take another gulp of wine, an even bigger one this time. "Not that I could count on."

"My family isn't exactly the supportive warm-and-fuzzy kind of clan."

"I know. I remember you telling me that. But they're powerful. *You're* powerful. And I'm not. Or rather, I'm not in the same way. I have my own powers. Anyway, I figured I'd tell Julia about you when she got older and would be able to stand up to you. When she was an adult. Then the years went by, and . . . Anyway, I did finally tell her. And you."

"Sharing that kind of news at a book signing isn't exactly the way I'd pictured it."

"Me either. But I figured it was my best chance to get close to you."

"You never thought to call me?"

Angel rolled her eyes. "Please. As if I'd be able to get through to you. Anyway, it all worked out in the end. You and Julia seemed to be getting along without too much conflict."

"I hardly got to know her before she took off with that biker guy," Adam complained.

"Luke is a good man."

"He turned down a large chunk of money from me."

"So Julia told me. That was a dumb move, Adam."

"I had to make sure he was in love with her and not her money."

"She doesn't have any money."

"As my only heir, she will have."

Angel stared at him in disbelief. "Surely you don't think she's going to run your empire, do you?"

"Surely you don't think she's going to be happy staying in that small-town library when she gets back?"

"It's Julia's life. Her choice. Not yours, not mine. We should stay out of it. That's what parents do."

"I wouldn't know. So what else are parents supposed to do?"

"Love unconditionally."

"The way you love Skye? Even when she does something wacky, like buying a movie theater?"

"I love both my daughters, equally and unconditionally."

"They aren't much alike."

"No, they aren't. But that doesn't matter."

"And how do you do that? Love unconditionally."

Angel shrugged. "You just do it."

To her surprise, Adam leaned forward and took her hand in his. "I might need your help in showing me the way. Think you can do that?"

He wanted her to help him become a better father. A better man. A better human being. How could she say no?

• • •

Skye stood before her belly-dancing students, wearing a short purple T-shirt and black leggings, her attention focused on her friend who'd just joined the class. "There's a reason it's called a shoulder punch and not a boob punch, Sue Ellen."

"Hold on a sec. My left boob just popped out of my lucky bra." Sue Ellen fixed the situation. "Okay, now I'm good to go. Where were we?"

"You were flashing us," Fanny Abernathy said with a toothless grin. She'd forgotten to put in her bridge again. "Is that a new move? Want us all to do it?"

"No, not really," Skye said quickly. "Okay, now keep

your posture straight and your chin up. Punch that shoulder, as if it were a fist."

"You mad at the sheriff again?" Fanny said. "Because you're sure punching as if you've got it in for someone."

"He came to her apartment," Sue Ellen told Fanny.

The octogenarian nodded. "So I heard."

Skye focused on the lesson. "Use your abdominal muscles to push your hips back. Circle. And circle. Now arms overhead in the same direction as your hips. Beautiful arms. Fluid snake arms."

"Yuck." Sue Ellen stopped in her tracks. "I hate snakes."

"I think they should just have at it and get it over with," Nancy announced, joining in the conversation for the first time.

"Who?" Sue Ellen furrowed her brows. "The snakes?"

"No. Skye and the sheriff."

"Now move in the other direction." Skye was determined not to get sidetracked. "Left, front, side, back. Sweep your arms over your head. Sweep and sweep."

"He'd sweep her off her feet if she'd let him."

"Maybe she'd rather sweep him off *his* feet."

Skye laughed. "Trust me, if I wanted Studly Do-Right in my bed, he wouldn't know what hit him. But that's not the case."

"Why not?" Nancy demanded, her hips rotating as directed.

"Why are you so eager to get him in my bed?" Skye kept moving as well.

"Well, let's just say that he's not the kind of guy you'd kick out for eating crackers in bed. Right, girls?"

A chorus of affirmative cheers filled the room.

To which Skye replied, "If you like him so much, then you go after him."

"I would if I were ten years younger," Nancy said.

"Me, too," Fanny said with another gap-toothed grin.

"Focus on your inner goddess, ladies," Skye ordered them.

After class, Sue Ellen approached Skye. "Are you sure all this boob shaking won't make 'the girls' sag or something?" Sue Ellen stared down at her breasts as she spoke.

"What's the matter? Are you afraid they're gonna shimmy right off?"

"No, the plastic surgeon assured me that that wouldn't happen." Sue Ellen clapped a hand over her mouth. "Forget I said that," she added before making a quick exit.

So Sue Ellen had had some help in the boob department. Interesting. Not something Skye would ever do. She was happy with her breasts as they were. Not that they were perfect or special in any way. She was simply okay with them.

Alone in the space, Skye danced. For herself. For her inner goddess. For all the women in the world who wanted to dance but still lacked the freedom to do so.

Slowly, she became aware of another presence. Nathan. Off-duty. In jeans and a T-shirt. Looking too damn good. He caught her right in the middle of her deep back bend, with her cleavage aimed directly at him.

He didn't appear to be unaffected. "I . . . uh . . . you . . ." Nathan mumbled.

Skye straightened up, deliberately taking her time.

"I thought your class was over." His voice was raspy.

"It is. We're all alone here."

"Right."

"Is it? Is it right?"

He didn't ask what she was talking about. Their sexual chemistry was thick in the air. "Do you care if it's right?"

"No." She barely got the word out before his mouth covered hers, totally consuming her.

His hunger would have surprised her, had she not felt the same singular, red-hot intensity herself.

Seconds later, he had her up against the wall, her breasts

pressed against his chest. Cupping her bottom, he lifted her. Skye wrapped her legs around his hips and ran her fingers through his hair as she held on.

Who knew he could make her feel so good? Beyond good. Wickedly divine. Deliciously decadent.

She could feel his arousal beneath the placket of his jeans. His crotch and hers were doing an ancient mating dance of their own—rubbing, thrusting, lunging. Her bare feet dug into the backs of his thighs as his tongue swept through her mouth, capturing her moans of pleasure.

Then it was over as quickly and unexpectedly as it had begun. He released her and stepped away just as Sue Ellen walked in. Skye hadn't heard the distinctive click of Sue Ellen's wedgies on the floor, but apparently Nathan had.

"Don't mind me," Sue Ellen told them airily. "I forgot my purse. You two just carry on with whatever you were doing."

Nathan's expression was remote. "I was just leaving."

Speechless for the moment, Skye watched him go. How dare he get her all ready to do the deed with him and then walk out on her?

"Did I interrupt something?" Sue Ellen asked.

Skye shook her head and vowed to wipe Nathan from her memory.

• • •

Two weeks after Owen gave Skye the winning lottery ticket, Sue Ellen burst into her apartment. "You were on TV again! They showed your picture and said you were a million-dollar instant winner from Rock Creek."

"Uh-huh." Skye wasn't the least bit impressed. She continued to pore over the Tivoli's architectural blueprints, determined not to think about Nathan and that hot embrace they'd shared after her class.

He'd been avoiding her since then. Fine by her. He wasn't the only man who could fill her heart's desires. Or her body's.

So, why wasn't she interested in anyone else?

Maybe she should just have sex with him and get it over with. Booting him out of her mind wasn't working as well as she'd hoped.

"We haven't had any kind of winner from Rock Creek in ages!" Sue Ellen raved. "Not since I won Miss Scrapple several years back."

"You mean Miss *Scrabble*, like the word game?"

"No way. I mean *scrapple*." At Skye's blank look, Sue Ellen added, "Come on, you've lived in PA for almost a year now and you've never heard of scrapple?"

"What is it?"

"A type of pork mush. You eat it for breakfast."

"You were Miss Pork Mush?"

"Among other titles." Sue Ellen pointed to the blueprints spread out in front of Skye. "What are you looking at?"

"The original plans for the theater. Isn't it wicked awesome?" Skye's voice reflected her enthusiasm.

Sue Ellen was not as impressed. "It looks pretty boring to me."

"Boring? Do you realize that the Tivoli was only the third theater in the entire country designed and built for movies with sound?"

"So, how old does that make this building? Like a hundred and fifty years old?"

"No. It was built in 1929."

"I was close. Do you think Mae West was here? I dressed up as her one Halloween when we were doing old movie stars. You know, that makes me think . . . maybe I should have a Halloween party this year. I still have that outfit. We could have the party at the theater."

"I don't think the renovations will be done by then."

"Done? What's to do? You just plug in the popcorn machine and stick in a DVD, or whatever you do to make the movies play."

"The equipment has to be updated."

Sue Ellen hoisted her bra straps. "I'd like to know whose equipment couldn't use some updating. Or uplifting." She squinted into the mirror above Skye's head. "Do you think my eyebrows are too far apart?"

"It's not something I think about, Sue Ellen."

"Sure. Because your eyebrows are fine."

"So are yours."

"You're just saying that to be polite." Skye's incredulous look made Sue Ellen laugh. "I'm sorry. You're right. I forgot who I was speaking to for a minute there. You don't say things to be polite."

"Damn right."

"So what about my eyebrows?"

"You're asking the wrong person."

"The story of my life." Sue Ellen slumped onto the round red couch. "I always seem to hook up with the wrong person. Why is that?"

"Again, you're asking the wrong person."

"Right. The silver lining is that you're more messed up than I am. Thanks." She bounced back up again. "I need to repay you for cheering me up. What can I do? I know. I could help you decorate the theater! Pick color schemes, that kind of stuff. I watch HGTV all the time."

Skye stared at her blankly. "What's HGTV?"

"Home and Garden TV." Sue Ellen sounded reverent. "It's on cable TV."

"I don't have cable."

"You don't have a television, period."

"I was getting too addicted to it when we were staying at my sister's house."

"There are worse things to get addicted to. Anyway, let's get back to my decorating. What do you think? And, okay, I know that the trailer where I'm living now is a little over the top. My mom loved Liberace and that Vegas style.

And I didn't have the money to redecorate it the way I wanted when they gave the trailer to me after they retired to Florida. That's not really my style—except for the velvet portrait of Elvis."

"The Tivoli really doesn't need redecorating. I'm going to restore it to the way it was in its glory days."

"I don't get why an edgy bad girl like you would be into old stuff like the Tivoli in the first place. It doesn't make sense."

Skye just shrugged. "I'm not into making sense. I'm into complicated."

"Fine. So you restore the theater and then what?"

"Then she's going to open a New Age institute here and show movies that inspire and feed the spirit," Angel announced as she joined them.

"That, or show triple-X porn films. Where's Toni?" Skye asked Angel.

"She insisted on staying with Algee at Cosmic Comics a little longer," Angel replied. "He said he'd bring her up in a few minutes."

"You're gonna show porn films?" Sue Ellen whispered, only now able to form the words.

Skye rolled her eyes. "Relax. I was only kidding."

"Right." Sue Ellen wrapped her arms around her middle and tried to look blasé. "I knew that. Well, if I can't help you with the decorating, how about the publicity? I'm good with that. Look at how many places picked up that story about my seeing the face of Jesus in that llama's fur."

"Lucy still hasn't forgiven you," Angel noted.

"Who's Lucy?"

"The llama."

"And she hasn't forgiven me?"

Angel shook her head. "Did you expect her to? When you never even bothered to give her an apology for all that unwanted attention you sent her way?"

Sue Ellen frowned. "I don't know how to apologize to a llama. Besides she's out on a farm someplace."

"It's nearby," Angel said. "Less than an hour away. I can drive you out there when I go visit them tomorrow. Then you can make the apology yourself."

"I don't know . . ." Sue Ellen shook her head. "What would I wear to apologize to a fuzzy animal?"

"The same thing you'd wear to apologize to a nonfuzzy one," Skye said.

Angel nodded. "Or a person."

"But don't wear white," Skye cautioned. "There's a lot of mud and dirt out there."

"Would jeans and a T-shirt be okay?" Sue Ellen asked.

"That should be fine." Angel patted her on the shoulder. "Now that she's pregnant, she's just a little sensitive."

Sue Ellen's eyes almost popped out of her head. "Oh, my lord! Skye is pregnant?"

"No, Lucy is."

"The llama," Skye reminded her.

Sue Ellen got all defensive. "I knew that."

"Knew what?" Algee asked as he joined them with Toni riding on his wider-than-an-entire-continent shoulders.

Sue Ellen answered, "That she's pregnant."

"The llama, not me," Skye said. "So don't go starting any rumors."

"I thought you didn't care what people said about you." Sue Ellen looked concerned. "Milton is still spewing all kinds of lies, you know. And now his wife has started doing the same thing."

"I wish you'd let me set him straight," Algee growled after swinging Toni to the ground.

"Set him straight? Who's crooked?" Toni asked.

"Republicans," Angel and Skye automatically replied.

"Hey!" Sue Ellen was offended. "I've dated some very nice Republicans."

Angel shook her head. "Don't tell Lucy."

"You're not going to tell me that your llama is a Democrat, are you?" Sue Ellen said.

Angel laughed. "Of course not."

"I should hope not."

"She's a reincarnated Independent voter."

• • •

"Hey, buddy, you're late!" Cole greeted Nathan the instant he entered a packed Nick's Tavern. It was almost ten at night and he'd hoped the celebratory activities might be over by now. "Glad you could finally make it."

"Yeah, well, you pretty much threatened to make my life miserable if I didn't."

Cole led him to the back of the tavern, where several tables had been shoved together. The area was separated from the rest of the room by the kind of bead curtains popular back when *Kojak* was in.

"Listen," Cole was saying, "if I have to show up at this bachelor party, so do you."

"He's *your* brother. And I thought you had to do more than just show up. I thought you organized this deal."

Cole shook his head. "I ended up having to delegate that honor to our cousin."

"Which cousin? Not . . . ?"

"Yeah, I'm afraid so. Butch. He was the only one with enough time on his hands to take care of it."

"The guy thinks he's Martha Stewart."

"Tell me something I don't know."

"Is that why there are little name tents on the table? Are those bow-tie-shaped sandwiches?"

"Afraid so."

"This is Nick's Tavern. Not exactly the Ritz." The only Ritz these guys knew about was the cracker.

"It's the best I could do. The VFW hall was booked for tonight. It was here or nowhere."

"Nowhere sounds good about now," Nathan muttered.

Cole pointed to the food. "Some of this stuff should be edible. Butch did all the cooking himself. Miniquiches, crab puffs, stuffed mushrooms . . ."

Yeah, right. The day Nathan ate a miniquiche was the day he turned in his service weapon, tossed in his handcuffs, and called it quits. "What about the entertainment?"

"Don't worry." Cole thumped him on the back. "I handled that myself. I think you'll be pleased."

A dozen burly guys were seated around the tables. They all greeted Nathan with varying degrees of enthusiasm, based, he suspected, on the number of alcoholic beverages they'd consumed so far. A beer keg sat at the end of the far table, looking incongruous among the dainty appetizers.

"You must try this," Butch declared, stuffing a crab puff into Cole's mouth.

One look from Nathan warned Butch that he'd better not try that maneuver on him.

Butch wisely backed away from him and focused on Cole. "Dee-lish, huh? I got the recipe from Martha's website."

"Recipes aren't a big deal at a bachelor party," Cole told him with his mouth full.

"Mine are," Butch declared. "Eat up, everyone. We've got lots left."

"Where's the entertainment?" The question voiced by half the party was accompanied by the banging of a number of beer mugs and bottles on the table, knocking the name tents onto the floor.

"Yeah, where's the entertainment?" the other half of the group demanded. "You promised us a show, Cole."

"Right." Cole checked his watch. "And it's almost showtime."

The bar was loud. But the minute Skye stepped out from the back room wrapped in a royal blue caftan, you could hear a pin drop. Next to drop was that caftan, revealing her costume.

Nathan almost didn't recognize her, with the long, dark-haired wig and the Cleopatra eye makeup she wore. But no one else had lips—or hips—like that. It was Skye, all right.

Nathan told himself he shouldn't have been surprised. But he was.

Skye was the entertainment. A flame ready to set off this powder keg of a group.

He had to step in. Right in front of her.

"What are you doing?" he demanded in an angry undertone.

"Belly dancing. Now get out of my way." She planted her hands on his chest.

His hands covered hers and he stood firm. "You just won a million dollars. Why are doing this?"

"Because I said I would. And because the money hasn't come through yet. Paperwork," she muttered. "I hate paperwork."

"Hey, Nathan, don't hog her all to yourself!" the other guys protested en masse.

"Yeah, this is supposed to be *my* bachelor party," Cole's brother said. "If anyone's gonna hog her, it should be me!"

"They've already had a lot to drink," Nathan warned Skye. "To wash down those God-awful crab puffs. So, do *not* get them all riled up."

"Who? Li'l ol' me?" She seductively tiptoed her fingers up Nathan's chest before catching him off balance and shoving him out of her way. "Ready or not, here I come, boys!"

A roar of approval filled the tavern and traveled down the block, garnering the attention of several passersby, who immediately rushed in to join the fun.

"Hey, this is a private party," Cole's brother complained as the crowd grew.

"Too late now," Nathan said, his eyes fixed on Skye the Seductress.

Every male in the place had his eyes fixed on her as she performed her dance, her hips shimmying as if they had a life of their own.

"Take it off!" One overeager oaf made a grab for her top.

She sidestepped him and glared, while keeping her hip shimmy going. "Hey, I am *not* a stripper. You wouldn't ask a ballet dancer to take off her tutu, would you?"

"Take it off!" the sloppy drunk repeated, shoving a ten-dollar bill down her cleavage while simultaneously attempting to rip off her sequined bra-top.

Before Nathan could make a move to help her, a totally pissed-off Skye shoved the drunk away from her. He stumbled a few steps before landing on the table, smashing everything in sight.

"Get off my crab puffs!" Butch howled. He might be a great cook, but he was an even better wrestler, having competed in the state finals four years in a row.

Fists started flying, and the fight was on.

Chapter Eight

· · · · · · · · · · ·

An hour later, Skye sat in Nathan's office, gazing at him without a flicker of remorse. "I guess that file on me just got a little thicker, huh?"

Nathan reminded himself that he was an officer of the law, and that regulations precluded him from using their own dark wigs to strangle belly-dancing seductresses. Not that Skye was wearing the wig at the moment. She had it stuffed in her huge WWF tote bag—World Wildlife Fund, not World Wrestling Federation—although the way she'd shoved that drunk in the bar, she'd probably be able to hold her own in any smackdown.

Instead of being concerned with Nathan, as he felt she should be, Skye was busy studying her surroundings. "Did you ever notice that the walls in your office are the color of a mud puddle? Not exactly conducive to positive energy. Have you thought of using a little feng shui in here? To make the place more harmonious?"

"It's not at the top of my to-do list, no."

"You should think about it. I could help you with that. I dabble a bit in feng shui. You've already made a good start by having your desk face the entrance."

He rested his elbows on the aforementioned desk and gave her one of his best "lawman" stares. It was actually something he'd learned and perfected in the Marine Corps. "I like to see who's coming at me."

"But you could do more," she blithely continued. "Put a lucky bamboo plant near the main entrance, and maybe add a water fountain."

"There's a water fountain out in the hallway."

"Not to drink from. I meant a water feature. I'm putting one in the lobby of the Tivoli. It's good feng shui. I should warn you that, even though I only dabble a bit, I totally do feng shui my way. I'm not good at following other people's rules."

"Yeah, I noticed that."

She finally focused her attention on him. "You're not going to try and blame tonight's little incident on me, are you?"

"I wouldn't call it a *little* incident."

"Compared to global warming—"

"Yeah, I know. You've made that comparison before."

"Yeah, well, it was nice of you to try and protect me."

"Nice? And what do you mean, 'try and protect you'? I *did* protect you." Nathan had yanked Skye to safety, out of the way of the mob at the bar, before he'd worked to break up the fight.

"If it makes you feel better to believe that you protected little ol' me, then you go right ahead." She reached across his desk to pat his arm.

His jaw clenched. "Have you noticed that, wherever you go, trouble follows?"

"Some people feel that way."

"It's got nothing to do with *feelings*. I'm stating facts here."

"The fact is that several drunken men started a brawl in Nick's."

"Because you incited them."

Her green eyes flashed. "Come again?"

"You heard me."

"Let me get this straight. You're blaming me? The old Eve-with-her-wickedly-tempting-ways-leading-Adam-astray story, is that it?"

"I'm just saying . . ."

"That you're an idiot."

"No, that's not what I was saying."

"It's what I'm saying!"

"It's what you're *yelling*."

Skye took several deep breaths. "You're doing this deliberately. I get that now. You're just trying to push my buttons. Well, forget it. I'm in control of my own buttons. There's no way I'm handing over that joystick to you."

Nathan almost choked.

"What's the matter, Sheriff?" She stood and sashayed over to perch on the corner of his desk. "Did wicked badgirl me push your Studly Do-Right buttons? Are you afraid I'm going to kiss you again?"

He made no reply.

"I don't belly dance to titillate men. I do it as a powerful and joyous artistic expression." She hopped off his desk. "Titillating men is merely a side benefit." She mocked him with a defiant shimmy of her hips.

That was it. He got up, marched to his office door, and yanked it open. "I think you've caused enough problems for one night. Go home. Take care of your daughter."

She slammed the door shut, but remained inside his office instead of leaving. "What is that crack supposed to mean?"

Nathan shrugged.

"Are you insinuating I don't take care of my daughter?"

He remained silent.

"Because I'm a damn good mother. And don't you forget it!" Whirling around, Skye pulled open the door and flounced out, almost mowing down Cole in the process.

"Wow." Cole stared after her and then fixed his sights on Nathan. "What did you say to her?"

"Nothing." Nathan headed back to his desk and sat down.

"Nothing? Come on." Cole dropped into the chair Skye had recently vacated. "You must have said something to make her go all ballistic like that."

"She was born ballistic."

"Uh-huh."

"I've never met a woman who could cause more trouble."

"You two do seem to rub each other the wrong way," Cole said.

"You've got that right."

Cole grinned. "Although, now that I think about it, you seemed to be rubbing each other just fine when she started dancing tonight."

"She told me I needed to get a lucky bamboo plant."

"Huh?"

"In my office. She told me I needed plants and a water element. To make the place more harmonious."

"Sounds like feng shui."

"Sounds like crap to me. This is the sheriff's department. We're not supposed to be harmonious here."

"Right."

"And I didn't say she was a bad mother."

"Right. Because I can see where your telling her that would definitely piss her off."

"She's too ballistic."

"So you said. I've never seen her the way she is with you, though."

"What are you talking about?"

"Tonight. She was all over you."

"She was trying to aggravate me."

"Is that what she was trying to do? Or seduce you? Sounds like she succeeded, either way."

"That's just the way she is."

"Not with me."

Nathan's eyes narrowed. "Do you want her to be that way with you?"

"What red-blooded guy wouldn't?" Cole said.

"Me. She's trouble. She's unpredictable. Too wild. Doesn't even think of the consequences before she acts."

Cole nodded wisely. "She's everything you're not."

"Exactly."

"Opposites do attract. Or so they say."

"I refuse to be attracted to her."

"Right. Does that really work?"

"Not very well," Nathan murmured in disgust.

"Yeah," Cole commiserated. "I didn't think so."

• • •

"Thanks for babysitting Toni for me tonight," Skye told Angel as she entered her apartment.

"No problem."

"Is she asleep?"

"Yes. How did the bachelor party go?"

Skye dumped her tote bag by the couch. "Things got a little rowdy in the end."

"How rowdy?"

"The sheriff hauled me off to the police station again. Although not in handcuffs this time. And then the dictator had the nerve to insinuate that I'm not a good mother! And this after I'd given him a few helpful feng shui tips for his office. But did he listen? No." Unable to stand still, Skye paced the living room's perimeter, sticking her finger into the soil around the jade plant to see if it needed water. "He already knows what he thinks, so don't bother confusing him with the facts. That's his philosophy. I mean, the man is a total prude. He actually tried to blame me for the fight at the bar tonight."

Angel stood in her path, forcing Skye to stop pacing. "Fight? This is the first I've heard about a fight."

Skye stepped around her and kept prowling. "I told you, things got a little rowdy."

"Rowdy is one thing. A fight is another."

"Well, that's why he hauled me off to jail. Not that he actually put me in a cell. We talked in his office."

"The one you gave him the feng shui suggestions for."

Skye nodded. "Exactly. Which he ignored."

"So how did he try to blame you for the fight?"

"He said I"—Skye paused for hand quotes—"*incited* the guys."

"Oh my." Angel shook her head. "That is rather regressive of him, isn't it?"

"The man lives in the Stone Age, I swear."

"Then you'll just have to enlighten him."

"The man doesn't want to see the light, Angel. He's got blinders on, and he's not taking them off for anyone."

Angel took Skye's hand and tugged her toward the kitchen. "Come have some hibiscus tea. Your aura and meridians must all be completely helter-skelter at the moment."

"I'm going to change out of my costume first. I didn't have time to do that before Nathan hauled me away. And I need a quick shower to get rid of the smell of cigarette smoke." Skye grimaced at the lingering scent on her skin from the bar.

Ten minutes later, she was back in the kitchen, wearing a thin, cotton shorty pajama set and smelling of ginger-spice body cream.

Skye and Angel talked about men and how dumb they could be sometimes. And how you frequently ended up loving them anyway. At least, that's what Angel said. Skye wasn't so sure.

"What's the deal with you and Adam? Are you still seeing him?"

Angel nodded and sipped her tea.

"Tyler still doesn't know?"

Angel shook her head.

"Do you plan on telling him?"

"Of course. I'm just not sure when."

"You know you're playing with fire, right? That's really more my territory than yours. I'm the reckless one in the family, not you."

"Julia might not agree with you."

"Like I'd care."

"She's your sister. You do care about her. I know it."

"*Half* sister."

"You say that as if it gives you permission to push her away."

"I don't need permission to do what I want."

"No, you never did," Angel said wistfully. "Not even as a kid. You were always full of initiative, independence, and assertiveness."

"That's what I want for Toni. I want her to have the confidence to explore and conquer the world for herself."

"And you've given her that."

"I hope so. Did I mention that Nathan accused me of being a bad mother?"

"Yes, you did. Is that what this conversation is about? Did he make you doubt your parenting abilities?"

"Did you ever doubt yours?"

Angel laughed. "Constantly."

"Really?"

"Absolutely. Once I met your father, Sash, things got better, because I had someone to share your birth with."

"Yeah, Sash was special." He'd died in Colombia, where he'd been participating in a project to save the natural resources there. Skye had been only ten at the time.

"He certainly was. And his presence made a big difference. I didn't have that in the beginning with Julia and you didn't have that with Toni."

"Toni's father was no Sash, though. Rex was a rebel musician in search of heavy-metal glory. A dramatic guitar man who ran screaming for the nearest exit the instant he heard I was pregnant. Not exactly Father of the Year material."

"Do you know where he is now?"

"Last I heard, he and his band Nasty were playing the bars in Bangkok. But that was two or three years ago."

"It's his loss not having Toni in his life."

"I'm glad he's not in her life. He had a way of ruining things. And people."

"Did he ruin you?"

"In some ways."

"What ways?"

"I was so sure I loved him. I trusted that he loved me in return. Stupid, stupid, stupid."

"We all make mistakes, Skye."

"Yeah, well, Rex wasn't a total mistake, because I have Toni. I guess everything happens for a reason."

Angel nodded her agreement.

"So maybe Rex was supposed to teach me a lesson," Skye said.

"And that lesson would be?"

"That I wasn't meant to settle down."

"By 'settle down,' you mean what, exactly? That you weren't meant to live in one place? You already knew that. Or did you learn that you weren't supposed to settle, period? Settle for anything less than the total love you deserve?"

As Angel hugged her, Skye knew that her mother was half right. Skye had no intention of settling. Not again. As for deserving total love . . . that was a trickier concept for her to wrap her bad-girl mind around.

Skye believed she deserved to be happy. And she deserved to follow her own rules. But total love? Maybe that required a goodness she didn't possess. Maybe that was reserved for people who colored inside the lines. People who were selfless and obedient. People like Julia.

"I'm sensing a shift in your aura." Angel looked at Skye with concern. "What is it? What are you thinking?"

Skye had no intention of telling her. Angel was a sensitive soul who felt everyone else's pain. Skye wasn't like that. Not that she wanted to cause anyone pain. She didn't. But she wouldn't change who she was for someone else. She *couldn't*. She'd done that with Rex, sublimating her goals for his.

So, yeah, maybe Angel was right. Rex *had* been a learning experience. By running out on her, he'd taught Skye that she was strong enough to make it on her own.

Not that Julia had ever given Skye credit for that, or that Skye's definition of "making it on her own" matched her sister's. Julia the librarian was all for conforming to a steady job. Skye's rebellious nature required that she find her own way.

And now Skye had a new project—the Tivoli Theater. Her focus should stay there and with Toni. Not on disapproving lawmen like Nathan.

"Skye?" Angel sighed. "Never mind. It's getting late. I should head home. Tyler will be waiting."

"Okay." Skye gathered their cups and put them in the sink. "Thanks again for coming over to babysit."

"Don't go to bed angry with Nathan, okay?" Angel said. "That just causes negative vibes."

As if on cue, there was a knock on the door.

"It's Nathan," Angel said.

Skye didn't ask how she knew. Experience had taught her that Angel was usually right.

• • •

Skye yanked open the door. Sure enough, it *was* Nathan. Still in the casual clothes he'd worn earlier at the bar. The perennial jeans and T-shirt. No slave to cutting-edge fashion, this guy.

"Have you come to give me another lecture?" she snapped.

"Hello, Nathan." Angel greeted him with a smile and tugged him inside. "I was just leaving, so you two can speak privately."

Skye had never seen her make such a fast getaway. Usually, speedy exits were *her* specialty, not Angel's.

And so Skye stood there, in her yellow shorty pajamas with the little llamas on them. A gift from Angel. Julia would have been horrified to stand before a man at midnight dressed the way Skye was, despite the fact that the pajamas covered her as well as a regular pair of shorts and a sleeveless shirt.

"I, uh, saw your lights on and I . . . uh . . . where's your daughter?" Nathan asked, looking around.

Skye's temper flared. "Is that why you came? To check on the welfare of my kid? Why? Do you think I've got her dangling out a window or something?"

"No. It was just a simple question. Why do you take everything I say the wrong way?"

"Why do you *say* everything the wrong way?"

"Because of this." Sliding his big hands around her head, Nathan pulled her to him. Her lips were parted when their mouths met, allowing his tongue undisputed entry.

His hands remained where they were, cradling her head.

Skye ran her hands all over him. She couldn't help herself. She tried reminding herself that the last time he'd held her in his arms, he'd ended up walking out on her, leaving her hot and damp and aching for him. It didn't work. She didn't seem to care about the past at the moment. The here and now was way too exciting.

"You drive me crazy, do you know that?" he mumbled against her mouth.

"Ditto," she mumbled back, stringing a line of heated kisses along his Mt. Rushmore jawline.

"When I saw that guy touching you, I wanted to flatten him."

"Me, too."

He brushed his fingers across her cheek. "You could have gotten hurt tonight."

"So could you." She kissed his fingertips.

"It's my job."

"Mmmm, don't remind me."

"This is crazy." His voice was husky as he nibbled on her ear.

"I agree." She tilted her head to grant him better access. "Totally crazy."

"We're complete opposites."

"Tell me about it."

"I didn't mean to come here tonight," he admitted.

"Yet here you are."

"I couldn't seem to stop myself."

"I feel the same way."

After that, words were discarded for actions. Only this time, Skye wasn't about to allow Nathan to take charge like he had before. If anyone was going up against the wall, it would be him. But en route, she decided the couch might be a better option. It was big and round.

Throw pillows went flying as they bounced onto the couch. Skye rolled until she was on top, which should have made undoing the buttons on her pajama top more difficult for Nathan, but somehow didn't.

Not that she minded having his big, warm hands on her bare breasts, his callused thumbs brushing over her nipples. Mmm, she didn't mind at all.

Tugging her down on top of him, he licked his way around the creamy mound of her breast before taking her nipple into his warm, wet mouth, tantalizing her with his surprisingly talented and creative tongue.

His hands were now free to pursue other treasures, sliding beneath the hem of her shorts to stroke her through her bikini underwear. Draped atop him as she was, she didn't think he'd be able to do half the things he was doing to her—provocative, wonderfully wicked things.

Nathan shifted his attention from her left breast to her right just as his finger slipped beneath the elastic edge of her skimpy underwear to plunder the damp depths of her femininity.

And, just like that, she came. Powerful surges seized her vulva or vagina—one of her V-parts was vibrating. No, *all* of them were. She panted and pulsed with delight.

Not satisfied with giving her just one orgasm, Nathan slowly built up her pleasure again . . . and again. A brush of his thumb, just so, up against her clitoris, sent spasms of bliss coursing through her.

When Skye finally caught her breath, she was drenched with satisfaction, yet still wanted him to come within her.

She was reaching for the zipper on his jeans when the sound of her daughter's sleepy voice stopped her.

"Mommy, what are you doing? Why are you squishing the kitten-book man like that?"

Nathan tumbled Skye onto the couch and shot to his feet. Or tried to. She suspected his hard-on had prevented him from moving as quickly or standing as straight as he would have liked.

"I . . . uh . . . you . . . uh . . ." Nathan looked frantically at Skye.

Still trying to collect the scattered molecules of her body after that last explosive orgasm he'd given her, Skye was unable to move.

"Mommy, were you turning him into a toad? Was he mean to you again?" Toni gave Nathan a glare that was fiercely protective of her mother.

"No, he wasn't mean. He was being very, very, *very* . . . nice."

Did Nathan just snort at her in a muffled sort of way?

"If he was nice, then why were you squashing him?" Toni asked.

"We were just fooling around," Skye said.

She definitely heard him snort this time.

Skye ignored him and focused on her daughter. This gave her the energy to get up from the couch and hurry over to Toni, who had her beloved Ta the Tiger clutched in one hand. "What's the matter, honey? Did you have a bad dream?"

Toni yawned, then said, "I heard noises."

"Must have been the television," Nathan mumbled.

Skye rolled her eyes. "We don't have a television."

His disbelieving look clearly said what kind of weirdo doesn't have a TV, but aloud he just said, "I'd better be going now."

"Don't you want to read me a story from the kitten book you gave me?" Toni asked him.

Every muscle in Nathan's face froze.

Taking pity on him—after all, the man had given her a Big O three-peat—Skye said, "He can't tonight. Maybe next time."

As she watched Nathan walk toward the door, she wondered if there would be a next time. Or if he'd retreat behind that thick wall he'd built around himself.

Chapter Nine

. . . .

"I think Haynes is having trouble with his sixth chakra," Brock, the jock quarterback, told Skye before the team's yoga class began. "Isn't that the one located between the eyes that gives you clear vision of the world around you? The third eye, right?"

Skye nodded. "That's right."

"Well, his third eye isn't working."

"What makes you say that?"

"Because the moron can't catch any pass I throw him," Brock drawled.

To which Haynes responded, "Maybe if you threw more accurately, I'd be able to catch your passes."

"Have you both been doing your visualizations?" Skye asked.

"I've been visualizing that new bootie-licious babe on the cheerleading squad," Brock said.

Skye wasn't impressed. "Maybe that's why you're having trouble with your passes."

Brock smirked. "My passes are always successful. Especially with the babes."

"Which would be fine if you were trying out for the cheerleading squad," Coach Spears growled. Where had *he* come from? The coach had a habit—or talent, depending on your point of view—of appearing out of nowhere. And the guy had eyes and ears in the back of his head. He missed nothing. It was uncanny. "Is that your plan, Brock? To become a cheerleader?"

Brock hung his head. "No, Coach."

"Then stay focused. Our opening game is next Friday. You're coming," he said curtly to Skye.

She didn't answer. She did not respond well to orders.

Coach Spears belatedly remembered that and decided to play the sympathy card. "The kids are counting on you."

One wave of his hand, and the team instantly looked at her en masse with sad puppy-dog eyes.

"Fine." Skye sighed. "I'll be there."

Now the guys were all high-fiving each other. She even saw a few exchanging dollar bills, as if they'd placed a bet on her answer.

She clapped her hands to get their attention. "Okay, remember what I said about yoga offering you a complete body workout, balancing the stresses of your football practices and correcting the tightness that might cause pulled hamstrings or knee injuries. So let's begin with your breathing . . ."

They knew the routine now. Some had even come up with their own names for a few of the poses.

"Now move into the Monkey forward bend."

"Monkey butt in air," they all translated.

"Warrior One," Skye continued. This series was their favorite. "Holding Warrior poses develops balance and concentration," Skye said as she did the pose with them. "You can overcome any obstacle. Smoothly moving now into Warrior Two. Spine straight. Exhale and bend your right knee. Good. Good. Breathe deeply."

And so she put the team through their paces. Watching them, she could see how they'd improved over the past few weeks. Their confidence had increased, as well as their ability to focus.

Coach Spears always disappeared during their workout, as if he were afraid Skye might try and press him onto a yoga mat and put him to work. But he always magically reappeared the moment they were done.

"I'm expecting great things from you." The coach gave them all a look, not unlike the variety that Sister Mary could come up with. It was a look that got results. "Do not disappoint me. Now hit the showers."

The team headed out of the gym like a herd of buffalo.

"You've done a good job with them," Coach Spears told Skye.

"So have you."

"I've got to tell you, I wasn't sure about this entire yoga thing."

So he'd told her every time she'd shown up.

"But I'm thinking, this is working," he admitted. "Of course, I'll think it works even better if we win that opening game."

"That's up to fate and karma."

"Fate and Karma? Are those linebackers on the Cougars team?"

"No."

"My team holds their own fate in their hands. And that better be all they're holding," he muttered with a dark look toward the exit leading to the showers. "Gotta go."

• • •

"Meditation is a way of living," Angel told Adam in the quietly rich confines of his inner office on the top floor of one of Philadelphia's premier buildings.

Adam said nothing, a look of concentration on his face. Angel had the uneasy feeling he was thinking about his business deals.

"Truth and beauty are infinite things," she continued brightly. "There is no formula for meditation."

"Well, there should be," Adam said. "Who the hell has the time to sit around trying to figure out truth, justice, and the American way?"

"I believe that's Superman's line. I don't think he was into meditation."

"What do you know about Superman?"

Angel thought his question sounded rather dismissive. And she was getting another hot flash, which aggravated her. But then, today, just about everything aggravated her. "A friend of mine owns a comic-book store."

"That shouldn't surprise me."

"Meaning?"

"Meaning you've got a lot of friends in unusual professions."

"I'm going to ignore that rude comment and continue our lesson."

"How long is it going to take for me to perfect this meditation thing?" Adam demanded impatiently.

"Is that your goal?"

"One of them."

"A goal is in the future. In order to meditate successfully, you need to live in the present. It's not a matter of effort or control."

"I'm all *about* effort and control."

"I had noticed that." Angel fingered the amethyst crystal around her neck. It was supposed to calm an overstressed mind, but, so far, it wasn't working. Maybe hot flashes blocked the crystal's healing force.

"I talked to Julia last night," Adam said abruptly.

"So she told me."

"Did you tell her we're seeing each other?"

"No. Did you?"

"I may have alluded to it."

"Why?"

"Why not?"

Angel unbuttoned the top button on her billowy Indian-cotton shirt. The thing was suffocating her, making her want to suffocate Adam.

She wasn't normally a violent person. But she wasn't normal at the moment.

What had made her think she could manage Adam? That she could turn him into a better man? A meditative man.

"I must have been delusional," she said softly.

"And that's why you don't want Julia knowing we're seeing one another?"

"You make it sound like we're a couple or something."

Adam raised an eyebrow. "Is the idea so outlandish?"

"Totally."

"Why?"

"What's wrong with you today?"

"Nothing. What's wrong with you?"

"A lot." She reached for her bottle of chilled water and took several gulps before placing the cold bottle against her wrist. Hadn't she read someplace that doing so would cool you down in the middle of a hot flash?

"Are you ill?" Adam asked.

Did he look concerned for her . . . or for himself?

"Don't worry. What I have isn't contagious."

"What is it?"

"Menopause," she snarled. "You wanna make something of it?"

He backed up as if she'd just turned into a she-wolf. "No."

"Good. Because I'm in no mood for a hassle."

"I can see that."

She unwrapped the scarf she had around her neck.

"What are you doing?" He eyed her cautiously, as if afraid she might use it to strangle him.

"I'm hot. What's the temperature in here?"

"I always keep the office at sixty-nine degrees."

The bottle against her wrist wasn't helping the coal furnace burning in her chest. So she splashed a little cold water down her shirtfront. Or that was her intention. The result was closer to a drenching than a splash. Her thin cotton shirt now clung to her breasts. She peeled it away from her skin and glared at Adam as if this were all his fault. "What are you looking at?"

"I . . . uh . . . perhaps I should wait outside until you . . . er . . . recover."

As Angel watched the door close behind him, she wondered how many people had the power to make billionaire Adam Kemp retreat from his own office. Not many, she was willing to bet. Which left her feeling strangely proud of herself.

• • •

Skye stood before the Tivoli Theater, her friends gathered around her. It was the Sunday before Labor Day. "I appreciate you coming here today to help me celebrate my finally getting possession of the theater." In honor of the big event, Skye had taped a length of ribbon across the Tivoli's dusty glass entrance doors. She'd also borrowed Toni's tiara, which she wore perched on top of her head as she addressed the small crowd—Angel, Sue Ellen, Lulu, Algee, and Tyler. And, of course, Toni, who had dressed up for the occasion by teaming her pink tutu with a pair of orange polka-dotted tights and a lime green top.

"It's Labor Day weekend, so it's fitting that we spend it working," Angel said.

Skye had asked everyone to wear work clothes, which meant different things to different people. To Tyler and Algee, it meant jeans and T-shirts. To Lulu, it meant wearing her "No Sense in Being Pessimistic. It Wouldn't Work Anyway" tank top and baggy black pants with metal studs on the pockets. But to Sue Ellen, it meant sculpted red nails with red and white stripes to match her red-and-white-striped bandeau top, red shorts, and red kitten-heeled sandals.

"Ready, everyone?" Skye said.

"Wait! I want a picture." Sue Ellen handed a disposable camera to Skye. "Take my picture. Make sure you get the nails in clearly." She turned her back to Skye and looked coquettishly over her shoulder, her chin resting on one hand.

"What are you doing?" Skye said.

"I'm posing. You know, the way all the big-name actresses do on the red carpet."

"Where's the red carpet?" Toni demanded. "I like red."

"Yes, where is the red carpet?" Sue Ellen asked. "I expected for this momentous occasion—"

"I'm saving it for the theater's reopening," Skye broke in, clicking the camera's shutter without paying much attention.

"Are you sure you got my nails?" Sue Ellen sent her a worried look. "I had my hand posed just right on my shoulder. And my eyebrows looked okay too, right?"

"Yeah, yeah," Skye muttered, passing the camera back to her. "Now where was I . . . ? Oh, yeah." Taking the small sewing scissors Angel handed her, she said in a tony English accent, "I declare this theater . . . open for work!" And with a royal wave, she cut the ribbon.

Everyone jumbled forward, but Skye had to unlock the front door first. "Hold on! Okay."

The door open, they all hurried inside. And were stunned into silence.

"Usually people look at a piece of property *before* they buy it," Algee noted. "You looked in here before buying, right?"

"Sort of. I wasn't seeing all the work that had to be done. I was seeing possibilities." Skye sounded a tad defensive.

"I think you were hallucinating," Sue Ellen said. "I hear you can do that if you drink too much carrot juice."

"An urban myth," Skye said.

"So is this place."

The lobby had seen better days, to put it mildly. Cobwebs dangled from the ceiling, and stalactites of dust hung in the corners. A once-white-but-now-grubby drop cloth haphazardly covered the concession stand's two glass cases. The walls and floor were dark and grungy, and there was an unmistakably musty smell in the air. Dust motes danced in the pale sunlight filtering in through the dirty glass entry doors.

"Well, it's mine now," Skye stated proudly.

Sue Ellen shook her head in disbelief. "Yes, it is . . . you poor lost soul."

"Thank you for your words of encouragement, Sue Ellen. As always, they are such a morale boost."

"If you're looking for a morale boost, get a manicure." Sue Ellen waved her acrylic nails at her.

Skye turned to another friend. "What do you think, Algee?"

"You're going to need some major elbow grease."

"I agree," Tyler said from beside him.

"I could smudge the interior for you," Angel offered. "Burn some dried sage and juniper to get rid of any negative energy that might be left behind."

Tyler looked around, frowning at the brass wall sconce barely clinging to the wall. "Speaking of energy, you're going to need an electrician to check out the entire system, and a plumber to check out the pipes."

"My granddad could help with that," Lulu said. "The electrical part, I mean. He's a retired electrician. He should be getting back from his biker rally in South Dakota in a few days. I'll have him give you a call when he does."

"Thanks, Lulu. And thanks, everyone, for agreeing to pitch in and help out today."

"I like that little ticket-booth thing there by the entrance," Lulu said. "Sweet."

"Where's the ice cream?" Toni demanded, pointing at a

picture of a Fudgsicle on the wall behind the concession stand.

"No ice cream," Skye replied. "They're all out."

Sue Ellen sneezed. "It sure is dusty in here."

"Well, the place has been closed up for a number of years," Skye said.

"You don't think it's haunted, do you?" Sue Ellen's eyes darted around the shadowy interior. "Like in *The Phantom of the Opera*? I never saw it, but I heard it had something to do with a haunted theater."

"I'd love to have a ghost," Skye said with enthusiasm.

Sue Ellen jumped as a florescent tube above the concession stand flickered off in a burst of blue light. "I knew it! This place *is* haunted."

"Maybe someone was murdered here once." Lulu used her best "spooky" voice, which was good enough to go on a Halloween recording. "Do you know how many murder victims know their attackers?"

"No, and I don't want to!" Sue Ellen backed up until she was at the entrance, her hands reaching behind her for the door handle. "I'm not feeling very well."

"Oh, don't be such a wimp," Lulu said.

"Come on. I think the realtor told me the rest of the light switches are in the office." Skye unlocked the door to a small room with paneling from the seventies, just like in Nick's Tavern. The photo on the wall was of former President Ronald Reagan. That was it as far as artwork went. A dented black file cabinet stood alongside a scarred oak desk in one corner. The top of the desk showed a number of cigarette burns as well as water stains from cups once placed on its surface.

A metal folding chair was placed behind the abused desk. Skye sat on the wobbly chair and faced her friends and family. "So, what do you think? Do I look like a business mogul?"

"Not in that outfit," Sue Ellen replied.

"Good. I don't want to be a mogul." Skye was wearing her "Got Brains" T-shirt and rattiest low-cut jeans. Not exactly Donald Trump Apprentice attire. "I wouldn't mind skiing some moguls, but that's another story."

"We should probably start with a list of repairs that need to be made," Tyler suggested. "You're going to have to hire professionals for some of the work or you won't meet the code requirements."

"Believe me," Skye assured him, "after getting zapped with a bolt of electricity a few weeks ago trying to fix our toaster, I have no intention of playing with that stuff. But the cleaning can be done by us. And some of the minor repairs."

"Did you see that vintage popcorn machine in the lobby?" Angel asked.

Skye nodded. "Of course, we're only going to sell organic popcorn."

Angel waved her hands. "And none of that fake butter stuff."

"Right," Skye agreed. "We'll have brewer's yeast. Or chili powder and lime zest."

Sue Ellen stared at Skye and Angel as if they'd stepped out of a *Friday the 13th* movie. "Brewer's yeast? Lime zest? On popcorn? That's just wrong. Who's going to buy that?"

"Anyone with good sense."

"We don't want customers with good sense, we want customers with good taste. Which is why you should use my decorating talents. I hate to brag, but"—Sue Ellen fluffed her hair—"I've been told that I have outstanding taste."

"Oh, please." Lulu popped the gum she was chewing. "You like velvet paintings of Elvis."

"They are art."

Lulu sighed, signaling that in her opinion Sue Ellen was hopeless. "I rest my case."

"Right, like you're the expert on what's tasteful," Sue

Ellen shot back. "You work in a comic-book store and you wear skulls in your ears."

"You're both creating negative energy within this space," Angel gently chastised them.

"Can we return to structural issues here?" Tyler's voice reflected his impatience.

"I'm with you, man." Algee just shook his head. "You really think that you can make this a successful business, Skye?"

"No, I thought I'd just burn a million dollars for the hell of it." Skye's voice reflected her growing aggravation. "I expected better from you of all people, Algee. Didn't everyone doubt your sanity for opening a comic-book store?"

Algee nodded sheepishly.

"And yet here you are, a successful businessman who recently opened a new store."

"A smaller one than in Serenity Springs," Algee pointed out. "There's nothing small about this place."

Sue Ellen raised her hand as if in class. Only she didn't wait to be called upon before speaking. "Tell me again why you think people will come here instead of going to that megaplex out past the interstate?"

"Because that's almost an hour's drive each way," Skye said. "Here, the people of Rock Creek can have a movie theater in their own downtown. That's more than Serenity Falls has."

"True." Sue Ellen's expression became more optimistic. "That alone is an excellent reason for doing this. We'll have a movie theater and they won't."

"Now that the lights are on, let's look at the grand auditorium, shall we?" Angel suggested.

Sue Ellen appeared confused. "The what?"

"The theater's seating area," Skye explained.

"Oh. Right."

Tyler held the door open for them as they filed into the auditorium and down the center aisle.

For the first time, Skye noticed the ragged holes in some of the seats and in the red velvet drapery flanking the stage. She also heard the unmistakable skitter of little rodent feet.

"Mice!" Sue Ellen shrieked, snatching Toni up in her arms. "This is no place for a child right now. I'll babysit her while you get things under control."

"Don't take her to Dairy Queen," Skye said as Sue Ellen jogged up the aisle toward the exit. "She got sick from eating too much ice cream the last time you took her there."

Sue Ellen just kept jogging, almost knocking down Sister Mary on her way out.

"I heard you could use a little extra elbow grease over here," the nun said. "So I brought a few volunteers." She'd rounded up a number of people who helped out at the thrift shop or had been fed at the soup kitchen. "We even brought our own buckets." She lifted them for everyone to see. "Where do you want us to get started?"

"In the lobby area," Skye said. "And thanks so much for coming to help!"

Tyler and Algee were already checking out the rows of seats, marking those that needed to be rebolted to the floor and those too far gone for repairs. The worst seemed to be in the front row.

"Remember that movie theater in Mendocino that had couches on the sides in the front row? I bet we could find a pair of comfy couches to use. And I could make some washable slipcovers for them," Angel said.

"That's a great idea. Thanks, Angel!" Skye gave her a grateful hug.

And so they all got to work. Scrubbing. Sweeping. Polishing.

Four hours later, great progress had been made. The cobwebs were gone. The razzle-dazzle marble floor in the lobby glowed. The red carpeting in the auditorium had been vacuumed, the velvet drapes removed for repairs. The sound track for their labor included selections ranging from

Sister Mary's dream-guy, Frank Sinatra, to Lulu's choice of Marilyn Manson, to Angel's fave, Enya. All the tunes were blasting from the speakers of the sound dock that held Lulu's iPod.

Skye paused beside Lulu, who was washing down the glass cases at the concession stand. "I didn't know you'd downloaded Frank."

Lulu just shrugged. "I knew Sister Mary likes his stuff. And it's kind of retro. So when I heard she might be helping out today, I went online."

Skye gave her a big hug. "You're wicked awesome."

Lulu grinned. "Yeah, I am."

"This place is great," Sister Mary enthused as she joined them. "There's an elegant ornateness to it. Can't you just imagine Cary Grant walking in?"

"If he does, hand him a mop," Algee said as he walked by with another bag of garbage.

"I don't envy whoever gets the job of cleaning that chandelier," Sister Mary confessed, pointing up.

"I love the saying over the doorway." Skye pointed to the recently uncovered discovery, hidden beneath layers of dirt. "'Don't give the people what they want, give them something better.' Roxy Rothafel."

"Who the hell is"—Lulu shot a guilty look at Sister Mary—"I mean, who the heck is Roxy Rothafel?"

"Don't know," Skye admitted. "I'll have to Google him tonight and find out. But for now, I'm just going to go out and check the marquee."

Skye had barely gotten outside when Toni launched herself at her. "Mommy! I got man-cured!"

Which immediately made Skye wish she could cure herself from the temptation of one man—Nathan. "Mancured, huh?"

"Yeah."

Skye gave her a sloppy kiss on her cheek, the kind that always made Toni crack up, before setting her back down.

"We had a great time. Toni got a manicure. Knowing you, I made sure the nail polish was a brand that isn't tested on animals. Look, it turned out great." Sue Ellen showed off Toni's newly painted green nails. "Toni picked out the color herself. To match your eyes."

"I don't have glitter in my eyes," Skye protested.

"Details, details. And guess who I ran into in the nail salon?"

"I have no idea."

"Milton's wife. She said he's still furious with you about the lottery-ticket thing."

"No surprise there."

The surprise came from Toni, who suddenly and without any warning darted straight out into the street.

Skye's heart stopped. A big red pickup truck was heading right for her little girl!

Before Skye could move, Nathan appeared out of nowhere with stunning speed to whisk Toni out of the way, barely missing getting hit by the vehicle as it sped by.

Skye was shaking as she ran across the street to join them, pulling Toni into her arms. "Baby, are you okay?"

"That was fun." Toni clapped her hands. "Let's do it again!"

"Little girls don't belong in the street without their mommy," Nathan firmly told Toni.

His authoritative voice instantly made the little girl's bottom lip jut out in pouting mode. "Mean man again," she said.

"You almost got hit by that truck." Nathan's voice was turning harder by the second. He redirected his attention from Toni to Skye. "Didn't you teach her not to run out into the street?"

Skye felt guilty enough without his accusing glare. There was so much she wanted to say. Sarcastic comments filled her head, but she couldn't seem to voice them. Instead, she simply gathered Toni in a tighter embrace and carried her back to the theater.

Only once they were inside did Skye's knees give out. She sank to the now clean floor of the lobby with Toni on her lap. Skye hugged her daughter fiercely, fighting back the tears while cradling her warm little body against hers.

Toni wriggled. "You're squishing me, Mommy."

Skye loosened her hold slightly. "Mommy needs a hug," she croaked unsteadily.

Toni responded to that, curling her arms around Skye's neck and cuddling close.

Sue Ellen stood beside them. "I'm so sorry! I didn't see Toni move. She went so fast. One minute she was with us, the next . . ."

"What happened?" Sister Mary demanded as she joined them.

"Toni ran out into the middle of the street," Sue Ellen said, "and was almost flattened by a pickup. Nathan saved her life."

The nun bent down beside Skye. "Are you okay?"

"I's fine," Toni answered brightly.

"I'm glad to hear that." Sister Mary's voice was gentle. "I was asking about your mommy, though."

Skye still had her face buried in Toni's hair to hide her tears.

Angel came racing into the lobby, knelt beside them, and took both Skye and Toni into her arms. "There now," Angel crooned. "It'll be okay."

"Why are you crying, Mommy?" Toni asked.

Skye still couldn't speak.

So Angel answered for her. "Because she's glad you weren't hurt."

"Mean man yelled at me." Toni sounded very offended.

"Because you were out in the street," Angel explained. "You know you're not supposed to do that. You could have been hurt."

Or killed. The close call shook Skye to her very core.

She kept hearing Nathan's accusing voice over and over again . . .

*   *   *

"Read me more, Mommy!" Toni sat perched on her twin bed with the soft unbleached cotton sheets.

Skye was perched beside her, the colorful Indian-cotton skirt she wore pooled around her feet.

Skye had done up the room to Toni's specifications. Hence the mural of kittens on the wall, the romping felines hand-painted on the lamp shade beside the bed, and the silhouettes of kittens along the side of the dresser.

"I've already read *Kitten's First Full Moon* to you three times."

Toni bounced on the bed. "Want to hear again!"

Skye was so relieved to have her daughter unharmed and by her side that she did what Toni wanted. But she hugged her first. For about the hundredth time.

Twenty minutes later, Toni finally fell asleep.

As Skye watched the steady rise and fall of her little girl's chest, a ticker-tape parade of panicked thoughts kept racing through her mind. What made her think she could do this mother gig? Skye wasn't empathetic like Angel, who was natural mother material. Angel, who had insisted on staying with Skye instead of going home with Tyler.

When Skye walked into the kitchen a few minutes later, Angel was waiting for her. "Did I ever tell you about the time you almost gave me a heart attack?" she asked, pouring Skye a mug of hibiscus tea and handing it to her.

Skye shook her head. Sinking onto a chair, she blindly watched the wisps of steam rising from her mug as if they might hold the secrets of the world.

"You were about Toni's age at the time," Angel said, "and you were fascinated with matches. Even then, you liked playing with fire—literally. I considered taking you to the local fire station for a kids' safety class they had. But I figured, even at that early age, you'd rebel against authority figures. So I had Sash talk to you. I'm not sure what he said to you, but you didn't play with matches anymore."

Skye wished she could remember what Sash had said to her, but she couldn't. And somehow that just incited her panic even more. She'd been ten when he died, and she still missed him. But the memory of the sound of his voice had faded over the years. How had that happened? *When* had it happened? She'd vowed to never forget him, and yet here she was, unable to call up his voice.

"I can't breathe. I need to get some air."

"Go ahead," Angel encouraged her. "I've got my crocheting here." She pointed to her tote bag filled with yarn and half-finished projects.

Skye grabbed the keys to the Tivoli on her way out of the apartment. When she entered the darkened theater, the emergency exit signs in the lobby were the only illumination.

A knock on the entry door behind her startled her. It was Nathan. "I was walking by and saw you come in here. Is something wrong? Are you okay?"

"I don't know."

As he entered the lobby, she realized he was limping slightly. "What's wrong?"

"Nothing. Old college football injury. I must have twisted it when . . . Anyway, I was just checking to make sure you were okay."

"I never thanked you for saving my daughter's life."

Her words clearly startled him.

"If you hadn't grabbed her . . ." Skye swallowed. "Anyway, thanks."

He shrugged awkwardly. "That's my job."

"Yeah, well . . ." Her voice trailed off.

He squinted into the darkness. "It looks like you got a lot done today."

"Here, I'll turn on some lights. The switches are this way." She led him into the office marked "Private."

He stumbled into her in the semidarkness.

That's all it took. Pivoting, she kissed him. He met her more than halfway. When she wrapped her legs around his hips, he maneuvered her to the desktop, where she shoved blueprints aside and pulled him down to her.

He removed her tank top and shoved up her skirt, sliding his hands along her bare thighs.

She tugged off his T-shirt and reached for the zipper on his Levi's.

"Wait." He placed his hand over hers. "I don't want you doing this out of gratitude for my saving your daughter."

"I've wanted to have sex with you ever since our first kiss."

"Is that all this is?" He raised his head to look down at her. "Sex?"

"Let's find out." Her hands returned to his zipper. "It's definitely not gratitude."

"No?" He slid his fingers beneath the elastic on her underwear. "You're not grateful?" He brushed his thumb through the crisp curls guarding the entrance to the damp cave of her sex.

"Yes, but I'm also hot—"

He slid his index finger inside her. "Yes, you are. I can tell. Real hot."

"Aren't you real hot too?" She tried to reach for him.

"Burning up." He spread her legs wider and moved her skirt up until it was bunched around her waist.

"Prove it," she challenged him.

He undid his zipper and shoved his jeans and tightywhities down. Hard and erect, his penis sprang forth as nature intended—wicked awesome.

"Condom?" she gasped.

"Where's your tote bag with the box of Trojan?"

"Upstairs."

"Good thing I've got a few in my pocket."

"You came prepared, huh?"

"Ever since I kissed you for the first time."

Words were replaced with actions as she helped him slide the condom on.

Seconds later, he entered her in a glorious rush. "I should go slow."

"Slow is good." She stopped him when he moved as if to withdraw, fiercely tugging him closer until he was embedded deep, *deep* within her. "Fast is even better."

His strong hands pinned her to the desk so she wouldn't fall off as he drove into her like a man possessed. She certainly responded like a woman possessed.

"No, don't stop," she moaned when he suddenly paused.

She saw pain on his face and remembered his sore knee. "Chair," she gasped. "Right behind you."

He didn't need any further guidance. Keeping her joined to him, he sank onto the chair.

"Ahhhh. Sweet." Her new position opened new channels of pleasure and satisfaction to her.

"You just like being on top," he growled.

"Mmmm," she agreed. "I like."

"How about this?" He gripped her bottom and thrust upward. "You like?" He thumbed her clitoris with seductive skill, working her arousal like a master artisan. "You like?"

She could only pant and nod blindly. "I . . . I . . ."

He swallowed her orgasmic scream as her vagina clenched around him, until, with one final, powerful plunge, he came apart in her arms.

Chapter Ten

· · · · · · · · · · · ·

Guilt. Nathan had it written all over his face. Not satisfaction. Not tenderness. Just guilt.

Skye wanted to know why, yet was strangely reluctant to ask. Which wasn't like her at all. Normally, she said whatever she wanted, whenever she wanted.

But this time was different. Nathan was different.

He was nothing like the guys in her past. Most had been moody nonconformists intent on doing their own thing. None had been a Mr. Responsible like Nathan.

Unlike the brooding types she'd gone for before, he had a quiet intensity, as if he refused to give himself permission to focus on himself and his inner pain.

Skye considered resting her forehead on his shoulder, closing her eyes, and ignoring reality. But she could feel the tension building in his body. And it wasn't sexual.

She slid off his lap awkwardly, noting that he was

unable to meet her eyes as he disposed of the condom and zipped up his jeans.

She wanted to pound on his bare chest and yell, *"Talk to me!"* But an unexpected wash of painful humiliation rushed over her. She felt cheap. Was he deliberately trying to make her feel that way?

Why? Why do that after he'd just made mind-blowing love to her?

Love? Or sex? Big difference.

"Did you love your wife?" The words just tumbled out of her mouth, as they so often did.

Nathan's expression closed up tighter than the funeral home after hours. "What kind of question is that?"

"What kind of answer is that?"

"Of course I loved my wife. She was *everything* to me."

His fierce words sliced into Skye like the paring knife that had slipped in her hand and resulted in her needing ten stitches a few years ago. She still had a scar on her palm. She rubbed her thumb over it now.

"What was she like?" Skye's unsteady voice sounded strange even to her own ears.

Nathan didn't notice. "She was golden. Blonde hair, light brown eyes that glowed when she laughed or smiled. And she did that a lot. She was sweet and . . ." His words dried up as he swallowed and looked away, clearly in the grip of a strong emotion.

When his gaze returned to Skye she could read the message there. *She was nothing like you.*

Skye had never been golden. Never been sweet. Not even as a kid. She'd always been a hell-raiser. A rebel.

She figured now she knew where his guilt came from. "You didn't betray her. Not by having sex with me, if that's what you were thinking."

"How would you know what I'm thinking?"

His tone of voice aggravated her. "Not because you'd

tell me anything, that's for sure." She took a deep breath. "All I'm trying to say is that you don't have to feel guilty. It's not as if you love me, or vice versa. We just shared a natural biological need, that's all."

"Why are you telling me this?"

"Because I don't want you to feel bad."

"Why should you care, if all we did was share a 'biological need'? You do that with a lot of guys?"

"Define *a lot*," she shot back angrily.

"Never mind."

"Don't ask the question if you don't want to hear the answer."

"I don't want to hear the answer."

This time, the knife slashed into Skye's heart without her even seeing the blow coming. Nathan didn't want to hear because he already knew what he thought.

Skye was usually the first to admit that she cultivated her bad-girl image, which was much worse than reality. She'd never cared what other people thought about her. The people she loved knew her and knew what was true about her.

The people she loved . . .

Oh no. No way she was adding Studly Do-Right to that group. Skye might be bad, but she wasn't stupid. She remembered thinking the very same thing the first time Nathan kissed her. Yet here she was, her body still tingling from having him embedded deep within her.

His hand suddenly cupped her cheek. "I'm sorry." His voice was gruff.

"For what?"

"For everything."

Which meant he was sorry he'd had sex with her. She probably wasn't as good at it as his saintly, beloved wife. The man clearly wasn't over the woman he'd adored and married.

So how did you respond to a guy who just told you he was

sorry for everything, including getting intimate with you?

"You can stuff your apology!" The fury of Skye's words was diluted by the sudden onset of tears. She quickly blinked them away.

"Hey, are you crying?" He tipped up her chin to get a better look at her face but she pulled away.

"Bad girls don't cry," she said roughly.

"Neither do cops."

"Not even when their wife dies?" There she went again. Speaking without thinking.

He stiffened. "Why this sudden interest in my past?"

"I'm trying to figure you out."

"Don't bother."

"Don't tell me what to do." She glared at him.

He glared right back.

"If I want to figure you out, I will," she said.

"Good luck."

"I never claimed it would be easy. You're complicated. And bossy."

"You're complicated and rebellious. And probably proud of it."

"Yeah, so? Your point is?"

"There's no talking to you," he muttered, yanking his T-shirt on over his head.

"Sure there is. I can talk just fine. You're the one with the communication problems."

His only response was a look of male impatience.

"The sex was great, but your postcoital pillow talk needs a lot of improvement!" she called after him as he walked out.

• • •

Work. Nathan immersed himself in it. He began in his office early the next morning. His office with the mud puddle walls, as Skye had called them. Dammit. The woman was everywhere.

Trying to figure him out, was she? Forget it. Not gonna happen. Nathan refused to let her get that close to him.

Of course, last night they'd physically been as close as a man and woman could be. But that was just a biological need. She'd said so herself.

So why had she gotten tears in her eyes? Was she feeling sorry for him? Or for herself for having sex with him?

Talk about complicated. She was a Rubik's Cube, a puzzle he'd never been good at working out.

"Did you eat breakfast?" Celeste demanded as she placed a healthy oatmeal bar on his desk.

He shoved the bar back at her.

She wrapped her arms around her sizable middle and stared at him as if he were a kid.

Nathan was tired of people telling him what to do. He was the sheriff, for God's sake. If anyone around here should be issuing orders, it was him."Get me the dispatcher logs for the past two days."

"I will if you eat something."

"Let me explain something to you, Celeste. I'm the boss. You're the employee."

"I know that. Now let me explain something to you. Breakfast is the most important meal of the day."

"Celeste . . ." His inflection warned her that he was fast losing what little patience he had.

"Fine. Be that way." She flounced out of his office, returning a few minutes later with the dispatcher information he'd requested. "Nothing exciting there. Lenore Trimble's parrot out in the Regency Trailer Park dialed 911 again for no reason. Oh, and a burglary was reported yesterday by Bernie Crampton."

"A burglary?" Finally, a crime he could sink his teeth into. "Why wasn't I notified immediately?"

"Because Bernie reported that the burglary occurred when his ex-wife came into his kitchen when he wasn't home, cooked up a batch of pork chops in apricot sauce, and ate them."

"Pork chops?"

"He said she stole them."

Nathan tossed down the file in disgust.

Celeste picked it up and hugged it to her chest. "I told you there was nothing exciting. Not like you saving that little girl's life. I heard about it this morning. How you swooped in to save the day."

Nathan flashed back to that moment when he'd seen Toni dash into the street, the pickup truck headed right for her. His blood ran cold at the memory. So he did what he always did when something cut too close to the bone. He slammed the hatch on those thoughts and focused on his work.

"Are you going to file a report against Skye?" Celeste asked. "Want me to notify the children's welfare department?"

"There's no need for that."

"You don't think that was child endangerment?"

"Her mother was right on the curb. The kid just darted off. Kids under seven can't be expected to remember street safety."

"That's why you have to hold on to them at all times. Any good mother could tell you that."

"Skye is a good mother. She loves her daughter."

Celeste sniffed. "I'm surprised to hear you defending her. After everything she's done. Like starting that fight over at the bar. Is that the behavior of a good mother?"

"She didn't start the fight." Sure, he'd as good as said so at the time, but once he'd cooled down some, he'd realized how stupid that was.

"That's not what I heard. I heard she started the fight. And I heard she never married the father of her child. That little girl was born out of wedlock."

"Not that unusual these days."

"That doesn't make it right. I also heard she might not even *know* who the father is."

Don't ask the question if you don't want to hear the answer. He hadn't asked . . . and now wished he had. Because he'd started to wonder if maybe Skye wasn't nearly as bad as she made out.

Or was that just wishful thinking on his part? Why did it even matter to him? Why did *she* matter?

And why had she brought up his wife Annie like that? How had she known he'd been feeling guilty?

Was the woman psychic or something?

She definitely was . . . something. Memories from last night filled his mind—her parted lips, her legs wrapped around his hips, the way she took him in, the way she tightened around him as she came.

He yanked his mind back to the present.

He coughed and had to clear his throat twice before he could speak. "Look, Celeste, I'd appreciate it if you didn't bad-mouth Skye."

Celeste sadly shook her head. "She's gotten to you, just like she got to poor Owen. Lenore Trimble is just beside herself over it all."

"Lenore Trimble, the widow with the parrot that dials 911? What does she have to do with it?"

"She and Owen were a couple before that hussy Skye came along with her belly-dancing ways."

"Celeste, I really don't have time to talk about the funeral director's love life."

"Of course not. You're the sheriff. An important man. Much too important to waste your time on that hussy Skye. I'll make sure she doesn't bother you."

"I wish," Nathan muttered under his breath as Celeste walked out of his office.

Nathan was actually able to spend the rest of the day on law enforcement work. Some of it paperwork, which never seemed to end. Some of it fieldwork, answering a domestic

violence call. Rock Creek might be small, but it suffered
from the same social maladies as the rest of the country,
just on a smaller scale.

After a twelve-hour day, Nathan headed home to the
unimpressive squat brick building also known as the Pine
Grove Apartments. There were only four apartments—two
downstairs, two up. He was the lessee of Apartment 1, located a mere block from the sheriff's office.

As he let himself in, he flicked on the lights and ignored
the stacks of unpacked boxes. He had a plasma TV, cable,
and a pair of black leather recliners. That's all he needed in
his living room.

That, and a pizza—half sausage, half pepperoni—
with everything on it. Which Cole was supposed to be
bringing . . .

A knock at door had Nathan heading in that direction.

"Love what you've done with the place since last time,"
Cole said, handing over the pizza.

"I'm not here much."

"No kidding? Really? I would never have guessed that."

"What? Like your place is decorated by a designer?"

"At least I don't have to use packing boxes as tables."

"I don't have to, I *choose* to."

"Yeah, right. That's my point. Why do you choose to?"

"You're a vet, not Dr. Phil."

"Thank God."

"Then stop with the stupid questions."

"I never ask stupid questions. So what game are we
watching tonight?"

"The White Sox." Growing up in Nebraska, Nathan had
seen the Chicago games on TV and gotten hooked. When
they'd won the World Series in 2005 he'd felt vindicated
for all those years he'd been a fan. "Women don't get this."

"Huh?" Cole paused with a slice of pizza midway to his
mouth. "They don't get baseball?"

"They try to figure you out."

"Who does?"

"Women."

"All of them or one in particular?"

"Why do they do that? Try to figure you out?"

"Because they want to know why you do the crazy stuff you do?"

Nathan yanked the rest of the pizza, still in the take-out box, away from his buddy. "What kind of answer is that?"

"Hey," Cole protested. "If you don't want to hear the answer, then don't ask the question."

Nathan stopped in his tracks. "That's what Skye said."

"She did? When?"

"Never mind." He set the pizza on one of his unpacked boxes.

"You know, it would be okay for you to settle down here in Rock Creek instead of just . . ."

"Just what?"

"Surviving."

"Surviving ain't bad," Nathan said carelessly. "Don't knock it."

"I'll bet Skye would be willing to help you unpack your stuff."

"Are you kidding? She'd probably want to do some weird feng shui thing here like she talked about doing in my office."

"I heard about her daughter running into the street and you saving her."

Nathan's throat clogged up and he dropped his slice of pizza back in the box. "Want a beer?" He headed for the fridge, which housed beer and pickles—that was it.

"Sure." Cole caught the can Nathan tossed to him. "So, how's it feel to be a big hero?"

"I wouldn't know."

"Was Skye suitably grateful that you'd saved her kid?"

Images flared through Nathan's mind once again, of Skye touching him, of him touching her . . .

"Yo, Nate." Cole waved his arms to get his attention.

"Huh?" He snapped back to the present. "Stop asking stupid questions."

"I already told you—"

"You don't ask stupid questions. Yeah, I heard you. Just watch the game."

As Nathan stared at the high-definition screen, which was so clear he could see the actual blades of grass in the ballpark, he was instead envisioning Skye.

• • •

"I've come for Gravity," Skye told Wally as soon as she entered the thrift shop on Tuesday afternoon. Today, he was wearing a shirt with little hula dancers on it and green tartan golfing pants.

"Are you taking her to your little girl now?"

"Yes."

"Gravity likes this basket, but you should wrap her up so she doesn't get scared when you carry her home in it. She has all her claws, you know."

The kitten hadn't gotten any cuter since the last time Skye had seen her. She still looked like a drunken painter had slapped orange paint on her black coat or dipped her in a large vat of creamy peanut butter.

Mmm, peanut butter. Skye's stomach growled. She hadn't eaten since the fruit and yogurt she'd had early that morning.

"So you've finally come to get your kitten," Sister Mary noted. "I meant to ask you about it at the theater the other day. But then I got distracted with . . ." Her voice trailed off. She didn't have to say the words. The image of Toni dashing out into the street still haunted Skye's dreams.

"Anyway, I'm glad you're here," Sister Mary continued. "I wasn't sure if you'd changed your mind about giving her to Toni."

"Because of what Toni did?"

"Because it's been a few weeks since you said you wanted the kitten."

Skye studied Gravity. "Yeah, she's gotten bigger, hasn't she?"

"Abs-o-tively." Wally beamed. "She's beautiful, huh?"

"Yeah, in her own way. Anway, I didn't change my mind. I just had a lot of things to do, you know? Like cashing in the lottery ticket and getting all that stupid paperwork filled out. Have I told you that I hate paperwork?"

"You may have mentioned it a time or two."

"Or ten," Wally said with a grin.

"And there was even more paperwork with the realtor," Skye said. "But now I'm the owner of the building, and I say we can have pets. I just wanted things to settle down a little before I brought Gravity into the picture."

"I can't see your life ever settling down."

"You're right." Skye rubbed the kitten's ear, which got Gravity purring up a storm. "I'm not the type to settle down."

"I didn't say that."

"You don't have to."

"You're taking my words the wrong way," Sister Mary protested.

Skye waved her hands. "Change of subject. I wanted to thank you again for bringing your work crew over to help out at the theater on Sunday."

"No problem. You've helped out at the soup kitchen plenty of times."

"Well, I'd better get going, so Gravity can meet Toni. I hope they're both ready for this."

Sister Mary patted her arm. "Good luck with that."

"Wait." Skye stopped in her tracks, the kitten still in her arms.

"What? Are you having second thoughts?"

"Yes. Not about the kitten, but the setup. I think I should tell Toni we're getting a kitten and then bring her here to see Gravity, and together we can bring her home. Yeah, I like that idea." She handed Gravity back to Wally. "I'll be right back."

Skye raced home to find Angel and Toni in the living room. Angel was working at the spinning wheel while Toni was working on a puzzle on the floor—a kitten puzzle.

"Hey, lovebug, I've got a surprise for you."

Toni leapt to her feet, her tiara tumbling to the floor as she looked around. "Where is it?"

"At the thrift shop."

Toni's face fell.

"I wanted to bring it home, but then decided to tell you about it first."

"If you tell me, it's not a surprise," the ever-clever Toni pointed out. The kid wasn't even five yet, and already she was brilliant.

"You know how you always wanted a kitten—"

Toni's shriek drowned out everything else. "YOU GOT ME A KITTEN?"

"Mm-hmm. But you've got to prove to me you're a big enough girl to take care of a kitten."

"I can. I can do it!"

"That means you can't run into the street like you did the other day. You must always wait for Mommy or Angel. Promise?"

Toni nodded solemnly.

"Okay, then let's go get Gravity."

Toni frowned. "Who's that?"

"The kitten. Her name is Gravity."

"She's a Gravity Girl. Let's go!" Toni grabbed Skye's hand and tugged her out the door. As she tried to keep up with her daughter, who faithfully held on to her hand and waited with her at the curb before crossing the street, Skye hoped to regain some of her own lost balance and focus. Because this was what was important to her—her daughter's happiness.

Not a sexy and infuriating cop.

• • •

"Go, Trojans, go!" the peppy girls along the sidelines yelled in unison as Skye and Lulu took their seats in the half-filled stadium.

"I hate cheerleaders." Lulu looked morose.

"So you've told me. A number of times."

"It bears repeating. I hate cheerleaders."

"How about the kicker? Do you hate him, too?"

Lulu shrugged. "He's bearable. What about the sheriff? Do you hate him?"

Skye mimicked Lulu's shrug. "Hate creates negative energy."

"That doesn't answer my question."

"Yeah, I know. I planned it that way."

"Yooo-hooo. Girls!" Sue Ellen was waving frantically at them, a tailgating nightmare in her bright purple Trojans' workout pants and matching long-sleeved hoodie. "Did you save me a seat?"

They hadn't, but there was plenty of empty space next to them.

Sue Ellen sat down and plopped two huge tote bags beside her. "I brought stuff."

"Yeah, I see that."

Sue Ellen pulled out a trio of "#1 Fan" foam hands, socking the people in the row in front of them. She blithely ignored their irritated stares. "Here, take these." She shoved the green foam at Skye and Lulu.

Next, she pulled out a giant *D* made of stiff cardboard, followed by a portion of picket fence.

Skye recognized it. "Isn't that from your garden at the trailer park?"

"Well, the fence part is. I'll put it back after the game."

"Why did you bring it with you?"

Sue Ellen held up the *D* and the fence side by side.

At Skye's blank look, she said, "*D*, fence. *De*fense. Get it?"

Skye nodded.

"Where's Toni?" Sue Ellen looked around. "I got her the cutest little football helmet."

"She's with Angel tonight."

"Wise move. Remember last fall, how she ran out into the middle of the wiener dog races in Serenity Falls? And then the other day, running out into the street like that. I swear, she nearly gave me white hair. I had to go home and get out the Nice'n Easy as a preventative measure. We certainly don't need her racing out into the middle of the football field tonight."

"She might do better than the Trojans' defensive line," Lulu said. "They stink."

"That may have been the case before I tutored them in the ways of yoga," Skye reminded her. "But now, they are enlightened warriors."

"Right."

"You'll see. Okay, why are they all running off like that?"

"It's the kickoff. The game is beginning." Lulu turned to study Skye. "You don't have a clue about this game, do you?"

"I know that sacks are something the coach wants a lot of."

Lulu attempted to give Skye a crash course in football for dummies, while Skye waved her foam hand like a wildly overcaffeinated cheerleader, bouncing to her feet to shout every few seconds.

Skye made it to the third quarter before having to take a potty break. So much for drinking all that chilled green tea she'd brought with her in a thermos. That stuff went right through you.

The port-a-potties were located to one side behind the stadium bleachers. Okay, *stadium* might be a bit of an exaggeration. The reality was a bunch of rows of bleachers along one side of a playing field. The other three sides were open.

The word *stadium* made Skye think of the Coliseum in Rome. Or the bizzaro job they'd done on Soldier Field in Chicago, which they'd driven by on their way from California to PA. Skye had liked the rest of the skyline of that city, but the stadium was too out there.

So Rock Falls didn't have a "stadium" per se, as much as it had a football field with a bleacher stand.

Potty break completed, Skye was taking a shortcut under the bleachers when she heard his voice. Nathan. Wearing a black T-shirt and jeans.

"I didn't expect to see you here," he said.

If he had, he probably would have gone elsewhere. He'd done a pretty good job of avoiding her since they'd had sex in her office at the Tivoli almost a week ago.

"Same here." Her voice was curt. "I wasn't expecting to see you."

"As the sheriff, I make a point of coming to the games. What's your excuse?"

She gave him a scathing look, one closely related to the Sicilian death stare. "If you're insinuating that I'm here to see you, then you are totally deranged. The team invited me. I taught them yoga, remember?"

"And belly dancing?"

"That was only to show flexibility. I focused on yoga."

Nathan seemed focused on her mouth. It was pretty dark beneath the bleachers, so she couldn't be sure. She did know that the sexual chemistry between them was still there, simmering. Like heat shimmers above a blacktop road in the August sun.

They both made the first move, meeting near a support beam. Nathan backed her up against it, kissing her as if she were a cool drink of water and he were a very thirsty man.

There in the shadows, he slid his tongue into her mouth with erotic stealth, while his hands stole beneath her paisley top to caress her breasts. If Nathan was surprised to find she was wearing a bra for once, he didn't say anything. She discovered that his touch was just as potent with silky lingerie acting as a seductive barrier.

She pulled his T-shirt out from the waistband of his jeans and slid her fingers up his spine. His skin was hot. Was that him panting, or was it her?

He nudged his knee between her legs and lifted her a bit, only to let her slide down his thigh. The ensuing friction, magnified by the denim of their jeans, was incredibly arousing.

She urged him to do it again. Oh, yeah . . .

The cheering inside her body was suddenly echoed by the crowd above them, bringing Skye back to earth with a bump. What was she doing, making out under the bleachers like some Nipplegate cheerleader?

She pushed him away and for once took the easy way out by making a run for it. Yes, fast exits were her specialty, but this ranked as one of her speediest. And shakiest. She just prayed her knees wouldn't give out before she returned to her seat. Nathan did not come after her.

"What took you so long?" Sue Ellen demanded. "You missed the touchdown! We're winning!" She hugged Skye while leaping up and down, then she quickly released her. "Oops! My boob just popped out of my lucky bra again." She wiggled around and got things back in order. "There, that's better."

"Brad got a field goal," Lulu told Skye. "You missed that, too."

"There was a line to use the port-a-potties."

Lulu raised a pierced eyebrow. "Really. Meet anyone interesting on your way there?"

"Why?"

"Because I saw the sheriff a little while ago. Did you know he'd be here?"

"No."

"Did you run into him?"

Did grabbing each other and making out under the bleachers count as "running into him"? Skye didn't think so, so she said, "No."

Lulu, the clever cynic, eyed Skye's kiss-swollen lips suspiciously before saying, "Would you tell us if you did?"

"Doubtful."

"I didn't think so."

The crowd roared. "Look! We won!" Sue Ellen and Lulu hugged each other, sandwiching Skye between them. "We won! Do you believe it?"

Yes, Skye could believe it. What she couldn't believe was that she'd made out with Nathan again. That kind of behavior made her worry that she might be both bad *and* stupid. Not a real good combo.

• • •

Two days later, Sue Ellen was once again bouncing with happiness. This time, she was doing it in Skye's living room. In a toga. "First the Trojans win their opening football game for the first time in ages, and now I get the totem party I always wanted for my birthday!"

"Why are you wearing a toga?" Lulu voiced the question, but Skye had been thinking it too.

"Silly girl. Everyone knows you wear a toga to a totem party, right?"

"Not really."

"Oh." Sue Ellen didn't appear too upset with this news. "Well, it's my party and I can wear a toga if I want to." She rubbed her hands together eagerly. "I haven't been this excited since I won the title of Miss Whoopie."

"What'd you do to win that?" Lulu asked. "Make out with the judges?"

"I thought you were Miss Scrapple," Skye said.

"I was. But I told you, that was just one of the titles I've won."

Skye didn't mention the title Sue Ellen had been known by in Serenity Falls—Our Lady of the Outlandish.

Skye knew all about being outlandish. She thrived on it. She'd been born too rebellious and had grown up too outspoken. These were pluses in her book.

Which was why Sue Ellen was her friend. Ditto for Lulu, who today was wearing a bowling shirt teamed with a black miniskirt and black combat boots.

Skye felt positively mundane dressed in lavender pedal pushers from the sixties and a paisley halter top.

"I planned a little something to kick things off," Sue Ellen said, pointing to the karaoke machine she'd brought with her.

Karaoke was a little unusual for a totem party, but then, so were togas. After all, it was Sue Ellen's party. Who was Skye to judge?

"I picked this song just for you, Skye." Sue Ellen grabbed the mike and started singing "Bad Girls" by Donna Summer.

Two seconds later, Lulu and Skye joined her. Of course, little Toni didn't want to be left out, so she bopped around with Ta the Tiger in hand, mimicking their movements before collapsing in giggles.

Sue Ellen, Lulu, and Skye continued to gyrate to the music, releasing their inner disco divas, with Angel as their audience.

Afterward, Sue Ellen's diva wanted feeding. "I'm starving," she announced.

Skye pointed to the set of tangerine-colored Fiestaware, a Serenity Falls garage-sale find. "I got out the good dishes for you," she said, giving her best Martha Stewart impersonation.

"And you plan on filling them with healthy food, I'll bet."

"You were hoping for Cheetos and Velveeta?" Skye countered.

"I suppose that would be too much to hope for," Sue Ellen replied, "despite the fact that it *is* my birthday."

"You suppose right."

Despite her initial hesitation, Sue Ellen was soon digging into the bean burritos, guacamole, and roasted eggplant dip Skye had prepared. Angel had offered to bring some of her yellow-squash cookies, but Skye had diverted her with a request for an organic fruit salad instead.

They all clustered around the kitchen table, Toni perched on Skye's lap, popping bits of cut-up pears and raspberries into her mouth.

"My birthday is coming soon, right, Mommy? Ta and I want a party like this one. Only with cake. And real tigers. And lots of kittens to keep Gravity company."

The singing and dancing had sent the kitten under Toni's bed, her favorite hideout when things got too chaotic for her Zen personality.

"Getting back to me," Sue Ellen said, "I want to achieve enlightenment and become a radiant being today. Can we get that accomplished in two hours?"

"No," Skye said bluntly.

"How about if we toss in some yoga?"

"Still no."

"Why not?"

"Because that's not how yoga works. You know that. You took yoga lessons from Angel."

"Yes, but I thought maybe they'd come up with a more efficient version by now. You know, the same way they develop faster computers all the time?"

Lulu just snapped her gum and rolled her eyes, which drew Sue Ellen's attention to her.

"I'm telling you, if you'd just let me work on your makeup . . ."

Lulu held up the large silver cross she wore around her neck and aimed it in Sue Ellen's direction. "Stay away from me with your wicked Mary Kay ways."

"Oh, I don't want to be a Mary Kay sales rep anymore," Sue Ellen assured her. "I was thinking more along the lines of a realtor. I mean, I already manage the Regency Trailer Park and do that so well that I really should branch out. I could begin in sales of double-wides. What do you think? Will this totem party tell me if that's a good idea?"

"No. This party is meant to remind you that we're all linked to our animal guides, and to accept the power that they offer us. To remind us that we're part of the Earth, that each creature has a place and an inherent skill of its own. Are you ready to answer some questions to help you chose your totem animal?"

"Sure, but I already know which one is mine."

"Is it an animal you feel an affinity with?" Skye asked.

Sue Ellen nodded emphatically. "Yes."

"Is it an animal you share characteristics with?"

"Yes. We're both cute."

"What animal are you thinking of?"

"A toy poodle."

Angel choked on her tea, which required Skye to pound her on the back.

"I'm surprised you didn't already know that." Sue Ellen sent them both a reprimanding look. "Didn't the tarot cards or something give you the answer?"

"My horoscope did say that today would be a very challenging day," Skye noted ruefully.

They all turned at the sound of someone knocking on the door. "Is that a surprise for me? A toy poodle, maybe?" Sue Ellen leapt to her feet and followed Skye to the door.

Skye opened it to find a Betty White clone standing there, complete with poodle-cut white hair, a floral dress, a string of pearls around her neck, and gold button earrings on her ears.

"Well, don't just stand there," the woman said. "Aren't you going to invite your grandmother inside?"

Chapter Eleven

· · · · · · · · · · ·

Who *was this crazy woman?* Skye was not impressed by her wild claim. "I don't have a grandmother."

"Of course you do," the woman replied. "You're looking at her."

"What kind of con is this?" Skye said.

The Betty White clone looked over Skye's shoulder, her attention focused on Angel. "Aren't you going to tell her the truth, Ethel?"

"Ethel?" Skye said. "Listen, you've definitely got the wrong place, lady. There's no Ethel living here."

"Yes, there is. I'm looking at her." The strange woman pointed at Angel.

"Angel," Skye began, "tell her . . ."

"Angel?" The older woman raised a perfectly sculpted eyebrow. "What kind of name is that? A bit presumptuous, don't you think, Ethel?"

"Angel is my chosen name."

"It sounds silly to me. I'm going to call you Ethel. It's what I named you."

"It's not my name anymore!"

Skye stared at her mother in astonishment. "What are you saying?"

"She's trying to tell you that she's my daughter, that I'm her mother. That you're my granddaughter and I'm your grandmother. My name is Violet Wright, by the way."

Skye shook her head. "No way."

"I assure you, my name is Violet Wright. Do you want to see my driver's license?"

"How did you find us?" Angel looked stunned.

"I saw a report on the news about a million-dollar lottery winner in Rock Creek, Pennsylvania. There was a picture of Skye."

"There's no way you could have recognized her," Angel said. "You haven't seen a picture of her since she was a child."

"You were standing beside her," Violet said. "I recognized *you*, Ethel."

Angel's face turned red. "Don't call me that."

Violet just shrugged. "As I said, it's your name."

"Why are you here?" Angel demanded. "Why did you leave California? You swore you'd never leave Bakersfield."

"Wait a second here." Skye held out her hands as if demanding a time-out. "Angel, are you saying this woman really is your mother?"

"Of course I'm her mother," Violet stated. "And her name is Ethel, not Angel."

"Who names their kid Ethel?" Skye said.

"A mother who wants to torture her child and have her spend her entire childhood ostracized," Angel replied.

"Oh, stop being such a drama queen," Violet said. "I named you after my beloved mother. Unlike you, Ethel, I know how to be a good daughter."

"What are you doing here?"

"I came for a visit." Violet pointed to the wheelie suitcase behind her.

"This really isn't a good time." Angel sounded a bit frantic.

"I can't wait for a good time," Violet retorted. "I might die tomorrow."

Angel's face reflected her concern. "Are you ill?"

"I'm old. Who knows how much time I have left."

"You're only seventy."

"Let's see how you feel when you reach the big seven-oh," Violet said. "Then we'll talk. Until then, you should ask me to sit down and offer me some tea. Or have you forgotten all the manners I tried to teach you?"

"I'm sorry." Angel seemed to crumble under the weight of her mother's obvious disapproval. "Come in. Let me help you." She took charge of the suitcase. "Skye, lead her to the couch so she can sit down."

"I don't need leading." Now Violet sounded cranky. She paused as she realized there were other people in the room.

"Hi there. I'm Sue Ellen and we were celebrating my birthday."

"Is that why you're wearing that silly outfit? And who is this?" Violet turned her laser gaze on Lulu.

"Your worst nightmare," Lulu drawled with a snap of her gum.

"Now, Lulu, don't pick on her," Sue Ellen said. "She's just a little old lady. She can't help it if she's crabby. She probably has bowel issues."

"That's one of the stupidest comments I've ever heard. And that is definitely the stupidest couch I ever saw," Violet declared, pointing at it in disdain.

Leaving Sue Ellen to handle Violet, Skye took Angel into the kitchen for a little one-on-one talk. "Why didn't you ever tell me I had a grandmother?"

"You've met her." Angel shot a nervous look in Violet's

direction while putting the tea kettle on to boil. "I think you can see why."

"Yeah, but still . . ."

"She makes me crazy," Angel quietly wailed. "I let her know when Julia and you were born, sent her pictures. She never acknowledged the letters I sent."

"Well, we did move around a lot."

"She never wrote back. My father disowned me when I left at seventeen. Said his daughter was dead. She'd never go against his wishes."

"He sounds like a real winner."

"The man was radioactive." Angel paused to take a few cleansing breaths.

Skye hugged her. "It's okay. You're safe now."

"Not with her around."

"Then I'll get rid of her."

"No, wait . . ."

"What are you two whispering about in there?" Violet called out. "It's not polite, you know, whispering behind my back that way. Come in here and face me."

"Why didn't you ever answer my letters?" The words poured out of Angel as she gathered the courage to confront her mother. "Why didn't you even acknowledge the birth of my daughters?"

"You know how your father felt about things."

Angel waved her hands dismissively. "Forget him. What about you?"

"He died a year ago," Violet said.

Angel paled.

"Of lung cancer," Violet calmly continued. "You know how he loved his cigarettes."

"Why didn't you tell me?" Angel whispered.

Violet shrugged. "The last address I had for you was in Alaska. The envelope came back marked 'addressee unknown.' "

"I meant when you got here. Why didn't you tell me right away?"

"I had to prove who I was to your daughter first. Anyway, as time went on, I got to thinking that maybe I should contact you. But I didn't know how. Then I saw the story on the TV."

"And suddenly contacting your family looked a lot more appealing now that a million dollars was involved, huh?" Skye said.

"You've raised a cynical daughter," Violet told Angel. "She also has questionable taste in her decorating choices." She shot another disapproving look at the couch before gingerly perching on the very edge.

Leave it to Toni to march right up to Violet and demand, "Who are you?"

"Who are you?"

"Toni. I bite. Skye is my mommy."

Violet blinked. "Ethel, you have a granddaughter?"

"Who's Ethel?" Toni asked, looking around. "Is she an invisible friend?"

"Of course not. She's your grandmother."

Toni narrowed her eyes. "Who are you?" she repeated.

Violet sat up straight. "I'm your great-grandmother."

Toni eyed her suspiciously. "What's so *great* about you?"

"Everything," Violet stated proudly. "As you'll find out for yourself soon enough."

"I don't think you're great. You've got mean eyes," Toni declared.

"Nonsense. You really should teach this child some manners, Ethel. She should show more respect when addressing her elders."

"A word of warning . . . ," Skye began.

"I should hope so."

"To you, not to Toni. You *really* don't want to insult my child."

The older woman sniffed her disapproval. "No offense intended, but . . ."

Sue Ellen shook her head and interrupted her. "Trust me on this. You don't want to insult Skye's kid. She gets very upset about that. I'm just trying to be helpful here."

"And who are you again?" Violet asked.

"The birthday girl. I'm also about to become a realtor, should you be interested in looking at a double-wide trailer. I could get you a really good deal—"

"Sue Ellen!" Skye grabbed her arm.

"What?"

"She's not moving here."

"I haven't made that decision yet," Violet said. "I feel a headache coming on. A nice cup of Darjeeling tea would be lovely."

Angel hurried into the kitchen. Skye followed her, while Sue Ellen engaged Violet in conversation. Toni and Lulu remained cautious observers.

"She'll have to stay with me at Julia's house." Angel spoke in a distracted undertone as she turned off the heat under the teakettle.

"Not if you don't want her there."

"Well, she can't stay here. There's no room, and Toni would end up biting her for sure. Not that I'd blame her."

"Don't let Violet force you into doing something you don't want to do."

"She's my mother. I don't know how to say no."

"Well, I sure do," Skye assured her. "I know how to say whatever I want, including *no* when the situation warrants it. And it seems like this situation warrants it."

Angel took a deep, cleansing breath. "Everything happens for a reason. Including her traveling here. Maybe the time has finally come for us to reach some kind of peaceful understanding." Seeing Skye's skeptical look, she added, "It could happen."

"Any other relatives you haven't told me about?"

"No. I'm an only child."

"No 'good girl' sister to egg you on, huh?"

"No. And you know Julia doesn't mean to—"

"Yeah, yeah. Forget about Julia and me. You're going to have your hands full as it is with Violet."

● ● ●

"I'll take it." Skye pointed to the ratty floral couch against the back wall in the thrift shop. She'd come shopping first thing Monday morning, to rid herself of the bad feeling left over from Violet's unexpected appearance the day before. Toni had come with her and was seated in a child's plastic chair, setting up a tea party for the toy animals.

"Are you sure?" Sister Mary eyed her dubiously.

"Positive. It's got good lines. Angel will make it look great in the front row of the theater."

"If you say so. I heard that Angel's mother is visiting from California. That must be nice for her," Sister Mary said.

"Not really. They haven't been . . . close."

"That's too bad. Well, perhaps this visit will make up for that."

"That's the stupidest couch I ever saw." Skye was startled by Toni's emphatic statement, until she realized her daughter was speaking to a plastic monkey, repeating Violet's words from the night before.

"She picked that up from Angel's mother, Violet," Skye told Sister Mary.

"So this Violet has definite ideas about decorating, hmm?"

"She has definitely *wrong* ideas about almost everything, from what I could tell."

"That's a shame."

"Yeah. Listen . . ." Skye looked around to make sure no one was near enough to overhear them. The shop had appeared empty when she'd walked in, but she remembered how she'd thought Cosmic Comics was safe, only to find Nathan lurking inside. "Nathan's not in here someplace, is he?" "Better safe than sorry" had never been her mantra, but just this once she figured it wouldn't hurt to ask.

"No." Sister Mary was clearly surprised by her question. "Why?"

"You know how I never wanted to hear about Nathan's past? Well, now I do."

"I didn't realize you didn't want to know before."

"A bunch of people tried to tell me about him—Sue Ellen, your sister . . ."

"So, why not go to one of them? Why come to me?"

"Because I figured you'd give me the most accurate answer."

"I'll try to, but the most accurate information would come from Nathan himself."

"I already tried to talk to him about it."

"And?"

"And all he told me was that he loved his wife and that she meant everything to him."

"She died in a car crash back in Nebraska. Before Nathan moved here."

"Was Nathan driving?"

"I don't believe so, no. He was working and heard the information about a crash come over the police radio. He never dreamed that his wife was involved at first, but he quickly found out when they listed the car's license number. He was at the scene shortly thereafter."

"He's still grieving for her."

"Grief is a unique thing, affecting every human being a little differently. Some people are able to pick up the pieces faster than others. And some never allow their emotions to come out, so they never really heal."

"Is that what you think is going on with Nathan?"

"I know he was devastated. My nephew Cole is Nathan's best friend and was rooming with him in college when he first met Annie. Cole was here when the accident occurred, but he flew out to Nebraska for the funeral. He's the one who convinced Nathan to come to Rock Creek and apply for the position of sheriff."

"Did they have any kids? Nathan and his wife?"

"No. Why do you ask?"

Skye didn't answer, not wanting to confess to the feelings she had about Nathan. And those feelings weren't just observations about the pain he carried within him. Something was going on there.

But something was also going on within Skye. Authority-figure guys like Nathan had never been her thing. So what was it about this particular man that got to her?

That's why she needed to figure him out. Not because she thought they had a future together. So she could get over whatever this was she had for him.

Opposites might attract, but they'd drive each other crazy over time. Nathan was a do-gooder who deserved someone equally respectable.

"Why this sudden interest in Nathan?" Sister Mary asked.

"I'm trying to figure him out," Skye admitted.

"Difficult to do with any man, but even more so with someone as reserved as Nathan. I think you'd be good for him."

Skye blinked at the nun with stunned disbelief. "Why do you think that?"

"You'd draw him out of his shell. Give him hope and enthusiasm for the future."

"I'd drive him crazy," Skye retorted. "I *do* drive him crazy."

"Exactly."

"Exactly what?"

"You get to him. Everyone has seen it. Right from that very first day."

"And why is that a good thing?"

"Because you shake up his world. He's spent the five

years since his wife's death refusing to put himself out there again."

"I can't really blame him for that."

"I'm not saying I blame him. I'm saying that it's as if he put himself in that coffin with his wife. He ended his life when she lost hers."

Skye rubbed away the sudden, stinging tears that Sister Mary's words evoked.

The nun patted her shoulder reassuringly. "I didn't mean to upset you."

"No, it's just . . ."

"Yeah, it is." Sister Mary understood Skye's unspoken sentiment.

Feeling like an idiot, Skye took a deep breath. "Thanks for telling me what you know."

"No problem. And, Skye, there's one more thing I know."

"What's that?"

"That Nathan would be good for you, too. He'd be your anchor and you'd be his kite. He'd keep you grounded and you'd give him hope to fly again."

"What makes you think I want to be grounded?"

Sister Mary just gave her a look.

"If I wanted to get grounded, I could do it on my own," Skye said defensively. "I don't want to be tied up like that."

"The town bad girl talking to a nun about being tied up." Sue Ellen shook her head as she joined them. "I never thought I'd hear such a thing. What are you two doing back here?"

"I'm buying that couch." Skye pointed to it.

Sue Ellen stared at it in horror. "You aren't!"

"I am."

"That couch is the Charlie Brown Christmas tree of couches."

"Yeah, it is," Skye cheerfully agreed. "And we're going to make it look beautiful."

"By burning it and putting it out of its misery?" Sue Ellen asked.

"Oh, ye of little faith," Sister Mary said.

"Hey, I go to church every Sunday." Sue Ellen was instantly on the defensive. "Not your church, but the Baptist one."

Sister Mary grinned. "I'm happy to hear that, but it's not what I meant. I was referring to the couch makeover."

"I like those makeover decorating shows on HGTV. Home and Garden TV," she clarified for the nun's benefit.

"Me, too."

Sue Ellen was stunned. "You watch HGTV?"

"Yes."

"I didn't think nuns did that."

"There's a lot you probably don't know about nuns. Like the fact that there are more nuns over seventy than there are under thirty."

"Hey, don't look at me," Skye said. "I wouldn't make a good nun."

"I would," Sue Ellen declared. "If I wasn't a Baptist and didn't look pale when not wearing jewel-tone colors. But should you ever want to buy a double-wide trailer, sister, then I'm your girl."

Sister Mary said dryly, "I'll keep that in mind."

As Skye led Toni out of the thrift shop, she wondered if she'd ever be able to keep Nathan out of her mind. The odds weren't looking real good at the moment.

• • •

Nathan sat in the squad car, filling out a status report on the noise complaint he'd just responded to. Usually, the Regency Trailer Park was a fairly quiet place, aside from Mrs. Trimble's 911-dialing parrot, but today the parrot had added something new to its repertoire. It had started shrieking obscenities through Mrs. Trimble's open window, causing her neighbors to complain.

"Wilson started watching cable TV without my realizing it," Mrs. Trimble tearfully explained. "He knows how to use the remote control."

"When he starts to rant, you might want to keep your windows closed," Nathan suggested.

"I'll do that. Thank you so much, Sheriff. Uhm, while you're here, I wanted to ask you about that woman who took Owen's money."

"What woman?" Nathan asked, though he was almost certain he knew who Mrs. Trimble was talking about.

"The one with the strange name. Skye, is it? An innocent-sounding name for someone who causes so much trouble."

"Do you know her?"

"I've never spoken to her, but I've seen her around town. Flaunting her body the way she does. Poor Owen didn't stand a chance."

Nathan knew the feeling. His own chances of being unaffected by Skye had long since evaporated.

"You keep an eye on her, Sheriff. She's up to no good, I just know it. Rock Creek would be better off without her sort."

Nathan left Mrs. Trimble's trailer, her words still ringing in his head. *Keep an eye on her.* He'd done more than that. He'd kept his hands on her, every inch of her. And he was aching to do it again.

Angry with himself over his temporary lapse in allowing Skye back into his thoughts, Nathan focused his attention on checking out the neighborhood as he drove back to the station. When he saw a group of kids hanging around a storage shed when they should have been in school, he stopped. Most of the kids took off, but he recognized them and would be speaking to their parents later. For now, he focused on the one he'd caught. Jay.

Nathan fixed him with the steely stare he'd perfected as a Marine. "Why aren't you in school?"

"School sucks."

"Does your mom know you're not in school?"

"She don't care. She don't care about nothing but—" Jay's mouth clamped shut.

Nathan knew his mom. She had a drinking problem and he'd been called in to break up a domestic dispute with her and a live-in boyfriend a couple of times. Nathan had gotten Jay involved with the Big Brother folks, and had thought that was working out.

He'd made a point of intervening with kids like Jay, taking them on field trips to the juvenile detention facilities to warn them away from the mistakes that others had made, before they did something they might regret the rest of their lives.

Nathan came from a family of do-gooders. It was something of a joke in the Thornton family. But also a matter of some pride.

So he sat there with Jay and listened to him. Sometimes, that's all it took to make a difference.

•　•　•

As Skye approached the Tivoli Theater, holding Toni by the hand, she noticed a biker parked out front. He wore jeans and a black leather vest with no shirt underneath, and he had more tattoos than Lulu. His head was covered with a bandanna and his white beard was shaggy. He hopped off his Harley and greeted her.

"You must be Skye. I'm Lulu's grandfather, Jerry. I just got back into town from South Dakota. Lulu tells me you could use my help."

"That's right. I bought the theater, and it needs renovating before I can reopen it. I heard you were an electrician."

Jerry nodded. "For twenty years. Want me to look things over for you?"

"That would be great."

"I can do it now if you've got the time."

"I've totally got the time." She led him inside the theater. "A lot of the main switches are in the office." Skye hadn't spent much time in there since she and Nathan had gotten intimate—not returning to the scene of the crime, so to speak. Not that sex between two consenting adults was a crime by any stretch of the imagination. At least, not in her book.

Nathan was working with an entirely different set of guidelines. He'd been married to a woman who was everything to him. Skye had never had that in her life. Never been married. Never found the one man who was everything to her.

In the past, she'd liked her guys dramatic—artistic and edgy. Like Toni's father, a musician and all-around player in search of heavy-metal glory. He'd certainly taken off fast enough after hearing the news that Skye was pregnant.

Given her history, it surprised Skye that she'd felt such intense chemistry with Nathan. And that chemistry hadn't diminished any because they'd had sex. If anything, it had increased.

And it also wasn't like her to avoid a place just because it reminded her of a man.

"What about the main fuse box or circuit breakers?" Jerry's question interrupted Skye's thoughts. She didn't usually indulge in thinking about past mistakes.

"I don't have a clue where those are," Skye admitted. "Tyler might know if he's around."

"That's okay. I'll find what I need."

She showed Jerry into the auditorium, where his attention became focused on the organ in the corner. "Oh, man, a Wurlitzer organ with four hundred and fifty pipes." He reverently ran his fingers over the keys before wincing at the sound. "I'd be glad to tune this for you."

"You know about this kind of stuff?"

Jerry nodded.

Tyler joined them, preventing Jerry from going on about the wonders of the organ as he'd clearly wanted to do. Skye left the two men together and took Toni with her into the lobby, where Angel met them with a picnic lunch of tofu hot dogs and roast-veggie sandwiches. They sat on metal folding chairs and drank iced green tea.

Afterward, Toni sat on an old quilt and played. She wasn't wearing her tiara today, which was rare for her.

With Toni busy, and Tyler and Jerry off in the backstage area, Skye felt free to quiz Angel. "How is it going with Violet?"

"She's having her hair done today. With Mabel."

Mabel was Serenity Falls' leading gossip.

"Everything she says will probably end up in Mabel's blog tomorrow," Skye noted.

"I warned her about that."

"And what about Tyler? Did you warn him about your dinner with Adam?"

"I haven't told him about any of the meetings."

"Meetings? As in more than one?"

"Mm-hmm."

"So you're sneaking around behind Tyler's back to see a capitalist pig?"

"It's not like that. I'm helping Adam become a better human being."

"By getting up close and intimate with him?"

"I am not having sex with him."

"Not yet."

"We just meet and talk sometimes."

"If it's all so innocent, why haven't you told Tyler about it?"

"Because he wouldn't understand."

"You've got that right. If I don't understand, he certainly won't."

"I don't understand why you're making such a big deal out of this."

"Because it *is* a big deal. Adam is trying to woo you over to the dark side."

"Oh, please." Angel rolled her eyes. "Quite the opposite is true. I'm trying to woo him over to the light."

"And how's *that* working?"

"Hard to tell for sure, but I'm making some improvements. He wants to learn how to meditate.

"I'd call that a pretty small improvement."

"It's a start."

"Exactly. And I don't want to see you get anything started with Adam."

"Not even his enlightenment?"

"He's probably just conning you about that."

"When did you become so cynical?"

"I was born that way."

"Yeah, you kind of were." Angel had to agree. "But it got worse when Rex left."

"You never quite get over the pain of being dumped that way. You definitely move on, but it changes you," Skye admitted.

"That's how I felt about Adam's dumping me. He didn't know I was pregnant, though, and Rex did. That makes a difference."

"The only difference I want to focus on at the moment is making a difference in this theater," Skye said. "It's going to be great when it's done. We can set up fund-raisers, feature a foreign-film night. We could even do our own version of the Sundance Film Festival and show short documentaries by brilliant, cutting-edge independent filmmakers. And we could do special displays here in the lobby, featuring local artists, starting with your fabric art—your scarves and hats and the wall hangings you're starting to explore. The Tivoli will be a showcase for dreams."

"And we Wright women have big dreams," Angel said proudly.

"Well, some of us do. You and I represent the wilder

side of the Wright women. Violet and Julia represent the prune-serious side."

"That's not fair to your sister."

"Fine. Whatever. I don't want to argue about her. I just want to savor this moment, creating a dream."

But later that night, the sound of breaking glass woke Skye, right in the middle of an incredibly sexy dream about Nathan. Her maternal instincts immediately clicked into action, and she ran to check on Toni first. But her daughter was sound asleep, Gravity cuddled at the foot of the bed, snoring slightly. So the kitten hadn't broken anything.

Moving into the living room and looking out the front window, she saw a dark figure down below, throwing something at the marquee of the theater. She yanked open the stubborn double-hung window and leaned out to yell, "Hey!"

The vandal turned tail and ran before Skye could get a good look at him . . . or her.

• • •

"I got a report of vandalism here at the theater," Nathan said as he walked into the lobby the next morning.

He was back in uniform, looking all official and exuding bossy vibes. Skye should have been totally turned off. Instead, she wanted to mess him up, ruffle his hair, tear open his shirt, and lick his warm skin.

"You've been avoiding me for a week now." The words were out before she could stop them. Her lack of an inner editor to monitor what she said had never bothered her, but it was starting to now. And it was all his fault.

"I saw you at the football game a few days ago."

"Yeah, and made out with me under the bleachers, only to shove me away."

"You pushed first," Nathan said.

Well, okay, he was right about that. She'd pushed first in order to be proactive. Skye was tired of being the one rejected. Better to be the dumpee and not the dumper. Better to be first to walk away. And better to stick to the facts, not the sex.

"Someone threw something at the marquee in the middle of the night and broke a bunch of the incandescent bulbs and some neon tubes. Or so Jerry tells me. I'm not an expert on neon."

"Jerry?"

"Jerry the electrician. Lulu's grandfather. He's also promised to tune the Wurlitzer."

"That's nice of him."

"Is that your suspicious voice? I can't tell for sure."

"No," he said mildly. "I was just making a comment."

"Not a snide comment?"

"No." Okay, now he didn't sound so mild. He sounded like he was getting aggravated.

Well, join the party, buddy.

"Was anything taken from inside the theater?" he asked. "Any sign of forced entry?"

"I don't think so."

"Can you show me the exits?"

Why? So you can head for one of them instantly? Hey, she didn't say that out loud. Maybe she was learning some restraint.

Wait a second, was that necessarily a good thing?

"The exits?" he prompted.

"Right. Well, the front doors, of course. And then the ones at the back of the theater, near the stage." She led him down the aisle and pointed to the two side fire doors and the two sets of double-wide doors on either side of the stage.

"What about the stage itself?" Nathan asked.

"What about it?"

He climbed the few steps leading up to the stage. The screen rolled up out of sight when not in use. Jerry had gotten that to work yesterday.

She followed Nathan onto the stage. "Pretty cool, huh? I can see this place as not only a movie theater but also a community center. We could do performances here of local groups." She sat at the edge of the stage, not caring if her black shorts got dusty, and let her legs dangle down. She stared out at the empty seats as if imagining them filled with an appreciative audience.

"Local groups?" To her surprise, he sat beside her. "You mean, like local belly dancers?"

"Among other things, yes." She started swinging her legs, excited with her plans for the future. "We could do fund-raisers. Special events." She turned to find him staring at her.

Something in his eyes made her abruptly say, "You think I'm the kind of girl you bang once and then forget about."

Her blunt words didn't shock him. "No, I don't." He cupped her cheek with his big hand. "You are definitely unforgettable."

She wasn't convinced until his lips replaced his hand, and he tenderly nibbled his way across her cheek with the sweetest string of kisses she'd ever experienced. Once his mouth reached her parted lips, things got hot pretty fast.

Presto, they were both horizontal on the stage, putting on a passionate performance starring dueling tongues and caressing hands. He stole the scene by undoing the buttons of her cherry-studded shirt, slowly pulling the edges apart as if opening the proscenium curtains at a movie premiere.

Skye wasn't wearing a bra. Nathan muttered his approval before bending down to swirl his tongue over her right nipple.

Which made it a very bad time for a hammer to come crashing down from someplace far above, almost hitting them both.

Chapter Twelve

. . . .

Nathan was on his feet with lightning speed. "Who else is in the building?"

He was totally the law enforcement officer now.

"No one." She sat up. "Why?"

"That hammer didn't fall by itself."

"It could have. Maybe it slipped off something. There are metal beams, rollers, and other stuff up there. Some of the guys were working in that area earlier this morning."

"What guys?"

"The guys that Tyler hired."

"What do you know about Tyler?"

Skye blinked. "Oh, come on. You don't think he left a hammer up there to fall on me, do you? How could he know I'd be making out on the stage with you at this exact time?"

"Maybe someone was watching us."

"Hope you enjoyed the show!" she shouted at the ceiling.

"This isn't a joke."

"Do I look amused?"

She looked like a woman who'd been made love to. Her lips were still swollen from his kisses, her blouse unbuttoned. She wasn't wearing a bra, so he could see her creamy breasts through the gaping material.

"Button up."

"You button up," she said, pointing to his shirt.

He quickly redid his buttons. She made no such move toward her own.

Nathan did a quick recon of the stage area to make sure they were indeed alone. When he returned, Skye was sitting just as he'd left her. "I'll need a list of people who don't want you opening the theater."

"What?"

"You heard me." He couldn't take staring at her breasts a second longer without touching them. So he bent down and tried to button her blouse himself.

But his bumbly fingers kept brushing her bare skin. Skye smacked his hand. Hard. Not because she was modest, but because she was pissed off at him. He was wise enough to know the difference. And to back off.

"You think someone is trying to sabotage my opening the theater?"

"It's a possibility."

"So is the Loch Ness monster, that doesn't mean that it's real. Well, okay, that one time I did visit Scotland, I really did see something in the water that day, so maybe the monster was a bad example."

Nathan was a little freaked to realize he was actually able to follow that garbled statement of hers. He knew her that well.

Irrelevant, his crime-fighting, former Marine self stated. *Complete the mission. Ignore distractions.* "Who might have it in for you?"

She shrugged, making her shirt gap a little more. "How should I know? I don't worry about things like that."

"Well, you should start worrying."

"Worrying creates negative energy."

"So does getting hit on the head with a hammer. That can create permanent brain damage."

"You've got brain damage if you think I'm going to back off renovating this theater." She was shouting at him.

"I never said you should do that."

"Is that your plan? To scare me into stopping?"

"My plan is to keep you safe." He yanked her into his arms and kissed her, open blouse and all. "Why can't you understand that?" he muttered against her mouth.

"Keeping me safe is just part of your job, right?"

"Kissing you is definitely *not* my job. It's my . . . pleasure."

"How do you know another tool won't fall on us if we keep this up?"

"I'm almost willing to take the risk." He tapped his index finger on the tip of her nose. "Almost. But not quite."

"Skye, what on Earth are you doing up there on that stage half naked like that?" a voice demanded from the aisle.

It was Violet Wright.

Nathan instantly released Skye.

Skye made the introductions. "Sheriff, meet my long-lost grandmother, Violet."

"I've never been lost in my life," Violet declared. "And I've never seen a more derelict theater."

"It used to look much worse," Skye said cheerfully.

"Somehow, that's not reassuring to me. You still haven't told me what you're doing, Skye."

"And I have no intention of doing so."

Nathan recognized that stubborn look in her eyes, even if her long-lost grandmother didn't. He could have warned her that ordering Skye to do anything only made her dig in her heels.

Violet sniffed. "Clearly, your mother didn't teach you to respect your elders." Her gaze fixed on Nathan. "What about you, young man? Are you really a sheriff?"

"Yes, ma'am."

"Then you should know better. What if someone else had walked in and found the two of you like that?" She waved a disapproving hand at them. Then, "Your blouse is unbuttoned, Skye." Now she sounded horrified.

Nathan could read Skye's mind. He could tell how tempted she was to yank open her blouse and flash the old lady.

But she didn't.

Instead, Skye gritted her teeth and buttoned her shirt. Crookedly. On purpose, he suspected. As a sign of rebellion.

He was getting to know his bad girl pretty well.

Halt right there, he ordered himself. She wasn't *his* at all. And he certainly wasn't hers.

She didn't even want him to be. Did she?

Why her? Why now? *Why not?*

Well, that last question had about twenty good answers, too damn many to go into right now with him facing down an infuriated grandmother.

He tried to make polite conversation. "Do you live around here, Violet?"

"No, I came all the way from Bakersfield, California."

"When she learned I'd won a million dollars," Skye added.

Violet's perfectly made-up face reflected her anger. "That's not the reason and you know it. I already explained—"

"I know what you told me," Skye interrupted. "That doesn't mean I believe it."

"I've never seen a girl so disrespectful."

Skye shrugged. "What can I say? I'm one of a kind."

Nathan was standing close enough to Skye to sense the tension in her body. He took note of her defensive body language.

"I hope you don't plan on raising your daughter to be this disrespectful," Violet said naughtily.

Big mistake. Nathan could have told the old lady that.

Skye reacted instantly, just as he'd known she would. "Don't you tell me how to raise my daughter! You were hardly a model mother yourself. Letting your husband kick your only child out of the house as a teenager. What kind of mother allows that?"

"A frightened one." Violet stared at them with stricken eyes before turning and walking out of the theater.

"Oh, shit." Skye sank onto the stage floor. "Shit, shit, shit!" She banged her clenched hand against the warped wood.

Nathan knelt beside her, taking her hand in his. "Talk to me."

"Why?" She sniffled. "So you can write it all down in your report for that thick file of yours?"

"Because you're hurting."

"Bad girls don't hurt."

"And I suppose they don't bleed, either, huh?" He pointed to the scratch on her arm.

"Gravity."

"Gravity made you bleed?"

"We got a new kitten. Her name is Gravity."

"Isn't that the kitten that Wally found over at the thrift store? The one that fell through the hole in the roof before it was repaired?"

"That's right. How did you know that?"

"It's my job to know what's going on in this town."

"What is going on?"

He was no dummy. He knew what she was asking. *What was going on between them?*

Problem was, he didn't have an answer. "I don't know," he admitted huskily.

"Yeah. Me, either."

Their eyes met and he drank her in, as if hoping to absorb her into every cell of his body. She was gazing at him exactly the same way. Whatever this was between them, they were both in danger of falling victim to its power.

Nathan had a hard time seeing Skye as a victim of anything.

There was a time when he'd been like that too. Until he'd become victim to a grief that had brought him to his knees.

As if sensing the darkening of his thoughts, Skye suddenly looked away and focused on their surroundings.

"You know, a lot of these old theaters have been either demolished or chopped up into cubelike compartments to watch a movie. The magic of a big auditorium like this is lost." She pointed to the deep blue ceiling where angels floated in a star-studded sky.

"So you're a bad girl who still believes in magic?"

"Yes," Skye said. "You always have to believe."

"Sometimes things happen that make you stop believing."

"Yeah, I know." She gently squeezed his hand. He didn't have to say that the death of his wife had made him stop believing in anything other than the letter of the law. She seemed to already know.

Nathan cleared his throat. "So, getting back to the matter of that hammer . . ."

"You don't think it was an accident?"

Nathan shook his head. "That's not what my gut is telling me. I'm going to check the hammer for fingerprints, see what turns up."

"How do you know someone wasn't after you?"

"Because last night, someone vandalized the Tivoli's marquee."

"And you think the two occurrences are related?"

"I intend to find out," Nathan said grimly. "You can rely on that."

• • •

"When is your mother leaving?" Tyler asked Angel as she fussed over Lucy the Llama.

They'd come in his pickup truck to visit the llamas on the farm. Angel welcomed the chance to get away from Julia's house, where Violet had settled in with disturbing ease.

"I wish I knew." At the moment, there was a lot that Angel wished. She wished for a healthy pregnancy for Lucy. She wished she knew a good way to tell Tyler about her time spent with Adam. She wished she knew what danger the tarot cards were foretelling for Skye.

She also wished for world peace and an end to hunger and global warming—but those were long-standing wishes.

The others were personal ones that kept her awake at night.

Well, okay, after Hurricane Katrina the prospect of global warming and the probability that it was intensifying hurricanes kept her awake at night. Even now, when many had forgotten the problems of the devastated Gulf Coast region, Angel continued to make regular donations to Habitat for Humanity in their quest to rebuild housing for those in need.

With her thoughts spiraling so far away, Angel had to concentrate on what Tyler was saying.

"Your mother is cramping my style." Tyler sounded irritated. "I can't make love to you with her in the house."

Angel sighed. "If you tried, she'd come after you with a butcher knife."

"She doesn't look the violent sort."

"Looks are deceiving."

"Yeah, I learned that when I was a prosecutor."

Angel turned to face him, her attention now one hundred percent focused on him. "I haven't mentioned anything about your prior life to my mother. She knows nothing."

"I appreciate that."

"I know you don't like talking about that period in your life. And that you still feel guilty about what happened with that last case."

Tyler's expression hardened. "The one where I was responsible for an innocent man's death."

"You thought you'd put the right man in prison. By the time you found out different, he'd taken matters into his own hands and hung himself in his cell. You're probably not ever going to stop blaming yourself for that, but I hope you can heal some of the pain. We're only human. We all make mistakes."

"Some people's mistakes are bigger than others."

"Yeah, I know." Angel sure knew she'd made more than her fair share of mistakes. And she knew the depth of Tyler's mistake went clear to the center of his soul, changing him forever.

"So, why didn't you ever mention anything about your mother before?" he asked.

"You've met her. She's a steamroller in June Cleaver clothing."

"Even so . . ."

"My father kicked me out of the house when I was seventeen. I stayed at a friend's house to finish high school and then headed for LA on my own. I took some classes at UCLA but never got a degree. And I got pregnant with Julia. You know the rest."

"Not really. What did your parents think about your getting pregnant?"

"They refused to even acknowledge that fact. I wrote a letter letting them know. Even sent a birth announcement and photo of Julia as a baby. Nothing. When he kicked me out, my father told me I was dead to him. And he stuck to that until he died."

"I'm sorry about that."

"I don't know what I am, aside from all messed up."

Angel started to cry. She was in hormone hell again, transported there with lightning speed.

"Hey, none of that."

"I can cry if I want to," she said fiercely.

Tyler immediately backpedaled. "Right. Sure you can."

"Don't think you can tell me what to do!"

"Wouldn't dream of it."

"Lucy and I are both having hormonal issues. Trust me, you really don't want to mess with us."

"Right."

Angel brushed away her tears. "Let's go make out in your pickup."

Tyler blinked. "Huh?"

"You heard me."

"Uh, we're on an Amish farm here."

"Oh, right." She nodded excessively. "Not the best place to make out. You're right. I wasn't thinking straight. That is happening to me more and more lately." She started to wail. "I try to keep the threads of my being from getting all tangled into knots, but nothing I do seems to work—yoga, meditation, getting my chakras in order. My meridians are totally messed up."

"Is this because of your mother or because of Adam?"

Angel's heart stopped. Had Tyler somehow found out about her meetings with Adam? "What do you mean?"

"You never did tell me why he called you that time."

She breathed again. Tyler didn't know the truth. "Listen, I really need you to be stable and normal right now and not go off on some rant about Adam, okay? You're my rock."

Tyler appeared very uncomfortable with this news.

"What?" Angel demanded. "What's wrong with being my rock?"

"I don't know that I'm that stable."

"Well, you'll just have to be. We can't both fall apart at the same time. What do you have to be upset about?" Her voice rose. Angel knew it but couldn't help herself. Hormone hysteria did that to a person. "*Your* mother isn't living with *you*. She's not planning on coming here, is she?"

"She died the day after I graduated law school. From breast cancer."

"I'm so sorry." Angel's voice was softer now. "What about your dad? Or your siblings?"

"I was an only child. My dad died a few years after my mom. So, no, I don't have any family that might suddenly drop in on me."

Angel wanted to tell him that he was lucky, but she realized how shallow that sounded. Was this how Julia had felt when Angel had descended on her unannounced? Totally freaked out?

She flipped open her cell phone.

"Who are you calling?" Tyler asked.

"Julia."

"Right now?"

"Yes. I've got something important to tell her."

"Hello?"

Angel heard seagulls in the background. "Julia, it's Angel. Where are you?"

"Along the coast in Oregon. I'd forgotten how beautiful it is out here."

"Listen, I've got something very important to say."

"This connection isn't real good," Julia said.

"Probably because I'm out in the countryside visiting with the llamas. Lucy is pregnant, you know."

"So you told me. Is that why you called?"

"No, I wanted to say I'm . . . I'm sorry I just showed up on your doorstep last year with no warning!" Angel burst into tears and handed the phone to a panicked Tyler.

"Hello, hello?" Julia was frantically saying.

"I . . . er . . . . it's me. Tyler, I mean," he said. "So how are you doing, Julia?"

"What's going on with my mom? Did you two have a fight?"

"No. She's just upset because her mother showed up."

Angel was making no-no motions with her hand, but it was too late.

"Her mother?" Julia sounded stunned.

Angel yanked the phone away. "Don't yell at me," she pleaded with Julia. "And don't get mad."

"I never yell. Well, almost never," Julia said. "So, along with a father I didn't know I had, I now have a grandmother, too? Any more relatives you're hiding in the closet?"

"No, this is it," Angel said in a small voice. "I didn't mean to tell you this way."

"Yeah, I've heard that before." Julia sighed. "I suppose Skye already knows?"

"Only because Violet—that's my mother—showed up on Skye's front doorstep unannounced."

"Gee, that sounds familiar."

"She heard Skye had won a million dollars in the instant lottery."

"Skye won a million dollars?!"

"I thought I told you."

"No, you didn't. But then, you and Skye have a special kind of relationship. I hope she's doing something sensible with the money, but I bet she's not."

"She is so. She's bought a movie theater."

"A what?"

"An old movie theater in Rock Creek. And she's restoring it."

"I don't believe this! You didn't try to talk her out of it . . . ? Never mind. Of course you didn't. You're the one who crashed and burned trying to sell tofu hot dogs in Fairbanks, Alaska, the heart of meat country."

"I didn't call to discuss my past entrepreneurial endeavors. I only wanted to say that I'm sorry I threw your orderly world into chaos when I showed up unannounced. I didn't realize how upsetting that could be until my own mother did the same thing to me."

"Why didn't you tell me about her?" Julia asked.

Angel filled her in on the story.

"How long is she staying?"

"I don't know. Tyler just asked me the same question."

"I think it's time Luke and I started thinking about going back to Serenity Falls," Julia said.

"Really? It would be great to see you again."

"Adam tells me the two of you have been getting along really well."

Angel gave Tyler a nervous look. "Yeah, well, we can talk about that later. Love you."

Julia sighed. "Yeah, I know. Same here."

Tyler handed Angel some rumpled but unused Kleenex from his jeans pocket. "You feel better now?"

She blew her nose and nodded.

"I'm glad." He gave her a quizzical look. "Want to tell me what that was all about?"

"Julia didn't know that I had parents."

"She thought you were hatched from an egg?"

"I mean, she didn't know they were still alive."

"Lies have a way of catching up with you," Tyler said with a shake of his head. "And usually not in a good way."

Angel knew. She'd lied to Julia about her biological father for all those years. She'd lied about her own *parents* . . . Well, not really. She'd simply avoided telling the truth. Surely that wasn't quite as bad? And now she'd used the same avoidance technique with Tyler regarding the time she'd spent with Adam.

What a complicated web she turned out to be spinning. Especially for someone who'd always thought she was leading such a truthful life.

•   •   •

Nathan stared at his computer screen. Several pairs of fingerprints had turned up from the hammer. One set belonged to Tyler.

And the info that had come up on the handyman had surprised Nathan. Tyler had once been a prosecutor in Chicago, a man on the fast track to success until a case had gone horribly wrong, resulting in an innocent man hanging himself in a jail cell.

So Tyler was someone else who'd stopped believing. Only he'd left his career behind instead of immersing himself in it the way Nathan had.

"Have you eaten lunch yet?" Celeste demanded as she entered his office.

"Yeah," Nathan said absently.

"Then why is your sandwich still sitting on your desk?"

"You're not my mother. I've *got* a mother, back in Nebraska."

"I should call her and tell her how badly you're taking care of yourself."

"You do, and you'll find yourself out of a job."

"Did you hear that Skye's grandmother is here for a visit? Well, actually, she's staying with Skye's mother over at Julia-the-librarian's house in Serenity Falls. Julia is the good daughter, you know."

"Really? I heard she took off on the back of a Harley with some guy."

"Not some guy—Luke Maguire. I heard he's a wild one. Anyway, I didn't come in here to gossip."

"That's reassuring."

"I came in to tell you there's someone to see you."

"Who?"

"That comic-book man."

"Algee is here? Show him in."

Algee came in and closed the door behind him, almost in nosy Celeste's face. He eased his Hulk-like body into the guest chair in Nathan's office before he spoke.

"Look, I'm not here to cause any hassle in the castle."

Nathan frowned. "I'm sorry, but I'm not following you."

"I talked to Luke about it, and he said I should talk to you."

"Luke?"

"Luke Maguire. He's a close buddy of mine. And a former Marine, and a former FBI Special Agent."

"I'm a former Marine myself." Nathan pointed to his "Semper Fi" mouse pad.

"I'm a former Navy man. Anyway, I'm worried about Skye."

"Because?"

"Because someone vandalized the Tivoli marquee. And Milton is still spreading lies about her, trying to make trouble. I offered to put the fear of God into him, but Skye strictly forbade me to do that."

"A wise move, actually."

"Sister Mary wanted to put the fear of God into him too, but again Skye said no. Nancy Crumpler, well, she wanted to set the mob on him, but Sister Mary didn't go along with that plan. Lulu just wanted to TP his office, but that's not going to do much. Of course, this was all before the vandalizing incident. Anyway, Luke said I should come talk to you. He read something about the vandalism in Mabel's online blog."

"Mabel?"

"She's the biggest gossip in Serenity Falls. Somehow, she heard about the incident. Mabel knows everything—we've just come to accept that. Anyway, Skye won't be happy I came behind her back to voice my concerns about her safety to you. That's what I meant by not causing a hassle in your castle."

"Skye's not in my castle."

"Yeah, right. If you don't want to talk about what's going on between the two of you, that's cool. I'm just saying I'm worried about her."

Nathan abruptly changed the subject. "What do you know about Tyler?"

"Tyler? He's a good dude. Rollerblades in the middle of the night sometimes when he can't sleep, but that's no big deal. Why are you asking?"

"Just checking out everyone who had access to the theater."

"Luke is close with Tyler. If there was something bad going on with him, Luke would have found out and done something about it. What about Milton?" Algee said.

"What about him?"

"Have you checked him out?"

"I've canvassed the area, and no one saw anyone near the theater that night."

"Skye did."

"Aside from her."

"You're not saying she lied about seeing someone, are you?" Algee demanded.

"Of course not. The vandalism is a fact. I just hope things don't get worse."

"So what are we going to do about it?"

"*We* aren't going to do anything about it. I'll take care of things."

Algee shook his head. "You jarheads are stubborn."

Nathan smiled. "Yeah, we are."

"So, how do you plan on taking care of Skye?"

"I'm working on that."

"Uh-huh. Well, I can tell you right now, she's not going to like whatever you come up with."

"I realize that. Who said I'm going to give her a choice?"

"She's going to hate that even more."

"Understood. But the bottom line is, I aim on keeping her safe."

"That's all I needed to hear." Algee stood and held out his hand. "If you require any help, you know where to find me."

Nathan rose and shook Algee's hand. "I appreciate it. And . . . it wouldn't hurt for you to keep an eye out for her as well."

"Understood."

"Just don't go putting the fear of God into anyone without my permission, okay?"

"You might want to tell Sister Mary that. I heard she looked furious when Milton walked into the thrift shop a couple minutes ago."

Nathan leapt to his feet. "Why didn't you tell me this earlier?"

"I figured a nun wasn't going to do anything criminal to him. Would she?"

Nathan sighed. "I'd better go find out."

• • •

Skye walked into the thrift shop to find Sister Mary yelling at Milton.

"You should be ashamed of yourself!"

"No, *you're* the one who should be ashamed! Defending a sinner like that Skye woman."

"Don't yell at Sister Mary and don't insult Skye," Wally warned him.

"Let he who is without sin cast the first stone," Sister Mary said.

"Don't you dare go quoting the Bible at me." Milton's face was turning as red as the cherries on Wally's shirt. "And don't give me that holier-than-thou look either. I'm not the villain here." He pointed at Skye. "She is!"

"Chill out, Milton." Skye slyly lowered her gaze. "Your bad vibe is showing."

Milton automatically looked down and checked his fly before realizing what she'd said. "I'm not the one who's bad. You are."

"So?"

"So you admit it? You're bad?"

"Sure I am."

"You heard her." Milton looked around at Sister Mary and Wally. "She just admitted—"

"The fact that some people think I'm bad. That doesn't mean I steal lottery tickets or that I'm a thief." Skye paused. Well, there was that shoplifting charge on her juvenile record. And she had told Julia she'd stolen one or two things made in child labor camps from a store in Serenity Falls, just to bring attention to that cause. But she'd been yanking Julia's chain a little on that one. Skye had sent a press release to the media about the conditions in such camps and listed the store selling the items. But she hadn't actually taken anything. Not that she hadn't been tempted.

Milton pounced on her momentary hesitation. "You want to swear with your hand on a Bible, in front of Sister Mary, that you've never stolen anything?"

"Don't answer that."

The command came from Nathan as he walked into the thrift shop. "What's going on here?"

Silence.

"Don't all of you answer at once."

"Milton was just showing off his bad vibe," Skye reported.

"Stop saying that! Make her stop saying that," Milton ordered Nathan.

"Milton was insulting Sister Mary," Wally volunteered.

"I did no such thing," Milton said vehemently.

"Sister Mary, would you care to insert a word or two here?" Nathan said.

"I was just chastising Milton for his bad behavior," she replied.

"And I told her I wasn't the one who's bad, she is." Milton again pointed at Skye.

"Which I readily admitted," Skye said.

"Yeah, I figured you would." Nathan sighed. "Listen, folks, why don't you all just calm down and head on back home. The party's over here."

"Party pooper," Skye drawled.

"Are you going to let her speak to you like that?" Milton demanded.

"It's a free country," Skye said. "At least, it was this morning."

"Still is," Nathan assured her. "Now I'm sure you all have more important things to do than stand around here and bicker."

"Bicker?" Skye raised an eyebrow. "What kind of a word is that?"

"Now she's picking on your word choices!" Milton's voice was shrill. "Are you just going to stand there and take it, Sheriff?"

"He doesn't have to," Syke said. "I'm leaving. *My* choice. I have a theater to restore." And she flounced out.

But the next morning, Skye entered the Tivoli with her daughter to find paint splashed all over the marble floor of the lobby and the walls.

Chapter Thirteen

· · · · · · · · · · · ·

"**Someone** was messy," Toni said.

"Come on, honey, let's leave." Skye's voice shook.

"Don't want to. Want to finger-paint."

Skye scooped Toni up in her arms. "This is the wrong kind of paint. You can finger-paint at home. We'll go there now."

She ran into Angel, Tyler, and Violet on her way out.

"I've never seen such messy painters." Violet's forehead wrinkled with disapproval as she looked around.

"What's going on here?" Tyler said to Skye.

"Someone must have broken in last night—" Skye began.

"Did you call the sheriff?"

She shook her head. "Not yet. I just got here."

Tyler took control of the situation, using Angel's cell phone to notify Nathan.

"I'm taking Toni upstairs," Skye said.

"I'll do that," Angel volunteered, taking Toni. "Maybe

you should stay here and talk to the sheriff when he comes."

"Nathan will be right over," Tyler said, handing the cell phone back to Angel.

"Don't leave her alone, please," Angel told Tyler.

"I won't. Don't worry."

Angel shivered. "I feel such negative energy in this space now. Do you feel it, Skye?"

Skye nodded.

"I don't feel anything," Violet said flatly.

Angel sighed. "That doesn't surprise me. Come on."

Violet refused to budge. "I want to stay here."

When Tyler went to check the auditorium for more damage, Violet cornered Skye. "Are you and this sheriff person serious? Because what you were doing on that stage looked very serious to me. Does Ethel know about this? Not that she'd think anything of it, given her history."

Skye's eyes narrowed for an only slightly toned-down version of her Sicilian death stare. "A word of warning," she said. "You do *not* want to insult my mother. And her name is Angel."

Violet sniffed, a sure sign she was peeved. "I'm just trying to be helpful. You don't have to jump all over me for being concerned about my granddaughter."

"And you don't have to insult my mother to make yourself feel better."

"That's not what I'm doing!"

"Isn't it?"

Violet was prevented from answering by Nathan's arrival. He had his cop face on.

"The back door was forced open," Tyler announced as he rejoined them.

Nathan took off with him to investigate, leaving Skye alone again with Violet.

Skye used the opportunity to address something that had been bothering her. "Why did you say the other day that you were frightened of your husband? Did he hit you?"

"He didn't have to. He believed a wife should obey her husband. It was part of our wedding vows, and he took it very seriously. To love and obey."

"Doesn't sound to me like he took the love part very seriously."

"He loved me in his own way, just as he loved Ethel before she got so rebellious . . . I don't want to talk about those days," she said abruptly.

Skye would have said more, but Owen showed up, his face filled with concern. "I saw Nathan rushing over here. Is everything okay?" He paused as he surveyed the theater's damaged lobby. "No, obviously, everything isn't okay. What happened?"

"Vandals broke in overnight. The sheriff is here now investigating."

"Skye, aren't you going to introduce me?" Violet patted her hair to make sure it was still in place. Since she used enough Aqua Net to choke an army, there was no chance of that hair helmet moving one iota.

"Owen, this is Violet, my long-lost grandmother. And this is my friend Owen."

"Owen, I'm so happy to meet you," Violet trilled. "And I appreciate your concern over my granddaughter's safety. I wasn't harmed in the attack either, thank heavens."

Skye rolled her eyes. "You weren't anywhere near the theater last night. You're staying with Angel over in Serenity Falls."

"Even so, I've been inside the theater."

"Yes, I know." Skye remembered all too well how Violet had walked in on her and Nathan. And even if she hadn't, Violet had taken great pleasure in reminding her.

"So, Owen." Violet batted her heavily mascaraed lashes at him. "What do you do here in Rock Creek?"

Skye answered on his behalf. "He owns the funeral home."

"Oh, my." More eyelash batting. "Well, that's a noble profession. You know, neither my daughter nor Skye have shown me around town. Perhaps you'd be willing to do that?"

Owen appeared flustered. "Well, I . . . uh . . . sure, I could do that. Not that there's much to see. Of course, we do have that World War II tank in Memorial Park. Well, it's more just a small, tank-size area than a real park."

"I was a young girl when the war started, but I still recall that time so vividly. Young people nowadays don't realize what sacrifices we've made for them."

Owen shook his head sadly. "A lot of men died in that war. I lost an older brother on the beaches of Normandy."

Owen had never told Skye that. Why was he confessing something so personal to Violet, of all people?

"I'm sorry for your loss." Violet comforted him with a hand on his arm, which looked Super-Glued there.

"It was a long time ago."

"And yet so fresh in our memories"

"Yes, it is."

"I'd love to see this memorial park. Do you think you'd have time today?" Violet asked.

"Well, business is slow at the moment," Owen admitted. "Not that I'm looking for people to die."

Violet patted his arm. "Of course not. I saw that sign outside your funeral home. The one about not hurrying, that you'll wait? Maybe people are taking that literally."

"I don't mind waiting."

"Young people these days do seem to mind waiting. But I'm with you, Owen. I think it's much more exciting to let the anticipation build. Don't you agree?"

Owen nodded and then checked his watch. "I have a few things to do first, but I could meet you here in two hours to give you a tour of the area. Would that work for you?"

"Absolutely. That will give me time to calm Skye." Violet's commiserating look was as fake as her eyelashes. "She depends on me so."

"She's lucky to have you here," Owen said. "Skye, let me know if there's anything I can do to help. I'll see you later, Violet."

The moment Owen left the theater, Skye confronted Violet. "What do you think you're doing, flirting with Owen like that?"

Violet primped, pulling out a mirrored lipstick case and outlining her lips before speaking. "What's the matter? Are you jealous?"

"Owen is a good friend of mine."

"Like the sheriff?" Violet snapped the lipstick case shut with an impatient snap. "Don't you think that's a bit greedy of you, wanting all the best men in this town for yourself?"

"Owen is nothing like Nathan."

"What are you going to do about Sheriff Nathan?" Violet asked.

"Why do you care?" Skye countered.

"Fine." Violet sniffed. "Don't tell me. I can see where this is going. You're as stubborn as your mother."

"Thanks for the compliment."

Violet sniffed again before turning on her heel to march out. Skye didn't even ask where she was going. She had other cosmic-sized problems to overcome.

Staring at the disturbing mess surrounding her, she kept wondering who would do such a thing. Roxy Rothafel's saying over the theater entrance—"Don't give the people what they want, give them something better"—seemed to mock her now. Plus, it reminded her that she still didn't know who the hell Roxy was. She hadn't Googled him yet. Another chore to add to her "to do" list, had she been the kind of person to keep such a thing, which she wasn't.

"Did you touch anything?" Nathan asked as he rejoined her.

"Just the front door when I unlocked it to come inside."

"Tyler was right, the back door was forced open. Most of the damage seems to be in this area though."

Skye thanked the fates for that. Replacing seats and carpeting or the screen would have been very expensive.

"Have you worked on that list of people who might not want you to succeed in this project?" Nathan said.

Skye shook her head.

"Tell me more about the run-in you had with Milton at the thrift shop yesterday."

"It was mostly between Milton and Sister Mary. I was just a bystander."

"I find that hard to believe."

His words, meant to tease her, she supposed, infuriated her. "No surprise there. You find just about everything about me hard to believe."

"That's not what I meant, and you know it."

"Do I? How am I supposed to know that? I may be good at reading some people's minds, but not yours. You keep it locked up tighter that those tighty-whities of yours."

"If you'll just calm down a second—"

"I'm not going to calm down. I'm pissed. Seriously pissed! We were just making progress here, and now look at it. Everything is a big mess."

"Did you hear anything suspicious last night?"

"No, nothing. But if I find out who did this, I'm going to kick some serious butt."

"That's my job. Who aside from Milton might be upset with you right now?"

"Right now, this very minute?"

"You know what I mean. When did Violet come to visit? Before or after the first vandalism incident?"

"So now you think my long-lost seventy-something grandmother is behind all this?"

"I'm not ruling anyone out."

"Except for Sister Mary."

"Not even her."

"She likes me."

"She could be angry that Owen didn't give the money to her charity instead of to you."

"But she's not. She told me so."

"I have to consider everyone a suspect."

"That's a terrible way to live."

"It works for me."

"Well, Owen can't be a suspect."

"Maybe he regrets giving you the money."

"Stop it." She put her hands to her ears. "I don't want to hear any more."

He gently tugged her arms down. "I think Milton is the most likely culprit. And I plan on having a little talk with him shortly. Meanwhile, I'm not real happy with you living right above the theater."

"Why not?"

"Because these incidents seem to be escalating, and by practically living on-site, you leave yourself and your daughter vulnerable. What if the guy who broke in here last night had decided to break into your apartment instead?"

"Are you deliberately trying to scare me?"

"I'm trying to make you face reality. And the reality is that you and Toni would be safer staying with your mom at your sister's house over in Serenity Falls."

"I'm not letting some idiot scare me out of my own home. Or my theater."

"It's the wise thing to do."

"It's the cowardly thing to do."

Nathan sighed. "I had a feeling you'd say that. Let me go talk to Milton and see what he has to say." He turned his attention to Tyler, who'd just joined them. "Can you keep an eye on things here?"

"Angel already told him not to leave me alone," Skye said.

"Good. I won't be long."

"If you think everyone is a suspect, then why aren't you suspicious of Tyler?"

"Because I know his background." Nathan walked out without saying anything more.

Which meant Skye had to get the information out of Tyler. "What was he talking about?"

"I suspect Nathan had me checked out."

"And?" she prompted.

"And he probably found out that I was once a prosecutor in Chicago."

Skye stared at him in astonishment. With his long gray hair gathered in a braid, no one looked more antiestablishment than Tyler. "You were a suit? A lawyer?"

"Yeah."

"So what happened? Does Angel know any of this?"

"She knows."

"Why keep it a big secret? Not that being a lawyer is something you'd want to brag about. I can understand that. Were you a Republican, too?"

"I refuse to answer that question on the grounds that I may incriminate myself," Tyler said wryly.

"A Republican lawyer. And look at you now. Long hair, ragged flannel shirts, and jeans. A rebel." Skye shook her head before giving him a fierce hug. "Good for you! I'm so proud of you!"

Tyler blinked. "Huh?"

"You knew you were on the wrong path, so you jumped off. That life path is what brought you here, though, so you really should honor it and not be ashamed of it."

"Yeah, so Angel has told me."

"People don't appreciate how smart she is."

"I do."

"I sure hope so." She also hoped that Tyler would understand when Angel finally confessed about her secret meetings with Adam. But for now, Skye had bigger problems to deal with.

• • •

"Yo, Milton, how's it going?" Nathan said as he walked into Milton's tidy accounting office without bothering to knock.

Milton, wearing a bow tie and suit as uptight as he was, did not look happy to see him. "What are you doing here?" His tone was belligerent.

"Your secretary wasn't at her desk, so I came on in."

"What do you want?"

Nathan took a seat across the desk from Milton. "Just thought I'd check in with you and see how you're doing."

"I find that highly unlikely given the fact that you were very uncooperative when I asked for your help with that situation with my uncle."

"In what way was I uncooperative?"

"I asked you to arrest that sleazy Skye woman."

"Yes, you did." Only years of training and self-discipline prevented Nathan from wrapping his fingers around Milton's scrawny little neck. Every honorable instinct he had urged him to defend Skye, even though he knew damn well that she wouldn't appreciate his sticking up for her. But beating up Milton wouldn't garner usable information, which was Nathan's primary reason for being here. "The thing is, I'm not allowed to do that without something known as due cause."

"Did my uncle send you here?"

"I haven't spoken to Owen recently. Have you?"

"No," Milton said curtly. "He wasn't exactly cordial to me the last time we spoke in your office."

"And that bothered you?"

"Of course it bothered me. He was treating me as if I were some kind of idiot, when I'm a highly respected professional." Milton pointed to the framed degrees on his wall. "I expect to be treated as such."

"As what?"

"As a highly respected professional."

"Me, too. I expect to be treated as a highly professional law enforcement officer."

"In that case, you'd be wise to act with more decorum."

"What do you mean?"

"I mean, people are talking about you and that woman."

"You mean Skye Wright? She's a highly professional businesswoman now that she owns the Tivoli Theater."

"The only profession she knows is the world's oldest profession," Milton sneered.

"You want to be careful making statements like that." Nathan's voice was taut. "She could sue you."

"Sue me for what?'

"For slander and defamation of character. And for being an asshole, if that were illegal . . . but unfortunately, it's not."

"Hey!" Milton's face turned red. "You've got no right coming in here and calling me names."

"You're correct. However, I do have a right to come in here and interrogate you. Unless you'd rather I took you down to the station to do that?"

"What are you talking about?"

"I'm talking about you, and your whereabouts last night."

"I was working late last night."

"Can anyone confirm that?"

"My wife. I told her I was here working late."

"Anyone see you here? Your secretary?"

"She went home at five."

"So, how late were you here?"

"I don't know. Until midnight, maybe."

"Really? That late? And it's not even tax time right now."

"I have a lot of work all year round to keep me busy."

"Yeah, it looks like it." Nathan noted Milton's clear desktop.

"I like order and tidiness," Milton said.

"Me, too. I'll tell you what I don't like. I don't like the idea that someone is deliberately trying to sabotage

Skye's efforts to rehab the Tivoli. That really pisses me off."

"I don't appreciate your choice of language," Milton primly informed him.

"Too bad. I don't appreciate vandalism and breaking and entering."

"I have no idea what you're talking about."

"Someone broke into the theater last night and defaced the lobby with paint."

"It wasn't me," Milton replied immediately, beads of sweat forming along his upper lip. "I was here last night. Working."

"Without any witnesses."

"I got home before one A.M. My wife can vouch for that."

"Still doesn't cover the hours before that."

"What time was the theater broken into?" Milton asked.

"We don't know."

Milton's earlier bravado returned. "Then it could have happened *after* one A.M., when I was home."

"It could. We're dusting for fingerprints now and following a few leads."

"You won't find my fingerprints there," Milton stated confidently.

"Maybe not. But we might find that whoever did break in was actually doing the dirty work for someone else. Someone who was working late or home in bed."

"Are you accusing me?"

"No. I was just stating a few possibilities."

"If you're exploring possibilities, you should look into Wally Purdy's past. You know, over at the thrift shop. He was a drunk, you know. Maybe he fell off the wagon and went a little crazy last night."

"Why should Wally want to vandalize the theater?"

"How should I know? Finding that out is your job, not mine."

"Yes, it is. And I *will* find out, Milton." Nathan gave him the steely glare honed and perfected during his years in the Marine Corps. "That's as certain as death and taxes."

*   *   *

Skye faced the football team the next day with eyes dry and scratchy from lack of sleep. She hadn't been able to rest much last night, fearing a repeat incident of vandalism and determined to stop it before it happened.

Tyler had called in a security company, which had installed a new system, along with motion-sensor lights near the rear exits. The lights had gone on twice—a prowling alley cat was the cause the first time, a garbage-looting raccoon the second.

Skye had spent the night sitting in a chair in her bedroom facing the window above the alley, ready to protect what was hers. Not the most restful of occupations.

She was *so* not ready for a hoard of sports-mad teenagers this morning.

"Are you coming to the game tomorrow night?" Brock the quarterback asked Skye. "You are, right? You're like our good-luck mascot."

Skye didn't really appreciate the comparison. She'd seen the team mascot, and the foam Trojan was not a pretty picture.

"We've been winning," Brock reminded her. "Coach says there's nothing like winning, and he's right. Coach is always right."

"Have you all been continuing with your yoga every day?" Skye asked.

"Yes!" they shouted in unison.

Skye winced. She was getting a serious headache. She turned on the Dave Matthews band and got started.

The familiar movements relaxed her, as they are intended to. As she went through the various poses, a degree of serenity slowly returned.

Her inner balance restored, Skye gathered her yoga mat after class and headed for the nearest exit. She was surprised to run into Algee in the locker-lined hallway. "What are you doing here?"

"Speaking to classes about a new project we've got going on."

"We?"

Algee nodded. "I saw what a difference you made with your yoga lessons and thought maybe there was more I could do to get involved. I read about this project that encourages kids to create their own comic books as an after-school program. I went to their website and got more information. Learned all the academic buzzwords, like how creating comic books fosters imagination, improves language skills, and builds vocabulary. They've cut the funding for art classes here in the Rock Creek school district, which sucks big-time, so this is a way for kids to express themselves artistically. Mostly younger kids, like in middle school, but I thought some ninth-graders might be interested too."

"It's a great idea, Algee! Hey, are you blushing?"

"Are you kidding?" he scoffed. "Black dudes don't blush."

"Yeah, right. Especially big, burly, ultratough black guys."

"Yeah, especially them."

"Is there anything I can do to help?"

"Like you don't already have your plate full? I heard about the vandalism at the theater. And that Tyler got a new security system installed for you yesterday, right after that last incident."

"Nathan wanted me to make a list of my enemies. Can you imagine?"

"Was it a long list?" Algee asked, utterly serious.

"I didn't make a list."

"Why not?"

"It's bad karma."

"So is getting vandalized."

"Yeah, so Nathan has told me."

"But you aren't listening to him."

"He's very bossy, have you noticed that?"

"So are you."

"Me?" She socked Algee's arm, wincing as she hit solid muscle. "I am not. I just have strong opinions about things, and I'm always right."

"Oh, well, that's different."

"Damn right. You know, once your comic-book project gets off the ground, we could do a display of some of your students' work in the theater lobby once we open. And maybe do a Spiderman/Batman movie marathon to highlight it or something."

"As long as it included *Batman Begins*."

"It would have to, or Sue Ellen and Lulu would run me over with the Batmobile."

"That is some kind of pink vehicle that Sue Ellen drives."

"Yes, well, Sue Ellen likes to make a splash wherever she goes."

"So do you. Listen." Algee's expression turned serious. "Nathan is a good guy. He already came to me about an at-risk kid named Jay that he thought would be a good candidate for the comic-book project. The guy knows everything that goes on in this town."

"Big Brother is watching, huh?"

"I don't think he sees himself as your big brother."

"No?"

"Not in this lifetime," Algee said. "You're not blind, girl. I'm not telling you anything new here."

"Nathan does everything by the book. He follows the rules. I break them."

"So?"

"So, that doesn't make for a good combination. Besides,

you're hardly in a position to be giving me advice on my love life. You are constantly going out with someone new."

Algee grinned. "I like to spread the joy around."

"You're just as leery of settling down as I am."

"Guilty as charged."

"I'm glad to hear you admit it."

"I've been meaning to thank you for recommending Lulu as an employee at Cosmic Comics Two. She's working out just fine."

"Another nonconformist."

"Who knows her graphic novels. She's a walking encyclopedia. I thought I knew a lot, but she blows me away."

"She has a younger brain."

"Ain't that the truth. Listen, I've got to go. But you be careful. And do what Nathan tells you."

"You're kidding, right?"

Algee shook his head. "This sabotage stuff is nothing to joke about. It's some serious shit."

It got even more serious in the middle of the night, when someone tried to set fire to the Tivoli Theater.

Chapter Fourteen

. . . .

Skye stood in front of the theater in the eerie predawn light, wearing low-cut jeans and a cropped tank top stating "When I Can't Sleep, I Count the Buckles on My Straight-jacket." The fire department had put out the flames, which had actually been confined to a pair of Dumpsters in the alley behind the theater.

The Tivoli was saved. For now . . .

Skye wrapped her arms around her bare midriff to ward off the chill.

"All right." Nathan's voice was hard when he spoke to her, matching his expression. "This does it. End of discussion. You and your daughter aren't safe staying upstairs in that apartment."

"I agree," Skye said. "Angel has already taken Toni to her place."

"Great. So you're moving to Serenity Falls temporarily."

"Like I said, Angel has taken Toni. But I'm staying."

"Don't you realize how dangerous this situation is?"

"And don't you realize how *important* this place is to me? What if you never find out who is behind all this? What am I supposed to do then, huh? Wait around indefinitely? Give up? No way!" she said fiercely. "I'm not doing that. End of discussion, to use your words."

The fire chief came up to them. "It was definitely arson," he said. "Good thing we caught it early, before much damage was done. It could have been worse."

Nathan and the chief walked away from Skye, talking quietly. There didn't seem much point in going back to sleep, so she grabbed her purse and car keys from upstairs and headed out of town to visit the llamas. Not usually her thing, but she felt the need to take a break from everything for an hour or two. Toni was safe with Angel. But Skye's state of mind was less secure, and it was too early to talk to Owen or Algee or Sue Ellen or Lulu. They were all bound to be still asleep. But the llamas would be awake.

By the time Skye reached the Amish farm where the llamas were being boarded, the sun was up, and so was the Miller family. In deference to them, she'd pulled on a denim shirt that covered her midriff, navel ring and all.

She waved to Mr. Miller as he headed into the milking barn, then made her way to the pens where the llamas were kept. "So, Lucy, how's the pregnancy going? I hear llamas take a year to have a baby. That sucks, huh? Bet you're surprised to see me. Don't worry, I'm not going to ask for your opinion on stuff the way Angel does."

Lucy stared at her with those big dark eyes surrounded by long feathery eyelashes.

"I needed to come out here to breathe. The smell of manure may make you gag, but it really clears the mind."

Ricky, the male llama in the pen next door, shuffled forward to greet her. "I haven't forgotten you. I brought you both some treats." As she shared a handful of her trail mix with the two animals, Skye tried to think who would want her out of town so much that they were willing to burn down the theater to accomplish it. Sure, in the past her auric field had interacted strongly with others', sometimes resulting in sparks . . . but never in arson.

Ricky gave her an indignant, sideways look, obviously peeved that she wasn't paying enough attention to him.

"You're such a *guy*," she said.

Which, of course, got her train of thought steaming nonstop for the Nathan-station.

"Can you believe that he actually ordered me out of my own building? Never mind. Forget it. I promised not to talk to you about my problems. I just needed a break, that's all. I'm better now, better able to meet obstacles, setbacks, and challenges. Which is a good thing, because I have a feeling there are going to be plenty of all three waiting for me back in Rock Falls."

• • •

On her way back into town an hour later, Skye ran into Nancy Crumpler at the Gas4Less, where the older woman was filling a Big Gulp–size cup with coffee. "I heard about the fire. Are you okay?"

Skye nodded.

"Do you have a minute?" Nancy asked. "I need to talk to you. Why don't you come with me to the store? I don't get any customers this early in the morning."

Only when Skye was seated in the chair behind the sales counter did Nancy stop drinking her coffee and begin to speak. "I thought I should tell you that some of the other business owners in town are acting like asses, trying to protect their own behinds by saying the theater is a threat to them."

"What?"

"Someone tried to burn the building down, right?"

"The fire wasn't that big."

"Because it was caught early. But Milton is trying to fan

the flames by making dire predictions about what could have happened."

Skye suspected Milton was doing more than just talking.

"He's saying the entire block could have gone up in flames," Nancy continued. "That's got folks nervous. I certainly did what I could first thing to quell such stupid speculation. It's just that some people are a little edgy."

"Join the club," Skye muttered.

"I heard you refused to move out."

"You heard right." Skye didn't even bother asking how Nancy had heard. She'd learned that small towns had their own rapid communications systems that rivaled anything the Internet could come up with.

"Good for you. Stick to your guns. It's tough being strong sometimes. Believe me, I know. When I said I wanted to move to Las Vegas to become a showgirl, I thought my parents would have a fit. They wanted me to settle down and get married. Or join the convent like my sister."

"As a kid, it must have been tough having a nun for a sister."

"Tell me about it."

"How did you deal with it? Did the two of you get along?"

"Fought like cats and dogs for decades," Nancy cheerfully confessed. "We still do, occasionally. You know what changed things for me? Finally realizing she needs me as much as I need her."

"Why? Because your being bad makes her look good?"

"Because your relationship with your sibling is the longest relationship you'll have in your life."

"There's a depressing thought."

"It doesn't have to be. The bottom line for me was, if I couldn't get things right with my sister, how could I get my other relationships right? Think about it, that's all I'm saying."

"And I'm saying that I have enough problems at the

moment without adding my oh-so-perfect sister to the mix," Skye said. She stood and gave Nancy a hug. "Thanks for the advice, though, even if I don't take it."

* * *

That evening, Skye decided it was time to cleanse her living environment of the negative energy that had been accumulating recently. She'd try to do the theater later. She'd already completed a thorough cleaning and organizing of her apartment. The space-clearing ritual would help her create a healthy flow of energy, or chi, within her space.

She'd placed clean-burning, nonparaffin candles in key locations around the living room, along with rock sea salt, which attracted stagnant energy, or *sha* chi. She'd sprinkled a line of the salt across the front threshold, as well as a small amount in various critical areas of the apartment.

The next step was clapping, which stirred up stale energy. Starting at the main entrance, she began clapping with her arms outstretched. She moved slowly around the perimeter of the room. She even clapped inside the coat closet by the front door, in case any stale energy was hiding out in there.

While carefully lighting a juniper wand, she kept her mind focused on her intention to clear and energize her space. Again moving slowly, she made her way around the room, saturating the atmosphere with the cleansing smoke, making sure to include areas under the Formica table in the dining area.

Juniper was well known as a purifying herb . . .

The high-pitched wail of the smoke detector in the living room ceiling shattered her peaceful meditation. It was immediately followed by the sound of pounding on her front door and Nathan yelling, "Open up!"

Okay, not exactly the way she'd planned things.

Skye almost tripped over a candle on her way to open

the door. She quickly assured Nathan everything was fine before heading for the smoke detector. It was about to make her go deaf.

Nathan went about the room extinguishing the candles. "What's going on in here? Are you trying to set the place on fire again?"

She stood on a chair and smacked the smoke detector button with a broom handle. The detector fell to the floor with a final squeal before lying there in pieces, as if she'd murdered it. "I was clearing my space of negative energy."

"By trying to burn it down?"

"I was practicing feng shui."

"With the smoke detector?"

"No. The smoke detector suffered collateral damage."

"Why aren't you at the football game?"

"The game . . . oh, shit!" Since Skye didn't wear a watch, she jumped off the chair, grabbed Nathan's arm, and looked at his watch. "It'll be almost over by now. I told the team I'd be there."

"Relax. I'm sure they'll understand, given the circumstances, that you weren't able to make it tonight."

Skye closed her eyes.

"You're not going to cry, are you?" Nathan sounded a tad desperate.

"Shhh. I'm channeling positive energy their way." She held out her hand in the universal command for silence. "Okay." She opened her eyes and looked around. "I still need to ring the tinghsa bells to fully saturate this space."

Nathan made a sweeping gesture with his arm in an invitation for her to continue. "Don't let me stop you."

For the first time, she noticed the sleeping bag and backpack he'd dumped by the front door. "What's going on? What are you doing here?"

"Moving in with you. It's the only way I can protect you."

Who was going to protect her from *him*? From falling for him? From connecting with him at a deeper level than she ever thought possible? That was the real danger here. Not the fire downstairs, but the fire burning deep in her heart. For him.

Skye could tell by the mulish look on Nathan's face that he expected her to fight him on this.

She hated being predictable.

So she said, "You don't leave the toilet seat or lid up, do you?"

He blinked.

"Because if you do, the deal is off."

He blinked again. Funny, she'd never noticed his thick, dark eyelashes before. She liked them. A lot.

"I can live by those rules," he finally said.

"Okay, then." Skye looked away, at a sudden and momentary loss for words. What had she just gotten herself into here?

"It would be helpful if you could provide me with your schedule."

"I don't even have a watch. What makes you think I have a schedule? It's not like I live my life according to a timetable the way you do."

"You don't know how I live my life," he protested.

"Because you won't tell me. But I'm right, aren't I? You find comfort in a schedule."

"You make it sound like some kind of security blanket."

"Isn't it?"

"I have a job. I can't just walk into the office whenever I feel like it. People need to know where I am and how to reach me."

"People? What people?"

"Celeste, for one. My deputies. The citizens of Rock Creek."

"So the *citizens* need to know where you are? Want me to lean out the window and let them know you're here with me?"

"No."

"I didn't think so."

"It's not like it's a secret. I told Celeste where I'd be, and she's not the most discreet person. So I'm discovering," he muttered.

"And what was her reaction to your moving in with me?"

"Why should you care?"

"I don't *care*. I'm *curious*. A big difference."

"It doesn't matter what her reaction was."

"Which means it was not a positive one."

"That would be an accurate statement."

"So what's the deal with her? She jealous?"

"No way. She's married."

"So? I heard she dotes on you."

"Who told you that?"

"I've got my sources."

"Celeste fusses over people she cares about."

"That must drive you nuts. Don't worry." She patted his arm. "I won't fuss over you." She moved her fingers to the buttons on his shirt, which she started undoing.

His brown eyes widened. "What are you doing?"

"Taking off your shirt. Or trying to."

He grabbed her wrists and held them still. "Why?"

"I said I wouldn't fuss over you. I never said I wouldn't have sex with you."

"You're part of an investigative case I'm working on."

"It doesn't feel like you're working on me at the moment, but that could change." She placed his hands on her breasts.

He actually fondled them a moment before pulling away. "It wouldn't be ethical."

Skye took a deep breath. What was she doing? Not a minute earlier, she'd told herself that he was dangerous to her, and now here she was, trying to seduce him. And not doing a very good job of it.

Sure, she didn't listen to other people, but she usually listened to her own inner goddess or diva, depending on what mood she was in. So what was the deal here?

Skye felt disoriented. She didn't realize that she was backing away from Nathan until she bumped into the side of the couch.

"Don't look like that," he said.

"Like what?"

"Like a puppy that's been kicked."

Okay, that was *so* not a good thing to tell her. His offensive words snapped her right back into reality. "I am *not* a puppy!" The urge to kick him had now totally replaced the urge to kiss him. "I was just trying to teach you a lesson."

"What lesson?"

"Not to mess with me."

"By telling me you want to have sex with me?"

"I wasn't serious," she informed him haughtily.

"You have a strange sense of humor."

"Yeah, so I've been told. I don't think this is going to work after all." She picked up his rolled sleeping bag and tossed it at him. "You should go home."

"I'm not going anyplace." He dumped the bag back on the floor. "But if you want to go to your sister's house in Serenity Falls, I'll give you a lift."

"I'm not going anywhere. I already told you that. No one is running me off like some stray dog."

Back to the canine motif again. Did this represent some message totem for her?

As far as she was concerned, the message was clear. Time to replace Seductress Skye with Skye the Super Sleuth. Time to go into Nancy Drew mode. She'd eat nails before admitting she'd read those books as a kid, having gotten a box of them from a thrift shop in Oregon. The versions she'd picked up had been the vintage books from the 1930s, the ones with blue cloth covers. In *The Password to Larkspur Lane*, Nancy had driven a roadster, worn bobby socks, and pondered clues.

These days, it would be cooler for Skye to think of herself as some sort of kick-butt heroine of comic-book fame. Anyone but Catwoman. That movie was too lame.

But she had a soft spot in her consciousness for good ol' crime solver Nancy Drew.

Whatever her secret identity as a crime solver, Skye could gather information on her own. She'd never believed in depending on the authorities to solve her problems. Why should this be any different?

She had to take a proactive stand in solving this crime, and get Nathan out of her apartment ASAP.

But she had some tinghsa-bell ringing to take care of first.

• • •

Nathan lay staring up at the crack in Skye's living room ceiling. It was well after midnight and he'd already memorized the ragged shape of that crack. Skye had turned off the lights at ten, with the curt warning, "Don't waste electricity."

He remembered those words. And he remembered the lights going out in his office, during his first run-in with Skye. Her daughter had switched off the lights then, plunging him into darkness.

At the time, he'd said he was accustomed to darkness. Which was true. But since he'd gotten involved with Skye . . . she brought a certain flash of fireworks along with her.

Involved? Is that what he was? When he'd heard the news of a fire at the theater, his gut had clenched at the possibility that Skye might have been hurt in the blaze.

So here he was. Camped out on her living room floor.

He tensed at the sound of her bare feet padding down the hallway toward him. Moonlight shone through the living room's gauzy curtains to highlight her as if by some kind of weird celestial magic.

She was wearing the same llama shorts and top she'd worn when he'd almost made love to her on the couch before they'd been interrupted by her daughter.

"You don't have to stay on the floor."

Was she inviting him into her bed? Did he have the strength to refuse?

"You can sleep in Toni's bed," she said.

"No way." The words came out more vehemently than he'd intended.

"Why not? Afraid of a little girl's room?"

Absolutely. He was more than afraid. Skye didn't have to know the reasons why. No one did.

"She loves that kitten book you got her."

Nathan didn't want to know. Didn't want to hear.

"You know, in some cultures, if you save someone's life, that person is beholden to you forever. A bond is created."

"Children that age can't be expected to remember street safety," he said as if by rote.

Skye came closer and studied him. "What's wrong?"

"Nothing."

"Liar," she said softly. "I can tell when something's wrong."

"Are you going to tell me you read minds now?"

"I can sense things."

"No more New Age stuff. I'm beat. I'm going to sleep." He tugged the sleeping bag up to his chin and turned his back on her. He'd been up all night, investigating the fire. And the night before that he hadn't slept much, torn by his obsession with Skye and residual guilt over Annie.

He hadn't felt guilty the few times a woman had come into his life prior to this. Probably because he knew she'd be right back out of it again real soon. Nothing permanent.

And Skye should have been like that. Temporary. She sure wasn't a card-carrying member of the white-picket-fence club.

But there was something about her that was different.

Well, actually, *everything* about her was different. From her short, spiky, yet surprisingly silky hair to her navel ring to her shimmying hips to her deliciously bare feet.

It wasn't just her appearance. Her behavior and thought

processes were also unique. She excelled at the unexpected.

Like tonight, when he'd shown up unannounced at her door. Instead of trying to toss him out on his ass, she'd blown his mind by talking about having sex with him.

And that was another thing. Skye never referred to it as "making love," the way most women did. Why was that? Did the word *love* scare her? Nathan couldn't imagine much frightening her. Then he remembered Skye's face when Toni had dashed into the street and almost been hit by that truck.

Stark terror. In his heart and on Skye's pale face, so ashen a few freckles had suddenly stood out. Raw fear had glazed her bottle-green eyes, obscuring all traces of their customary defiance.

Once Toni was out of danger and back at her side, Skye had recovered quickly. Or appeared to. And that night, Skye had had "sex" with him.

He should have been fine with that. Should have been laid-back about it. Should have been satisfied.

Instead, he was as confused as ever. And he hated that.

This had happened days ago. So why was Nathan thinking about it now? He should be focusing on how to find the vandal or vandals intent on sabotaging the theater renovation.

"You scowl a lot. Did you know that?" Skye said.

Yeah, he knew. He'd had plenty of things in his life to scowl about, to beat his fists on the ground and howl with grief about. But, as he'd learned in the Marine Corps, you sucked it up and managed. Failure was not an option.

No excuses.

No exceptions.

Sighing, Skye turned around and headed back to her bed, while Nathan battled his inner demons and his growing fascination with a belly-dancing bad girl.

• • •

The minute Nathan left for work the next morning, Skye set to work on her crime-fighting agenda. She'd just started brainstorming when Sue Ellen showed up. "Where were you last night? You missed an incredible game. The Trojans were behind by two touchdowns with only five minutes to go. Somehow they scored twice and the game went into overtime. Brad the kicker won the game for them. Even Lulu thought it was awesome."

"I was distracted by the fire."

"Fire?" Sue Ellen's lavishly made-up eyes widened. "What fire?"

"Here at the theater. How could you not know about it?"

"Why didn't you call me on my cell to tell me? I was out of town taking a realtor course all day yesterday. I barely got back in time for the game last night."

"Lulu didn't tell you about the fire?"

"I was focused on the game and wasn't really paying attention to what she was saying. Don't you think the coach is a manly man?" Noting Skye's expression, she said, "Never mind. Tell me about this fire. How did it start?"

"Someone set it."

"Who?"

"We don't know yet, but I aim on finding out."

"Why do you have a sleeping bag rolled up in the corner?"

"It's not mine. It's Nathan's."

"You and Nathan made out in a sleeping bag?"

"No, he stayed in the living room to protect me."

"From what? He doesn't have any STDs, does he?"

"Not that I know of. Can we focus here, Sue Ellen?"

"Sure. What are we focusing on?"

"I'm going to find out who's trying to sabotage my opening the theater."

"I think it's Milton."

"So do I. Now we have to prove it."

"I've got the perfect way to do that. Follow me."

Fifteen minutes later, they stood in the alley behind Milton's two-story brick home.

"I'm going to give you a lesson in garbology," Sue Ellen told her before putting on latex gloves. She handed another pair to Skye. "Good thing I keep these in my car, huh?"

"The pink Batmobile has many secrets," Skye agreed. To avoid detection, they'd parked a few blocks away. "How did you get to be an expert on the subject of garbology? Don't tell me you were once Miss Refuse?"

"Of course not. Although I was once crowned Miss Chow Chow."

"Isn't that some kind of dog?"

"No, it's a relish."

"Have you noticed a food motif in all your pageant titles?"

"What can I say? I told you I've got good taste. Ah, now this is what you want to look for. Incriminating papers." Sue Ellen triumphantly held up some slips of paper.

"Those are coupons from Gas4Less."

"And some of them have been cut out. Which proves that Milton is both neat and cheap."

"What if his wife cut them out?"

"Are you kidding? Robin is not the tidy sort. I know. The girls at the nail salon tell me these things. His wife would have ripped out the coupons, not cut them. It's these little details that make the difference in crime solving. Let's keep looking. Thank heavens for recycling! I *hate* having to go through dirty garbage. Presorting makes it so much easier."

Skye was about to ask for more details about Sue Ellen's "dirty garbage" days, but was distracted when her friend pulled out another sheaf of paper and waved it at her. "Look at this!"

"I'm trying to," Skye muttered, "but you keep moving it around. What is it?"

"Sears has a sale on boots. Look at this black suede pair with the heel . . ."

"Will you concentrate here?" Skye yanked the sale flyer away from her. "And keep your voice down. Someone could hear us. Or see us, since it *is* the middle of the morning."

"Everyone on this block works. No one is around."

"Wait a second. Isn't today Saturday? That means people are home."

"Right. At home, not in the alley. We'll be fast. Stop worrying. Aha!" Sue Ellen pounced again.

Skye was not impressed with her find. "A subscription invoice for *Playboy*. Torn in half and thrown away. That doesn't help us. I'm beginning to think this wasn't such a good idea after all."

"Only *beginning* to?" Nathan drawled behind her.

Sue Ellen shrieked. "Mercy, Sheriff! Sneaking up on a person like that is liable to give them a heart attack."

"What are you ladies doing?"

"Studying garbology," Sue Ellen explained.

"Making sure everyone is recycling," Skye said at the same time.

"Right." Sue Ellen nodded. "Studying garbology *and* making sure everyone is recycling."

"We're multitasking," Skye said.

Sue Ellen sighed. "And we're in trouble, right?"

"Save the investigating for the professionals, ladies," Nathan ordered them sternly. "The next time I find you playing amateur detective, I won't be as lenient."

Once they were back in the Batmobile, Sue Ellen pulled a handful of papers out from under her blouse. "I guess the trick is not letting him find us."

Skye gave her a high five. "You're learning, grasshopper."

•   •   •

"Is it true?" Fanny Abernathy demanded in belly-dancing class a few days later.

"Is what true?" Skye was a bit distracted because she'd run late from her yoga class at the high school. She hadn't planned on the class being as successful as it was. Coach Spears insisted she continue with it or risk breaking the team's winning streak. He was still antsy about the loss they'd almost suffered in their last game, when Skye had been a no-show.

As for her Nancy Drew gig, that wasn't going very well. None of the papers Sue Ellen had hidden in her cleavage had been incriminating. As an accountant, Milton was too smart to leave a paper trail and not to shred anything that might link him to the crimes.

"There's a rumor going around that you and the sheriff have set up housekeeping."

Skye snorted. "That makes it sound like we're doing dishes together."

"Are you *doing* each other?" Sue Ellen asked.

The other women shrieked.

Sue Ellen just looked at them. "What? You were all wondering the same thing, so don't try to pretend otherwise."

"Ladies, we have a teenager present." Fanny clapped her arthritic hands over Lulu's ears. Lulu had joined the class only this week.

"Oh, please. She knows more about sex than the rest of us do," Sue Ellen said.

"Damn right." Lulu shifted Fanny's hands away from her face. "Do you know how many suicides are caused by bad sexual experiences—"

Sue Ellen shoved Fanny aside and clapped her hand over Lulu's mouth. "No, and we don't want to know any of your depressing statistics. This is a belly-dancing class. We're supposed to be focusing on our inner divas."

"And not choking our friends," Skye added, gently removing Sue Ellen's hand.

"Right. Sorry about that." Sue Ellen put her arm around Lulu and gave her a gentle hug. "Let me make it up to you by showing your grandfather a double-wide trailer."

"How does that make up for assaulting me?" Lulu

demanded, stepping away from Sue Ellen as if fearing for her safety.

"I could get him a good deal."

"He's already got a trailer."

"I know. Over in Broken Creek Trailer Park. But that's not a good location, and you know what they say about real estate. Location, location, location."

"Can we get back to the subject of Skye doing the sheriff?" Lulu asked hopefully.

"Doing *what* with the sheriff?" Fanny asked, reaching into her ear to turn up her hearing aid. "I can't hear you."

"You're whistling," Lulu told her.

"No, I'm not," Fanny protested.

Lulu pointed to her ear.

"Oh, the hearing aid." Fanny adjusted it again.

"I don't think it's anyone's business what the sheriff and Skye are doing together in the privacy of her bedroom," Nancy Crumpler said, jumping into the conversation for the first time. "If the two of them want to try out every pose in the Kama Sutra, that's their business."

"Damn right," Skye agreed.

"Smooth move," Sue Ellen said to Nancy. "Now you've got Skye admitting she and Nathan are practicing the Kama Sutra in her bedroom."

"What about your grandmother?" Fanny asked Skye. "Is she doing it?"

"With the *sheriff*?" Sue Ellen looked ready to pass out.

"No," Fanny said. "Belly dancing. Does she do it?"

Skye shrugged. "I have no idea."

"She's definitely not doing it with the sheriff," Nancy said.

Fanny frowned. "Skye isn't?"

"I meant her grandmother."

"I'm confused," Fanny admitted.

"Which is why we need to focus our attention back on belly dancing," Skye said. Normally, she didn't mind a little anarchy in class, but for some reason it was bothering her today. Probably because she was frustrated by her lack of sleuthing skills. And the fact that Nathan was keeping an eagle eye on her activities.

"You did promise to tell us whether you yanked the sheriff into your bed," Sue Ellen reminded Skye.

Skye glared at her. "Tell me again why we're friends?"

"Because you like me."

"Not at the moment I don't."

"Remember who taught you about garbology."

"And remember how we got caught."

"Now what are they talking about?" Fanny asked.

"I have no idea," Nancy confessed.

"I had no idea this is what you guys did in belly-dancing class," Lulu said with a snap of her gum.

"It's *not* what we do in belly-dancing class. Positions, ladies," Skye ordered.

"Don't you talk about the history of belly dancing and stuff? You know, about Little Egypt, the dancer who performed at the Chicago World's Fair or something way back in the 1890s. And how she, like, totally rocked."

"You missed that class," Nancy said. "But it sounds like you already know about it."

"I've been reading up on it," Lulu admitted.

"I didn't want to mention it before, but you've got some dirt on your neck, dear," Fanny told Lulu.

"It's not dirt. It's a tattoo of a spiderweb."

"Does it wash off?"

"No."

Fanny just shook her head. "That's a shame. When you get older, you'll have to wear turtleneck sweaters to hide it."

"No way. My grandfather has more tattoos than I do."

"Yes, but it's different for men, isn't it?"

"What is?"

"Everything."

"Not anymore."

"Don't the boys still play football while the girls stand on the sidelines and cheer?"

"I hate cheerleaders," Lulu growled.

"Lulu likes the kicker, though," Sue Ellen said. "Ouch! What'd you hit me for?"

Lulu snapped her gum in aggravation. "Can't you keep a secret?"

"Of course I can. I know that Nancy isn't really a size eight, but a size ten." Sue Ellen clapped her hand over her mouth before giving Lulu an accusatory look. "Now look what you've made me do!"

"I do not wear a size ten!" Nancy said indignantly.

"There's nothing wrong with a size ten, or with any size," Skye said. "I hate the way popular culture has given women such a poor self-image. We're all *supposed* to be different. That's the beauty of it."

Nancy nodded slowly. "Remember that great Dove commercial that premiered during the Super Bowl when the Steelers won? The one with all the different young girls worrying that they were ugly or fat or something else? And how every girl deserves to feel good about herself. It really touched me deeply. Got me a little teary-eyed. Or was that because of Mick Jagger's performance during the half-time show? I'm not sure now."

Lulu's eyes bugged out. "You're a Stones fan?"

"That surprises you?" Nancy said.

"Well, yeah," Lulu replied. "Your sister is a nun."

"So everyone keeps telling me," Nancy grumbled. "I'm *not* my sister."

"I hear you," Skye said. "I'm not *my* sister, either."

"Maybe not," Julia said from the doorway. "But don't forget who taught you how to belly dance." She proudly pointed to herself. "Me."

Chapter Fifteen

. . . .

"Is it true?" Fanny asked. "Is your sister really a belly-dancing librarian?"

"So she says."

"Did she really teach you to belly dance?"

"And play poker," Julia added.

Lulu looked impressed. "I thought you were supposed to be the good-girl sister."

"She is," Skye stated, irritation in her voice. "What are you doing here?" she asked Julia.

To which her good-girl, near-perfect half sister replied, "I came back because I heard you were in trouble."

Her comment immediately annoyed Skye. "And you always come charging in to save the day when I screw up, huh?"

"I used to," Julia replied.

"Yeah, well, Nathan is doing that now," Sue Ellen said. "He's our town sheriff. And he's doing it with Skye."

"Sue Ellen." Julia's gaze was frosty. "I see you're as controversial as ever."

"And I see you still haven't forgiven me for that llama incident back in Serenity Falls. Which is a shame, because Lucy has forgiven me."

"Lucy?"

"Lucy the Llama. You know she's pregnant, right?"

Fanny gasped. "Skye is pregnant?"

"No, the llama is," Nancy explained.

Fanny tapped her hearing aid and looked confused. "What llama?"

"Shhh. I'll tell you later," Nancy said.

"Don't treat me like I'm some silly old woman. You know I only lost my hearing last year when I used that power saw without the proper safety measures of earphones. Now my darn kids won't let me use power tools anymore. Won't let me climb up on the roof to clean the gutters anymore either. They don't let me have any fun."

"They let you take belly-dancing lessons."

Fanny snorted. "Thank heavens for small favors."

"You rock," Lulu told Fanny with admiration. "I thought you were a 'plays well with others' kind of person, but you're really a 'runs with scissors.' That's wicked awesome!"

Fanny looked skeptical. "I hope that's a compliment."

"It is," Lulu assured her.

Despite their earlier rocky moment about Lulu's spiderweb tattoo, the youngest and oldest members of Skye's class suddenly bonded—just like that.

Sometimes it happens that way, Skye thought. People make a connection. She, Sue Ellen, and Lulu might seem unlikely allies, but there was just a connection between the three of them that made their relationship work.

Skye and Nathan's relationship was *not* destined to work. That didn't seem to make the connection between them weaken or disappear, though.

And the connection between Skye and her sister had been broken so long ago, Skye wasn't sure she remembered it at all.

She stared at Julia, still not quite able to believe she was back. She didn't look any different. Well, okay, maybe a little. Instead of her usual uptight librarian's clothes with tidy Peter Pan collars, Julia was wearing a Stanley Idaho T-shirt and jeans. No visible tattoos or piercings, though.

"I'm in the middle of class," Skye pointed out.

"Nonsense. Your sister has been gone for months. You two should talk," Fanny insisted. "We can end the class early, right, everyone?"

They all nodded.

"I don't want to end class early." Skye realized she sounded as petulant as Toni when she was demanding more ice cream, but she didn't care. She wasn't ready to face Julia yet.

That didn't mean she was afraid of her. No way.

• • •

"Adam, what are you doing here?" Angel stared at him with dismay. She'd never dreamed that he'd just show up on Julia's doorstep in Serenity Falls without calling first. That wasn't like him at all. He looked totally out of place in his designer business suit and silk tie.

"I heard our daughter Julia is back."

"She is, but she's not home at the moment. She's gone to Rock Creek to see Skye. You should have called first."

"I'll wait for her."

He walked in and stopped when he saw Violet, who instantly recognized him. "You're Adam Kemp. I saw you on *Good Morning America* once. What are you doing here?"

Adam frowned. "Who are you?"

"Ethel's mother."

"Who's Ethel?"

"She is." Violet pointed at Angel. "Even though she calls

herself Angel now, her birth certificate gives her name as Ethel. Did I hear you right earlier when you called Julia "our daughter"? Does that mean that you and Ethel . . . ?"

"Mother, don't you want to go watch *The Price Is Right*?" Angel sounded desperate. "You're missing it."

Violet refused to budge. "I don't care. You're telling me you had a love child with a billionaire? I assume it *was* out of wedlock."

"You didn't tell her?" Adam said to Angel.

Violet stared at Angel in disbelief. "Why aren't you rich? You don't have to be living this way, hand to mouth."

"I'm not living hand to mouth. My fabric arts business is doing really well."

"Pfft." Violet waved her words away. "You could be rolling in money. Should have been, all these years."

"Money isn't important to me."

"Well, your father and I sure could have used some to make our retirement years a little easier."

"He disowned me decades ago. Are you saying that I could have *bought* my way back into his good graces?"

"No, you're right." Violet seemed to diminish in size. "He was a stubborn man. Once he'd made up his mind, there was no going back. You're right."

Angel didn't know what to say to that.

Adam had no such problem. "The information about my family life and my relationship with Julia is confidential. I don't want to hear that you've tried to sell it to some media rag."

Violet drew herself back up to her full height, which, at four-foot-eleven, wasn't all that tall. "I don't air my family's dirty laundry in public. I've never done that in seventy years and I don't aim on starting now."

"Glad to hear it."

"Why didn't you do a better job at looking after my daughter?" Violet leveled her best accusatory glare at Adam.

Angel knew firsthand how powerful that look could be. That's why she stepped in to defend him. "Adam didn't know. I didn't tell him I was pregnant. He didn't know about Julia until a year ago."

Violet's expression was etched with remorse. "Did you hate your father so much that you wanted to prevent your own daughter from having one?"

"No. My father had nothing to do with my decision." *Or had it?* Angel had never considered the impact her own estrangement from her father might have on her life, or on her decisions.

But Sash had been a great father to Julia during his lifetime, even though she wasn't his biological child. So she had had a paternal influence in her life—a loving, nonjudgmental paternal influence.

Unlike Angel, who'd grown up under the thumb of a man drunk on power. Maybe that's why she'd avoided Adam like the plague. Because of her fear of becoming subjugated to another man's autocratic authority.

Violet stared at Angel as if able to read her mind. "Your father had a way of making others do what he wanted, no matter what. Believe me, I know."

"Then why stay?"

"Because I'd made a vow before God."

"Which is why I never got married. Because I don't want any part of a vow that would make you stay in a situation like that."

"So you're blaming me for ruining your life, is that it?"

"No, that's not it."

"Then, what?"

"If I could interrupt here for a moment?" Adam said. "It seems to me that with this information about your past, Angel, a lot of things are starting to make more sense."

"What do you mean?"

"I mean, if you grew up with a bastard for a father, then it makes sense that that would affect your decision-making process, and that you'd have issues, as they say. No offense intended, ma'am," he said to Violet.

"None taken," she said wearily. "Sometimes, it seems you just can't make up for past mistakes."

Angel knew what her mother meant. Angel had wondered if she'd ever be able to make up for not telling Julia about Adam, or for not telling him about Julia.

But she'd had no idea that her mother had ever considered such a thing, that she even acknowledged that mistakes had been made. This was all a revelation to her. Talk about an aha moment.

• • •

Skye was having her own aha moment with her sister. *Half* sister. An aha-I-want-to-hit-you moment.

"You couldn't wait until my class was over to come barging in here?" Skye said the minute they were alone.

"Forgive me for being worried about you," Julia shot back.

"No way. I don't forgive you."

"No surprise there. You've always had a chip on your shoulder the size of Oregon."

"And you've always tried to knock it off."

"No, I haven't. I am not into confrontations the way you are. Not at all. In fact, usually I try to avoid them at all costs."

"So why come here, then? Why make me look like an idiot in front of my class?"

Julia was clearly stunned. "Since when do you care what your class or anyone else thinks?"

"I don't."

Yet, for all Skye claimed she didn't care, Julia always came to mind whenever Skye did something. How Julia wouldn't think this or that. Wouldn't think Skye was smart. Wouldn't think she was making good decisions. Wouldn't wear that top with that skirt. Wouldn't get her navel pierced. Wouldn't get pregnant by a self-centered musician with no staying power.

In a sudden, different kind of aha moment, Skye realized she had to make peace with her sister or she'd never find peace within herself. Nancy had tried to tell her, but Skye hadn't been ready to listen then.

Skye couldn't keep living her life trying to aggravate Julia. For one thing, it was too damn easy to do. For another, it meant Skye wasn't harnessing her own power, but was instead reacting to Julia. Or doing something to make Julia react to her.

Suddenly, it all made sense to Skye in a strange, convoluted kind of way. The paths she'd chosen in the past. The decisions she wanted to make in the future. They all hinged on Julia.

Of course. She always had been the dominant one.

Not that she'd ever admit it.

Right now, Julia was staring at Skye as if trying to figure her out. Was this how Nathan felt when Skye stared at him, trying to figure him out? Like a bug under a microscope.

Well, it was different with Nathan, of course, because there was the whole man-woman-sexual-attraction thing going on with him.

Which reminded her: Where was Julia's bad-boy Luke? "Why are you here alone? Did your other half dump you?"

Okay, maybe not the least confrontational line to open a dialogue of reunion with her sister. *Half* sister.

"Luke went to see the sheriff about the vandalism."

Skye's eyes widened. "Luke went to see Nathan? Why didn't you tell me that earlier? We've got to stop him."

"Why's that?"

"Because. He'll talk to Nathan."

"That was the point, yes."

"No, he'll *talk* to him."

"What are you afraid Luke might tell Nathan?"

"I'm not afraid."

"It wouldn't kill you to admit it if you were."

"Yes, it would," Skye said under her breath.

"You always did hate admitting you were afraid. Remember when you used to get nightmares as a little kid? Even then, you refused to say you were scared. Instead, you insisted on sleeping in my bed, claiming it was somehow better than yours."

"Forget about that. We have to go stop Luke from talking to Nathan."

"I've learned that it's almost impossible to stop Luke from doing something he wants to do."

"You come with me. We have to convince him."

Skye rushed out of the community center, not changing out of the leggings and cropped T-shirt she wore in class, her coin-adorned chiffon hip scarf jingling. Julia rushed after her.

When they reached the station, guard-dog Celeste was there, barring the way to Nathan's office. "The sheriff is busy at the moment."

"Oh, okay. We'll wait," Julia said.

"No, we won't." Skye grabbed her by the hand and yanked her past a furious Celeste.

"You can't go in there!" Celeste protested.

Skye ignored her and walked in to find Luke and Nathan shooting the breeze like a couple of good ol' boys.

"Hello, ladies. You must be Julia." Nathan stood and came over to greet her.

"Sure, be nice to her," Skye muttered in disgust. "After all, she's the *good* sister. You never get up when *I* come barging into your office."

"Ever think there might be a physical reason for that?" Luke said lazily. "Maybe the guy is trying to hide the fact you turn him on. Why the shocked expression, Skye? This from the woman who as soon as she met me demanded to know if I was having sex with her sister?"

"I . . . I . . ." Skye sputtered. Temporarily unable to

voice her opinion, she opted for walking over to Luke and smacking his arm as hard as she could before hugging him. "Welcome back."

"Sure, hug him. After all, he's the *bad* boy," Julia said. "You never gave *me* a hug."

"I could have told you that you'd never turn her into a bad girl," Skye informed Luke.

"I don't know." His gaze fell on Julia with enough heat that even Skye could feel it. "She's bad in all the best possible ways."

Julia blushed. Then she surprised Skye by walking up to Luke and kissing him. Her sister had never been one for public displays of affection before.

Skye's eyes met Nathan's as she remembered every kiss they'd shared, each hotter than the one before. Would the day ever come when Nathan would kiss her in front of an audience instead of beneath the bleachers or behind closed doors?

"Get a room, you guys," she finally told her sister and Luke.

Julia broke away from Luke with a laugh, but he kept his arms looped around her waist.

"So, Luke, what were you and Nathan talking about when we walked in?" Skye tried to sound casual.

"The stubbornness of a Wright woman."

"Oh, please." Skye rolled her eyes. "We are not stubborn."

"Well, *I'm* not," Julia said. "But you are."

"Yeah, right. This from the woman who refused to give up her Pop-Tarts."

Luke just grinned. "Nathan and I have decided you're *both* stubborn, each in your own adorable way."

Skye narrowed her eyes at him. "That ranks right up there on the sexist-meter with the idiotic phrase 'You're so cute when you're mad.'" She paused a moment before adding, "Of course, maybe my half sister isn't bothered by that. I mean, after all, she put her life on hold to follow her man around the country because that's what he wanted."

"It's what *I* wanted," Julia said. "Which you would have known if you'd bothered to come see me before I left."

"If you recall, we weren't exactly on the best of terms back then."

Julia ignored Skye's words and focused her attention on Nathan. "So, are you and my sister seeing each other?"

"Yeah, we're seeing each other. In fact, we're *looking* at each other right now," Skye drawled.

"She's part of an investigative case I'm working on," Nathan said.

Julia nodded. "Luke told me about the sabotage incidents at the theater."

Nathan's cop face returned. "There was a fire the night before last."

"Angel told me. She also told me that you've moved in with Skye to protect her."

"It's a temporary measure, until we catch the perpetrator."

"I've already offered Nathan my law enforcement expertise, such as it is," Luke said. "Not that a burnt-out former FBI Special Agent might provide that much assistance."

"Yes, you would," Julia said loyally.

"So what else did you and Nathan talk about?" Skye asked Luke.

"The Steelers."

"And the White Sox," Nathan added.

"What did you think we were going to talk about?" Luke asked. "Afraid I was going to ask the lawman here what his intentions are regarding you?"

Skye gave a short laugh. "Like you're in any position to be asking that. You haven't even stated your own intentions about Julia."

"Oh, I plan on marrying her," Luke stated confidently. "I just haven't decided when."

Julia looked stunned.

Skye gave Luke a you-poor-s.o.b. look. "Even I, rebel that I am, know that you're supposed to *ask* the woman first. And by the expression on Julia's face, I'm guessing you skipped that critical step. Bad move, Luke. You're screwed now."

"She knew. Right? You knew, Julia."

"How was I supposed to know?" she retorted. "You never mentioned a word about getting married until just now."

"Yeah, but you're a traditional woman. You must have been thinking of marriage."

"No, not really. And what do you mean, I'm 'traditional'? You say that as if it were some sort of bad trait."

"See what I meant about Wright women being stubborn?" Luke said in a knowing aside to Nathan, who wisely kept his mouth shut.

Skye just stood back and watched as Julia, who was slow to anger but did have a temper, began a major meltdown. "It's not a matter of being stubborn. It's a matter of respecting my feelings! Or don't they matter to you, Luke? Was Skye right? Am I just the little woman dutifully following behind my man? Is that all I am to you?"

Luke, belatedly realizing he was in deep shit, tried to pull Julia into his arms.

She shoved him away. "Don't touch me! We're arguing. You can't distract me by kissing me. That's not going to work!"

Skye grinned at Luke. "Only back in town a few hours, and already you've messed up."

"This is your fault," he said.

"Don't you dare blame my sister!" Julia was getting angrier by the second. "It's not her fault that you're impossible sometimes."

"Only sometimes?" Skye said, before Nathan gently but firmly clapped his hand over her mouth.

It didn't stay there long, because Skye stomped hard on his foot and bent his little finger backward in a self-defense move Nathan instantly recognized.

The moment he released her, she pivoted to angrily jab her index finger in the middle of his chest. "Don't you ever do that again! Do not *ever* manhandle me or try to shut me up! I have the right to speak. So does my sister. So do women all around the world! Come on, Julia."

Skye and Julia paused by the door, looking over their shoulders at the two men before saying in unison and with equal irritation, "Idiots."

They then marched out of the office together, leaving the men shaking their heads in bewilderment.

• • •

Skye and Julia held a postmortem in the back booth at Angelo's Pizza.

"I can't believe the way they treated us," Julia said.

"I can't believe how good this pizza is," Skye replied. "Do you know how long it's been since I've had a greasy pizza like this? Years and years."

"For a bad girl, you sure do eat healthy."

"Your body is a temple, and you should honor it by only allowing pure foods to enter."

"Yeah, yeah. So are you going to eat that last piece or not?"

"It's mine!" Skye growled, grabbing it and stuffing it into her mouth.

"That sheriff must really be something if he drove you to eat pizza," Julia remarked. "Tell me about him."

"He's anal-retentive."

"Cute, though."

"*Cute* is for kittens and teddy bears. He's hot and sexy. But I don't care how sexy Studly Do-Right is." Skye took another drink of her beer. "We have nothing in common."

"Neither did Luke and I when we first got together."

"Yeah, and look how good you two are doing."

Julia sighed. "Why do men have to be so . . . ?"

"Malelike?"

"Their brains are wired differently."

"Yeah, they're wired to their penises."

"Skye!" Julia looked around in horror, but no one seemed to be paying them any attention.

"What? You want me to use euphemistic phrases instead of the real thing?"

"I'd like you to use a little decorum."

"That word isn't in my vocabulary."

Julia rolled her eyes. "Neither is common sense. What on Earth possessed you to buy a dilapidated movie theater?"

"It's a palace of dreams."

"That's something Angel would say. A palace of dreams, huh? Talk about using euphemistic phrases . . ."

"You haven't even seen the theater," Skye protested.

"I saw it when we rode into town."

"On the back of your bad boyfriend's Harley. Not that you have what it takes to be a biker babe."

"How would you know? You haven't seen or talked to me in over six months."

"You could have called me. The phone works both ways."

"I didn't know if you'd talk to me," Julia said.

"Same here," Skye admitted.

"You never did say why you were in such a hurry to stop Luke from talking to Nathan."

"I panicked, okay?"

"Really? Wow. That's a big step for you. To admit you panicked. You never do that."

"Never panic?"

"Never admit to it. So what were you panicked about?"

"I didn't know what Luke might tell Nathan about me."

"And you care what Nathan thinks. But you should know that Luke would never say anything bad about you."

No, but Luke saw past Skye's defenses, and he might reveal the fact that she wasn't as tough as she made out. She didn't want Nathan to know that. She was already too vulnerable where he was concerned.

"You're in love with him," Julia murmured softly.

"No way."

"Yes way."

"Then I'm not only bad, I'm really, *really* stupid, because Nathan still loves his dead wife. Shit." Skye bent forward until her forehead thumped the edge of the table. "I'm totally screwed."

Chapter Sixteen

· · · · · · · · · · · · ·

"**Stop** that!" Julia ordered. "Sit up and take a deep breath. Come on, where's that Skye attitude? Since when has being screwed ever stopped you from going after what you want?"

"Since I met him. Well, not right at first." Skye straightened up and looked around, suddenly nervous. "We can't talk more here. Someone might overhear us."

"Okay, now I'm seriously worried. Who are you, and what have you done with my sister?"

"*Half* sister," Skye said unsteadily.

Julia reached across the table and grabbed her hand. "You've been my sister for a quarter of a century," she said fiercely. "Biology isn't changing that now."

"Okay, that's it." Skye furiously blinked back tears. "If we're going to get sappy, we need to do it in private. We can't go to my place. Nathan will be there."

"And we can't go to my place in Serenity Falls, because Violet will be there."

"I've got an idea . . ."

•   •   •

Half an hour later, Skye turned her rusty Toyota into a pull-off along the two-lane highway leading out of town. The mid-September night was warm and clear. The sky, away from the lights of Rock Creek, was filled with stars, reminding her of the Tivoli's glistening celestial ceiling.

She grabbed an old quilt from the backseat and placed it and her huge Peruvian tote on the hood of the car. A minute later, she and Julia were sitting with their backs propped against the windshield, just like they'd done as kids. They'd made a quick stop at Gas4Less on the way out of town to pick up comfort food—Pop-Tarts for Julia and pumpkin seeds for Skye.

"You know," Julia said in between bites, "the irony of this situation hasn't escaped me."

"I never thought it would. Tell me again—which situation were you referring to, exactly? We've got so many going on."

"I meant our grandmother and Angel."

"What's ironic about Violet and Angel?"

"The fact that Violet drives Angel crazy, that she's the total opposite of everything Angel stands for."

"Violet drives *everyone* crazy."

"That may be, but she especially gets to Angel. Just like Angel especially gets to me. You've got it good, because you and Angel always had this special kind of bond."

"Don't give me that poor-little-good-girl speech. I'm not in the mood."

"I'm just saying that you should value how special your relationship with Angel is."

"I do."

Julia sighed and opened another packet of Pop-Tarts. "Life is funny, you know?"

"Oh, yeah, it's just stinking hysterical."

"I read somewhere that we re-create stressful emotional situations in our lives until we resolve the issues that gives them power over us."

"Have I ever told you that you read too much?"

"Frequently. But I think it's true."

"That you read too much? Totally, it is true."

"No, I meant about the need to resolve old emotional issues or end up forever repeating mistakes of the past."

"Meaning *my* mistakes, since I'm the sister who's good at that."

"You don't get to own the mistake card. I've made plenty too." Julia turned to face her. "I was really jealous of you, did you realize that?"

"No way."

"You were closer to Angel than I could ever be. You two think alike and always did. And you have a little girl who adores you. And I was jealous and still am of the way you don't seem to care what other people think. You obey your own set of rules. While it often drives me nuts, it's also something I wish I had the courage to do. It's something I'm working on, which is why Luke's comments about my being traditional really bothered me."

"You weren't bothered by the fact that he just assumed you wanted to get married and that he figured he'd ask you when he felt like it?"

"Yeah, that pissed me off too."

Skye laughed. "Such language! You wild woman, you."

"Do you ever look in the mirror and wonder if your butt looks too big?" Julia abruptly asked.

"Not really. But then, I don't have a big butt."

"Are you saying I do?" Julia suddenly started to cry. "Well, I'm going to get a lot bigger all over, because I think I'm pregnant!"

"Okay, if you're going to learn to be a bad girl, the first lesson is no crying. And no skipping birth control."

"It was just the one time . . ."

"That's all it takes. Believe me, I know." Skye reached into her tote bag in search of a tissue. She found a receipt from Gas4Less, a flyer from Cosmic Comics, and the still unopened box of Trojan condoms she'd had with her when Nathan first stopped her for speeding. No time to think about that now. "So, what are you going to do?" She stopped her search when she realized that Julia had found a tissue on her own. "I suggest you first make sure you really are pregnant."

"I took two of those home pregnancy tests yesterday. They were both positive."

"Maybe you should see a doctor."

"I should see a mental health provider for doing something this crazy!"

"Well, the good news is that Luke wants to marry you, so that should make you feel better."

"What if Luke doesn't want this baby?"

"If he loves you, he'll love the baby you made together. Have you guys ever talked about having kids?"

Julia shook her head. "And you know that Luke's childhood was not a pleasant one. He was just a kid when his mom died, and his dad started beating him after that. How am I going to tell him?"

"The mayor of Serenity Falls used to call him a bad seed, right? Well, tell Luke that his seeds are pretty good after all. Damn fertile, in fact. Want me to tell him?" Skye offered.

"No! If you do, I'll tell Nathan you love him!"

"Okay, okay, calm down. I won't say anything. But you should tell Luke, and the sooner, the better. Look at the mess Angel has gotten herself into by hiding the truth."

"You mean by not telling me Adam was my real father?"

"Or telling us about Violet. And you know that Angel is seeing Adam."

"Yes, he told me."

"Well, Angel hasn't told Tyler, and I have a feeling he's not going to be too happy about it when he finds out."

"Great."

"So let's recap, shall we? I may be in love with a by-the-book lawman still in love with his dead wife. You're pregnant by a bad-boy biker dude who may not want kids. And Angel is lying to her current lover about seeing her former lover. That about wrap it up?"

"Yeah."

"We're all screwed."

• • •

Nathan was waiting for Skye when she walked into her apartment. "Where have you been?"

"Angelo's Pizza."

"You never go to Angelo's Pizza."

"I did tonight. And then I went out on a drive to talk to my sister. You want to make something out of it?"

Nathan wisely backed off and waited until she'd taken a shower and changed into a tank top and shorts before approaching her again. "I've compiled a preliminary list of possible suspects for you to look over."

"Didn't I tell you?" Skye towel-dried her short hair until the ragged chunks fell into place, framing her face. "Milton did it. Angel said the tarot cards strongly indicate he's guilty."

"Afraid that won't stand up in court."

"And his auras are really negative."

"Again, not evidence I can use. Take a look at the list."

Skye read off the names. "Mrs. Trimble? I don't even know her."

"She has a thing for Owen, apparently, and feels you stole him from her."

"What about your assistant, Celeste? Why is she on here?"

"She's not a big fan of yours."

"Owen, Sister Mary, Violet," she read aloud. "I'm surprised you don't have Angel on here too."

"I considered it."

"I'm glad to see you crossed off Tyler's name."

"Luke vouched for him. And for Algee."

"If you don't trust anyone, how do you know that Luke isn't lying to you?"

"I had him checked out too."

"Of course you did. I should have known. You don't think Lulu or Sue Ellen or Nancy Crumpler are possible suspects?"

"You're right." He took the sheet of paper from her and began writing on it. "I should add them."

She grabbed it away from him. "That's not what I meant. Nancy would never suspect her friends."

"Nancy Crumpler?"

"Yeah, right." Skye wasn't about to admit that she'd actually been thinking of Nancy Drew. "Why don't you believe that Milton is the guilty one?"

"I never said I didn't believe that. But as a law enforcement officer, I need to look at all the evidence."

"We've got evidence? You didn't tell me that."

"You can get that *C.S.I.* look out of your eyes," Nathan said.

Skye only knew about the show from the issue of *TV Guide* she'd picked up at Gas4Less because one of the actors on the cover, George Eads—Nick Stokes on *C.S.I.*—looked a lot like Nathan.

"Talk to me about the evidence," she said.

"We don't have anything definitive yet."

"Well, that sucks." Skye flung herself onto the couch. An instant later, Gravity jumped onto her lap and started purring. "Maybe I should have had Angel take Gravity with her so she'd be safe too."

"Let me get this straight. You're worried about the cat but not about yourself?"

"She's still a kitten. I can look after myself."

"Which brings me to the garbology incident on Saturday morning."

"We're not doing that anymore."

"I'm very glad to hear it."

"I thought you would be."

"So what are you doing instead?"

She blinked at him with feigned innocence. "I have no idea what you mean."

"You know exactly what I mean."

"Yes, I do. And I plan on ignoring you."

"Ignoring me, huh?" Nathan sat beside her and moved closer until she could feel his warm breath tingling her ear. "How's that plan working?

She pushed him away. "You said we couldn't have sex."

"I didn't say we couldn't make out like maniacs."

"No, *I'm* saying that."

"Why?"

"I don't have to tell you my reasons." She paused as Gravity jumped down, clearly uneasy about the prospect of getting sandwiched between two humans. "You're here to do a job, and that's all. You've made that very clear. You have a schedule to keep—*mmmph!*"

Nathan's mouth covered hers without any advance warning. Not that knowing his tongue was about to do a tango with hers would have made her take immediate defensive action, but Skye liked to think it could . . . possibly . . . maybe . . . have happened. She might have protested. Not likely, but still . . .

He didn't kiss like an uptight cop. Why was that? He didn't have the lips of an uptight anything. His lower lip was full and yummy. She nibbled it a bit, then stopped so he could stroke his tongue across the roof of her mouth.

Where had a hunky side of beef from the cornfields of Nebraska learned to French-kiss like a pro? She'd have to ask him sometime . . . some *other* time, when he wasn't doing all these delicious things to her.

Nathan eventually broke off the kiss to rest his forehead against hers. "You're right," he murmured.

"Of course I am." Her voice was unsteady. "Uh, about what?"

"It's tough to stop with just one kiss. Making out probably isn't a good idea."

"Yeah." Like she'd been a fan of good ideas all her life. "Right." She jumped to her feet. "Let's play poker instead."

He leaned back on the couch and blinked. "Poker?"

"Yeah. You know, a card game where players bet on the hands they hold."

"I'm pretty good at poker."

"Really?" *Fresh meat*, Skye thought to herself. The poor guy didn't stand a chance. Because she was better than pretty good at poker. She was *damn* good.

• • •

Skye surveyed the pile of matchsticks in front of her on the Formica table. "Okay, time to cash in *my* chips now. Remember, we were not playing for money or for matches. We were playing for truths. For each matchstick, you need to tell me a truth."

"Today is Wednesday."

"A truth about yourself. I already told you that I don't like the taste of eel. Now it's your turn."

"I'm sheriff of Rock Creek."

"A truth that I don't already know about you," she reminded him.

He appeared stymied by her request.

"Hey, nobody twisted your arm to get you to play truth poker with me."

"I didn't know I'd be facing a New Age cardsharp," Nathan grumbled.

"Lucky you." Skye grinned. "Come on," she said, holding out her hand and wiggling her fingers. "Pay up."

"I don't like eel either," he finally said with a charming smile intended to coax the clothing right off her.

"No distracting me with your dimple, 'cause that bluff ain't gonna work."

"I do not have a dimple." At first, Nathan seemed highly insulted by her accusation, but then the flash of the dimple gave him away.

"Aha, there it is again."

"What about you?" he said.

"What about me?"

"No distracting me with flashes of cleavage."

"If I wanted to distract you, I'd do this." She lifted her tank top and flashed him.

"That works." His voice was hoarse.

"But distracting you wasn't my goal. Having you pay up is. Come on, another truth I don't know about you."

Silence.

"Why is this so difficult for you?" she demanded in exasperation.

He shifted uncomfortably in his chair. "I'm not into exposing truths about myself for anyone to see."

"Is that what I am? Just anyone? Thanks for the clarification," she said bitterly.

"I didn't mean that the way it sounded."

"Yeah, you did. Whenever I get too close emotionally, you slam the door on me. Fine." Skye gathered their cards and stuffed them back into the box. "Whatever. Welch on your bets. See if I care."

But she did care, and that was becoming a bigger problem all the time.

• • •

Unable to sleep, Nathan stared up at the all-too-familiar crack in Skye's living room ceiling. He was an idiot. He knew he'd hurt her by his inability to open up to her. But he didn't know how to fix it.

There was no changing him. Women usually thought they could do that to a guy—change the fundamental basis of his character. He'd seen it as a cop plenty of times. The woman who thought she could cure the guy of his drinking or drug habit. The woman who thought that, even though the guy had beaten his other girlfriends, he wouldn't beat her. They'd all been wrong.

The point was to accept someone the way they were. Faults and all.

Could he do that with Skye? Accept her as she was?

As much as Nathan told himself that she wasn't getting to him, the truth was, she'd already made it through his first line of defense and was in danger of breaching his inner sanctum.

She seemed unfazed by his attempts to keep her in line. Probably because she knew they were futile.

He wasn't in charge of the world. It was a lesson learned the hard way, when Annie had died. He'd thought that he'd been in charge of a perfectly planned-out life back then. One truck running a red light was all it took to annihilate that belief. He was actually in charge of very little.

Had he been a better man, he'd have told Skye a key truth tonight—that the reason her daughter freaked him out was because Annie had been four months pregnant when she'd died in that accident five years ago. Which meant that Toni was about the age their child would have been had Annie lived and given birth.

But he never talked about that with anyone. *Ever.* Because saying the words out loud might make him crumble.

Crumbling, like failure, was not an option.

Nathan never thought it would still be this gut-wrenching so many years later. That smacked of weakness, to his way of thinking. He should have recovered by now. Sister Mary told him once that he couldn't recover by jamming his emotions into a dark pit and refusing to acknowledge them. They just festered there without ever healing.

Well, hell. Tough shit. He'd never been a touchy-feely kind of guy. That's why the Marine Corps had appealed to him so much. The few, the proud, the Marines. The Corps values of honor, courage, and commitment matched the values he'd been taught from childhood.

The Marine Corps saying—Sweat dries, blood clots, bones heal. Suck it up, Marine!—was a creed Nathan followed. It had served him well up to this point, allowing him to get up every morning and keep going. Never give up, never give in.

As for his personal life . . . well, he hadn't had much of one until Skye had come belly dancing into his world. Well, she might be able to belly dance her way into his bed, but no way was she belly dancing her way into his heart. That door was permanently closed.

Rehashing the past wasn't his thing. He wasn't sure what was wrong with him tonight, but he knew that, somehow, it was all Skye's fault that he felt this way.

A sudden noise from the bedroom had him up and moving swiftly down the hallway. The door to Skye's room was open. Pale moonlight filtered through the sheer curtains. He really should talk to her about security issues, including the need for drapes that prevented anyone from seeing inside.

She'd kicked off the covers and was turning restlessly, obviously dreaming. Looking down at her, he was struck by how different she looked, and not just because her short hair was sticking up at odd angles. She looked . . . vulnerable.

Maybe he wasn't the only one adept at building walls.

She could look so tough that he was surprised by how innocent she appeared right now, the kitten curled up on the blanket next to her.

He didn't mean to sit on the bed and watch her, but he did. He didn't mean to tuck the sheet around her when she snuggled next to him in her sleep, but he did. He didn't mean to fall asleep there . . . but he did.

• • •

Skye was dreaming about Nathan again. She knew it was a dream because he wasn't being bossy. Instead, he was sweet and comforting, his body spooned against hers.

Her eyelids fluttered open. *There was a man in her bed. Mmm, nice.*

Her eyelids fluttered closed.

Wait a second. She sat up and wiped the sleep from her eyes. *Nathan was in her bed.* Sleeping on top of the covers.

Which made it highly unlikely that they'd somehow done the deed in their sleep.

Murmuring her name, Nathan tugged her back down into his arms. Even asleep, the guy was trying to tell her what to do. Not that she minded tremendously right at this particular moment.

She couldn't get back to sleep. Not when she'd seen how wicked awesome he looked wearing low-slung pajama bottoms and nothing else. Lying with her back against his chest prevented her from getting a really good look at him. But his arms were wrapped around her, so she could study those for a moment. And his hands. He had nice hands, for a bossy guy.

His fingernails were neatly clipped but not buffed. This was no metrosexual male into the latest Armani suits and newest-model Infiniti. These were the callused hands of a worker. A man who knew how to use tools. And a gun.

That last one might be a turn-on for some women. She'd heard the talk around town, that women had chased after Nathan because he was a cop, and that he'd ignored them.

Probably because he still loved his wife. His dead wife. The perfect one who was nothing like Skye.

So what was Nathan doing in her bed, then?

She suddenly wanted to boot him out.

Then he nuzzled her neck.

What kind of wimp was she to go all weak because

he . . . oh, that was more than nuzzling. That was his hand slipping under her pajama top and cupping her bare breast.

Did he even know who he was fondling? Did he think he was in bed with his wife? Was he dreaming of her while he was touching Skye?

Infuriated by the possibility, she jabbed her elbow into his stomach.

That got a reaction from the horny beast. "Ooof! What'd you do that for?" he demanded with typical male outrage.

"I want your eyes open when you touch me! I want you to be damn sure it's me you're touching!"

"Huh?" He blinked and gave her that men-are-from-Mars-women-are-from-another-galaxy-entirely look.

"Mommy, we're here!" Toni shrieked from the living room.

Nathan leapt out of the bed, almost falling on his face when his feet got tangled in the covers.

"Smooth move," she said sarcastically.

He tugged at his pajama bottoms, covering up his outie navel right before Toni burst into Skye's bedroom. "Angel and me came to visit with you." She bounced onto the bed and launched herself at Skye. "I missed you and Gravity."

"We missed you, too, lovebug."

"Why is Mr. Kitten-Book Man here? Did he bring me another book?"

"His name is Nathan. And no, he didn't bring you another book."

"Why not?"

"You avaricious little squirt." Skye blew a raspberry on Toni's arm.

"What's av-icious mean?"

"Avaricious means you expect presents all the time."

"Not all the time. Just *most* of the time." Toni looked around. "Where's Gravity?"

"I think she flew under the bed when you came roaring in here."

"I didn't come roaring in. This is a roar." Toni imitated a lion before modestly adding, "I did that good, didn't I?"

"Where's your tutu?" Skye asked, noticing for the first time that her daughter was wearing a regular short set, even if the top and bottom didn't match.

"I don't have to wear it all the time, Mommy," Toni solemnly informed her.

"Right."

Toni's attention returned to Nathan, who stood frozen, with a certain deer-in-the-headlights look about him. "So, if you're not here to give me a book, how come you're in my mommy's bedroom?"

"Gravity," Skye said. "He came to see Gravity."

"Where's his clothes?" Toni asked.

"In the living room with his sleeping bag."

Toni bounced up and down on the mattress. "Are we going camping?" Without waiting for an answer, she scooted off the bed and grabbed Nathan by the hand. "Come with me," she imperiously ordered him.

To give him credit, Nathan went with Toni without a word of protest. The look on his face was something else, though. Part panic, part resignation.

"Hi, Nathan," Angel said calmly as she passed them in the hallway, on her way into the bedroom to give Skye a plateful of muffins. "These turned out really good. Blueberry-wheat-bran. Try one."

Angel had never been one to judge Skye, so the fact that she'd had a man in her bedroom didn't faze her at all. "What are you doing here?" Skye said.

"Toni missed you. She insisted on coming over to see you. I figured it would be safe, with Nathan staying here and all."

Skye could hear the excited murmuring of Toni's voice even if she couldn't hear the words themselves. Nathan didn't seem to be talking much. No surprise there.

But she *was* surprised to find them, heads together in

mutual concentration, on the floor in Toni's kitty bedroom a few minutes later. Toni knew the story of *Kitten's First Full Moon* well enough that she could tell it to Nathan as she pointed to the illustrations on each page.

And since she was Skye's child, she added a few elements of her own. "This is the moon. It lives in the sky. It's a full moon. See how it's all big and round? You can smile, you know," she told Nathan, patting his cheek with her hand. "I don't mind."

He closed his eyes as if he were in pain.

"Uh-oh. That's how I look when I got to go poo and it won't come out," Toni confided with another pat to his cheek.

Nathan's eyes flew open, and he suddenly started laughing. He laughed so hard he ended up in a pile on the floor with Toni perched on his bare chest, tickling him.

"Do it again!" she yelled. "Laugh some more and make me bounce up and down."

He laughed so hard, tears poured from his eyes.

Toni scrambled off his chest to stare down at him in concern. "Why are you crying? Did you pee in your pants?"

That started another round of his laughter before, gasping for breath, Nathan sat up and tried to regain his composure. He leaned forward and rested his forehead on his bent knees while inhaling gulps of air.

"I'm better now." He sat up straight and looked at Skye. The earlier look of panic and pain was gone. She glimpsed the warmth in his eyes.

The door to his soul had opened.

Skye smiled. "Yeah," she said softly. "I think you *will* be better now."

· · ·

The next afternoon, Skye sat on the cream-colored couch in Julia's picture-perfect living room and studied the rest of her family. Four generations of Wright women in one room. A regular estrogen-fest.

Angel was crocheting beside her on the couch, while Toni and Julia were playing with Ta the Tiger on the floor. On Skye's way in earlier, Julia had pulled her aside and reminded her not to say anything to anyone about the pregnancy, because she hadn't told Luke yet. Then she'd hugged Skye, who still found it weird but kind of neat that she and her sister had bonded by sharing secrets while sitting on the hood of Skye's car and staring up at the night sky.

And there was Violet, the family matriarch, regally enthroned in a high-back armchair. She might look like Betty White, but she often acted like Miss Piggy, with her diva-like sense of entitlement. Yet there were some signs that Violet was transforming.

"You know, in the beginning I wasn't sure how I felt about having a badass for a granddaughter," she suddenly announced.

"Mom!" Angel protested.

"You must be talking about me," Julia noted dryly, which made Skye crack up.

"What? I got that right, didn't I? That's the proper term, isn't it?"

"Sure is," Skye agreed.

"Who's a badass?" Toni demanded.

Violet pressed her hand to her mouth. "I forgot that little pitchers have big ears," she said sheepishly.

"Who has a bad ass and big ears?" Toni insisted.

"Ta the Tiger," Angel replied.

"Ta's ears aren't big," Toni protested.

Angel swiftly changed the subject. "Who's ready for some sweet-potato muffins with candied ginger?"

Toni jumped to her feet. "I want candy."

Angel noted the adults' lack of similar enthusiasm. "These came out much better than my squash cookies," she assured her daughters and mother.

"That's not a real high bar you're setting there," Julia noted.

"My squash cookies are famous," Angel protested.

"Infamous," Julia said.

Skye had heard enough about the cookies. "Hey, Julia, before I forget, have you ever heard of someone named Roxy Rothafel? There's a quote from him above the entrance to the Tivoli. I've been meaning to Google him, but since you're a librarian and know everything, I thought you might have heard of him."

"I know who he is," Violet said. "Samuel Lionel Rothafel. He's the genius behind the design concept for the interior of Radio City Music Hall. Don't look so surprised—I'm not dumb. I know how to read."

"She asked me to get her a bunch of books from the library on movie theater history earlier today," Julia explained.

"Figured I might as well know what you're doing there at the Tivoli." Violet's look was a clear reminder that she'd seen what Skye and Nathan had been doing onstage that day.

"Yeah, Violet has seen firsthand the kind of activities we're engaged in at the Tivoli," Skye said with a challenging look in return.

"Are you sure that sheriff can protect you from harm?"

Skye was surprised to see genuine concern in Violet's eyes. So surprised, she momentarily didn't know what to say.

"Nathan is a good man," Angel said. "All the signs say so."

"You're not talking about those little rocks again, are you?" Violet pooh-poohed the idea with a sour-lemon face.

"They're runes."

"Runes, prunes—I don't care what you call them. I need more realistic assurances that Skye will be safe."

"Nathan will make sure of it," Julia said. "He's a professional. He knows what he's doing."

Skye wondered if Nathan knew what he was doing to *her*. Cuddling in bed with her and then laughing with her daughter—the devious man was making her fall for him. So, okay, maybe she'd already fallen for him and was now up to her armpits in deep shit. Up to her armpits in love. She couldn't even think about it.

Luckily, Violet distracted her. "I've got a bit of good news to share," she said.

"You're going back to Bakersfield?" Julia socked Skye's arm and sent her a warning look. "What?"

"I don't know when I'm going back," Violet said.

"I've been looking into getting my own place," Angel abruptly announced. "Now that Julia and Luke are back, I mean. I'd like someplace out in the country where the llamas and I can have space to tread lightly on the Earth."

"What about Tyler?" Skye asked. "Only you and the llamas will be going to your new place?"

"I haven't spoken to Tyler about this yet."

"Yeah, that's a problem," Skye said, her tone making it clear that this wasn't the only thing Angel needed to run past Tyler.

"If we can please get back to my good news?" Violet was getting impatient. "Ethel . . . uh . . . Angel, do you remember Ellie Mather who I play bridge with? Anyway, her daughter is best friends with someone who works for Nicole Kidman. I sent one of your scarves, the fuzzy aqua and purple one, to Ellie's daughter. Her friend saw it and loved it, so Ellie lent it to her. That's when Nicole saw it. And, well, to make a long story short, Nicole loved it. She wants you to make one for her."

"Are you serious?"

"Of course I am. Well, actually, Nicole borrowed it and was photographed wearing it. Apparently it's caused a big to-do in the fashion world, with people scrambling to figure out who the designer is. Ellie phoned me, asking what your line of scarves is called. I said Angel Designs. And that's what we've got up on the website."

"Website?" Angel said faintly, clearly stunned by this turn of events.

"Yes, well, I didn't have the foggiest how those things work, but Lulu designed the site and has taught me a lot. We got a thousand hits the first hour it went live, and then the server crashed because of the heavy traffic. But Lulu's got everything up and running again."

Angel stared at her mother as if the old woman had been invaded by aliens.

"And Sue Ellen is almost a realtor, so she pulled a few strings and looked up some properties you might be interested in." Violet handed Angel several sheets of paper. "You'll be starting a cottage industry, so you'll need room for the offices of Angel Designs in that farmhouse of yours. By the way, your scarves are now going for five hundred dollars. Each."

Angel choked and had a coughing fit.

"One actually went for a lot more than that on eBay," Violet continued. "I figure that you should be the creative force behind Angel Designs, and I'll be the financial brains. I'm no Adam Kemp—not yet. But I think I've got a good head on my shoulders."

"But, five hundred dollars?" Dazed, Angel shook her head. "That seems like price gouging. I've been charging much less than that. More like twenty-five dollars."

"It's valuing yourself and your creative work, not price gouging."

"I'm not into money—"

"I know that," Violet interrupted her. "And you can still do your other work, your wall hangings, and set your own prices. But Angel Designs are exclusive."

"I'm not into exclusive," Angel protested. "I'm into *in*-clusive. You shouldn't have done all this without asking me first."

"A badass move on my part," Violet stated, to everyone's surprise.

Violet surprised them all again the very next day, when she cornered Milton outside Angelo's Pizza and threatened him with a squirming frog.

Chapter Seventeen

. . . .

"**Milton** here is terrified of frogs. Aren't you, Milton?"
Violet waved the fidgeting frog closer to his face.

Milton whimpered and shrank back against the storefront.

Violet showed no mercy. "This nonsense has been going
on long enough. You've been terrorizing my granddaughter
with your vandalism of her theater. Don't you know that
the Tivoli has a quote from the man who designed the Radio City Music Hall, where the Rockettes still perform today? But do you care about things like that? Noooo." Violet
wiggled the frog menacingly. "And what about Owen, huh?
How do you think your behavior reflects on him? Badly,
that's how."

Skye stood beside Violet, unable to believe what she
was hearing or seeing. She'd had no idea this was what her
grandmother was planning when she'd insisted that Skye
come with her for a little stroll around town.

She had expected Violet to ask for her help in convincing

Angel of the merits of Angel Designs as an exclusive business venture. Skye still had a hard time imagining Nicole Kidman wearing one of Angel's scarves, but she had Googled it last night and found the photos. *And* found the website that Lulu had designed. It was wicked awesome.

But this . . . frog-dangling incident. This came out of nowhere. And it, too, was wicked awesome to watch.

Violet looked somewhat incongruous bullying Milton while wearing her pearl necklace and gold button earrings, trim navy blue pants, and kelly green sweater set. Skye wondered if her grandmother had chosen green to match her accessory, the frog.

Her *grandmother*. Suddenly Skye was thinking of her that way and not as Violet, some stranger from Bakersfield. She had noticed that her grandmother had used Angel's chosen name yesterday instead of Ethel. Definite progress there.

And now this.

Violet continued her rant. "Stop your silly whimpering and just be a man, Milton! Confess you were stupid and that you were petty and mean and vicious and cruel and spiteful, and that you were behind all the sabotaging incidents at my granddaughter's theater. Come on, Milton." She moved the frog closer. "I'm losing patience here. I'm seventy. Time becomes a precious commodity at my age."

A crowd started to gather.

"What's going on?" Sister Mary asked.

"Skye's badass grandmother is kicking Milton's butt," Lulu said.

"It looks like she's holding a frog," Sister Mary said.

"She is," Fanny noted as she joined them. "That was my idea. I heard from Owen that Milton is terrified of frogs."

"You rock!" Lulu high-fived Fanny.

"Yeah, but I don't like holding frogs," Fanny admitted. "Violet said she didn't mind, though."

"She's handling him like a pro. Where did you get a frog?"

"I can't reveal the secrets of our operation," Fanny said.

"I got it for her," latecomer Sue Ellen claimed, jiggling into position to get a better view.

"Get out." Lulu wasn't convinced. "You hate slimy stuff."

"Yeah, but frogs aren't slimy. Not to me. I've handled them since I was a kid. There are lots of them in the creek behind the trailer park. I named this one Fred."

"Then why aren't *you* the one dangling Fred the Frog in front of Milton?" Lulu asked.

"Violet insisted on doing it herself. Something about defending her family's honor and better late than never, whatever that means."

Skye overheard all these conversations while still staring at Violet, blown away by her grandmother's *High Noon* showdown with the bad guy.

"This is your last chance, Milton." Violet's voice had turned steely. "In another minute, Fred here is going to be doing a tap dance on your chest hair, if you have any."

"That's enough," Nathan said as he moved through the crowd to stand beside Violet. "You can stop torturing him with that frog now. Milton's wife Robin came to see me."

"To turn him in?" Violet asked hopefully.

"To confess," Nathan replied.

"To confess to what?" Violet said. "That she'd been an idiot to marry him?"

"That she was behind the sabotage."

"Why would she do that?" Skye demanded.

"The juvenile delinquent she hired to start the fire decided to blackmail her," Nathan explained. "Rather than give in to his exorbitant demands, she decided to confess."

"No, not that. I meant why would she want to sabotage the theater in the first place?"

"So you would leave and Milton would shut up and stop obsessing about you."

"She could have gotten Milton to shut up by smothering

him in his sleep," Skye declared angrily. "She didn't have to involve me."

"She loves her husband."

Skye shook her head. "See, this is why I never want to get married."

"So, you don't have to threaten him with Fred the Frog any longer." Nathan gently lowered Violet's frog-bearing arm.

Milton sank onto the pavement, then pointed a shaking finger at Violet. "Arrest her! And her sleazy-slut grand-daughter, too."

Violet raised the frog again. "You watch your mouth or I'll wash it out with Fred here!"

"You heard her!" Milton shrieked. "She's threatening me."

"It's a frog, Milton, not a nine-millimeter Glock. Besides, you're not in the clear here yourself. You've known about your wife's activities for several days now and said nothing. That makes you an accessory to the crime." Nathan hauled him to his feet. "Come along. You have the right to remain silent . . ."

As Nathan led an incoherent Milton away, Violet returned Fred to Sue Ellen, who cuddled the frog close and rubbed his head until his eyes closed in ecstasy.

While not as wildly happy as Fred the Frog, Skye definitely liked the idea of a badass grandmother. "I didn't know you had it in you," she told Violet.

"I guess you've rubbed off on me."

"I'm glad." Skye hugged her.

"Yeah." Her grandmother hugged her back. "Me, too."

• • •

"I can't believe this," Celeste said of the mayhem in the sheriff's office. Milton sat wailing in a chair, while his wife yelled at him to shut up and their attorney advised both of them to keep quiet and behave.

"Robin signed a written confession with her attorney present," Nathan said.

Celeste just kept shaking her head. "I can't believe she was involved in the first place. Being married to Milton must have driven her over the edge, that's all I can say."

"That doesn't excuse her actions."

"I didn't say it did. Good thing she made the right choice and confessed."

Nathan nodded, but the truth was that he'd already had contact earlier that morning with the sixteen-year-old who'd done the dirty work. The boy had turned on Robin, giving her up. So she would have been caught even if she hadn't come in on her own.

The turning point in the case had come when Jay overheard the teen bragging about the money he was going to come into. Jay had done the right thing: He'd told Nathan. Nathan was very proud of him, and had told him so. Here was a kid at risk who'd taken the right road when he'd come to that fork that always presents itself. Now that Algee was working with him, getting him involved in the comic-book project, Jay was making great progress.

Someone else striving to make progress was Deputy Sheriff Timmy Johnson, who had been deliberately trying to stay below Nathan's radar for weeks now, ever since Nathan had reprimanded him for not giving Skye a ticket any of the times he'd stopped her for speeding.

Mayberry had Barney and Rock Creek had Timmy. Which made Nathan what—Andy Griffith? Nathan simply couldn't relate to that idea.

The next few hours were filled with processing the paperwork on the two suspects and overseeing their transfer to the county jail. Things had barely settled down for a moment when Cole strolled into Nathan's office, turning the chair around in order to rest his arms on the back. "I hear you thwarted an assault by frog earlier today. I thought I'd stop by to see if Fred the Frog needed any medical attention after all the excitement."

"How did you know his name was Fred?"

"I hear things."

"The aforementioned amphibian is in protective custody."

"Yours?"

"No, Sue Ellen's."

Cole frowned. "She's not seeing any mystical visions in the frog's skin, is she?"

"Not the last time I checked, no."

"Glad to hear it. I think we've had enough hysteria around here to last us a while."

"What's with this *we* business?" Nathan wanted to know. "What excitement have you had?"

"A ferret got loose in the examining room and took a chunk out of my arm. Apparently, it has an aversion to men in white coats holding needles."

"I don't blame it."

"I should have known you'd take the ferret's side over my own."

"You probably nudged it into the dark side."

"It sure sounds like Milton nudged his wife into the dark side." Cole leaned forward. "Getting back to you, do you plan on keeping your sleeping bag parked in Skye's apartment?"

"I haven't had time to think about it."

"You don't have to stay at her place to protect her anymore, right?"

"Right."

"So now you can seduce her instead. Or let her seduce you."

"Maybe if you got a life of your own, you wouldn't be so fascinated with mine," Nathan retorted.

"Nah, I'd still be interested. Have you told Celeste she was a suspect?"

"What?" Celeste demanded from the partially open

doorway before barging into the room. "You actually thought I was a suspect?"

"It wasn't personal," Nathan assured her. "You've been around long enough to know that I needed to consider every possibility in this case. And you'd made your negative opinion about Skye known to me."

"Because I was trying to protect you from her. Well, forget that!" Celeste's eyes spat fire behind her big glasses. "You two deserve each other! Now eat your lunch." She tossed a plastic-wrapped sandwich onto his desk and marched out.

• • •

"You should have seen Violet. She was wicked awesome," Skye was telling Angel, Julia, and Luke as they joined the crowd still gathered in front of Angelo's Pizza. "Where's Toni?" she asked Angel.

"Algee has her at the store. I wasn't sure what was going on down here, so I didn't want to bring her with us until I knew it was safe."

"You know what this means, right? That Toni can come back home now that the danger is over." Skye did a happy hip jiggle before something else occurred to her. Turning to her grandmother, she said, "How did you know that Milton would be here at Angelo's so you could confront him?"

"Owen told me Milton always eats pizza for lunch on Fridays."

"Good thing you caught him before he went in and ate, or he probably would have projectile-vomited when he saw that frog," Lulu said.

Violet nodded. "I thought of that, which is why I did confront him before he ate."

"So it was Milton's wife, not Milton," Angel murmured thoughtfully. "The tarot cards just indicated that he was responsible for the danger. How is Owen taking it?"

"I have to go check on him," Violet declared, hurrying away toward the funeral home.

"I can't believe she threatened a guy with a frog," Luke said.

"Why's that?" Julia abruptly demanded. "Because traditional women don't do that sort of thing? I suppose they don't get pregnant, either, huh? Yes, that's right. I'm *pregnant*!" She looked around at the crowd. "Did everyone hear me?"

"Not me," Fanny said. "Let me adjust my hearing aid a little."

"She's knocked up," Lulu told Fanny in a loud voice.

"Skye?"

"No, Julia, her good-girl sister."

"I didn't want to tell you this way!" Julia wailed.

"That's okay." Fanny patted her shoulder.

"I think she meant she didn't mean to tell Luke this way," Skye told Fanny before returning her attention to Julia. "Just think of all the fun stories you'll be able to tell your kid."

Luke still looked poleaxed.

"Hello?" Skye waved a hand in front of his face. "Anyone home in there?"

"Pregnant?" he repeated hoarsely. "With a baby?"

"No, with a frog," Skye retorted in exasperation. "Of course with a baby. You better hug my sister soon, because she's terrified you don't want to have kids. And seeing as how you messed up the marriage-proposal thing—"

Without further ado, Luke took Julia's hand in his and dropped to one knee, right there in the middle of the cracked sidewalk, in front of everyone.

"I've been carrying this around for days, waiting for the right moment," Luke said, pulling a ring box out of his jeans pocket.

"And for some reason, he thought the pavement outside Angelo's was the most romantic spot possible," Skye teased.

Luke ignored her and held out the box to Julia before opening it with a flourish. The box . . . was empty.

"Shit!" Luke muttered, reaching back into his pocket to pull out the ring. "I'm not good at this romantic stuff. So I'll be brief. Julia, I love you. Baby or no baby. Will you marry me?"

"Yes." She pulled him to his feet. "Yes, I will marry you, Luke Maguire."

"You may now kiss the pregnant bride," Skye said in a solemn voice.

The crowd applauded as Luke gladly complied.

• • •

Nathan didn't have time to think about his personal life or his sleeping arrangements with Skye because his day was filled with one incident after another. They were short-staffed: One of their three part-time deputy sheriffs was getting an emergency appendectomy.

So it was Nathan who had to check out a landlord-tenant dispute in a rental house, followed by a crime-prevention speech at the middle school, followed by a noise complaint at the Broken Creek Trailer Park. Meanwhile, Deputy Sheriff Timmy Johnson caught two speeders and then managed traffic when one of the traffic lights leading out to the interstate went off-line.

It was evening before things settled down enough for Nathan to leave the office, although his cell phone and pager were always on should he be needed.

He'd barely made it out of the building when he was called back because of a major pileup on the interstate. A semi had jackknifed, involving five other vehicles in an accident. Every available officer was requested.

The EMTs, ambulance, and fire truck were already en route. Nathan jumped into the squad car and turned on the siren and flashing lights, all the while willing his rabid sense of déjà vu to stay under control. But when he arrived at the crash site and found the pile of badly crumpled cars, he almost lost it.

•   •   •

"A baby," Luke was saying in awe for about the fiftieth time. The family had all gathered in Skye's apartment for a celebration dinner of veggie quesadillas and mango-cucumber salad. Violet brought Owen, who had been hesitant to intrude and was so apologetic about the trouble Milton had caused.

Skye had stopped him. "You have nothing to be sorry for. You made my dream for the Tivoli Theater a reality. There's no way I can thank you. Not even with that lifetime pass that I promised you." She gave him a huge hug.

He seemed to be more comfortable now, as he sat beside Violet on one of the kitchen chairs.

Momma-to-be Julia was enthroned on the regal round couch, Luke glued to her side. "A baby," he repeated again, placing his hand on her still-flat stomach.

"I know," Julia said. "It's awesome, isn't it?"

"Yeah. And terrifying."

She smiled. "Yeah, that, too."

"Are you okay with all this?" Luke asked.

Julia nodded. "Are you? I know we didn't plan—"

"Since when do I plan?" Luke countered. "You're the one who makes notes to yourself."

"She still does that?" Skye shook her head in mock disappointment. "I thought maybe she'd outgrow that."

Julia tossed a small embroidered pillow at her.

Toni leapt into the air and caught it before running away down the hallway, the pillow clutched in her arms.

"Soon Toni will have a little cousin to play with," Angel said fondly.

"She'll have grown out of her biting stage by then, right?" Julia's face reflected her concern.

"Probably," Angel said. "I should start crocheting a toy for the baby."

"You won't have much time, with all those orders pouring in on your website," Violet said.

Angel fingered her amethyst pendant. "I can't get used to that concept. I haven't made a final decision about it yet."

"Well, it's been quite an evening," Luke suddenly announced, tugging Julia to her feet. "But my fiancée and I are going to head out now over to my old apartment above Maguire's for a little alone time."

"Congratulations," Tyler told him with a pat on his back.

"Thanks, man."

Angel's face was beaming as she watched Julia and Skye hug. "Is it my imagination, or are things more serene between the two of you?"

"Our relationship is in a better place now, I think," Julia admitted.

"I no longer always want to kick her butt," Skye agreed.

"I'm so glad." Angel hugged both her daughters.

"You think you can cope with both me and Lucy the Llama being pregnant at the same time?" Julia teased her.

"Yes. Dr. Flannigan is helping out with Lucy. He's the local vet. You'll want a natural home-birth yourself, of course," Angel said.

"No, I want lots of drugs to make the pain go away," Julia stated firmly. "And Pop-Tarts."

"Their baby, their choices," Tyler reminded Angel.

"Always. With input and information from women like me who have walked that path before."

"There's plenty of time to talk about all that stuff later," Luke declared, quickly heading for the nearest exit. "Come on, Julia, time to go."

• • •

Skye was in the theater's private office, doing some work on a grant Owen had suggested she apply for. She hated paperwork. But if it could help her get the theater restored, then it was worth it. She supposed.

She'd missed the football game tonight but heard the Trojans had won anyway. Good. Lesson well learned, grasshoppers.

Before Skye had come down here to the theater, Angel and Tyler had offered to stay with Toni until she returned. Tyler was crunching numbers about possible farmhouses on the market, while Angel was consulting the runes. Owen had driven Violet back to Serenity Falls.

Skye had given Toni a bath and listened to her daughter recite *Kitten's First Full Moon* twice before Toni had finally settled down. "When is Nathan coming back?" she asked sleepily.

"I don't know." His sleeping bag was still in her living room.

"I like his laugh," Toni murmured. "Nice laugh."

Gravity purred in agreement as she cuddled against Toni's legs.

Skye had to agree. She liked Nathan's laugh too. She also liked the way his eyes crinkled at the corners when he smiled. And the way his dimple flashed. She was still surprised by how long it had taken for her to discover that dimple. Probably because he hadn't smiled much in her presence.

The reward of his smile and his laughter was worth the effort. She'd tickle him senseless if it meant seeing his eyes crinkle and that dimple flash.

Oh, yeah, she had it bad.

As if conjured up by her thoughts, Nathan walked into her office. She hadn't seen him since he'd dragged Milton off hours and hours ago. He'd changed from his uniform into a black T-shirt and jeans.

"So the loon's wife was behind the sabotage all along, huh? Except for that incident with the hammer. Luke told me that appears to have been an accident." She noticed

Nathan's face pale at the word *accident*. "Hey, are you okay?" She got up and moved closer, putting her hand on his arm. "What's wrong?"

"Nothing," he said curtly.

"Then why aren't you happy? The crime is solved. Your job is done. I thought you'd be on top of the world. Geez, talk about a buzz killer—"

"So you're looking for a buzz, are you?"

Two seconds later he had her up against the wall, pinning her between the vintage Cary Grant posters for *Suspicion* and *Indiscreet* as his mouth consumed hers. The kiss wasn't sweet or cute, but raw and shameless. He drew her up until she was on tippy-toes. She kicked off her sandals when they got in the way.

Nathan was no suave and debonair Cary. He was a man possessed, reaching under her short, swirly skirt with his big, hot hands and tearing off her skimpy underwear. She responded by undoing the zipper on his jeans and shoving them and his tighty-whities out of the way.

Her Peruvian tote bag was on the desk beside her. She blindly reached inside and by some miracle was able to immediately locate the pack of condoms. He ripped open the box and removed one. She helped him roll it on.

Nathan immediately backed her against the wall again, pressing intimately against her. She reached down and guided him in. Once he was deep inside her, he lifted her until she wrapped her legs around his waist, her hands gripping his shoulders as she held on for dear life.

This new position created an erotic angle, so that each of his powerful thrusts generated increasingly intense shards of savage pleasure.

His eyes were closed, his face etched with some emotion she couldn't name.

She gasped his name as her orgasm gripped her and she gripped him.

And then it was over. He lowered her until her feet

touched the floor and then he stepped away, turning his back as he took care of removing the condom and returning his clothes to their regular positions.

The hem of Skye's skirt fell from her waist to cover her private parts, still tingling from his possession of her.

This time, instead of guilt, regret was written all over Nathan's face when he finally turned to face her. "I shouldn't have come here. This was a mistake."

Words like daggers into her soul.

"Do *not* apologize," Skye said fiercely, "or, I swear, I *will* hurt you badly." She paused to take a deep breath, shoving the pain into the back of her mind. He hadn't hurt her physically, but he'd struck a deathblow to her heart. "It ends here." She took another ragged breath. "You're always going to compare me with your perfect wife, and that's a race I can never win. You've cast me in the role of a wicked Eve, tempting you off the straight and narrow path. Well, forget it. I'm not playing that game anymore. It ends here." She turned her back on him and walked out—her feet bare, her dignity shredded, her inner diva on the verge of annihilation.

Chapter Eighteen

. . . .

Skye refused to cry. She refused to give in to the tears that threatened to pour down her face. Instead, she returned to her apartment and greeted Angel and Tyler as if nothing had changed.

Tyler bought it.

Angel didn't.

"What's happened? Something terrible has happened, I can tell. Your auras . . ." Angel shook her head in concern and hurried to Skye's side.

Damn auras, Skye thought. *Always giving her away.* She pinned a happy smile on her face. "I'm fine."

Tyler wisely decided it was time for him to get a little fresh air and left the two women alone.

"Talk to me," Angel said.

Skye curled up on the couch, hugging a soft silk pillow to her chest. "You've heard that saying—Good girls go to heaven, bad girls go wherever they want?"

Angel shook her head. "No."

"Well, maybe I made it up. I can't remember. The thing is, I can go wherever I want. Except into Nathan's heart."

"Why's that?"

"Because he won't let me in. I thought he would, but . . ."

"What happened? Did he come to the theater tonight?"

"Yes."

"And the sex was so good it scared you?"

Angel had never been shy about discussing sex with her daughters. Which was fine by Skye, although it freaked Julia out.

"Since when would great sex scare me?" Skye countered.

"Since you've fallen in love with the guy you're having great sex with."

"Did Julia tell you?"

"Julia knows about this?"

"She knows I might be in love with Nathan. But I'll get over him," Skye vowed fiercely.

"Well, the answer is no, Julia didn't tell me you were in love with Nathan. Your face when you walked in the door told me. Actually, I knew long before that. You two were meant to be together, but were bound to hit some rocky patches. The tarot cards indicated as much."

"There are rocky patches, and then there are boulders the size of Colorado. The man is still in love with his dead wife."

"He told you this?"

Skye nodded. "He said he loved her and that she was his everything. And that she was nothing like me."

"So?"

"So, she was golden. I'm not. I'm a rebel. I may be able to tempt him into having sex with me, but not into falling in love with me."

"Why shouldn't he fall in love with you?"

"There are tons of reasons."

"Give them to me." Angel curled up on the couch beside her. "Starting with the one that scares you the most."

Leave it to Angel to get right to the heart of the matter. There was no bullshitting her.

The bottom line was that Skye had never had a man love her the way she needed to be loved . . . but was afraid she didn't *deserve* to be loved.

Yes, Skye believed she deserved to be happy. She deserved to follow her own rules. But real love? Maybe that required a goodness she didn't possess. Maybe that was reserved for people who colored inside the lines. Golden people, like Nathan's dead wife, Annie. And do-gooders like Nathan.

"Talk to me," Angel urged, squeezing Skye's shoulders in a universal maternal sign.

"What scares me the most is that I—" Skye shook her head, unable to continue for a moment. "What if I'm not meant to find real love? What if I never do?"

"Then fate would have something bigger in mind for you. But I don't think that's the case."

"The tarot cards aren't always right. They indicated Milton was the saboteur. And remember, they also said that garlic gelato would be a big hit at your gelato store, and instead it totally bombed. Like I'm totally bombing in the love department. The sex is great. It's the other stuff that gets messed up."

"So what happened tonight?"

"I told Nathan that it ended here. That he couldn't just show up and have hot, wall-banging sex in my private office and then say he was sorry or that it shouldn't have happened."

"Hot, wall-banging sex, huh? Maybe Nathan was concerned that he might have hurt you?"

"He hurt me by saying the things that he did. It's over. I've learned enough from my past mistakes to know when it's time to cut my losses and end it."

"But in the past, you weren't in love with the man."

"Sometimes I thought I was."

"The same way you're in love with Nathan?"

"No." Skye slowly shook her head. "There's never been anyone like Nathan."

"Exactly. And that's why you don't have a manual to fall back on here. A way to read him."

"Even getting a fix on his auras is difficult," Skye said.

"Yes, I've noticed that myself. In some ways he's like Tyler. Not just regarding the wall-banging sex," Angel said with a grin. "But also in that Nathan is a man of few words. Not someone who opens up easily."

"Not someone who opens up at all."

"I wish there were something I could do to make the pain go away."

Skye leaned her head on Angel's shoulder. "Thanks for always being here for me. I don't tell you that enough, I know."

"Of course I'm here for you. That's what parents do. Love unconditionally."

"What about men? Do they ever do that with the women in their lives? Love unconditionally?"

"I believe so. It can happen. And you certainly deserve to have it happen to you. Because that kind of love is the kind that you are capable of giving, and therefore are very deserving of receiving." Angel hugged her tightly. "And don't you ever forget it."

• • •

Early the next morning, Angel insisted that Skye go off with Sue Ellen and Lulu to a nearby farmer's market, as planned. The only change was that Angel took Toni to visit the llamas instead of letting the little girl go with Skye.

Skye suspected it was so that she could talk to her friends about Nathan if she needed to.

It was a perfect Saturday morning, and the market was

in full swing. A crisp September breeze had set the fall leaves dancing in the air. Some of the trees were beginning to get a golden glow about them. Blue tarps tied to supporting poles covered the various stalls selling organic produce from local family farms. Other stalls offered fall flowers as well as homemade baked goods and jams. Dried corn and assorted gourds were also set out in artistic displays.

By mid-October, the hardwood trees on the surrounding hillsides would begin boasting magnificent hues of red, yellow, and gold. Skye knew because she'd arrived in Pennsylvania in late October, missing the peak colors of fall. She'd been looking forward to seeing them this year.

Having grown up and lived mostly on the West Coast, the concept of four seasons with different vibes for the various times of the year was one that appealed to Skye.

The vegetable stand in front of them did not appear to have a similar appeal for Sue Ellen, who was eyeing the produce suspiciously.

"Do you want to try some of the eggplant?" Skye asked.

"I don't eat anything purple," Sue Ellen stated firmly.

"You don't eat anything that doesn't come out of a can or a box," Lulu scoffed. She'd exchanged her skull earrings for skeleton ones, and was wearing her baggy black pants with the metal studs. Her goth look caused some curious looks from passersby. So did the saying on her T-shirt. EARTH FIRST! WE'LL STRIP-MINE THE OTHER PLANETS LATER.

Since Pennsylvania had long been coal-mining country, the sentiment conveyed was one that hit home.

Also hitting home for Skye was the fact that it really was over between her and Nathan.

"What is that?" Sue Ellen pointed to a basket filled with odd-shaped tan-colored things.

"Ginger."

"It looks obscene."

"Only if you have a dirty mind."

"What about this?" Sue Ellen demanded. "You can't claim that *this* isn't obscene."

"It's a cucumber."

"It's huge. That's just not right."

"I'll tell you what's not right," Lulu declared. "Whatever is going on between Nathan and Skye."

"Nothing is going on," Skye said.

"That's what I mean. All those sparks led to nothing?"

"It led to hot, wall-banging sex in my office at the Tivoli, right between two Cary Grant posters." Skye's internal editor was definitely not on duty at the moment.

Sue Ellen eyed her uncertainly. "You're kidding, right?"

"She doesn't look like she's kidding." Lulu's forehead wrinkled in concern, making her pierced eyebrow stand out even more. "She looks like she's going to cry."

"Skye never cries," Sue Ellen declared. "Right, Skye?"

And just like that, the tears came.

"Now look what you did to Skye," Lulu said accusingly. "You made her cry!"

"How?" Sue Ellen was clearly at a loss. "What did I say?"

"You insulted her vegetables. You know how she feels about her organic vegetables and the farmer's market. And you go and make fun of eggplants, ginger, and cucumbers the first five minutes you're here."

"The wildberry jam looks good," Sue Ellen noted, moving on to the next stall. "Want me to buy some?" she asked Skye. "I'll buy a case if you want me to."

"Come on." Lulu led Skye over to the benches set out nearby. "What's going on? Why are you crying if you and Nathan had wall-banging sex? He didn't have wall-banging sex in your office with someone else, did he?"

"No."

"Was he no good at it?"

"He was wicked awesome," Skye admitted.

Lulu shook her head. "So the problem is . . . ?"

"I'm stupid," Skye wailed.

"So? Men usually go for stupid women. Ow!" Sue Ellen rubbed her arm where Lulu had pinched it. "What was that for? It's not like that fact is a secret or anything."

"It's not true," Lulu said. "Do you know how many men prefer smart women?"

"No, and neither do you, so don't even try pretending that you do," Sue Ellen retorted.

"I don't want to talk about it anymore," Skye declared, scrubbing the tears away.

"You haven't really talked about it at all yet," Sue Ellen pointed out.

"Change the subject," Skye ordered.

"Okay. Do you know how many people squander their lottery winnings within a few short years?" Lulu asked.

"No, and I don't want to know," Sue Ellen said.

"Seventy percent. I read an article on the Internet about a woman who won five million and is now broke, living in a trailer park somewhere."

Sue Ellen bristled. "There's nothing wrong with living in a trailer park."

"Is that where you'd live if you had five million dollars?" Lulu asked.

"No way!"

"How is this information supposed to cheer me up?" Skye demanded.

Lulu snapped her gum. "You didn't say we were supposed to cheer you up."

"We need chocolate for that," Sue Ellen said. "A Blizzard would be good. Is there a Dairy Queen around here?"

"Skye doesn't eat stuff like that," Lulu reminded her.

"Which is why she needs cheering up."

• • •

"This is the last time we're doing this," Angel informed Adam as he got out of his limo. Toni had fallen asleep in the backseat of Angel's VW van, and Angel stood close enough to keep an eye on her in case she woke up.

Adam looked at the farmhouse at the end of the long drive they were standing on. "Is that why you had us meet at this out-of-the-way place?"

"This isn't an out-of-the-way place, it's a piece of property I'm thinking of buying."

"And you wanted my opinion of it?"

"No, I really couldn't care less about your opinion."

"Then you won't be upset to hear that I'm reconciling with my wife."

"No, I won't be upset." Angel wondered if she'd driven him back into his wife's arms by having a fit in his office the way she had, throwing cold water on herself as if she were on fire. "I'm glad for you. Glad that the meditation made you realize what's important in your life."

"I don't know that I'd go that far."

Angel sighed. "You know, it wouldn't kill you to admit that I helped you."

"You scared me. When you went ballistic in my office like that."

Okay, that answered *that* question. "Well, whatever I did to motivate you, I'm glad it worked. I hope you and your wife will do well together."

"Yeah, me, too. I guess I was sort of going through some kind of midlife crisis or something."

"That happens."

"To you, too?"

"In wanting to recapture the past? No, that wasn't an affliction I had, thank heavens."

"Julia told me she's pregnant. I'm going to be a grandfather."

"Yes, you are. And you better not mess that up."

"Mess what up? Luke and Julia? They're getting married. The guy should have come to me and asked for my permission first."

"No, he shouldn't have. He doesn't need your permission. No one in this family does. They don't need my permission either. Remember, being a parent means—"

"Loving your kids unconditionally. Yeah, yeah—I know. So, what do you think about their getting married?"

"I'm happy for them."

"Do you see yourself ever getting married?"

"No, I really don't."

"What about that bum in your life?"

"He's not a bum." Angel instantly defended Tyler. "He's an incredible man."

"If he's that incredible, why don't you marry him?"

"Well, for one thing, he hasn't asked. But even if he did, I don't want to get married. I've spent my life refusing to be hemmed in by arbitrary traditions like marriage. I don't like the formality of it. I prefer a spiritual meeting of souls."

"Well, if you ever change your mind, here's the name of my attorney. He does a great job on prenups, in case this latest business venture of yours really takes off. I saw the website and heard that Hollywood is going crazy over your scarves."

"Apparently so."

"You don't sound too thrilled."

"I have conflicting feelings about it."

"Now there's something new," Adam said. "You having conflicting feelings."

"What's that supposed to mean?"

"Just that I never met anyone so averse to success."

"At other people's expense."

"Who are you hurting by being successful? All those other business ventures you had, didn't you want them to thrive and be a success?"

"Well, yes, but—"

"But what?"

"I don't know if I'm any good at being successful."

"Listen, if you can teach a type-A like me to meditate, even a little bit, then you've got what it takes to be successful at anything."

Angel was on the verge of crying. "Really?"

"Entrepreneurs don't cry."

"New Age entrepreneurs do," she retorted before hugging him good-bye.

As Adam drove away, Angel opened the van door to check on Toni.

"Was that a capitalist pig?" Toni asked sleepily, pointing to the departing limo.

"No, that was just a man."

"A man you're still in love with?" Tyler demanded from the other side of the van.

Angel jumped a foot in the air. "Tyler! What are you doing here?"

"Following you. I parked down by the road and hiked in."

Angel was stunned. "Why?"

"Because I wanted to know what you were up to and you weren't telling me. I've known for some time now that something was going on, and I suspected it involved Adam. So I came to see for myself."

"Did you hear what I told him?"

"Yeah, I did."

"Then you should know that he's going back to his wife. I don't have any feelings for him. I love you. You're my soul mate."

Instead of saying she was his soul mate too, Tyler said, "Did you want to get married?"

"What?" She blinked at him. "No. What made you think that?"

"You did point out that I hadn't asked you."

"And then I added that I don't want to get married. Honestly, I don't."

"Not even to your soul mate?"

"What's a soul mate?" Toni demanded, hopping out of the van to join them.

"A person who drives you crazy," Angel muttered, feeling another hot flash coming on. Turning to confront Tyler, she jabbed his chest with her finger. "No, I don't want to get married, period! But I do want and expect that when I tell a man he's my soul mate, he reciprocates and tells me the same!"

"You already know you're my soul mate," Tyler said.

"Too little, too late, mister!" Angel scooped up Toni and snapped her into her car seat.

"She's mad at you," Toni told Tyler.

"Yes, she is. And I deserve it." Tyler spun Angel around before dropping to his knee in the gravel-covered drive. He winced at the stones digging into his jeans.

"What are you doing? I told you I don't want to get married! Honestly!" Angel tried to tug him to his feet but he refused to budge.

"I'm proposing that we *not* get married, but that we remain soul mates for the rest of our lives. What do you say?"

Angel blinked away tears as she pulled Tyler up and into her arms. "I say that's the kind of nontraditional proposal I've been waiting a lifetime for! And the answer is yes!"

• • •

Nathan knew he needed help. He just wasn't sure where to get it. His buddy Cole was certainly no expert in the relationship department.

He considered consulting with Luke and Tyler, who appeared to have had some success in dealing with the Wright women.

Luke seemed to be a happy camper. He and Julia were engaged and they had a baby on the way. Tyler and Angel also seemed well suited to each other. Even Owen and Violet had danced to Owen's Benny Goodman records, or so the funeral director had confessed to him not two seconds ago.

"In case you were wondering why I had that certain pep in my step," Owen said.

"No, I wasn't wondering." Nathan's thoughts were instead consumed with Skye and how deeply he'd hurt her the night before with his bumbling attempt to make things right.

When he'd returned from the accident scene, he'd been an emotional mess. Sure, he'd been to other crash sites since Annie's death, but none as bad as that one yesterday. There had been three fatalities.

So he'd gone to Skye and had sex with her to heal himself. Taken advantage of her. Tossed her up against the wall as if she weren't worthy of tender foreplay.

That's why he'd said what he had. He couldn't get the look on her face out of his mind. And then she'd accused him of always comparing her to Annie, saying that that was a race she could never win. And that he only saw Skye as a wicked Eve tempting him to do bad.

Didn't she see that *he* was the one who'd tempted *her*? Who'd mistreated her?

He had to make it up to her. Because the minute she'd walked out on him, he'd known in his head what he'd suspected deep in his heart for some time now. That he loved her.

Now he just needed to convince Skye of that fact. But how?

Chapter Nineteen

. . . .

After the farmer's market, Skye drove her friends back to Rock Creek in her trusty, rusty Toyota. The trunk of the car was filled with a bushel basket holding a variety of apples, and bags of veggies.

"Hey, isn't this the road where Nathan stopped you and gave you that ticket?" Sue Ellen asked.

"He didn't actually give me a ticket, just a hard time." Which he'd been giving her ever since.

"A hard time? As in wall-banging-sex hard time? Ow!" Sue Ellen turned to glare at Lulu in the backseat. "Why did you hit me *this* time?"

"Even I know that what you asked Skye was totally inappropriate."

"In that case, you better fasten your seat belts, girls," Sue Ellen noted. "We may be in for a bumpy ride."

"Why are you quoting old movies?" Skye demanded.

Sue Ellen pointed to the rearview mirror. "See anything interesting in there?"

Flashing red lights. Again. Skye was not amused. "Shit!"

Lulu swiveled to look out the back window. "Were you speeding?"

"I don't know." Skye pulled over and came to a stop.

"Maybe it's Deputy Sheriff Timmy Johnson," Lulu said.

But it wasn't. It was Studly Do-Right Nathan.

"Ladies."

Skye angrily shoved open the door, almost smashing it into his crotch. "What do you think you're doing?" She jumped out of the car. "Why did you stop us?"

"Because you're disturbing the peace. My peace of mind, body, and soul."

Skye rolled her eyes. "That's the lamest thing I ever heard!"

Not exactly the reaction Nathan had been hoping for.

He looked to Sue Ellen and Lulu, who'd gotten out of the car on the other side, for guidance.

"It is pretty lame," Lulu agreed.

"I thought it was kinda romantic," Sue Ellen said.

"That's what I was aiming for." Nathan put his hands on Skye's shoulders, but she pushed him away.

"Oh, no you don't!" Skye was furious. "You are not getting off that easily."

Sue Ellen spoke next. "Skye wouldn't tell us what you did to her after you had wall-banging sex in her office," Sue Ellen said, "but it must have been something bad, because she cried at the farmer's market. Ow!" Sue Ellen gave Lulu her own version of the Sicilian death stare. "*Stop hitting me!*"

"How did you know where to find me?" Skye demanded.

"I called Sue Ellen."

Skye belatedly recalled a muffled cell phone conversation Sue Ellen had had as they were leaving the market.

She turned to her friend. "You conspired with him?"

"Just listen to what he has to say." Sue Ellen jumped into the driver's seat of the Toyota, which was still running. "Get in!" she ordered Lulu, who quickly complied.

And they took off, leaving Skye standing there with Nathan. She wasn't wearing a belly-dancing costume this time, just jeans and a hand-knit blue sweater from Peru.

Nathan appeared to be at a loss for words. No surprise there.

Skye started walking away. It was only a mile or two into town. She could make it on her own.

"Wait."

Something about the tone of his voice made her pause for a moment. Then she started walking again.

"*Please* wait."

"For what?" She pivoted to confront him. "Wait for what? For you to come to your senses? For you to climb out of that coffin you put yourself into when your wife died?"

"You don't pull your punches, do you."

"You're only now noticing that?"

"I notice everything about you."

"Because you're a lawman, and that's what lawmen do—notice details and put them in their reports."

"No, not because I'm a lawman. Because I'm a man in love with you."

"Yeah, right." She wasn't buying that for one second.

"Why don't you believe me?"

"Because not twenty-four hours ago you told me that having sex with me was a mistake, that it shouldn't have happened."

"It shouldn't have happened the way it did, with me taking advantage of you."

"What are you talking about?"

"There was a terrible pileup on the interstate last night," Nathan said. "Multiple cars and a jackknifed semi. Three fatalities."

"And that reminded you of your wife's accident?"

"It reminded me that life is short. You have plans. You have a life. You don't expect it all to change in the blink of an eye. But it can and it does. I was still messed up when I came to you last night."

"So you had sex with me to forget your wife."

"No. You don't get it. I had sex with you to prove I was still alive."

"Well, gee, glad I could help you with that," Skye said with biting sarcasm, before turning on her heel and marching away.

"I should have been making love to you to prove that I love you."

She turned to face him again. "You say you love me, but you can't even talk to me about your past."

"I'm never going to be the kind of guy who spills his guts."

"And I'm never going to be the kind of woman who is obedient and conservative. So if that's what you want—"

"It's not. I want you."

"Then you have to stop slamming the door on me. You have to start sharing at least some of your thoughts and feelings. Not spilling your guts—I get that. But at least a little sharing."

"Okay." He swallowed hard. "Annie was pregnant when she died in that crash. If she'd lived, our child would have been about Toni's age now."

Skye's caught her breath. "So that's why I kept sensing pain in you whenever you saw my daughter."

"Until that last time, when Toni cracked me up. It's like I was finally able to let the past go."

Skye nodded. She'd seen that in his expression. He'd opened up like never before, letting her see the man behind the barriers. But not for long.

"Give me another chance," he pleaded huskily.

He was letting her in again, allowing her to see the

essence of himself, the man he was. "I think I can manage that. But you won't be able to manage me. I'm not manageable."

He moved closer to her and gently ran his fingers down her cheek. "Are you persuadable?"

"Possibly."

"Then can I persuade you to come back to my place to continue this conversation is a more private setting?"

"Aren't you working?"

"I'm off-duty today."

"So your pulling me over . . . ?"

"Was not an official act and no doubt broke at least a dozen regulations."

"I don't plan on filing any complaints. So you want us to go to your place? Just for conversation?"

"If that's all you want."

"We'll see." Skye wasn't about to promise anything yet. But she figured the fact that he was willing to take her to his home was a big step. A few minutes later, they walked into Nathan's apartment. Skye gulped. "You live *here*?"

"Yeah." Nathan dropped his keys onto the empty kitchen counter and secured his weapon before turning to look at her. "Can I get you something to drink?"

She looked over his shoulder into the empty fridge. "You've got beer and pickles."

"Yeah. I'm not home much. I work a lot."

"Uh-huh. I don't need anything to drink at the moment, thanks."

"Me either." He closed the fridge and ushered her toward the living room and his pair of leather recliners. When she was seated, he said, "I don't welsh on bets. I still owe you ten truths about myself. So here goes. I'm a White Sox fan. I'm no good at decorating. I like Heineken beer and Angelo's half-sausage, half-pepperoni pizza with everything on it. I've used my job as an excuse to avoid having a life. I don't want to do that anymore."

When he paused, she said, "That's six." She got out of her recliner and went to him, settling on his lap and curving her hand along his square jaw. "You owe me four more."

He gently tugged her closer so that her head rested on his shoulder. "I counted five, so I owe you five more."

"I was counting your statement about not welshing on bets as one of your truths. So you've got four to go."

Nathan stared down at this unpredictable, outspoken, rebellious woman and realized how lucky he was to have found her. His road to discovering he loved her had been a bumpy one. He'd made mistakes. But he'd also made progress. He'd reached out to her. And he'd finally moved on from his old life. Several days ago, he'd removed the boxes of household goods left over from his marriage and donated them to a Gulf Coast charity that Sister Mary had recommended.

And now he had Skye here. After his blunder last night, he hadn't known if this moment would come. But he hadn't been about to stand still and let any more time go by without having her by his side. So he'd taken immediate action. And here she was, cuddled against him.

Not that he thought he was on easy street. He knew he had to work hard to regain her trust. "Okay, four more truths. I'm constantly amazed by you. I love the way you dance and have no idea how you are able to move your hips the way you do. I will never forget the way you danced down Barwell Street the night you won the lottery. And I know how deeply I hurt you last night by saying what I did, but don't know how to make it up to you."

"You're making a damn good start," she noted unsteadily.

Nathan tipped her face up to his and kissed her. As always, it was hot and passionate. But now, tenderness also played a huge part. He gently wooed her with his lips, and when she finally parted her own, he didn't immediately entangle her tongue with his but instead built up to that point with little nibbles and seductive licks.

"We're not rushing things this time," he murmured against her mouth.

"Mmmm." She unbuttoned his shirt and peeled it off his broad shoulders.

"We are not rushing things," he vowed, even as he lifted her sweater over her head. She wasn't wearing a bra.

They left a trail of clothing on the way to his bedroom.

His bed was big. And soon it was very rumpled, as they rolled around on it with reckless abandon.

Kneeling before her, Nathan drew her forward, draping her legs over his shoulders and licking his way up her inner thigh, licking his way to paradise. Her heels dug into his shoulders as he launched her clear to the Milky Way.

"Where did you learn to do that?" she gasped when finally able to form words once again.

There was a hint of wicked humor in his brown eyes that she hadn't seen before. "I heard this rumor about you, me, and something to do with the Kama Sutra. So I did some investigating."

"I want to do some investigating too," she murmured, changing positions so that he was prone and she was perched atop his thighs, frankly admiring his very aroused male anatomy. "Do you have a name for this fella here?" She ran her thumb over the tip. "Mr. Happy? Mr. Big? The Private Investigator?"

"You choose."

"Mr. Big seems to suit just fine. Look, he likes that." She caressed him more intimately now. "How about you? Do you like that?" She looked Nathan in the eye.

"Should I speak to your mother?"

"Huh?" Skye was momentarily speechless. "About Mr. Big? No, I don't think that will be necessary. She told me all about the birds and the bees a *looooong* time ago."

"I meant, to ask permission to court you."

"Is that what you call this?" She stroked him again. "Courting?"

"I'm serious."

"I can tell." She gave his anatomy an approving look.

He grabbed her hands and held them. "This is more than sex. I love you."

"No, you don't."

"Yes, I do. Trust me, I know how I feel."

"You're thinking with Mr. Big now."

"No, I'm not."

"Are you going to finish what you started, or just talk about it?"

Despite Nathan's vow not to rush things, when she tempted him while putting on the condom for him, he growled deep in his throat and rolled so that she was beneath him. One powerful thrust and he was in, setting a seductive tempo that had her clenching around him as her orgasm hit her hard and strong. Seconds later, he stiffened, shouted her name, and collapsed in her arms.

Afterward, she cuddled against him in an orgasm-induced glow. "Do you realize that this is the first time we've ever done it in a bed?"

"Do you realize how much I love you?"

She cut him off with a wave of her hand. "You don't have to say that."

"I mean it."

Skye sat up, refusing to listen to him.

Nathan caught her arm. "Oh, no you don't. You're not running away from this." The next thing she knew, he had her secured to the wooden slats on the headboard of his bed with a pair of pink fuzzy handcuffs.

"Do I want to know where you got these?" she said. "Have you used them before?"

"They're brand-new. A gag gift for Cole's brother at his bachelor party, but I never got around to giving them to him."

He knew she could get out of them anytime she wanted. She read that much in his expression. She could also read his dogged determination to make his feelings for her known.

"I love you," he said. "Why is that so hard for you to believe?"

"Because I'm nothing like your perfect wife."

"I know that. She's my past. You're my future."

Skye shook her head, tears threatening, afraid to believe him.

"I'm not sure how a woman like you got to be a woman like you, but I love the woman you are. So, stop being difficult and say, 'Yes, Nathan darling, I do believe you love me, and I love you, too.'"

"You know I don't respond well to orders," she reminded him, blinking back a teardrop or two at the sight of him looking at her as if she were his entire world. No one had ever looked at her that way before.

"How about pleading and begging?" He nibbled his way around her mouth.

Her voice got huskier. "That might work."

He lowered his head to her breasts, where he sucked her nipple into his mouth and did the most amazing things, almost making her come again right there on the spot.

"Yeah . . . that . . . works," she panted.

"You're a very mouthy woman. I figure you need a mouthy man to keep you happy."

"You don't talk much."

"I don't have to. Actions speak louder than words." He shifted his mouth to her belly, licking his way around her navel ring before heading lower.

And then she was a goner. Her mouthy man was giving her pleasure like she'd never known until she'd met him.

She slipped out of the handcuffs to reach for him.

Much later, she propped her hands on his chest and gazed down at his face. "How do you know this isn't just sex?"

"Because it's something more. It's something here." He shifted her hand until it was right over his heart. "And here." He moved their joined hands to her breast, over her heart. "Scary, I know. Believe me, I know. But the greatest rewards come from the things that scare you the most."

"So you're one of my greatest rewards, huh?"

"You're certainly my greatest reward. You've brought hope back into my life."

"The kite and the anchor," she murmured. At Nathan's quizzical look, she added, "Something Sister Mary told me. That you grounded me, providing me with an anchor so I didn't scatter into a million pieces, and that I gave you hope so you could learn to fly again."

"Sister Mary is a wise woman."

"Yeah, she's pretty awesome . . . for a nun. And you're wicked awesome . . . for a lawman."

Six weeks later . . .

"Tonight's the night," Nathan said.

"Yeah, I know. I thought it would never get here." Skye stared up at the Tivoli Theater's brilliant marquee. Instead of REOPENING SOON, it read GRAND OPENING TONIGHT.

"Are you nervous?"

"No. Are you?"

He laughed. It was a sound she heard often these days. And appreciated every single time. Ditto for the humorous glint in his eyes and the crinkles at the corners. As for his dimple, well, she was a huge fan.

Skye loved this man. She still found it amazing. And him, too. Aggravating at times, to be sure. But still amazing. And always wicked awesome.

"You ready for the big night?" he asked as they walked into the lobby.

"Abs-o-tively."

"Been hanging out with Wally again, huh?"

"He's a natural behind the concession stand. Listen, do

you hear that?" She tilted her head toward the auditorium.

"Is that . . . ?"

"Yes, it's Jerry playing 'Stairway to Heaven' on the four hundred and fifty–pipe organ he tuned and restored. Sweet, huh?"

"Have I told you how beautiful you look tonight?"

Skye looked down at the vintage red dress she was wearing, a throwback to the fifties, when the Tivoli was still in its heydey. "You're just glad that I'm not wearing my belly-dancing costume."

"I rather like that costume."

"I know you do." She wore it for him often.

"Do you have any more interviews to do?"

"Sue Ellen is handling the press."

"I can't believe that Sue Ellen got the folks at Carpet World to donate a red carpet for the opening."

"No hassle in the castle tonight," Algee said, coming up to them, a huge smile flashing across his face. "Looking good."

"Yes, you are, as always," Skye teased before hugging him. "Thanks again for arranging the 'History of the Comic Book' exhibit in the lobby."

"I'm the one who should be thanking you for letting the kids in the comic-book project display their artwork here."

"And I should be thanking you for doing a fund-raising event here next weekend for the no-kill animal shelter," said Cole, looking good in a suit and tie.

"I see you dressed up for the occasion tonight," Nathan said slyly.

"And I see you dressed down," Cole shot back, pointing to Nathan's jeans and black T-shirt.

"Hey, I'm wearing a jacket."

"Be still my heart."

Angel and Toni came hurrying across the lobby to meet them. "I'm so glad we finally got the water element working," Angel said.

"Dragon!" squealed Toni, pointing to the water fountain before leaping into Nathan's arms.

"I'm just glad you got rid of that awful naked Adonis fountain that Sue Ellen unearthed at the flea market," Nathan said to Skye. "Where did that thing end up?"

"In front of the Regency Trailer Park, I believe."

"They're starting to line up outside," Lulu called from inside the ticket booth. "Nancy and Sister Mary are first in line. No, wait, they just let Fanny cut in front of them. And behind them are Owen and Violet, holding hands." Lulu snapped her gum. "Looks like Coach Spears has got the entire football team out there too."

"We handed out flyers at Maguire's Pub to tell them about the opening here tonight," Luke said.

"And I posted a flyer at the library," Julia added. "Here and in Serenity Falls."

"Is that a Pop-Tart in your mouth?" Angel demanded.

Julia clenched her teeth and shook her head.

"A limo has just pulled up outside," Lulu announced.

"Angelo's Pizza delivering by limo now?" Cole asked.

Adam and his wife waved at them before skipping the line and coming inside. "I thought we'd come see what all the talk was about."

"I thought I'd never get here!" Sue Ellen patted her Mae West wig in place, then stared at them with disapproval. "Why aren't you guys in costume? Nathan was supposed to dress as Batman, Algee as the Incredible Hulk, and Skye as Wonder Woman."

"We never agreed to that plan," Nathan said.

"I'm glad to see that Toni, at least, dressed appropriately." She nodded her approval of Toni's princess outfit, complete with tiara and yellow Paddington Bear rain boots. "But those boots just don't go with that outfit. She should take them off . . ."

"I bite," Toni growled as Sue Ellen reached for her footwear.

"Fine, then." Sue Ellen quickly backed away. "Be a fashion blunder."

"Aren't you going to comment on my outfit?" Lulu asked, swirling to show off her black metal-studded mini-skirt, boots, and bowling shirt.

"I've given up on you," Sue Ellen said before catching sight of Adam and his wife, both of them impeccably dressed. "Mr. Kemp!" She made a beeline for him and shook his hand. "Listen, I know about some great real estate in this area that I think would make a perfect investment for you. Have you ever thought of purchasing a double-wide trailer?"

Skye shook her head. "Okay, places, everyone. It's time. Where is Tyler?"

"Hiding out in the projection room, checking the equipment," Angel said.

"Smart man," Nathan noted with a grin.

"Wait!" Skye said suddenly.

"Why? What's wrong?"

"Nothing." Skye looked around at her family and friends before letting her gaze rest on the man she loved. "This is just one of those perfect moments I want to memorize for the rest of my life."

"It's just the first of many," Nathan promised her. "Now, let's open those doors and kick some butt. You ready?" He held out his hand.

She took it and twined her fingers through his. "Bad girls are always ready . . . for anything."

"Including love?"

"*Especially* love."

Turn the page for a special preview
of Cathie Linz's next novel

Big Girls Don't Cry

Coming soon from Berkley Sensation!

. . . .

Broke and skinny beat out broke and chunky every time. Leena Riley was convinced of it. She should know. She was a size sixteen, plus-size model in a Twizzle-stick, size-zero world.

How ironic that now she was down on her luck, she was forced to return to her down-on-its-luck hometown of Rock Creek, Pennsylvania. Leena hadn't been back since she'd left for the big city of Chicago at eighteen and honestly hadn't missed the place one bit.

Things had changed . . . a little. The Tivoli Theater was open again. The nail salon and comic book store were new additions. And there was a new vet in town. Looking for a receptionist. Leena pulled the help wanted sign out of the window as she strolled into the animal clinic.

She needed this job. It was this or work the graveyard shift at Gas4Less. Rock Creek wasn't exactly a hotbed of financial opportunities.

But the vet's office appeared to be a hotbed of total mayhem. Leena ducked as a parrot dive-bombed her while a beagle howled in the corner accompanied by a yowling cat in a carrier. Another cat, the biggest one Leena had ever seen, hissed from atop a metal file cabinet while a pair of wiry terriers yelped at the pissed-off mega-feline from down below.

The situation called for drastic measures. No problemo. Her sister Sue Ellen was the Queen of Drastic Measures so Leena instantly knew what had to be done. Putting two fingers in her mouth, Leena let out an ear-piercing whistle that made cabs on Chicago's Mag Mile squeal to a stop beside her.

The room instantly fell silent. Realizing that would only last a second or two, Leena spoke quickly. Her dad had done a stint in the Marine Corps and had never lost his drill-sergeant voice. She mimicked him as she barked out orders. "Okay, terriers and owners outside. Beagle and owner in there." She pointed to an empty exam room. "Parrot, come here." She held out her hand and—miracle of miracles—the bird obediently flew onto it with a flurry of feathers. "Cats, as you were."

A tattoo-covered older biker dude in a leather vest and jeans moved forward. "Thanks for catching that old buzzard!"

"This your parrot?" Leena asked.

"It's a friend's. Mrs. Trimble asked me to bring the stubborn buzzard to see the doc here for a checkup. She'd have my ass if he flew out the door or something."

"Why isn't he in a cage?"

The senior citizen biker dude shifted awkwardly from one booted foot to the other while guiltily pointing to the cage. "I . . . uh . . . have a hard time seeing creatures jailed."

Leena calmly opened the cage door and carefully set the parrot inside. "Keep the cover over the cage if you have trouble looking at him."

"You're good with animals."

"I've worked with a few in my time." One grabby photographer at a lingerie photo shoot several months ago certainly came to mind.

The senior biker held out his beefy hand. "The name's Jerry."

"Leena Riley." Yeah, right. Leena. Another joke since she hadn't been *lean* a day in her life. In school they'd mocked her by chanting that she should have been named Lotsa Riley.

Of course, it hadn't helped that she'd grown up in the poorest mobile home in the Regency Trailer Park. Sure, it was supposed to be ritzier than the Broken Creek Trailer Park, but that really wasn't saying much.

The two trailer parks had a rivalry going similar to the rivalry between Rock Creek and Serenity Falls. Leena had read somewhere that Serenity Falls had recently been listed as one of the best small towns in America. Which made Rock Creek the ugly stepsister yet again.

Not that her own older sister Sue Ellen saw things that way. Of course, Sue Ellen saw things no one else did, like the face of Jesus in the fur of a llama.

Leena loved her older sister, but she didn't understand her. Few people did. Which was why Sue Ellen earned the nickname Our Lady of the Outlandish.

Baby sister Emma was the one with the brains and fancy job title in the family. Leena was the one with the big dreams, very few of which had actually come true. Not that she'd told her sisters that. No, her reports to them had been filled with plenty of optimism and major exaggerations.

Which made her homecoming all the more humiliating.

Leena was still reeling from the bigger-they-are-theharder-they-fall jokes that had been thrown her way when her modeling agency had fired her. The Image Plus Modeling Agency in Chicago was no Wilhemina.

"And you're no Kate Dillon," her agent Irene had shot back at her before showing her the door.

Okay, so Kate was one of the leading plus-sized models. And okay, so Leena's assignments weren't photo shoots for *French Vogue* or even Lane Bryant. That didn't mean she was a total failure.

What about that layout for the Sears spring sales catalogue? last year? That had gone well, once the photographer and makeup artist had recovered from hurling after eating bad sushi they'd had catered in.

Before she could think of her other professional accomplishments, Leena was almost knocked down by a nun on the run who flew into the waiting room and rushed up to a family hidden from view by a large ficus.

Leena heard someone say, "Is he dead?"

Great. Her first day on the job and someone has to bite the dust on her watch. Not a good omen. Should she call 911?

"You called me here to give last rites," the nun, whom Leena now recognized as Sister Mary, said.

"Yes," a little girl replied.

"To a hamster?"

"Not just any hamster," the little girl explained. "To Harry the Hamster."

"I can't give last rites to a hamster," Sister Mary said.

"What's going on out here?"

Leena stared at the hunk in the white lab coat who'd just drawled that question. She knew this guy. She recognized the wicked twinkle in his blue eyes. Cole Flannigan.

She thought he'd be bartending in some tropical hotspot by now, his Hawaiian shirt hanging open to reveal his muscular chest. At least his chest had been muscular the last time she'd seen it. Of course that had been almost a decade ago.

Still, he didn't look like he'd gained a beer belly yet. In fact, his worn jeans made him look lean and extremely bedable. By a lean and equally bedable babe. Not by her, broke and chunky Leena Riley.

Had her career really taken off the way she'd told her sisters it had, why then things would have been different.

Then she'd have had the confidence to stroll right up to Cole and kiss him silly, had she wanted to.

Her lack of confidence had to do with her empty bank account, not her body image.

Well, okay, maybe it did have something to do with her body image. I mean, she wasn't a saint . . . or a nun.

"You want to know what's going on here?" Sister Mary repeated. "I was just telling your patients that I can't give last rites to a hamster."

"What about a special prayer?" the little girl asked.

"I told you that Harry is just fine," Cole reminded the family. "You didn't have to call in Sister Mary."

"Well, since I'm here, I might as well say a prayer." Sister Mary spoke bent down and spoke quietly to the little girl and Harry the Hamster. So quietly that Leena couldn't hear what she said but it made the kid feel better, judging by the shy smile she gave the nun.

"Your next patient is in exam room one," Leena efficiently announced.

"Really?" Cole pinned her with a stare. "And you are?"

"Your new receptionist."

Cole raised an eyebrow. "You're applying for the job?"

"No, you're *hiring* me," Leena stated confidently.

"Why is that?"

"Because you need me," Leena told him. "I'm here to rescue you from utter chaos."

"Sounds good to me," Sister Mary declared. "It's not like you've had people knocking down your door demanding to work here, Cole."

"No, she's the first," Cole agreed. He studied Leena for a moment. "Have we met before?"

Leena hesitated, unsure how to answer that question. She'd beaten him up once when she was in the sixth grade and he'd hung out with a bunch of younger kids who'd called her fat. Now probably wasn't the best time to admit that fact, however.

Too late. "Wait a second." Cole snapped his fingers. "Aren't you Sue Ellen's sister Leena?"

Right. Like that's how she wanted to be known for the rest of her life. As Sue Ellen's sister.

That was one of the reasons she'd left. Because she was sick and tired of always being referred to as Sue Ellen's sister. Or Sue Ellen's fat sister. Or Sue Ellen's chubbo sister. "I'm Leena Riley."

"I thought you were in Chicago doing modeling or something like that."

He made it sound like she was pole dancing on Rush Street. "That's right. I was."

"And now you want the job as my receptionist? Why?"

"Do you really care?" Leena retorted as another bunch of patients and animals entered the already overcrowded waiting room and the phone started to ring. Chaos was threatening to return.

"No. You're hired. For the day. We'll talk about the future after that."

Oh yeah. How the mighty had fallen. All the way from cover model on the spring Sears catalogue to small-town vet receptionist. Not exactly a lateral career move by any stretch of the imagination.

But it would do in a crunch. And she was definitely in a crunch.

Leena Riley, rising star reverting back to Leena the Loser.

No, she refused to think like that. She couldn't afford to go down that road. It led nowhere.

Of course, some might think that Rock Creek qualified as nowhere.

But at least she had a job. For today. And that's all she could handle for the moment. Today. Tomorrow would have to take a number.

After getting their names, Leena pulled the files on the patients waiting in the waiting room and then went outside to check on the two terriers and owners she'd banished out there. Luckily the spring weather was warm enough that they weren't shivering in their boots, had they been wearing any. Leena was wearing a lovely pair of Italian leather Prada boots she'd gotten at a sample sale.

They looked good at a photo shoot, and went great with her jeans and crisp white wrap shirt, but were perhaps not the best choice for a vet's office. Not when one of the banished terriers decided to squat and pee on Leena's leather-encased right foot.

"Oh, I'm so sorry," the owner, a harried-looking woman in her forties, declared. "Oscar gets a nervous bladder whenever we come to the vet."

The other terrier started gnawing on Leena's left boot.

Suddenly the job at the graveyard shift of Gas4Less was looking a lot more appealing.

• • •

Cole finished with his last patient, a Siamese male named Si who needed his shots updated, and headed out toward the empty waiting room.

He was surprised to find Leena still there. He'd have thought she'd taken off screaming when the Great Dane with anxiety issues had come in two hours ago. Or the depressed boa constrictor.

Instead, there she was. Standing behind the U-shaped desk of the receptionist area, looking totally out of place. But looking good. Her dark blonde hair brushed her shoulders in what was no doubt an expensive cut. Ditto for her perfect manicure.

She'd always had a bossy streak, which was no doubt how she'd gotten that Great Dane to behave. It hadn't made him behave when they'd been kids. He was ashamed to recall how he'd made fun of her weight and how she'd flattened him with a lucky sucker punch. He'd been two years younger than her—a cocky fourth grader.

"You still pack a mean right hook?" Cole asked as he handed her the file on his last patient.

"If necessary, yes." She stared him down, which gave him a good look at her gorgeous blue eyes. "I hope my actions that day taught you a valuable lesson."

"Which was?"

"That if you say something cruel, it will come back to bite you in the ass."

"I suppose I should be thankful you didn't do that and only punched me."

"Yes, you should. I was suspended from school for a week because of you."

"And yet here you are, begging me for a job."

"Wrong. Here I am, saving you from trouble yet again."

"That's why you came back to Rock Creek from Chicago? To save me?"

"Do you need saving?"

"Do you?" Cole countered.

Leena shrugged. "I gave up looking for a knight in shining armor to save me ages ago. These days, I save myself."

"And you also save overworked vets."

"That's right."

"Even though you have no experience working in a vet's office."

"I have experience booking appointments." As a model she'd usually been on the other end of the booking arrangements, dealing with bookers scheduling photo shoots. But how hard could this side of things be? Her organizational skills were very good. Everyone said so.

Even in kindergarten she'd organized the other kids' cubbies. And in their mobile home, at age eight Leena had moved all the contents of the kitchen cabinets into a more efficient arrangement.

By the time Leena was a teenager, she'd perfected time management so that she knew exactly how long to study for a test to get a B or a C.

Emma was the A student in the family. So Leena hadn't wasted her time on academic matters. Instead, after reading an article in a magazine about plus-size models, she'd focused on learning everything she could about the modeling industry. She'd gone to model shows and model talent searches at shopping malls all over the state.

And when she'd graduated from Rock Creek High, she'd packed her bags and headed to Chicago with her portfolio under her arm—consisting of several headshots and one full-length shot.

She could still remember her excitement at driving her used Toyota down Chicago's famous Lake Shore Drive, seeing all those tall buildings lining Lake Michigan. Someday, she'd promised herself, she'd live in one of those pricy condos along the Gold Coast.

Instead, she'd ended up sharing a small apartment with two other girls on the outskirts of the Ukraine Village area of Chicago.

"So you have experience booking appointments," Cole was saying, which made her wandering attention snap back to him. The man was hard to ignore. His light brown hair had a bit of a wave to it and was totally rumpled, giving him that I-just-got-out-of-bed look that worked very well for him. She wondered if he slept in the nude.

She probably should be paying attention to his questions instead of imagining him starkers. She'd known him when they'd been kids. Surely that should make her immune to his charming ways, right? Come on, she'd beat the guy up once.

So why were her hormones humming like queen bees zipping around a hive?

She should know better than to judge a person by their looks.

But then Cole's charm went beyond his looks. It was also generated by the way he talked, that sexy drawl he'd mastered when his voice had deepened during adolescence.

"Hello?" He waved his big hands in front of her face. "Anyone home in there?"

"Sorry." Leena blinked. "I was . . . uh . . . thinking about . . . uh . . . something else."

"Your Prada boots?"

"How did you know they were Prada?"

"One of my patients told me. The terrier owner."

"Ah, Oscar . . . the terrier with the nervous bladder."

"You've got a good memory."

"I never forget a bitch named Oscar who ruined my Pradas."

"They named her Oscar before they realized the dog was a she not a he. And then they refused to rename her."

"Which is probably why the dog has a nervous bladder. Gender identification issues."

His laughter caught her by surprise.

"A sense of humor is a requirement for this job," he said.

"So have I passed the audition?"

"I still can't figure out why you'd want to work for me when you're a model. Something happen in Chicago?"

Leena shrugged. "Lots of things happen in Chicago."

"And you don't plan on telling me about them? You don't think as your prospective employer, that I've got a right to know?"

Leena was prevented from answering by the dramatic arrival of her sister Sue Ellen, who burst onto the scene as she always did, with maximum effect.

"It's true! You're really here! You've come back home!" Sue Ellen engulfed her in a mighty python hold that squeezed the air out of Leena's lungs. "Why didn't you tell me you were coming? We could have set up a special welcome celebration. A parade or something. And what on earth are you doing over here at the vet's office? Did you get a pet while you were in Chicago? Is it one of those designer dogs? Don't tell me, let me guess. Is it a schnoodle? A labradoodle? A Yorkipoo? Is it sick? Is that why you're here?"

"I don't have a dog."

"Some exotic pet then? A lynx maybe?"

"I don't have any pets."

Sue Ellen frowned and released her. "Then why are you in the vet's office? Unless you came to see him?" She jabbed her thumb in Cole's direction. "I thought you didn't like him. Didn't you beat him up once?"

Leena tried not to squirm. "That was a long time ago."

"And you came here to apologize?" Sue Ellen beamed proudly. "Isn't that just like you? Even though you're a big star now, you still remember the little people you beat up along the way."

"Hey, watch who you're calling little," Cole protested.

"Well, of course you're taller now, Cole," Sue Ellen said. "Leena probably couldn't take you down with just one punch like she did then."

"It was a sucker punch," Cole growled.

Sue Ellen patted his arm. "Yeah, that's what Luke claimed that time Julia hit him before they were married."

"Who are they?" Leena asked, trying to follow her sister's line of thought, which was never an easy task.

"My friend Skye's sister and brother-in-law. I can't wait to introduce them all to my famous sister," Sue Ellen said, before admitting, "I never bragged about you before because Skye and her family are a little weird about makeup and stuff. But now that you're here, they can see for themselves how great you are." Sue Ellen paused to take a much-needed breath. "But I still don't know what you're doing in the vet's office."

"She's here about a job," Cole replied.

Sue Ellen frowned. "What kind of job could a supermodel do for you? She knows Iman, you know."

Which wasn't a lie . . . exactly. Leena knew *of* Iman. Who didn't? The famous supermodel was married to rock star David Bowie. She possessed a tall graceful elegance that Leena could never even aspire to.

But Leena had aspired to the world of plus-size modeling and thought she'd made her mark.

"Then maybe Iman should give her a job," Cole retorted.

"Don't be silly." Sue Ellen smacked Cole's arm. "My sister doesn't need a job. She's one of the most successful models in Chicago. Tell him, Leena."

Leena sighed and wished she could sink through the floor. But years of posing in front of a camera had given her the ability to mask her inner emotions. "I'm having a temporary reversal of fortunes," she said. "Which requires my returning home for a short period of time."

"How short?" Cole demanded suspiciously. "I don't want to hire you as my receptionist only to have you take off a few days later."

"What do you mean reversal of fortunes?" Sue Ellen demanded. "Do you have a gambling problem?"

"No, of course not." Leena answered her sister's question first because it was the easiest. "I don't gamble."

"You taking off to Chicago was a gamble."

Okay, so Sue Ellen had her there. Apparently her question wasn't as easy as Leena first thought. Which left Cole's question. "I wouldn't leave without giving two weeks notice."

"So you'd work two days and then give two weeks notice?" he countered.

"I anticipate being here through the summer." The words actually made Leena feel ill saying them. But the bottom line was that unfortunately, it would take her that long to get her act together financially to climb out of debt enough to start over.

She'd used her organizational skills to come up with a timeline that charted out the least amount of time she'd have to spend in Rock Creek. And given the salary this position was offering, proudly displayed on that Help Wanted sign she'd seen, it would take her a couple of months to regain control of her life.

The job paid well for Rock Creek, which surprised her at first. Apparently she wasn't the only one a little desperate. The vet seemed to have trouble getting the position filled. Not that she planned on asking why no one in town wanted to work for him.

Not yet.

"So are you accepting my offer to help you?" she asked Cole.

"How are you going to help him?" Sue Ellen demanded.

"By working as my receptionist," Cole replied.

"No way! Stop right there. No way is my sister working in a crummy vet's office. Not that you're a crummy vet," Sue Ellen hastily assured Cole. "I didn't mean that. I just meant that your office is crummy. Not that it's dirty, although it smells like dog urine in here."

"That's from my boots." Leena looked down at her ruined footwear. "Oscar peed on one of them earlier. I tried to clean it off . . ."

Sue Ellen glared at Cole. "You allowed a dog to pee on my sister? Do you have any idea who you're dealing with here? She's *famous*! She is *not* someone to be peed upon!"

Cole shrugged, his mouth curved as if he were holding back a smile. If he laughed at her, Leena would have to punch him again. Instead he drawled, "I can't guarantee it won't happen again."

"Then she is not working here," Sue Ellen stated firmly. "Come on, Leena, let's go."

Leena recognized Sue Ellen's bossy big-sister mode. Sue Ellen was ten years older than Leena and she took her job as the elder sibling very seriously.

But Leena had no intention of being bossed around. Not unless it was by someone who was signing her paycheck.

Cole, curse his twisted soul, just stood there, arms crossed across his chest, a stupid grin on his face. She could read his mind. *Whatcha gonna do now, big girl?*

Okay, maybe the "big girl" bit at the end was her own

interpretation, but the challenging look in his admittedly sexy blue eyes was definitely being broadcast to her loud and clear.

"I'll be back in the morning," she told him firmly.

"The office opens at nine," he replied, "but staff should show up at eight-thirty."

"No problem." Right. Talk about a huge lie. Leena had tons of problems. Boatloads of them. But at least she had a job. Now she just needed to find somewhere to stay.

"You're staying with me, right?" Sue Ellen said. "You know that Mom and Dad gave me their trailer. I haven't had a lot of time to redecorate it yet because I've been getting my real estate license. I'm sure I'm going to pass that test this next time around. Anyway, you can stay in your old bedroom."

Just kill me now. Leena reached through the open window of her blue Miata for a paper bag from her front seat and started breathing into it.

"What are you doing?" Sue Ellen demanded.

Leena just shook her head and held up her finger in the universal sign of *wait a minute, I'll be right with you.* Right after she had a nervous breakdown.

"She's hyperventalating," Cole said as he joined them in the parking lot.

"You're a doctor, do something to help her!" Sue Ellen shoved him toward Leena, almost knocking her down in the process.

The second Cole put his hands on her waist to steady her, Leena instantly wished she was thinner. Or richer. Or both.

She lowered her hands, and the paper bag, to remove his fingers from her body before he measured her further.

The rustling crush of the bag mimicked her rustling heartbeat.

His hands left her waist, but only to move to her shoulders in order to pull her even closer.

"What are you do—mmmbbb!"

His lips covered hers, muffling the rest of her words and answering her question. He was kissing her. Gently, softly, seductively, but this was a kiss all right. No mistaking that.

He didn't try to tongue-down right there in the middle of the parking lot, in front of her sister. No, he was just tempting her, exploring infinite possibilities before releasing her.

Just breathe, Leena told herself, inhaling a ragged gulp of air.

Grinning, Cole gently lifted the paper bag back to her mouth.

Leena batted it away and glared at him. If the man was amusing himself at her expense, he'd live to regret it, regardless of how awesome a kisser he was.

"Do you always kiss your employees?" Leena demanded.

Cole's grin widened. "You're not officially an employee until you fill out the paperwork tomorrow."

"You were kissing my sister?" Sue Ellen stared at him in disbelief.

"Just practicing a little mouth-to-mouth recesitation, ma'am."

"Well, go practice it on someone else." Leena lifted her chin to give him her best haughty Queen of the Universe look. "I don't need you rescuing me."

"Yeah, so you said earlier. You've come to rescue *me*, right? You know, I think I could get used to that idea." One final devastatingly sexy grin and then he was gone, sauntering around the corner of the building and out of sight— but not out of Leena's mind.

Which left her with the sinking feeling she'd just jumped out of the frying pan smack dab into the fire.